W9-AEY-001

Obscure Destinies

WILLA CATHER

Obscure Destinies

Historical Essay by
KARI A. RONNING

Explanatory Notes by
KARI A. RONNING

Textual Essay by
FREDERICK M. LINK
with Kari A. Ronning
and Mark Kamrath

University of Nebraska Press

LINCOLN

© 1998 by the University of Nebraska Press
All rights reserved
Manufactured in the United States of America

⊖ The paper in this book meets the minimum requirements
of American National Standard for Information Sciences —
Permanence of Paper for Printed Library Materials,
ANSI Z39.48-1984.

Library of Congress Cataloging-in-Publication Data
Cather, Willa, 1873–1947.
Obscure destinies / Willa Cather; historical essay by Kari
A. Ronning; explanatory notes by Kari A. Ronning; textual
essay by Frederick M. Link with Kari A. Ronning
& Mark Kamrath.
p. cm. – (Willa Cather scholarly edition)
Includes bibliographical references.
ISBN 0-8032-1430-8 (cloth: alk. paper)
1. Nebraska – Social life and customs – Fiction.
2. Cather, Willa, 1873–1947. Obscure destinies.
3. Nebraska – In literature. I. Ronning, Kari, 1949–.
II. Link, Frederick M. III. Kamrath, Mark. IV. Title.
V. Series: Cather, Willa, 1873–1947. Works, 1992.
PS3505.A87O25 1998 813'.52–dc21
98-13549 CIP

CONTENTS

Preface

THE objective of the Willa Cather Scholarly Edition is to provide to readers — present and future — various kinds of information relevant to Willa Cather's writing, obtained and presented according to the highest scholarly standards: a critical text faithful to her intention as she prepared it for the first edition, a historical essay providing relevant biographical and historical facts, explanatory notes identifying allusions and references, a textual commentary tracing the work through its lifetime and describing Cather's involvement with it, and a record of changes in the text's various editions. This edition is distinctive in the comprehensiveness of its apparatus, especially in its inclusion of extensive explanatory information that illuminates the fiction of a writer who drew so extensively upon actual experience, as well as the full textual information we have come to expect in a modern critical edition. It thus connects activities that are too often separate — literary scholarship and textual editing.

Editing Cather's writing means recognizing that Cather

was as fiercely protective of her novels as she was of her private life. She suppressed much of her early writing and dismissed serial publication of later work, discarded manuscripts and proofs, destroyed letters, and included in her will a stipulation against publication of her private papers. Yet the record remains surprisingly full. Manuscripts, typescripts, and proofs of some texts survive with corrections and revisions in Cather's hand; serial publications provide final "draft" versions of texts; correspondence with her editors and publishers helps clarify her intention for a work, and publishers' records detail each book's public life; correspondence with friends and acquaintances provides an intimate view of her writing; published interviews with and speeches by Cather provide a running public commentary on her career; and through their memoirs, recollections, and letters, Cather's contemporaries provide their own commentary on circumstances surrounding her writing.

In assembling pieces of the editorial puzzle, we have been guided by principles and procedures articulated by the Committee on Scholarly Editions of the Modern Language Association. Assembling and comparing texts demonstrated the basic tenet of the textual editor — that only painstaking collations reveal what is actually there. Scholars had assumed, for example, that with the exception of a single correction in spelling, *O Pioneers!* passed unchanged from the 1913 first edition to the 1937 Autograph Edition. Collations revealed nearly a hundred word changes, thus providing information not only necessary to establish a critical text and to interpret how Cather composed, but also basic to interpreting how her ideas about art changed as she matured.

Cather's revisions and corrections on typescripts and page proofs demonstrate that she brought to her own writing her extensive experience as an editor. Word changes demonstrate her practices in revising; other changes demonstrate that she gave extraordinarily close scrutiny to such matters as capitalization, punctuation, paragraphing, hyphenation, and spacing. Knowledgeable about production, Cather had intentions for her books that extended to their design and manufacture. For example, she specified typography, illustrations, page format, paper stock, ink color, covers, wrappers, and advertising copy.

To an exceptional degree, then, Cather gave to her work the close textual attention that modern editing practices respect, while in other ways she challenged her editors to expand the definition of "corruption" and "authoritative" beyond the text, to include the book's whole format and material existence. Believing that a book's physical form influenced its relationship with a reader, she selected type, paper, and format that invited the reader response she sought. The heavy texture and cream color of paper used for *O Pioneers!* and *My Ántonia*, for example, created a sense of warmth and invited a childlike play of imagination, as did these books' large dark type and wide margins. By the same principle, she expressly rejected the anthology format of assembling texts of numerous novels within the covers of one volume, with tight margins, thin paper, and condensed print.

Given Cather's explicitly stated intentions for her works, printing and publishing decisions that disregard her wishes represent their own form of corruption, and an authoritative edition of Cather must go beyond the sequence of words and punctuation to include other matters: page format, paper stock, typeface, and other features of design. The volumes in the Cather Edition respect those intentions insofar as possible within a series format that includes a comprehensive scholarly apparatus. For example, the Cather Edition has adopted the format of six by nine inches, which Cather approved in Bruce Rogers's elegant work on the 1937 Houghton Mifflin Autograph Edition, to accommodate the various elements of design. While lacking something of the intimacy of the original page, this size permits the use of large, generously leaded type and ample margins — points of style upon which the author was so insistent. In the choice of paper, we have deferred to Cather's declared preference for a warm, cream antique stock.

Today's technology makes it difficult to emulate the qualities of hot-metal typesetting and letterpress printing. In comparison, modern phototypesetting printed by offset lithography tends to look anemic and lacks the tactile quality of type impressed into the page. The version of the Scotch typeface employed in the original edition of *Obscure Destinies*, were it available for phototypesetting, would hardly survive the transition. Instead, we have chosen Linotype Janson Text, a modern rendering of the type used by Rogers. The subtle adjustments of stroke weight in this reworking do much to retain the integrity of earlier metal versions. Therefore, without trying to replicate the design of single works, we seek to represent Cather's general preferences in a design that encompasses many volumes.

In each volume in the Cather Edition, the author's specific intentions for design and printing are set forth in textual commentaries. These essays also describe the history of the texts, identify those that are authorial, explain the selection of copy-texts or basic texts, justify emendations of the copy-text, and describe patterns of variants. The textual apparatus in each volume — lists of variants, emendations, explanations of emendations, and end-of-line hyphenations — completes the textual story.

Historical essays provide essential information about the genesis, form, and transmission of each book, as well as supply its biographical, historical, and intellectual contexts. Illustrations supplement these essays with photographs, maps, and facsimiles of manuscript, typescript, or typeset pages. Finally, because Cather in her writing drew so extensively upon personal experience and historical detail, explanatory notes are an especially important part of the Cather Edition. By providing a comprehensive identification of her references to flora and fauna, to regional customs and manners, to the classics and the Bible, to popular writing, music, and other arts — as well as to relevant cartography and census material — these notes provide a starting place for scholarship and criticism on subjects long slighted or ignored.

Within this overall standard format, differences occur

that are informative in their own right. The straightforward textual history of *O Pioneers!* and *My Ántonia* contrasts with the more complicated textual challenges of *A Lost Lady* and *Death Comes for the Archbishop*; the allusive personal history of the Nebraska novels, so densely woven that *My Ántonia* seems drawn not merely upon Anna Pavelka but all of Webster County, contrasts with the more public allusions of novels set elsewhere. The Cather Edition reflects the individuality of each work while providing a standard of reference for critical study.

WILLA CATHER

Obscure Destinies

CONTENTS

Neighbour Rosicky

Neighbour Rosicky

I

WHEN Doctor Burleigh told neighbour Rosicky he had a bad heart, Rosicky protested.

"So? No, I guess my heart was always pretty good. I got a little asthma, maybe. Just a awful short breath when I was pitchin' hay last summer, dat's all."

"Well now, Rosicky, if you know more about it than I do, what did you come to me for? It's your heart that makes you short of breath, I tell you. You're sixty-five years old, and you've always worked hard, and your heart's tired. You've got to be careful from now on, and you can't do heavy work any more. You've got five boys at home to do it for you."

The old farmer looked up at the Doctor with a gleam of amusement in his queer triangular-shaped eyes. His eyes were large and lively, but the lids were caught up in the middle in a curious way, so that they formed a triangle. He did not look like a sick man. His brown face was creased but not wrinkled, he had a ruddy colour in his smooth-shaven cheeks and in his lips, under his long brown moustache. His hair was thin and ragged around his ears, but very little grey. His forehead, naturally high and crossed by deep parallel lines, now ran all the way up to his pointed crown. Rosicky's face had the habit of looking interested, — suggested a contented disposition and a reflective quality that was gay rather than grave. This gave him a certain detachment, the easy manner of an onlooker and observer.

"Well, I guess you ain't got no pills fur a bad heart, Doctor Ed. I guess the only thing is fur me to git me a new one."

Doctor Burleigh swung round in his desk-chair and frowned at the old farmer. "I think if I were you I'd take a little care of the old one, Rosicky."

Rosicky shrugged. "Maybe I don't know how. I expect you mean fur me not to drink my coffee no more."

"I wouldn't, in your place. But you'll do as you choose about that. I've never yet been able to separate a Bohemian from his coffee or his pipe. I've quit trying. But the sure thing is you've got to cut out farm work. You can feed the stock and do chores about the barn, but you can't do anything in the fields that makes you short of breath."

"How about shelling corn?"

"Of course not!"

Rosicky considered with puckered brows.

"I can't make my heart go no longer'n it wants to, can I, Doctor Ed?"

"I think it's good for five or six years yet, maybe more, if you'll take the strain off it. Sit around the house and help Mary. If I had a good wife like yours, I'd want to stay around the house."

His patient chuckled. "It ain't no place fur a man. I don't like no old man hanging round the kitchen too much. An' my wife, she's a awful hard worker her own self."

"That's it; you can help her a little. My Lord, Rosicky, you are one of the few men I know who has a family he can get some comfort out of; happy dispositions, never quarrel among themselves, and they treat you right. I want to see you live a few years and enjoy them."

"Oh, they're good kids, all right," Rosicky assented.

The Doctor wrote him a prescription and asked him how his oldest son, Rudolph, who had married in the spring, was getting on. Rudolph had struck out for himself, on rented land. "And how's Polly? I was afraid Mary mightn't like an American daughter-in-law, but it seems to be working out all right."

9

"Yes, she's a fine girl. Dat widder woman bring her daughters up very nice. Polly got lots of spunk, an' she got some style, too. Da's nice, for young folks to have some style." Rosicky inclined his head gallantly. His voice and his twinkly smile were an affectionate compliment to his daughter-in-law.

"It looks like a storm, and you'd better be getting home before it comes. In town in the car?" Doctor Burleigh rose.

"No, I'm in de wagon. When you got five boys, you ain't got much chance to ride round in de Ford. I ain't much for cars, noway."

"Well, it's a good road out to your place; but I don't want you bumping around in a wagon much. And never again on a hay-rake, remember!"

Rosicky placed the Doctor's fee delicately behind the desk-telephone, looking the other way, as if this were an absent-minded gesture. He put on his plush cap and his corduroy jacket with a sheepskin collar, and went out.

The Doctor picked up his stethoscope and frowned at it as if he were seriously annoyed with the instrument. He wished it had been telling tales about some other man's heart, some old man who didn't look the Doctor in the eye so knowingly, or hold out such a warm brown hand when he said good-bye. Doctor Burleigh had been a poor boy in the country before he went away to medical school; he had known Rosicky almost ever since he could remember, and he had a deep affection for Mrs. Rosicky.

Only last winter he had had such a good breakfast at Rosicky's, and that when he needed it. He had been out all night on a long, hard confinement case at Tom Marshall's, — a big rich farm where there was plenty of stock and plenty of feed and a great deal of expensive farm machinery of the newest model, and no comfort whatever. The woman had too many children and too much work, and she was no manager. When the baby was born at last, and handed over to the assisting neighbour woman, and the mother was properly attended to, Burleigh refused any breakfast in that slovenly house, and drove his buggy — the snow was too deep for a car — eight miles to Anton Rosicky's place. He didn't know another farm-house where a man could get such a warm welcome, and such good strong coffee with rich cream. No wonder the old chap didn't want to give up his coffee!

He had driven in just when the boys had come back from the barn and were washing up for breakfast. The long table, covered with a bright oilcloth, was set out with dishes waiting for them, and the warm kitchen was

11

full of the smell of coffee and hot biscuit and sausage. Five big handsome boys, running from twenty to twelve, all with what Burleigh called natural good manners, — they hadn't a bit of the painful self-consciousness he himself had to struggle with when he was a lad. One ran to put his horse away, another helped him off with his fur coat and hung it up, and Josephine, the youngest child and the only daughter, quickly set another place under her mother's direction.

With Mary, to feed creatures was the natural expression of affection, — her chickens, the calves, her big hungry boys. It was a rare pleasure to feed a young man whom she seldom saw and of whom she was as proud as if he belonged to her. Some country house-keepers would have stopped to spread a white cloth over the oilcloth, to change the thick cups and plates for their best china, and the wooden-handled knives for plated ones. But not Mary.

"You must take us as you find us, Doctor Ed. I'd be glad to put out my good things for you if you was expected, but I'm glad to get you any way at all."

He knew she was glad, — she threw back her head and spoke out as if she were announcing him to the whole prairie. Rosicky hadn't said anything at all; he merely smiled his twinkling smile, put some more coal on the fire, and went into his own room to pour the Doctor a little drink in a medicine glass. When they were all seated, he watched his wife's face from his end of the table and spoke to her in Czech. Then, with the instinct of politeness which seldom failed him, he turned to the Doctor and said slyly: "I was just tellin' her not to ask you no questions about Mrs. Marshall till you eat some breakfast. My wife, she's terrible fur to ask questions."

The boys laughed, and so did Mary. She watched the Doctor devour her biscuit and sausage, too much excited to eat anything herself. She drank her coffee and sat taking in everything about her visitor. She had known him when he was a poor country boy, and was boastfully proud of his success, always saying: "What do people go to Omaha for, to see a doctor, when we got the best one in the State right here?" If Mary liked people at all, she felt physical pleasure in the sight of them, personal exultation in any good fortune that came to them. Burleigh didn't know many women like that, but he knew she was like that.

When his hunger was satisfied, he did, of course, have to tell them about Mrs. Marshall, and he noticed what a friendly interest the boys took in the matter.

Rudolph, the oldest one (he was still living at home then), said: "The last time I was over there, she was lifting them big heavy milk-cans, and I knew she oughtn't to be doing it."

"Yes, Rudolph told me about that when he come home, and I said it wasn't right," Mary put in warmly. "It was all right for me to do them things up to the last, for I was terrible strong, but that woman's weakly. And do you think she'll be able to nurse it, Ed?" She sometimes forgot to give him the title she was so proud of. "And to think of your being up all night and then not able to get a decent breakfast! I don't know what's the matter with such people."

"Why, Mother," said one of the boys, "if Doctor Ed had got breakfast there, we wouldn't have him here. So you ought to be glad."

"He knows I'm glad to have him, John, any time. But I'm sorry for that poor woman, how bad she'll feel the Doctor had to go away in the cold without his breakfast."

"I wish I'd been in practice when these were getting born." The Doctor looked down the row of close-clipped heads. "I missed some good breakfasts by not being."

The boys began to laugh at their mother because she flushed so red, but she stood her ground and threw up her head. "I don't care, you wouldn't have got away from this house without breakfast. No doctor ever did. I'd have had something ready fixed that Anton could warm up for you."

The boys laughed harder than ever, and exclaimed at her: "I'll bet you would!" "She would, that!"

"Father, did you get breakfast for the doctor when we were born?"

"Yes, and he used to bring me my breakfast, too, mighty nice. I was always awful hungry!" Mary admitted with a guilty laugh.

While the boys were getting the Doctor's horse, he went to the window to examine the house plants. "What do you do to your geraniums to keep them blooming all winter, Mary? I never pass this house that from the road I don't see your windows full of flowers."

She snapped off a dark red one, and a ruffled new green leaf, and put them in his buttonhole. "There, that looks better. You look too solemn for a young man, Ed. Why don't you git married? I'm worried about you. Settin' at breakfast, I looked at you real hard, and I seen you've got some grey hairs already."

"Oh, yes! They're coming. Maybe they'd come faster if I married."

"Don't talk so. You'll ruin your health eating at the hotel. I could send your wife a nice loaf of nut bread, if you only had one. I don't like to see a young man getting grey. I'll tell you something, Ed; you make some strong black tea and keep it handy in a bowl, and every morning just brush it into your hair, an' it'll keep the grey from showin' much. That's the way I do!"

Sometimes the Doctor heard the gossipers in the drug-store wondering why Rosicky didn't get on faster. He was industrious, and so were his boys, but they were rather free and easy, weren't pushers, and they didn't always show good judgment. They were comfortable, they were out of debt, but they didn't get much ahead. Maybe, Doctor Burleigh reflected, people as generous and warm-hearted and affectionate as the Rosickys never got ahead much; maybe you couldn't enjoy your life and put it into the bank, too.

II

WHEN Rosicky left Doctor Burleigh's office he went into the farm-implement store to light his pipe and put on his glasses and read over the list Mary had given him. Then he went into the general merchandise place next door and stood about until the pretty girl with the plucked eyebrows, who always waited on him, was free. Those eyebrows, two thin

India-ink strokes, amused him, because he remembered how they used to be. Rosicky always prolonged his shopping by a little joking; the girl knew the old fellow admired her, and she liked to chaff with him.

"Seems to me about every other week you buy ticking, Mr. Rosicky, and always the best quality," she remarked as she measured off the heavy bolt with red stripes.

"You see, my wife is always makin' goose-fedder pillows, an' de thin stuff don't hold in dem little down-fedders."

"You must have lots of pillows at your house."

"Sure. She makes quilts of dem, too. We sleeps easy. Now she's makin' a fedder quilt for my son's wife. You know Polly, that married my Rudolph. How much my bill, Miss Pearl?"

"Eight eighty-five."

"Chust make it nine, and put in some candy fur de women."

"As usual. I never did see a man buy so much candy for his wife. First thing you know, she'll be getting too fat."

"I'd like dat. I ain't much fur all dem slim women like what de style is now."

"That's one for me, I suppose, Mr. Bohunk!" Pearl sniffed and elevated her India-ink strokes.

When Rosicky went out to his wagon, it was beginning to snow, — the first snow of the season, and he was glad to see it. He rattled out of town and along the highway through a wonderfully rich stretch of country, the finest farms in the county. He admired this High Prairie, as it was called, and always liked to drive through it. His own place lay in a rougher territory, where there was some clay in the soil and it was not so productive. When he bought his land, he hadn't the money to buy on High Prairie; so he told his boys, when they grumbled, that if their land hadn't some clay in it, they wouldn't own it at all. All the same, he enjoyed looking at these fine farms, as he enjoyed looking at a prize bull.

After he had gone eight miles, he came to the graveyard, which lay just at the edge of his own hay-land. There he stopped his horses and sat still on his wagon seat, looking about at the snowfall. Over yonder on the hill he could see his own house, crouching low, with the clump of orchard behind and the windmill before, and all down the gentle hill-slope the rows of pale gold cornstalks stood out against the white field. The snow was falling over the cornfield and the pasture and the hay-land, steadily, with very little wind, — a nice dry snow. The graveyard had only a light wire fence about it and was all overgrown with long red grass. The fine snow, settling into this red grass and upon the few little evergreens and the headstones, looked very pretty.

It was a nice graveyard, Rosicky reflected, sort of snug and homelike, not cramped or mournful, — a big sweep all round it. A man could lie down in the long grass and see the complete arch of the sky over him, hear the wagons go by; in summer the mowing-machine rattled right up to the wire fence. And it was so near home. Over there across the cornstalks his own roof and windmill looked so good to him that he promised himself to mind the Doctor and take care of himself. He was awful fond of his place, he admitted. He wasn't anxious to leave it. And it was a comfort to think that he would never have to go farther than the edge of his own hayfield. The snow, falling over his barnyard and the graveyard, seemed to draw things together like. And they were all old neighbours in the graveyard, most of them friends; there was nothing to feel awkward or embarrassed about. Embarrassment was the most disagreeable feeling Rosicky knew. He didn't often have it, — only with certain people whom he didn't understand at all.

Well, it was a nice snowstorm; a fine sight to see the snow falling so quietly and graciously over so much open country. On his cap and shoulders, on the horses' backs and manes, light, delicate, mysterious it fell; and with it a dry cool fragrance was released into the air. It meant rest for vegetation and men and beasts, for the ground itself; a season of long nights for sleep, leisurely breakfasts, peace by the fire. This and much more went through Rosicky's mind, but he merely told himself that winter was coming, clucked to his horses, and drove on.

When he reached home, John, the youngest boy, ran out to put away his team for him, and he met Mary coming up from the outside cellar with her apron full of carrots. They went into the house together. On the table, covered with oilcloth figured with clusters of blue grapes, a place was set, and he smelled hot coffee-cake of some kind. Anton never lunched in town; he thought that extravagant, and anyhow he didn't like the food. So Mary always had something ready for him when he got home.

After he was settled in his chair, stirring his coffee in a big cup, Mary took out of the oven a pan of *kolache* stuffed with apricots, examined them anxiously to see whether they had got too dry, put them beside his plate, and then sat down opposite him.

Rosicky asked her in Czech if she wasn't going to have any coffee.

She replied in English, as being somehow the right language for transacting business: "Now what did Doctor Ed say, Anton? You tell me just what."

"He said I was to tell you some compliments, but I forgot 'em." Rosicky's eyes twinkled.

"About you, I mean. What did he say about your asthma?"

"He says I ain't got no asthma." Rosicky took one of the little rolls in his broad brown fingers. The thickened nail of his right thumb told the story of his past.

"Well, what is the matter? And don't try to put me off."

"He don't say nothing much, only I'm a little older, and my heart ain't so good like it used to be."

Mary started and brushed her hair back from her temples with both hands as if she were a little out of her mind. From the way she glared, she might have been in a rage with him.

"He says there's something the matter with your heart? Doctor Ed says so?"

"Now don't yell at me like I was a hog in de garden, Mary. You know I always did like to hear a woman talk soft. He didn't say anything de matter wid my heart, only it ain't so young like it used to be, an' he tell me not to pitch hay or run de corn-sheller."

Mary wanted to jump up, but she sat still. She admired the way he never under any circumstances raised his voice or spoke roughly. He was city-bred, and she was country-bred; she often said she wanted her boys to have their papa's nice ways.

"You never have no pain there, do you? It's your breathing and your stomach that's been wrong. I wouldn't believe nobody but Doctor Ed about it. I guess I'll go see him myself. Didn't he give you no advice?"

"Chust to take it easy like, an' stay round de house dis winter. I guess you got some carpenter work for me to do. I kin make some new shelves for you, and I want dis long time to build a closet in de boys' room and make dem two little fellers keep dere clo'es hung up."

Rosicky drank his coffee from time to time, while he considered. His moustache was of the soft long variety and came down over his mouth like the teeth of a buggy-rake over a bundle of hay. Each time he put down his cup, he ran his blue handkerchief over his lips. When he took a drink of water, he managed very neatly with the back of his hand.

Mary sat watching him intently, trying to find any change in his face. It is hard to see anyone who has become like your own body to you. Yes, his hair had got thin, and his high forehead had deep lines running from left to right. But his neck, always clean shaved except in the busiest seasons, was not loose or baggy. It was burned a dark reddish brown, and there were deep creases in it, but it looked firm and full of blood. His cheeks had a good colour. On either side of his mouth there was a half-moon down the length of his cheek, not wrinkles, but two lines that had come there from his habitual expression. He was shorter and broader than when she married him; his back had grown broad and curved, a good deal like the shell of an old turtle, and his arms and legs were short.

He was fifteen years older than Mary, but she had hardly ever thought about it before. He was her man, and the kind of man she liked. She was rough, and he was gentle, — city-bred, as she always said. They had been shipmates on a rough voyage and had stood by each other in trying times. Life had gone well with them because, at bottom, they had the same ideas about life. They agreed, without discussion, as to what was most important and what was secondary. They didn't often exchange opinions, even in Czech, — it was as if they had thought the same thought together. A good deal had to be sacrificed and thrown overboard in a hard life like theirs, and they had never disagreed as to the things that could go. It had been a hard life, and a soft life, too. There wasn't anything brutal in the short, broad-backed man with the three-cornered eyes and the forehead that went on to the top of his skull. He was a city man, a gentle man, and though he had married a rough farm girl, he had never touched her without gentleness.

They had been at one accord not to hurry through life, not to be always skimping and saving. They saw their neighbours buy more land and feed more stock than they did, without discontent. Once when the creamery agent came to the Rosickys to persuade them to sell him their cream, he told them how much money the Fasslers, their nearest neighbours, had made on their cream last year.

"Yes," said Mary, "and look at them Fassler children! Pale, pinched little things, they look like skimmed milk. I'd rather put some colour into my children's faces than put money into the bank."

The agent shrugged and turned to Anton.

"I guess we'll do like she says," said Rosicky.

III

MARY very soon got into town to see Doctor Ed, and then she had a talk with her boys and set a guard over Rosicky. Even John, the youngest, had his father on his mind. If Rosicky went to throw hay down from the loft, one of the boys ran up the ladder and took the fork from him. He sometimes complained that though he was getting to be an old man, he wasn't an old woman yet.

That winter he stayed in the house in the afternoons and carpentered, or sat in the chair between the window full of plants and the wooden bench where the two pails of drinking-water stood. This spot was called "Father's corner," though it was not a corner at all. He had a shelf there, where he kept his Bohemian papers and his pipes and tobacco, and his shears and needles and thread and tailor's thimble. Having been a tailor in his youth, he couldn't bear to see a woman patching at his clothes, or at the boys'. He liked tailoring, and always patched all the overalls and jackets and work shirts. Occasionally he made over a pair of pants one of the older boys had outgrown, for the little fellow.

While he sewed, he let his mind run back over his life. He had a good deal to remember, really; life in three countries. The only part of his youth he didn't like to remember was the two years he had spent in London, in Cheapside, working for a German tailor who was wretchedly poor. Those days, when he was nearly always hungry, when his clothes were dropping off him for dirt, and the sound of a strange language kept him in continual bewilderment, had left a sore spot in his mind that wouldn't bear touching.

He was twenty when he landed at Castle Garden in New York, and he had a protector who got him work in a tailor shop in Vesey Street, down near the Washington Market. He looked upon that part of his life as very happy. He became a good workman, he was industrious, and his wages were increased from time to time. He minded his own business and envied nobody's good fortune. He went to night school and learned to read English. He often did overtime work and was well paid for it, but somehow he never saved anything. He couldn't refuse a loan to a friend, and he was self-indulgent. He liked a good dinner, and a little went for beer, a little for tobacco; a good deal went to the girls. He often stood through an opera on Saturday nights; he could get standing-room for a dollar. Those were the great days of opera in New York, and it gave a fellow something to think about for the rest of the week. Rosicky had a quick ear, and a childish love of all the stage splendour; the scenery, the costumes, the ballet. He usually went with a chum, and after the performance they had beer and maybe some oysters somewhere. It was a fine life; for the first five years or so it satisfied him completely. He was never hungry or cold or dirty, and everything amused him: a fire, a dog fight, a parade, a storm, a ferry ride. He thought New York the finest, richest, friendliest city in the world.

Moreover, he had what he called a happy home life. Very near the tailor shop was a small furniture-factory, where an old Austrian, Loeffler, employed a few skilled men and made unusual furniture, most of it to order, for the rich German housewives up-town. The top floor of Loeffler's five-storey factory was a loft, where he kept his choice lumber and stored the odd pieces of furniture left on his hands. One of the young workmen he employed was a Czech, and he and Rosicky became fast friends. They persuaded Loeffler to let them have a sleeping-room in one corner of the loft. They bought good beds and bedding and had their pick of the furniture kept up there. The loft was low-pitched, but light and airy, full of windows, and good-smelling by reason of the fine lumber put up there to season. Old Loeffler used to go down to the docks and buy wood from South America and the East from the sea captains. The young men were as foolish about their house as a bridal pair. Zichec, the young cabinet-maker, devised every sort of convenience, and Rosicky kept their clothes in order. At night and on Sundays, when the quiver of machinery underneath was still, it was the quietest place in the world, and on summer nights all the sea winds blew in. Zichec often practised on his flute in the evening. They were both fond of music and went to the opera together. Rosicky thought he wanted to live like that for ever.

But as the years passed, all alike, he began to get a little restless. When spring came round, he would begin to feel fretted, and he got to drinking. He was likely to drink too much of a Saturday night. On Sunday he was languid and heavy, getting over his spree. On Monday he plunged into work again. So he never had time to figure out what ailed him, though he knew something did. When the grass turned green in Park Place, and the lilac hedge at the back of Trinity churchyard put out its blossoms, he was tormented by a longing to run away. That was why he drank too much; to get a temporary illusion of freedom and wide horizons.

Rosicky, the old Rosicky, could remember as if it were yesterday the day when the young Rosicky found out what was the matter with him. It was on a Fourth of July afternoon, and he was sitting in Park Place in the sun. The lower part of New York was empty. Wall Street, Liberty Street, Broadway, all empty. So much stone and asphalt with nothing going on, so many empty windows. The emptiness was intense, like the stillness in a great factory when the machinery stops and the belts and bands cease running. It was too great a change, it took all the strength out of one. Those blank buildings, without the stream of life pouring through them, were like empty jails. It struck young Rosicky that this was the trouble with big cities; they built you in from the earth itself, cemented you away from any contact with the ground. You lived in an unnatural world, like the fish in an aquarium, who were probably much more comfortable than they ever were in the sea.

On that very day he began to think seriously about the articles he had read in the Bohemian papers, describing prosperous Czech farming communities in the West. He believed he would like to go out there as a farm hand; it was hardly possible that he could ever have land of his own. His people had always been workmen; his father and grandfather had worked in shops. His mother's parents had lived in the country, but they rented their farm and had a hard time to get along. Nobody in his family had ever owned any land, — that belonged to a different station of life altogether. Anton's mother died when he was little, and he was sent into the country to her parents. He stayed with them until he was twelve, and formed those ties with the earth and the farm animals and growing things which are never made at all unless they are made early. After his grandfather died, he went back to live with his father and step-mother, but she was very hard on him, and his father helped him to get passage to London.

After that Fourth of July day in Park Place, the desire to return to the country never left him. To work on another man's farm would be all he asked; to see the sun rise and set and to plant things and watch them grow. He was a very simple man. He was like a tree that has not many roots, but one tap-root that goes down deep. He subscribed for a Bohemian paper printed in Chicago, then for one printed in Omaha. His mind got farther and farther west. He began to save a little money to buy his liberty. When he was thirty-five, there was a great meeting in New York of Bohemian athletic societies, and Rosicky left the tailor shop and went home with the Omaha delegates to try his fortune in another part of the world.

IV

PERHAPS the fact that his own youth was well over before he began to have a family was one reason why Rosicky was so fond of his boys. He had almost a grandfather's indulgence for them. He had never had to worry about any of them — except, just now, a little about Rudolph.

On Saturday night the boys always piled into the Ford, took little Josephine, and went to town to the moving-picture show. One Saturday morning they were talking at the breakfast table about starting early that evening, so that they would have an hour or so to see the Christmas things in the stores before the show began. Rosicky looked down the table.

"I hope you boys ain't disappointed, but I want you to let me have de car tonight. Maybe some of you can go in with de neighbours."

Their faces fell. They worked hard all week, and they were still like children. A new jack-knife or a box of candy pleased the older one as much as the little fellow.

"If you and Mother are going to town," Frank said, "maybe you could take a couple of us along with you, anyway."

"No, I want to take de car down to Rudolph's, and let him an' Polly go in to de show. She don't git into town enough, an' I'm afraid she's gettin' lonesome, an' he can't afford no car yet."

That settled it. The boys were a good deal dashed. Their father took another piece of apple-cake and went on: "Maybe next Saturday night de two little fellers can go along wid dem."

"Oh, is Rudolph going to have the car every Saturday night?"

Rosicky did not reply at once; then he began to speak seriously: "Listen, boys; Polly ain't lookin' so good. I don't like to see nobody lookin' sad. It comes hard fur a town girl to be a farmer's wife. I don't want no trouble to start in Rudolph's family. When it starts, it ain't so easy to stop. An American girl don't git used to our ways all at once. I like to tell Polly she and Rudolph can have the car every Saturday night till after New Year's, if it's all right with you boys."

"Sure it's all right, Papa," Mary cut in. "And it's good you thought about that. Town girls is used to more than country girls. I lay awake nights, scared she'll make Rudolph discontented with the farm."

The boys put as good a face on it as they could. They surely looked forward to their Saturday nights in town. That evening Rosicky drove the car the half-mile down to Rudolph's new, bare little house.

Polly was in a short-sleeved gingham dress, clearing away the supper dishes. She was a trim, slim little thing, with blue eyes and shingled yellow hair, and her eyebrows were reduced to a mere brush-stroke, like Miss Pearl's.

"Good evening, Mr. Rosicky. Rudolph's at the barn, I

guess." She never called him father, or Mary mother. She was sensitive about having married a foreigner. She never in the world would have done it if Rudolph hadn't been such a handsome, persuasive fellow and such a gallant lover. He had graduated in her class in the high school in town, and their friendship began in the ninth grade.

Rosicky went in, though he wasn't exactly asked. "My boys ain't goin' to town tonight, an' I brought de car over fur you two to go in to de picture show."

Polly, carrying dishes to the sink, looked over her shoulder at him. "Thank you. But I'm late with my work tonight, and pretty tired. Maybe Rudolph would like to go in with you."

"Oh, I don't go to de shows! I'm too old-fashioned. You won't feel so tired after you ride in de air a ways. It's a nice clear night, an' it ain't cold. You go an' fix yourself up, Polly, an' I'll wash de dishes an' leave everything nice fur you."

Polly blushed and tossed her bob. "I couldn't let you do that, Mr. Rosicky. I wouldn't think of it."

Rosicky said nothing. He found a bib apron on a nail behind the kitchen door. He slipped it over his head and then took Polly by her two elbows and pushed her gently toward the door of her own room. "I washed up

33

de kitchen many times for my wife, when de babies was sick or somethin'. You go an' make yourself look nice. I like you to look prettier'n any of dem town girls when you go in. De young folks must have some fun, an' I'm goin' to look out fur you, Polly."

That kind, reassuring grip on her elbows, the old man's funny bright eyes, made Polly want to drop her head on his shoulder for a second. She restrained herself, but she lingered in his grasp at the door of her room, murmuring tearfully: "You always lived in the city when you were young, didn't you? Don't you ever get lonesome out here?"

As she turned round to him, her hand fell naturally into his, and he stood holding it and smiling into her face with his peculiar, knowing, indulgent smile without a shadow of reproach in it. "Dem big cities is all right fur de rich, but dey is terrible hard fur de poor."

"I don't know. Sometimes I think I'd like to take a chance. You lived in New York, didn't you?"

"An' London. Da's bigger still. I learned my trade dere. Here's Rudolph comin', you better hurry."

"Will you tell me about London some time?"

"Maybe. Only I ain't no talker, Polly. Run an' dress yourself up."

The bedroom door closed behind her, and Rudolph

34

came in from the outside, looking anxious. He had seen the car and was sorry any of his family should come just then. Supper hadn't been a very pleasant occasion. Halting in the doorway, he saw his father in a kitchen apron, carrying dishes to the sink. He flushed crimson and something flashed in his eye. Rosicky held up a warning finger.

"I brought de car over fur you an' Polly to go to de picture show, an' I made her let me finish here so you won't be late. You go put on a clean shirt, quick!"

"But don't the boys want the car, Father?"

"Not tonight dey don't." Rosicky fumbled under his apron and found his pants pocket. He took out a silver dollar and said in a hurried whisper: "You go an' buy dat girl some ice cream an' candy tonight, like you was courtin'. She's awful good friends wid me."

Rudolph was very short of cash, but he took the money as if it hurt him. There had been a crop failure all over the county. He had more than once been sorry he'd married this year.

In a few minutes the young people came out, looking clean and a little stiff. Rosicky hurried them off, and then he took his own time with the dishes. He scoured the pots and pans and put away the milk and swept the kitchen. He put some coal in the stove and shut off the draughts, so the place would be warm for them when they got home late at night. Then he sat down and had a pipe and listened to the clock tick.

Generally speaking, marrying an American girl was certainly a risk. A Czech should marry a Czech. It was lucky that Polly was the daughter of a poor widow woman; Rudolph was proud, and if she had a prosperous family to throw up at him, they could never make it go. Polly was one of four sisters, and they all worked; one was book-keeper in the bank, one taught music, and Polly and her younger sister had been clerks, like Miss Pearl. All four of them were musical, had pretty voices, and sang in the Methodist choir, which the eldest sister directed.

Polly missed the sociability of a store position. She missed the choir, and the company of her sisters. She didn't dislike housework, but she disliked so much of it. Rosicky was a little anxious about this pair. He was afraid Polly would grow so discontented that Rudy would quit the farm and take a factory job in Omaha. He had worked for a winter up there, two years ago, to get money to marry on. He had done very well, and they would always take him back at the stockyards. But to Rosicky that meant the end of everything for his son. To be a landless man was to be a wage-earner, a slave, all your life; to have nothing, to be nothing.

Rosicky thought he would come over and do a little carpentering for Polly after the New Year. He guessed she needed jollying. Rudolph was a serious sort of chap, serious in love and serious about his work.

Rosicky shook out his pipe and walked home across the fields. Ahead of him the lamplight shone from his kitchen windows. Suppose he were still in a tailor shop on Vesey Street, with a bunch of pale, narrow-chested sons working on machines, all coming home tired and sullen to eat supper in a kitchen that was a parlour also; with another crowded, angry family quarrelling just across the dumb-waiter shaft, and squeaking pulleys at the windows where dirty washings hung on dirty lines above a court full of old brooms and mops and ash-cans. . . .

He stopped by the windmill to look up at the frosty winter stars and draw a long breath before he went inside. That kitchen with the shining windows was dear to him; but the sleeping fields and bright stars and the noble darkness were dearer still.

V

ON the day before Christmas the weather set in very cold; no snow, but a bitter, biting wind that whistled and sang over the flat land and lashed one's face like fine wires. There was baking going on in the Rosicky kitchen all day, and Rosicky sat inside, making over a coat that Albert had outgrown into an overcoat for John. Mary had a big red geranium in bloom for Christmas, and a row of Jerusalem cherry trees, full of berries. It was the first year she had ever grown these; Doctor Ed brought her the seeds from Omaha when he went to some medical convention. They reminded Rosicky of plants he had seen in England; and all afternoon, as he stitched, he sat thinking about those two years in London, which his mind usually shrank from even after all this while.

He was a lad of eighteen when he dropped down into London, with no money and no connexions except the address of a cousin who was supposed to be working at a confectioner's. When he went to the pastry shop, however, he found that the cousin had gone to America. Anton tramped the streets for several days, sleeping in doorways and on the Embankment, until he was in utter despair. He knew no English, and the sound of the strange language all about him confused him. By chance he met a poor German tailor who had learned his trade in Vienna, and could speak a little Czech. This tailor, Lifschnitz, kept a repair shop in a Cheapside basement, underneath a cobbler. He didn't much need

38

an apprentice, but he was sorry for the boy and took
him in for no wages but his keep and what he could pick
up. The pickings were supposed to be coppers given
you when you took work home to a customer. But most
of the customers called for their clothes themselves, and
the coppers that came Anton's way were very few. He
had, however, a place to sleep. The tailor's family lived
upstairs in three rooms; a kitchen, a bedroom, where
Lifschnitz and his wife and five children slept, and a
living-room. Two corners of this living-room were curtained off for lodgers; in one Rosicky slept on an old
horsehair sofa, with a feather quilt to wrap himself
in. The other corner was rented to a wretched, dirty
boy, who was studying the violin. He actually practised
there. Rosicky was dirty, too. There was no way to be
anything else. Mrs. Lifschnitz got the water she cooked
and washed with from a pump in a brick court, four
flights down. There were bugs in the place, and multi-
tudes of fleas, though the poor woman did the best she
could. Rosicky knew she often went empty to give another potato or a spoonful of dripping to the two hungry, sad-eyed boys who lodged with her. He used to
think he would never get out of there, never get a clean
shirt to his back again. What would he do, he won-

dered, when his clothes actually dropped to pieces and the worn cloth wouldn't hold patches any longer?

It was still early when the old farmer put aside his sewing and his recollections. The sky had been a dark grey all day, with not a gleam of sun, and the light failed at four o'clock. He went to shave and change his shirt while the turkey was roasting. Rudolph and Polly were coming over for supper.

After supper they sat round in the kitchen, and the younger boys were saying how sorry they were it hadn't snowed. Everybody was sorry. They wanted a deep snow that would lie long and keep the wheat warm, and leave the ground soaked when it melted.

"Yes, sir!" Rudolph broke out fiercely; "if we have another dry year like last year, there's going to be hard times in this country."

Rosicky filled his pipe. "You boys don't know what hard times is. You don't owe nobody, you got plenty to eat an' keep warm, an' plenty water to keep clean. When you got them, you can't have it very hard."

Rudolph frowned, opened and shut his big right hand, and dropped it clenched upon his knee. "I've got to have a good deal more than that, Father, or I'll quit this farming gamble. I can always make good wages railroading, or at the packing house, and be sure of my money."

"Maybe so," his father answered dryly.

Mary, who had just come in from the pantry and was wiping her hands on the roller towel, thought Rudy and his father were getting too serious. She brought her darning-basket and sat down in the middle of the group.

"I ain't much afraid of hard times, Rudy," she said heartily. "We've had a plenty, but we've always come through. Your father wouldn't never take nothing very hard, not even hard times. I got a mind to tell you a story on him. Maybe you boys can't hardly remember the year we had that terrible hot wind, that burned everything up on the Fourth of July? All the corn an' the gardens. An' that was in the days when we didn't have alfalfa yet, — I guess it wasn't invented.

"Well, that very day your father was out cultivatin' corn, and I was here in the kitchen makin' plum preserves. We had bushels of plums that year. I noticed it was terrible hot, but it's always hot in the kitchen when you're preservin', an' I was too busy with my plums to mind. Anton come in from the field about three o'clock, an' I asked him what was the matter.

" 'Nothin',' he says, 'but it's pretty hot, an' I think I

won't work no more today.' He stood round for a few minutes, an' then he says: 'Ain't you near through? I want you should git up a nice supper for us tonight. It's Fourth of July.'

"I told him to git along, that I was right in the middle of preservin', but the plums would taste good on hot biscuit. 'I'm goin' to have fried chicken, too,' he says, and he went off an' killed a couple. You three oldest boys was little fellers, playin' round outside, real hot an' sweaty, an' your father took you to the horse tank down by the windmill an' took off your clothes an' put you in. Them two box-elder trees was little then, but they made shade over the tank. Then he took off all his own clothes, an' got in with you. While he was playin' in the water with you, the Methodist preacher drove into our place to say how all the neighbours was goin' to meet at the schoolhouse that night, to pray for rain. He drove right to the windmill, of course, and there was your father and you three with no clothes on. I was in the kitchen door, an' I had to laugh, for the preacher acted like he ain't never seen a naked man before. He surely was embarrassed, an' your father couldn't git to his clothes; they was all hangin' up on the windmill to let the sweat dry out of 'em. So he laid in the tank where he was, an' put one of you boys on top of him to cover him up a little, an' talked to the preacher.

"When you got through playin' in the water, he put clean clothes on you and a clean shirt on himself, an' by that time I'd begun to get supper. He says: 'It's too hot in here to eat comfortable. Let's have a picnic in the orchard. We'll eat our supper behind the mulberry hedge, under them linden trees.'

"So he carried our supper down, an' a bottle of my wild-grape wine, an' everything tasted good, I can tell you. The wind got cooler as the sun was goin' down, and it turned out pleasant, only I noticed how the leaves was curled up on the linden trees. That made me think, an' I asked your father if that hot wind all day hadn't been terrible hard on the gardens an' the corn.

" 'Corn,' he says, 'there ain't no corn.'

" 'What you talkin' about?' I said. 'Ain't we got forty acres?'

" 'We ain't got an ear,' he says, 'nor nobody else ain't got none. All the corn in this country was cooked by three o'clock today, like you'd roasted it in an oven.'

" 'You mean you won't get no crop at all?' I asked him. I couldn't believe it, after he'd worked so hard.

" 'No crop this year,' he says. 'That's why we're havin' a picnic. We might as well enjoy what we got.'

"An' that's how your father behaved, when all the neighbours was so discouraged they couldn't look you

43

in the face. An' we enjoyed ourselves that year, poor as
we was, an' our neighbours wasn't a bit better off for
bein' miserable. Some of 'em grieved till they got poor
digestions and couldn't relish what they did have."

The younger boys said they thought their father had
the best of it. But Rudolph was thinking that, all the
same, the neighbours had managed to get ahead more,
in the fifteen years since that time. There must be
something wrong about his father's way of doing things.
He wished he knew what was going on in the back of
Polly's mind. He knew she liked his father, but he knew,
too, that she was afraid of something. When his mother
sent over coffee-cake or prune tarts or a loaf of fresh
bread, Polly seemed to regard them with a certain suspicion. When she observed to him that his brothers had
nice manners, her tone implied that it was remarkable
they should have. With his mother she was stiff and on
her guard. Mary's hearty frankness and gusts of good
humour irritated her. Polly was afraid of being unusual
or conspicuous in any way, of being "ordinary," as she
said!

When Mary had finished her story, Rosicky laid aside
his pipe.

"You boys like me to tell you about some of dem
hard times I been through in London?" Warmly en-

couraged, he sat rubbing his forehead along the deep creases. It was bothersome to tell a long story in English (he nearly always talked to the boys in Czech), but he wanted Polly to hear this one.

"Well, you know about dat tailor shop I worked in in London? I had one Christmas dere I ain't never forgot. Times was awful bad before Christmas; de boss ain't got much work, an' have it awful hard to pay his rent. It ain't so much fun, bein' poor in a big city like London, I'll say! All de windows is full of good t'ings to eat, an' all de pushcarts in de streets is full, an' you smell 'em all de time, an' you ain't got no money, — not a damn bit. I didn't mind de cold so much, though I didn't have no overcoat, chust a short jacket I'd outgrowed so it wouldn't meet on me, an' my hands was chapped raw. But I always had a good appetite, like you all know, an' de sight of dem pork pies in de windows was awful fur me!

"Day before Christmas was terrible foggy dat year, an' dat fog gits into your bones and makes you all damp like. Mrs. Lifschnitz didn't give us nothin' but a little bread an' drippin' for supper, because she was savin' to try for to give us a good dinner on Christmas Day. After supper de boss say I can go an' enjoy myself, so I went into de streets to listen to de Christmas singers. Dey

45

sing old songs an' make very nice music, an' I run round after dem a good ways, till I got awful hungry. I t'ink maybe if I go home, I can sleep till morning an' forgit my belly.

"I went into my corner real quiet, and roll up in my fedder quilt. But I ain't got my head down, till I smell somet'ing good. Seem like it git stronger an' stronger, an' I can't git to sleep noway. I can't understand dat smell. Dere was a gas light in a hall across de court, dat always shine in at my window a little. I got up an' look round. I got a little wooden box in my corner fur a stool, 'cause I ain't got no chair. I picks up dat box, and under it dere is a roast goose on a platter! I can't believe my eyes. I carry it to de window where de light comes in, an' touch it and smell it to find out, an' den I taste it to be sure. I say, I will eat chust one little bite of dat goose, so I can go to sleep, and tomorrow I won't eat none at all. But I tell you, boys, when I stop, one half of dat goose was gone!"

The narrator bowed his head, and the boys shouted. But little Josephine slipped behind his chair and kissed him on the neck beneath his ear.

"Poor little Papa, I don't want him to be hungry!"

"Da's long ago, child. I ain't never been hungry since I had your mudder to cook fur me."

"Go on and tell us the rest, please," said Polly.

46

Neighbour Rosicky

"Well, when I come to realize what I done, of course, I felt terrible. I felt better in de stomach, but very bad in de heart. I set on my bed wid dat platter on my knees, an' it all come to me; how hard dat poor woman save to buy dat goose, and how she get some neighbour to cook it dat got more fire, an' how she put it in my corner to keep it away from dem hungry children. Dere was a old carpet hung up to shut my corner off, an' de children wasn't allowed to go in dere. An' I know she put it in my corner because she trust me more'n she did de violin boy. I can't stand it to face her after I spoil de Christmas. So I put on my shoes and go out into de city. I tell myself I better throw myself in de river; but I guess I ain't dat kind of a boy.

"It was after twelve o'clock, an' terrible cold, an' I start out to walk about London all night. I walk along de river awhile, but dere was lots of drunks all along; men, and women too. I chust move along to keep away from de police. I git onto de Strand, an' den over to New Oxford Street, where dere was a big German restaurant on de ground floor, wid big windows all fixed up fine, an' I could see de people havin' parties inside. While I was lookin' in, two men and two ladies come out, laughin' and talkin' and feelin' happy about all dey been eatin' an' drinkin', and dey was speakin' Czech, — not like de Austrians, but like de home folks talk it.

"I guess I went crazy, an' I done what I ain't never done before nor since. I went right up to dem gay people an' begun to beg dem: 'Fellow-countrymen, for God's sake give me money enough to buy a goose!'

"Dey laugh, of course, but de ladies speak awful kind to me, an' dey take me back into de restaurant and give me hot coffee and cakes, an' make me tell all about how I happened to come to London, an' what I was doin' dere. Dey take my name and where I work down on paper, an' both of dem ladies give me ten shillings.

"De big market at Covent Garden ain't very far away, an' by dat time it was open. I go dere an' buy a big goose an' some pork pies, an' potatoes and onions, an' cakes an' oranges fur de children, — all I could carry! When I git home, everybody is still asleep. I pile all I bought on de kitchen table, an' go in an' lay down on my bed, an' I ain't waken up till I hear dat woman scream when she come out into her kitchen. My goodness, but she was surprise! She laugh an' cry at de same time, an' hug me and waken all de children. She ain't stop fur no breakfast; she git de Christmas dinner ready dat morning, and we all sit down an' eat all we can hold. I ain't never seen dat violin boy have all he can hold before.

"Two three days after dat, de two men come to hunt me up, an' dey ask my boss, and he give me a good report an' tell dem I was a steady boy all right. One of dem Bohemians was very smart an' run a Bohemian newspaper in New York, an' de odder was a rich man, in de importing business, an' dey been travelling togedder. Dey told me how t'ings was easier in New York, an' offered to pay my passage when dey was goin' home soon on a boat. My boss say to me: 'You go. You ain't got no chance here, an' I like to see you git ahead, fur you always been a good boy to my woman, and fur dat fine Christmas dinner you give us all.' An' da's how I got to New York."

That night when Rudolph and Polly, arm in arm, were runnning home across the fields with the bitter wind at their backs, his heart leaped for joy when she said she thought they might have his family come over for supper on New Year's Eve. "Let's get up a nice supper, and not let your mother help at all; make her be company for once."

"That would be lovely of you, Polly," he said humbly. He was a very simple, modest boy, and he, too, felt vaguely that Polly and her sisters were more experienced and worldly than his people.

VI

THE winter turned out badly for farmers. It was bitterly cold, and after the first light snows before Christmas there was no snow at all, — and no rain.

March was as bitter as February. On those days when the wind fairly punished the country, Rosicky sat by his window. In the fall he and the boys had put in a big wheat planting, and now the seed had frozen in the ground. All that land would have to be ploughed up and planted over again, planted in corn. It had happened before, but he was younger then, and he never worried about what had to be. He was sure of himself and of Mary; he knew they could bear what they had to bear, that they would always pull through somehow. But he was not so sure about the young ones, and he felt troubled because Rudolph and Polly were having such a hard start.

Sitting beside his flowering window while the panes rattled and the wind blew in under the door, Rosicky gave himself to reflection as he had not done since those Sundays in the loft of the furniture-factory in New York, long ago. Then he was trying to find what he wanted in life for himself; now he was trying to find what he wanted for his boys, and why it was he so hungered to feel sure they would be here, working this very land, after he was gone.

They would have to work hard on the farm, and probably they would never do much more than make a living. But if he could think of them as staying here on the land, he wouldn't have to fear any great unkindness for them. Hardships, certainly; it was a hardship to have the wheat freeze in the ground when seed was so high; and to have to sell your stock because you had no feed. But there would be other years when everything came along right, and you caught up. And what you had was your own. You didn't have to choose between bosses and strikers, and go wrong either way. You didn't have to do with dishonest and cruel people. They were the only things in his experience he had found terrifying and horrible; the look in the eyes of a dishonest and crafty man, of a scheming and rapacious woman.

In the country, if you had a mean neighbour, you could keep off his land and make him keep off yours. But in the city, all the foulness and misery and brutality of your neighbours was part of your life. The worst things he had come upon in his journey through the world were human, — depraved and poisonous specimens of man. To this day he could recall certain terrible faces in the London streets. There were mean people everywhere, to be sure, even in their own country town here. But they weren't tempered, hardened, sharpened, like the treacherous people in cities who live by grinding or cheating or poisoning their fellow-men. He had helped to bury two of his fellow-workmen in the tailoring trade, and he was distrustful of the organized industries that see one out of the world in big cities. Here, if you were sick, you had Doctor Ed to look after you; and if you died, fat Mr. Haycock, the kindest man in the world, buried you.

It seemed to Rosicky that for good, honest boys like his, the worst they could do on the farm was better than the best they would be likely to do in the city. If he'd had a mean boy, now, one who was crooked and sharp and tried to put anything over on his brothers, then town would be the place for him. But he had no such boy. As for Rudolph, the discontented one, he would give the shirt off his back to anyone who touched his heart. What Rosicky really hoped for his boys was that they could get through the world without ever knowing much about the cruelty of human beings. "Their mother and me ain't prepared them for that," he sometimes said to himself.

These thoughts brought him back to a grateful consideration of his own case. What an escape he had had, to be sure! He, too, in his time, had had to take money for repair work from the hand of a hungry child who let it go so wistfully; because it was money due his boss. And now, in all these years, he had never had to take a cent from anyone in bitter need, — never had to look at the face of a woman become like a wolf's from struggle and famine. When he thought of these things, Rosicky would put on his cap and jacket and slip down to the barn and give his work-horses a little extra oats, letting them eat it out of his hand in their slobbery fashion. It was his way of expressing what he felt, and made him chuckle with pleasure.

The spring came warm, with blue skies, — but dry, dry as a bone. The boys began ploughing up the wheat-fields to plant them over in corn. Rosicky would stand at the fence corner and watch them, and the earth was so dry it blew up in clouds of brown dust that hid the horses and the sulky plough and the driver. It was a bad outlook.

The big alfalfa-field that lay between the home place and Rudolph's came up green, but Rosicky was worried because during that open windy winter a great many Russian thistle plants had blown in there and lodged. He kept asking the boys to rake them out; he was afraid their seed would root and "take the alfalfa." Rudolph said that was nonsense. The boys were working so hard planting corn, their father felt he couldn't insist about the thistles, but he set great store by that big alfalfa-field. It was a feed you could depend on, — and there was some deeper reason, vague, but strong. The pecu-

liar green of that clover woke early memories in old
Rosicky, went back to something in his childhood in the
old world. When he was a little boy, he had played in
fields of that strong blue-green colour.

One morning, when Rudolph had gone to town in
the car, leaving a work-team idle in his barn, Rosicky
went over to his son's place, put the horses to the
buggy-rake, and set about quietly raking up those thistles. He behaved with guilty caution, and rather enjoyed stealing a march on Doctor Ed, who was just then
taking his first vacation in seven years of practice and
was attending a clinic in Chicago. Rosicky got the thistles raked up, but did not stop to burn them. That
would take some time, and his breath was pretty short,
so he thought he had better get the horses back to the
barn.

He got them into the barn and to their stalls, but the
pain had come on so sharp in his chest that he didn't try
to take the harness off. He started for the house, bending lower with every step. The cramp in his chest was
shutting him up like a jack-knife. When he reached the
windmill, he swayed and caught at the ladder. He saw
Polly coming down the hill, running with the swiftness
of a slim greyhound. In a flash she had her shoulder
under his armpit.

"Lean on me, Father, hard! Don't be afraid. We can get to the house all right."

Somehow they did, though Rosicky became blind with pain; he could keep on his legs, but he couldn't steer his course. The next thing he was conscious of was lying on Polly's bed, and Polly bending over him wringing out bath towels in hot water and putting them on his chest. She stopped only to throw coal into the stove, and she kept the tea-kettle and the black pot going. She put these hot applications on him for nearly an hour, she told him afterwards, and all that time he was drawn up stiff and blue, with the sweat pouring off him.

As the pain gradually loosed its grip, the stiffness went out of his jaws, the black circles round his eyes disappeared, and a little of his natural colour came back. When his daughter-in-law buttoned his shirt over his chest at last, he sighed.

"Da's fine, de way I feel now, Polly. It was a awful bad spell, an' I was so sorry it all come on you like it did."

Polly was flushed and excited. "Is the pain really gone? Can I leave you long enough to telephone over to your place?"

Rosicky's eyelids fluttered. "Don't telephone, Polly. It ain't no use to scare my wife. It's nice and quiet here, an' if I ain't too much trouble to you, just let me lay still

till I feel like myself. I ain't got no pain now. It's nice here."

Polly bent over him and wiped the moisture from his face. "Oh, I'm so glad it's over!" she broke out impulsively. "It just broke my heart to see you suffer so, Father."

Rosicky motioned her to sit down on the chair where the tea-kettle had been, and looked up at her with that lively affectionate gleam in his eyes. "You was awful good to me, I won't never forgit dat. I hate it to be sick on you like dis. Down at de barn I say to myself, dat young girl ain't had much experience in sickness, I don't want to scare her, an' maybe she's got a baby comin' or somet'ing."

Polly took his hand. He was looking at her so intently and affectionately and confidingly; his eyes seemed to caress her face, to regard it with pleasure. She frowned with her funny streaks of eyebrows, and then smiled back at him.

"I guess maybe there is something of that kind going to happen. But I haven't told anyone yet, not my mother or Rudolph. You'll be the first to know."

His hand pressed hers. She noticed that it was warm again. The twinkle in his yellow-brown eyes seemed to come nearer.

56

Neighbour Rosicky

"I like mighty well to see dat little child, Polly," was all he said. Then he closed his eyes and lay half-smiling. But Polly sat still, thinking hard. She had a sudden feeling that nobody in the world, not her mother, not Rudolph, or anyone, really loved her as much as old Rosicky did. It perplexed her. She sat frowning and trying to puzzle it out. It was as if Rosicky had a special gift for loving people, something that was like an ear for music or an eye for colour. It was quiet, unobtrusive; it was merely there. You saw it in his eyes, — perhaps that was why they were merry. You felt it in his hands, too. After he dropped off to sleep, she sat holding his warm, broad, flexible brown hand. She had never seen another in the least like it. She wondered if it wasn't a kind of gypsy hand, it was so alive and quick and light in its communications, — very strange in a farmer. Nearly all the farmers she knew had huge lumps of fists, like mauls, or they were knotty and bony and uncomfortable-looking, with stiff fingers. But Rosicky's was like quicksilver, flexible, muscular, about the colour of a pale cigar, with deep, deep creases across the palm. It wasn't nervous, it wasn't a stupid lump; it was a warm brown human hand, with some cleverness in it, a great deal of generosity, and something else which Polly could only call "gypsy-like," — something nimble and lively and sure, in the way that animals are.

Polly remembered that hour long afterwards; it had been like an awakening to her. It seemed to her that she had never learned so much about life from anything as from old Rosicky's hand. It brought her to herself; it communicated some direct and untranslatable message.

When she heard Rudolph coming in the car, she ran out to meet him.

"Oh, Rudy, your father's been awful sick! He raked up those thistles he's been worrying about, and afterwards he could hardly get to the house. He suffered so I was afraid he was going to die."

Rudolph jumped to the ground. "Where is he now?"

"On the bed. He's asleep. I was terribly scared, because, you know, I'm so fond of your father." She slipped her arm through his and they went into the house. That afternoon they took Rosicky home and put him to bed, though he protested that he was quite well again.

The next morning he got up and dressed and sat down to breakfast with his family. He told Mary that his coffee tasted better than usual to him, and he warned the boys not to bear any tales to Doctor Ed when he got home. After breakfast he sat down by his window to do some patching and asked Mary to thread several needles for him before she went to feed her chickens, — her eyes were better than his, and her hands steadier. He lit his pipe and took up John's overalls. Mary had been watching him anxiously all morning, and as she went out of the door with her bucket of scraps, she saw that he was smiling. He was thinking, indeed, about Polly, and how he might never have known what a tender heart she had if he hadn't got sick over there. Girls nowadays didn't wear their heart on their sleeve. But now he knew Polly would make a fine woman after the foolishness wore off. Either a woman had that sweetness at her heart or she hadn't. You couldn't always tell by the look of them; but if they had that, everything came out right in the end.

After he had taken a few stitches, the cramp began in his chest, like yesterday. He put his pipe cautiously down on the window-sill and bent over to ease the pull. No use, — he had better try to get to his bed if he could. He rose and groped his way across the familiar floor, which was rising and falling like the deck of a ship. At the door he fell. When Mary came in, she found him lying there, and the moment she touched him she knew that he was gone.

Doctor Ed was away when Rosicky died, and for the first few weeks after he got home he was hard driven.

59

Every day he said to himself that he must get out to see that family that had lost their father. One soft, warm moonlight night in early summer he started for the farm. His mind was on other things, and not until his road ran by the graveyard did he realize that Rosicky wasn't over there on the hill where the red lamplight shone, but here, in the moonlight. He stopped his car, shut off the engine, and sat there for a while.

A sudden hush had fallen on his soul. Everything here seemed strangely moving and significant, though signifying what, he did not know. Close by the wire fence stood Rosicky's mowing-machine, where one of the boys had been cutting hay that afternoon; his own work-horses had been going up and down there. The new-cut hay perfumed all the night air. The moonlight silvered the long, billowy grass that grew over the graves and hid the fence; the few little evergreens stood out black in it, like shadows in a pool. The sky was very blue and soft, the stars rather faint because the moon was full.

For the first time it struck Doctor Ed that this was really a beautiful graveyard. He thought of city ceme-teries; acres of shrubbery and heavy stone, so arranged and lonely and unlike anything in the living world. Cities of the dead, indeed; cities of the forgotten, of the "put away." But this was open and free, this little square of long grass which the wind for ever stirred. Nothing but the sky overhead, and the many-coloured fields running on until they met that sky. The horses worked here in summer; the neighbours passed on their way to town; and over yonder, in the cornfield, Rosicky's own cattle would be eating fodder as winter came on. Nothing could be more undeathlike than this place; nothing could be more right for a man who had helped to do the work of great cities and had always longed for the open country and had got to it at last. Rosicky's life seemed to him complete and beautiful.

New York, 1928

Old Mrs. Harris

Old Mrs. Harris

I

MRS. David Rosen, cross-stitch in hand, sat looking out of the window across her own green lawn to the ragged, sunburned back yard of her neighbours on the right. Occasionally she glanced anxiously over her shoulder toward her shining kitchen, with a black and white linoleum floor in big squares, like a marble pavement.

"Will dat woman never go?" she muttered impatiently, just under her breath. She spoke with a slight accent — it affected only her *th's*, and, occasionally, the letter *v*. But people in Skyline thought this unfortunate, in a woman whose superiority they recognized.

Mrs. Rosen ran out to move the sprinkler to another spot on the lawn, and in doing so she saw what she had been waiting to see. From the house next door a tall, handsome woman emerged, dressed in white broadcloth and a hat with white lilacs; she carried a sunshade and walked with a free, energetic step, as if she were going out on a pleasant errand.

Mrs. Rosen darted quickly back into the house, lest her neighbour should hail her and stop to talk. She herself was in her kitchen housework dress, a crisp blue chambray which fitted smoothly over her tightly corseted figure, and her lustrous black hair was done in two smooth braids, wound flat at the back of her head, like a braided rug. She did not stop for a hat—her dark, ruddy, salmon-tinted skin had little to fear from the sun. She opened the half-closed oven door and took out a symmetrically plaited coffee-cake, beautifully browned, delicately peppered over with poppy seeds, with sugary margins about the twists. On the kitchen table a tray stood ready with cups and saucers. She wrapped the cake in a napkin, snatched up a little French coffee-pot with a black wooden handle, and ran across her green lawn, through the alley-way and the sandy, unkept yard next door, and entered her neighbour's house by the kitchen.

The kitchen was hot and empty, full of the untempered afternoon sun. A door stood open into the next room; a cluttered, hideous room, yet somehow homely. There, beside a goods-box covered with figured oilcloth, stood an old woman in a brown calico dress,

66

washing her hot face and neck at a tin basin. She stood with her feet wide apart, in an attitude of profound weariness. She started guiltily as the visitor entered.

"Don't let me disturb you, Grandma," called Mrs. Rosen. "I always have my coffee at dis hour in the afternoon. I was just about to sit down to it when I thought: 'I will run over and see if Grandma Harris won't take a cup with me.' I hate to drink my coffee alone."

Grandma looked troubled, — at a loss. She folded her towel and concealed it behind a curtain hung across the corner of the room to make a poor sort of closet. The old lady was always composed in manner, but it was clear that she felt embarrassment.

"Thank you, Mrs. Rosen. What a pity Victoria just this minute went down town!"

"But dis time I came to see you yourself, Grandma. Don't let me disturb you. Sit down there in your own rocker, and I will put my tray on this little chair between us, so!"

Mrs. Harris sat down in her black wooden rocking-chair with curved arms and a faded cretonne pillow on the wooden seat. It stood in the corner beside a narrow spindle-frame lounge. She looked on silently while Mrs. Rosen uncovered the cake and delicately broke it with her plump, smooth, dusky-red hands. The old lady

did not seem pleased, — seemed uncertain and appre-
hensive, indeed. But she was not fussy or fidgety. She
had the kind of quiet, intensely quiet, dignity that
comes from complete resignation to the chances of life.
She watched Mrs. Rosen's deft hands out of grave,
steady brown eyes.

"Dis is Mr. Rosen's favourite coffee-cake, Grandma,
and I want you to try it. You are such a good cook
yourself, I would like your opinion of my cake."

"It's very nice, ma'am," said Mrs. Harris politely, but
without enthusiasm.

"And you aren't drinking your coffee; do you like
more cream in it?"

"No, thank you. I'm letting it cool a little. I generally
drink it that way."

"Of course she does," thought Mrs. Rosen, "since
she never has her coffee until all the family are done
breakfast!"

Mrs. Rosen had brought Grandma Harris coffee-
cake time and again, but she knew that Grandma
merely tasted it and saved it for her daughter Victoria,
who was as fond of sweets as her own children, and
jealous about them, moreover, — couldn't bear that special dainties should come into the house for anyone but
herself. Mrs. Rosen, vexed at her failures, had deter-

mined that just once she would take a cake to "de old lady Harris," and with her own eyes see her eat it. The result was not all she had hoped. Receiving a visitor alone, unsupervised by her daughter, having cake and coffee that should properly be saved for Victoria, was all so irregular that Mrs. Harris could not enjoy it. Mrs. Rosen doubted if she tasted the cake as she swallowed it, — certainly she ate it without relish, as a hollow form. But Mrs. Rosen enjoyed her own cake, at any rate, and she was glad of an opportunity to sit quietly and look at Grandmother, who was more interesting to her than the handsome Victoria.

It was a queer place to be having coffee, when Mrs. Rosen liked order and comeliness so much: a hideous, cluttered room, furnished with a rocking-horse, a sewing-machine, an empty baby-buggy. A walnut table stood against a blind window, piled high with old magazines and tattered books, and children's caps and coats. There was a wash-stand (two wash-stands, if you counted the oilcloth-covered box as one). A corner of the room was curtained off with some black-and-red-striped cotton goods, for a clothes closet. In another corner was the wooden lounge with a thin mattress and a red calico spread which was Grandma's bed. Beside it was her wooden rocking-chair, and the little splint-bottom chair with the legs sawed short on which her darning-basket usually stood, but which Mrs. Rosen was now using for a tea-table.

The old lady was always impressive, Mrs. Rosen was thinking, — one could not say why. Perhaps it was the way she held her head, — so simply, unprotesting and unprotected; or the gravity of her large, deep-set brown eyes, a warm, reddish brown, though their look, always direct, seemed to ask nothing and hope for nothing. They were not cold, but inscrutable, with no kindling gleam of intercourse in them. There was the kind of nobility about her head that there is about an old lion's: an absence of self-consciousness, vanity, preoccupation — something absolute. Her grey hair was parted in the middle, wound in two little horns over her ears, and done in a little flat knot behind. Her mouth was large and composed, — resigned, the corners drooping. Mrs. Rosen had very seldom heard her laugh (and then it was a gentle, polite laugh which meant only politeness). But she had observed that whenever Mrs. Harris's grand-children were about, tumbling all over her, asking for cookies, teasing her to read to them, the old lady looked happy.

As she drank her coffee, Mrs. Rosen tried one subject after another to engage Mrs. Harris's attention.

"Do you feel this hot weather, Grandma? I am afraid you are over the stove too much. Let those naughty children have a cold lunch occasionally."

"No'm, I don't mind the heat. It's apt to come on like this for a spell in May. I don't feel the stove. I'm accustomed to it."

"Oh, so am I! But I get very impatient with my cooking in hot weather. Do you miss your old home in Tennessee very much, Grandma?"

"No'm, I can't say I do. Mr. Templeton thought Colorado was a better place to bring up the children."

"But you had things much more comfortable down there, I'm sure. These little wooden houses are too hot in summer."

"Yes'm, we were more comfortable. We had more room."

"And a flower-garden, and beautiful old trees, Mrs. Templeton told me."

"Yes'm, we had a great deal of shade."

Mrs. Rosen felt that she was not getting anywhere. She almost believed that Grandma thought she had come on an equivocal errand, to spy out something in Victoria's absence. Well, perhaps she had! Just for once she would like to get past the others to the real grandmother, — and the real grandmother was on her guard, as always. At this moment she heard a faint miaow. Mrs. Harris rose, lifting herself by the wooden arms of her chair, said: "Excuse me," went into the kitchen, and opened the screen door.

In walked a large, handsome, thickly furred Maltese cat, with long whiskers and yellow eyes and a white star on his breast. He preceded Grandmother, waited until she sat down. Then he sprang up into her lap and settled himself comfortably in the folds of her full-gathered calico skirt. He rested his chin in his deep bluish fur and regarded Mrs. Rosen. It struck her that he held his head in just the way Grandmother held hers. And Grandmother now became more alive, as if some missing part of herself were restored.

"This is Blue Boy," she said, stroking him. "In winter, when the screen door ain't on, he lets himself in. He stands up on his hind legs and presses the thumb-latch with his paw, and just walks in like anybody."

"He's your cat, isn't he, Grandma?" Mrs. Rosen couldn't help prying just a little; if she could find but a single thing that was Grandma's own!

"He's our cat," replied Mrs. Harris. "We're all very fond of him. I expect he's Vickie's more'n anybody's."

"Of course!" groaned Mrs. Rosen to herself. "Dat Vickie is her mother over again."

Here Mrs. Harris made her first unsolicited remark. "If you was to be troubled with mice at any time, Mrs. Rosen, ask one of the boys to bring Blue Boy over to you, and he'll clear them out. He's a master mouser." She scratched the thick blue fur at the back of his neck, and he began a deep purring. Mrs. Harris smiled. "We call that spinning, back with us. Our children still say: 'Listen to Blue Boy spin,' though none of 'em is ever heard a spinning-wheel — except maybe Vickie remembers."

"Did you have a spinning-wheel in your own house, Grandma Harris?"

"Yes'm. Miss Sadie Crummer used to come and spin for us. She was left with no home of her own, and it was to give her something to do, as much as anything, that we had her. I spun a good deal myself, in my young days." Grandmother stopped and put her hands on the arms of her chair, as if to rise. "Did you hear a door open? It might be Victoria."

"No, it was the wind shaking the screen door. Mrs. Templeton won't be home yet. She is probably in my husband's store this minute, ordering him about. All the merchants down town will take anything from your daughter. She is very popular wid de gentlemen, Grandma."

Mrs. Harris smiled complacently. "Yes'm. Victoria was always much admired."

At this moment a chorus of laughter broke in upon the warm silence, and a host of children, as it seemed to Mrs. Rosen, ran through the yard. The hand-pump on the back porch, outside the kitchen door, began to scrape and gurgle.

"It's the children, back from school," said Grandma. "They are getting a cool drink."

"But where is the baby, Grandma?"

"Vickie took Hughie in his cart over to Mr. Holliday's yard, where she studies. She's right good about minding him."

Mrs. Rosen was glad to hear that Vickie was good for something.

Three little boys came running in through the kitchen; the twins, aged ten, and Ronald, aged six, who went to kindergarten. They snatched off their caps and threw their jackets and school bags on the table, the sewing-machine, the rocking-horse.

"Howdy do, Mrs. Rosen." They spoke to her nicely. They had nice voices, nice faces, and were always courteous, like their father. "We are going to play in our back yard with some of the boys, Gram'ma," said one of the twins respectfully, and they ran out to join a troop of schoolmates who were already shouting and racing over that poor trampled back yard, strewn with velocipedes and croquet mallets and toy wagons, which was such an eyesore to Mrs. Rosen.

Mrs. Rosen got up and took her tray.

"Can't you stay a little, ma'am? Victoria will be here any minute."

But her tone let Mrs. Rosen know that Grandma really wished her to leave before Victoria returned.

A few moments after Mrs. Rosen had put the tray down in her own kitchen, Victoria Templeton came up the wooden sidewalk, attended by Mr. Rosen, who had quitted his store half an hour earlier than usual for the pleasure of walking home with her. Mrs. Templeton stopped by the picket fence to smile at the children playing in the back yard,—and it was a real smile, she was glad to see them. She called Ronald over to the fence to give him a kiss. He was hot and sticky.

"Was your teacher nice today? Now run in and ask Grandma to wash your face and put a clean waist on you."

II

THAT night Mrs. Harris got supper with an effort—had to drive herself harder than usual. Mandy, the bound girl they had brought with them

75

from the South, noticed that the old lady was uncertain and short of breath. The hours from two to four, when Mrs. Harris usually rested, had not been at all restful this afternoon. There was an understood rule that Grandmother was not to receive visitors alone. Mrs. Rosen's call, and her cake and coffee, were too much out of the accepted order. Nervousness had prevented the old lady from getting any repose during her visit.

After the rest of the family had left the supper table, she went into the dining-room and took her place, but she ate very little. She put away the food that was left, and then, while Mandy washed the dishes, Grandma sat down in her rocking-chair in the dark and dozed.

The three little boys came in from playing under the electric light (arc lights had been but lately installed in Skyline) and began begging Mrs. Harris to read *Tom Sawyer* to them. Grandmother loved to read, anything at all, the Bible or the continued story in the Chicago weekly paper. She roused herself, lit her brass "safety lamp," and pulled her black rocker out of its corner to the wash-stand (the table was too far away from her corner, and anyhow it was completely covered with coats and school satchels). She put on her old-fashioned silver-rimmed spectacles and began to read. Ronald lay down on Grandmother's lounge bed, and the twins, Albert and Adelbert, called Bert and Del, sat down against the wall, one on a low box covered with felt, and the other on the little sawed-off chair upon which Mrs. Rosen had served coffee. They looked intently at Mrs. Harris, and she looked intently at the book.

Presently Vickie, the oldest grandchild, came in. She was fifteen. Her mother was entertaining callers in the parlour, callers who didn't interest Vickie, so she was on her way up to her own room by the kitchen stairway.

Mrs. Harris looked up over her glasses. "Vickie, maybe you'd take the book awhile, and I can do my darning."

"All right," said Vickie. Reading aloud was one of the things she would always do toward the general comfort. She sat down by the wash-stand and went on with the story. Grandmother got her darning-basket and began to drive her needle across great knee-holes in the boys' stockings. Sometimes she nodded for a moment, and her hands fell into her lap. After a while the little boy on the lounge went to sleep. But the twins sat upright, their hands on their knees, their round brown eyes fastened upon Vickie, and when there was anything funny, they giggled. They were chubby, dark-skinned little boys, with round jolly faces, white teeth, and yellow-brown eyes that were always bubbling with fun unless

77

they were sad, — even then their eyes never got red or weepy. Their tears sparkled and fell; left no trace but a streak on the cheeks, perhaps.

Presently old Mrs. Harris gave out a long snore of utter defeat. She had been overcome at last. Vickie put down the book. "That's enough for tonight. Grandmother's sleepy, and Ronald's fast asleep. What'll we do with him?"

"Bert and me'll get him undressed," said Adelbert. The twins roused the sleepy little boy and prodded him up the back stairway to the bare room without window blinds, where he was put into his cot beside their double bed. Vickie's room was across the narrow hallway; not much bigger than a closet, but, anyway, it was her own. She had a chair and an old dresser, and beside her bed was a high stool which she used as a lamp-table, — she always read in bed.

After Vickie went upstairs, the house was quiet. Hughie, the baby, was asleep in his mother's room, and Victoria herself, who still treated her husband as if he were her "beau," had persuaded him to take her down town to the ice-cream parlour. Grandmother's room, between the kitchen and the dining-room, was rather like a passage-way; but now that the children were upstairs and Victoria was off enjoying herself somewhere,

Old Mrs. Harris

Mrs. Harris could be sure of enough privacy to undress. She took off the calico cover from her lounge bed and folded it up, put on her nightgown and white nightcap.

Mandy, the bound girl, appeared at the kitchen door.

"Miz' Harris," she said in a guarded tone, ducking her head, "you want me to rub your feet for you?"

For the first time in the long day the old woman's low composure broke a little. "Oh, Mandy, I would take it kindly of you!" she breathed gratefully.

That had to be done in the kitchen; Victoria didn't like anybody slopping about. Mrs. Harris put an old checked shawl round her shoulders and followed Mandy. Beside the kitchen stove Mandy had a little wooden tub full of warm water. She knelt down and untied Mrs. Harris's garter strings and took off her flat cloth slippers and stockings.

"Oh, Miz' Harris, your feet an' legs is swelled turrible tonight!"

"I expect they air, Mandy. They feel like it."

"Pore soul!" murmured Mandy. She put Grandma's feet in the tub and, crouching beside it, slowly, slowly rubbed her swollen legs. Mandy was tired, too. Mrs. Harris sat in her nightcap and shawl, her hands crossed in her lap. She never asked for this greatest solace of the day; it was something that Mandy gave, who had nothing else to give. If there could be a comparison in absolutes, Mandy was the needier of the two, — but she was younger. The kitchen was quiet and full of shadow, with only the light from an old lantern. Neither spoke. Mrs. Harris dozed from comfort, and Mandy herself was half asleep as she performed one of the oldest rites of compassion.

Although Mrs. Harris's lounge had no springs, only a thin cotton mattress between her and the wooden slats, she usually went to sleep as soon as she was in bed. To be off her feet, to lie flat, to say over the psalm beginning: *"The Lord is my shepherd,"* was comfort enough. About four o'clock in the morning, however, she would begin to feel the hard slats under her, and the heaviness of the old home-made quilts, with weight but little warmth, on top of her. Then she would reach under her pillow for her little comforter (she called it that to herself) that Mrs. Rosen had given her. It was a tan sweater of very soft brushed wool, with one sleeve torn and ragged. A young nephew from Chicago had spent a fortnight with Mrs. Rosen last summer and had left this behind him. One morning, when Mrs. Harris went out to the stable at the back of the yard to pat Buttercup, the cow, Mrs. Rosen ran across the alley-way.

"Grandma Harris," she said, coming into the shelter

of the stable, "I wonder if you could make any use of this sweater Sammy left? The yarn might be good for your darning."

Mrs. Harris felt of the article gravely. Mrs. Rosen thought her face brightened. "Yes'm, indeed I could use it. I thank you kindly."

She slipped it under her apron, carried it into the house with her, and concealed it under her mattress. There she had kept it ever since. She knew Mrs. Rosen understood how it was; that Victoria couldn't bear to have anything come into the house that was not for her to dispose of.

On winter nights, and even on summer nights after the cocks began to crow, Mrs. Harris often felt cold and lonely about the chest. Sometimes her cat, Blue Boy, would creep in beside her and warm that aching spot. But on spring and summer nights he was likely to be abroad skylarking, and this little sweater had become the dearest of Grandmother's few possessions. It was kinder to her, she used to think, as she wrapped it about her middle, than any of her own children had been. She had married at eighteen and had had eight children; but some died, and some were, as she said, scattered.

After she was warm in that tender spot under the ribs, the old woman could lie patiently on the slats, waiting for daybreak; thinking about the comfortable rambling old house in Tennessee, its feather beds and hand-woven rag carpets and splint-bottom chairs, the mahogany sideboard, and the marble-top parlour table; all that she had left behind to follow Victoria's fortunes.

She did not regret her decision; indeed, there had been no decision. Victoria had never once thought it possible that Ma should not go wherever she and the children went, and Mrs. Harris had never thought it possible. Of course she regretted Tennessee, though she would never admit it to Mrs. Rosen: — the old neighbours, the yard and garden she had worked in all her life, the apple trees she had planted, the lilac arbour, tall enough to walk in, which she had clipped and shaped so many years. Especially she missed her lemon tree, in a tub on the front porch, which bore little lemons almost every summer, and folks would come for miles to see it.

But the road had led westward, and Mrs. Harris didn't believe that women, especially old women, could say when or where they would stop. They were tied to the chariot of young life, and had to go where it went, because they were needed. Mrs. Harris had gathered from Mrs. Rosen's manner, and from comments she occasionally dropped, that the Jewish people had an altogether different attitude toward their old folks; therefore her friendship with this kind neighbour was almost as disturbing as it was pleasant. She didn't want Mrs. Rosen to think that she was "put upon," that there was anything unusual or pitiful in her lot. To be pitied was the deepest hurt anybody could know. And if Victoria once suspected Mrs. Rosen's indignation, it would be all over. She would freeze her neighbour out, and that friendly voice, that quick pleasant chatter with the little foreign twist, would thenceforth be heard only at a distance, in the alley-way or across the fence. Victoria had a good heart, but she was terribly proud and could not bear the least criticism.

As soon as the grey light began to steal into the room, Mrs. Harris would get up softly and wash at the basin on the oilcloth-covered box. She would wet her hair above her forehead, comb it with a little bone comb set in a tin rim, do it up in two smooth little horns over her ears, wipe the comb dry, and put it away in the pocket of her full-gathered calico skirt. She left nothing lying about. As soon as she was dressed, she made her bed, folding her nightgown and nightcap under the pillow, the sweater under the mattress. She smoothed the heavy quilts, and drew the red calico spread neatly over all. Her towel was hung on its special nail behind the curtain. Her soap she kept in a tin tobacco-box; the children's soap was in a crockery saucer. If her soap or towel got mixed up with the children's, Victoria was always sharp about it. The little rented house was much too small for the family, and Mrs. Harris and her "things" were almost required to be invisible. Two clean calico dresses hung in the curtained corner; another was on her back, and a fourth was in the wash. Behind the curtain there was always a good supply of aprons; Victoria bought them at church fairs, and it was a great satisfaction to Mrs. Harris to put on a clean one whenever she liked. Upstairs, in Mandy's attic room over the kitchen, hung a black cashmere dress and a black bonnet with a long crêpe veil, for the rare occasions when Mr. Templeton hired a double buggy and horses and drove his family to a picnic or to Decoration Day exercises. Mrs. Harris rather dreaded these drives, for Victoria was usually cross afterwards.

When Mrs. Harris went out into the kitchen to get breakfast, Mandy always had the fire started and the water boiling. They enjoyed a quiet half-hour before the little boys came running down the stairs, always in a good humour. In winter the boys had their breakfast in the kitchen, with Vickie. Mrs. Harris made Mandy eat the cakes and fried ham the children left, so that she would not fast so long. Mr. and Mrs. Templeton breakfasted rather late, in the dining-room, and they always had fruit and thick cream, — a small pitcher of the very thickest was for Mrs. Templeton. The children were never fussy about their food. As Grandmother often said feelingly to Mrs. Rosen, they were as little trouble as children could possibly be. They sometimes tore their clothes, of course, or got sick. But even when Albert had an abscess in his ear and was in such pain, he would lie for hours on Grandmother's lounge with his cheek on a bag of hot salt, if only she or Vickie would read aloud to him.

"It's true, too, what de old lady says," remarked Mrs. Rosen to her husband one night at supper, "dey are nice children. No one ever taught them anything, but they have good instincts, even dat Vickie. And think, if you please, of all the self-sacrificing mothers we know, — Fannie and Esther, to come near home; how they have planned for those children from infancy and given them every advantage. And now ingratitude and coldness is what dey meet with."

Mr. Rosen smiled his teasing smile. "Evidently your sister and mine have the wrong method. The way to make your children unselfish is to be comfortably selfish yourself."

"But dat woman takes no more responsibility for her children than a cat takes for her kittens. Nor does poor young Mr. Templeton, for dat matter. How can he expect to get so many children started in life, I ask you? It is not at all fair!"

Mr. Rosen sometimes had to hear altogether too much about the Templetons, but he was patient, because it was a bitter sorrow to Mrs. Rosen that she had no children. There was nothing else in the world she wanted so much.

III

MRS. Rosen in one of her blue working dresses, the indigo blue that became a dark skin and dusky red cheeks with a tone of salmon colour, was in her shining kitchen, washing her beautiful dishes — her neighbours often wondered why she used her best china and linen every day — when Vickie Templeton came in with a book under her arm.

"Good day, Mrs. Rosen. Can I have the second volume?"

"Certainly. You know where the books are." She spoke coolly, for it always annoyed her that Vickie never suggested wiping the dishes or helping with such household work as happened to be going on when she dropped in. She hated the girl's bringing-up so much that sometimes she almost hated the girl.

Vickie strolled carelessly through the dining-room into the parlour and opened the doors of one of the big bookcases. Mr. Rosen had a large library, and a great many unusual books. There was a complete set of the Waverley Novels in German, for example; thick, dumpy little volumes bound in tooled leather, with very black type and dramatic engravings printed on wrinkled, yellowing pages. There were many French books, and some of the German classics done into English, such as Coleridge's translation of Schiller's *Wallenstein.*

Of course no other house in Skyline was in the least like Mrs. Rosen's; it was the nearest thing to an art gallery and a museum that the Templetons had ever seen. All the rooms were carpeted alike (that was very unusual), with a soft velvet carpet, little blue and rose flowers scattered on a rose-grey ground. The deep chairs were upholstered in dark blue velvet. The walls were hung with engravings in pale gold frames: some of Raphael's "Hours," a large soft engraving of a castle on the Rhine, and another of cypress trees about a Roman ruin, under a full moon. There were a number of water-colour sketches, made in Italy by Mr. Rosen himself when he was a boy. A rich uncle had taken him abroad as his secretary. Mr. Rosen was a reflective, unambitious man, who didn't mind keeping a clothing-store in a little Western town, so long as he had a great deal of time to read philosophy. He was the only unsuccessful member of a large, rich Jewish family.

Last August, when the heat was terrible in Skyline, and the crops were burned up on all the farms to the north, and the wind from the pink and yellow sand-hills to the south blew so hot that it singed the few green lawns in the town, Vickie had taken to dropping in upon Mrs. Rosen at the very hottest part of the afternoon. Mrs. Rosen knew, of course, that it was probably because the girl had no other cool and quiet place to go — her room at home under the roof would be hot enough! Now, Mrs. Rosen liked to undress and take a nap from three to five, — if only to get out of her tight corsets, for she would have an hourglass figure at any cost. She told Vickie firmly that she was welcome to come if she would read in the parlour with the blind up only a little way, and would be still as a mouse. Vickie came, meekly enough, but she seldom read. She would take a sofa pillow and lie down on the soft carpet and look up at the pictures in the dusky room, and feel a happy, pleasant excitement from the heat and glare outside and the deep shadow and quiet within. Curiously enough, Mrs. Rosen's house never made her dissatisfied with her own; she thought that very nice, too.

Mrs. Rosen, leaving her kitchen in a state of such perfection as the Templetons were unable to sense or to admire, came into the parlour and found her visitor sitting cross-legged on the floor before one of the bookcases.

"Well, Vickie, and how did you get along with *Wilhelm Meister*?"

"I like it," said Vickie.

Mrs. Rosen shrugged. The Templetons always said that; quite as if a book or a cake were lucky to win their approbation.

"Well, *what* did you like?"

"I guess I liked all that about the theatre and Shakspere best."

"It's rather celebrated," remarked Mrs. Rosen dryly. "And are you studying every day? Do you think you will be able to win that scholarship?"

"I don't know. I'm going to try awful hard."

Mrs. Rosen wondered whether any Templeton knew how to try very hard. She reached for her work-basket and began to do cross-stitch. It made her nervous to sit with folded hands.

Vickie was looking at a German book in her lap, an

illustrated edition of *Faust*. She had stopped at a very German picture of Gretchen entering the church, with Faustus gazing at her from behind a rose tree, Mephisto at his shoulder.

"I wish I could read this," she said, frowning at the black Gothic text. "It's splendid, isn't it?"

Mrs. Rosen rolled her eyes upward and sighed. "Oh, my dear, one of de world's masterpieces!"

That meant little to Vickie. She had not been taught to respect masterpieces, she had no scale of that sort in her mind. She cared about a book only because it took hold of her.

She kept turning over the pages. Between the first and second parts, in this edition, there was inserted the *Dies Iræ* hymn in full. She stopped and puzzled over it for a long while.

"Here is something I can read," she said, showing the page to Mrs. Rosen.

Mrs. Rosen looked up from her cross-stitch. "There you have the advantage of me. I do not read Latin. You might translate it for me."

Vickie began:

> "Day of wrath, upon that day
> The world to ashes melts away,
> As David and the Sibyl say.

"But that don't give you the rhyme; every line ought to end in two syllables."

"Never mind if it doesn't give the metre," corrected Mrs. Rosen kindly; "go on, if you can."

Vickie went on stumbling through the Latin verses, and Mrs. Rosen sat watching her. You couldn't tell about Vickie. She wasn't pretty, yet Mrs. Rosen found her attractive. She liked her sturdy build, and the steady vitality that glowed in her rosy skin and dark blue eyes, — even gave a springy quality to her curly reddish-brown hair, which she still wore in a single braid down her back. Mrs. Rosen liked to have Vickie about because she was never listless or dreamy or apathetic. A half-smile nearly always played about her lips and eyes, and it was there because she was pleased with something, not because she wanted to be agreeable. Even a half-smile made her cheeks dimple. She had what her mother called "a happy disposition."

When she finished the verses, Mrs. Rosen nodded approvingly. "Thank you, Vickie. The very next time I go to Chicago, I will try to get an English translation of *Faust* for you."

"But I want to read this one." Vickie's open smile darkened. "What I want is to pick up any of these books and just read them, like you and Mr. Rosen do."

The dusky red of Mrs. Rosen's cheeks grew a trifle deeper. Vickie never paid compliments, absolutely never; but if she really admired anyone, something in her voice betrayed it so convincingly that one felt flattered. When she dropped a remark of this kind, she added another link to the chain of responsibility which Mrs. Rosen unwillingly bore and tried to shake off — the irritating sense of being somehow responsible for Vickie, since, God knew, no one else felt responsible.

Once or twice, when she happened to meet pleasant young Mr. Templeton alone, she had tried to talk to him seriously about his daughter's future. "She has finished de school here, and she should be getting training of some sort; she is growing up," she told him severely.

He laughed and said in his way that was so honest, and so disarmingly sweet and frank: "Oh, don't remind me, Mrs. Rosen! I just pretend to myself she isn't. I want to keep my little daughter as long as I can." And there it ended.

Sometimes Vickie Templeton seemed so dense, so utterly unperceptive, that Mrs. Rosen was ready to wash her hands of her. Then some queer streak of sensibility in the child would make her change her mind. Last winter, when Mrs. Rosen came home from a visit to her sister in Chicago, she brought with her a new cloak of the sleeveless dolman type, black velvet, lined with grey and white squirrel skins, a grey skin next a white. Vickie, so indifferent to clothes, fell in love with that cloak. Her eyes followed it with delight whenever Mrs. Rosen wore it. She found it picturesque, romantic. Mrs. Rosen had been captivated by the same thing in the cloak, and had bought it with a shrug, knowing it would be quite out of place in Skyline; and Mr. Rosen, when she first produced it from her trunk, had laughed and said: "Where did you get that? — out of *Rigoletto?*" It looked like that — but how could Vickie know?

Vickie's whole family puzzled Mrs. Rosen; their feelings were so much finer than their way of living. She bought milk from the Templetons because they kept a cow — which Mandy milked, — and every night one of the twins brought the milk to her in a tin pail. Whichever boy brought it, she always called him Albert — she thought Adelbert a silly, Southern name.

One night when she was fitting the lid on an empty pail, she said severely:

"Now, Albert, I have put some cookies for Grandma in this pail, wrapped in a napkin. And they are for Grandma, remember, not for your mother or Vickie."

"Yes'm."

When she turned to him to give him the pail, she saw

93

two full crystal globes in the little boy's eyes, just ready to break. She watched him go softly down the path and dash those tears away with the back of his hand. She was sorry. She hadn't thought the little boys realized that their household was somehow a queer one.

Queer or not, Mrs. Rosen liked to go there better than to most houses in the town. There was something easy, cordial, and carefree in the parlour that never smelled of being shut up, and the ugly furniture looked hospitable. One felt a pleasantness in the human relationships. These people didn't seem to know there were such things as struggle or exactness or competition in the world. They were always genuinely glad to see you, had time to see you, and were usually gay in mood — all but Grandmother, who had the kind of gravity that people who take thought of human destiny must have. But even she liked light-heartedness in others; she drudged, indeed, to keep it going.

There were houses that were better kept, certainly, but the housekeepers had no charm, no gentleness of manner, were like hard little machines, most of them; and some were grasping and narrow. The Templetons were not selfish or scheming. Anyone could take advantage of them, and many people did. Victoria might eat all the cookies her neighbour sent in, but she would give away anything she had. She was always ready to lend her dresses and hats and bits of jewellery for the school theatricals, and she never worked people for favours.

As for Mr. Templeton (people usually called him "young Mr. Templeton"), he was too delicate to collect his just debts. His boyish, eager-to-please manner, his fair complexion and blue eyes and young face, made him seem very soft to some of the hard old money-grubbers on Main Street, and the fact that he always said "Yes, sir," and "No, sir," to men older than himself furnished a good deal of amusement to by-standers.

Two years ago, when this Templeton family came to Skyline and moved into the house next door, Mrs. Rosen was inconsolable. The new neighbours had a lot of children, who would always be making a racket. They put a cow and a horse into the empty barn, which would mean dirt and flies. They strewed their back yard with packing-cases and did not pick them up.

She first met Mrs. Templeton at an afternoon card party, in a house at the extreme north end of the town, fully half a mile away, and she had to admit that her new neighbour was an attractive woman, and that there was something warm and genuine about her. She wasn't in the least willowy or languishing, as Mrs. Rosen had usually found Southern ladies to be. She was high-spirited and direct; a trifle imperious, but with a shade of diffidence, too, as if she were trying to adjust herself to a new group of people and to do the right thing.

While they were at the party, a blinding snowstorm came on, with a hard wind. Since they lived next door to each other, Mrs. Rosen and Mrs. Templeton struggled homeward together through the blizzard. Mrs. Templeton seemed delighted with the rough weather; she laughed like a big country girl whenever she made a mis-step off the obliterated sidewalk and sank up to her knees in a snow-drift.

"Take care, Mrs. Rosen," she kept calling, "keep to the right! Don't spoil your nice coat. My, ain't this real winter? We never had it like this back with us."

When they reached the Templetons' gate, Victoria wouldn't hear of Mrs. Rosen's going farther. "No, indeed, Mrs. Rosen, you come right in with me and get dry, and Ma'll make you a hot toddy while I take the baby."

By this time Mrs. Rosen had begun to like her neighbour, so she went in. To her surprise, the parlour was neat and comfortable — the children did not strew things about there, apparently. The hard-coal burner threw out a warm red glow. A faded, respectable Brus-

96

sels carpet covered the floor, an old-fashioned wooden clock ticked on the walnut bookcase. There were a few easy chairs, and no hideous ornaments about. She rather liked the old oil-chromos on the wall: "Hagar and Ishmael in the Wilderness," and "The Light of the World." While Mrs. Rosen dried her feet on the nickel base of the stove, Mrs. Templeton excused herself and withdrew to the next room, — her bedroom, — took off her silk dress and corsets, and put on a white challis négligée. She reappeared with the baby, who was not crying, exactly, but making eager, passionate, gasping entreaties, — faster and faster, tenser and tenser, as he felt his dinner nearer and nearer and yet not his.

Mrs. Templeton sat down in a low rocker by the stove and began to nurse him, holding him snugly but carelessly, still talking to Mrs. Rosen about the card party, and laughing about their wade home through the snow. Hughie, the baby, fell to work so fiercely that beads of sweat came out all over his flushed forehead. Mrs. Rosen could not help admiring him and his mother. They were so comfortable and complete. When he was changed to the other side, Hughie resented the interruption a little; but after a time he became soft and bland, as smooth as oil, indeed; began looking about him as he drew in his milk. He finally

97

dropped the nipple from his lips altogether, turned on his mother's arm, and looked inquiringly at Mrs. Rosen.

"What a beautiful baby!" she exclaimed from her heart. And he was. A sort of golden baby. His hair was like sunshine, and his long lashes were gold over such gay blue eyes. There seemed to be a gold glow in his soft pink skin, and he had the smile of a cherub.

"We think he's a pretty boy," said Mrs. Templeton. "He's the prettiest of my babies. Though the twins were mighty cunning little fellows. I hated the idea of twins, but the minute I saw them, I couldn't resist them."

Just then old Mrs. Harris came in, walking widely in her full-gathered skirt and felt-soled shoes, bearing a tray with two smoking goblets upon it.

"This is my mother, Mrs. Harris, Mrs. Rosen," said Mrs. Templeton.

"I'm glad to know you, ma'am," said Mrs. Harris. "Victoria, let me take the baby, while you two ladies have your toddy."

"Oh, don't take him away, Mrs. Harris, please!" cried Mrs. Rosen.

The old lady smiled. "I won't. I'll set right here. He never frets with his grandma."

When Mrs. Rosen had finished her excellent drink, she asked if she might hold the baby, and Mrs. Harris placed him on her lap. He made a few rapid boxing motions with his two fists, then braced himself on his heels and the back of his head, and lifted himself up in an arc. When he dropped back, he looked up at Mrs. Rosen with his most intimate smile. "See what a smart boy I am!"

When Mrs. Rosen walked home, feeling her way through the snow by following the fence, she knew she could never stay away from a house where there was a baby like that one.

IV

VICKIE did her studying in a hammock hung between two tall cottonwood trees over in the Roadmaster's green yard. The Roadmaster had the finest yard in Skyline, on the edge of the town, just where the sandy plain and the sage-brush began. His family went back to Ohio every summer, and Bert and Del Templeton were paid to take care of his lawn, to turn the sprinkler on at the right hours and to cut the grass. They were really too little to run the heavy lawn-mower very well, but they were able to manage because they were twins. Each took one end of the handle-bar, and they pushed together like a pair of fat Shetland ponies. They were very proud of being able to keep the lawn so nice, and worked hard on it. They cut Mrs. Rosen's grass once a week, too, and did it so well that she wondered why in the world they never did anything about their own yard. They didn't have city water, to be sure (it was expensive), but she thought they might pick up a few velocipedes and iron hoops, and dig up the messy "flower-bed," that was even uglier than the naked gravel spots. She was particularly offended by a deep ragged ditch, a miniature arroyo, which ran across the back yard, serving no purpose and looking very dreary.

One morning she said craftily to the twins, when she was paying them for cutting her grass:

"And, boys, why don't you just shovel the sand-pile by your fence into dat ditch, and make your back yard smooth?"

"Oh, no, ma'am," said Adelbert with feeling. "We like to have the ditch to build bridges over!"

Ever since vacation began, the twins had been busy getting the Roadmaster's yard ready for the Methodist lawn party. When Mrs. Holliday, the Roadmaster's wife, went away for the summer, she always left a key with the Ladies' Aid Society and invited them to give their ice-cream social at her place.

This year the date set for the party was June fifteenth.

Old Mrs. Harris

The day was a particularly fine one, and as Mr. Holliday
himself had been called to Cheyenne on railroad business, the twins felt personally responsible for everything. They got out to the Holliday place early in the
morning, and stayed on guard all day. Before noon the
drayman brought a wagon-load of card-tables and folding chairs, which the boys placed in chosen spots under
the cottonwood trees. In the afternoon the Methodist
ladies arrived and opened up the kitchen to receive the
freezers of home-made ice-cream, and the cakes which
the congregation donated. Indeed, all the good cake-
bakers in town were expected to send a cake. Grandma
Harris baked a white cake, thickly iced and covered
with freshly grated coconut, and Vickie took it over in
the afternoon.

Mr. and Mrs. Rosen, because they belonged to no
church, contributed to the support of all, and usually
went to the church suppers in winter and the socials in
summer. On this warm June evening they set out early,
in order to take a walk first. They strolled along the
hard gravelled road that led out through the sage toward the sand-hills; tonight it led toward the moon, just
rising over the sweep of dunes. The sky was almost as
blue as at midday, and had that look of being very near
and very soft which it has in desert countries. The

moon, too, looked very near, soft and bland and inno-
cent. Mrs. Rosen admitted that in the Adirondacks, for
which she was always secretly homesick in summer, the
moon had a much colder brilliance, seemed farther off
and made of a harder metal. This moon gave the sage-
brush plain and the drifted sand-hills the softness of
velvet. All countries were beautiful to Mr. Rosen. He
carried a country of his own in his mind, and was able to
unfold it like a tent in any wilderness.

When they at last turned back toward the town, they
saw groups of people, women in white dresses, walking
toward the dark spot where the paper lanterns made a
yellow light underneath the cottonwoods. High above,
the rustling tree-tops stirred free in the flood of
moonlight.

The lighted yard was surrounded by a low board
fence, painted the dark red Burlington colour, and as
the Rosens drew near, they noticed four children standing close together in the shadow of some tall elder
bushes just outside the fence. They were the poor
Maude children; their mother was the washwoman, the
Rosens' laundress and the Templetons'. People said
that every one of those children had a different father.
But good laundresses were few, and even the members
of the Ladies' Aid were glad to get Mrs. Maude's ser-

vices at a dollar a day, though they didn't like their children to play with hers. Just as the Rosens approached, Mrs. Templeton came out from the lighted square, leaned over the fence, and addressed the little Maudes.

"I expect you children forgot your dimes, now didn't you? Never mind, here's a dime for each of you, so come along and have your ice-cream."

The Maudes put out small hands and said: "Thank you," but not one of them moved.

"Come along, Francie" (the oldest girl was named Frances). "Climb right over the fence." Mrs. Templeton reached over and gave her a hand, and the little boys quickly scrambled after their sister. Mrs. Templeton took them to a table which Vickie and the twins had just selected as being especially private — they liked to do things together.

"Here, Vickie, let the Maudes sit at your table, and take care they get plenty of cake."

The Rosens had followed close behind Mrs. Templeton, and Mr. Rosen now overtook her and said in his most courteous and friendly manner: "Good evening, Mrs. Templeton. Will you have ice-cream with us?" He always used the local idioms, though his voice and enunciation made them sound altogether different from Skyline speech.

"Indeed I will, Mr. Rosen. Mr. Templeton will be late. He went out to his farm yesterday, and I don't know just when to expect him."

Vickie and the twins were disappointed at not having their table to themselves, when they had come early and found a nice one; but they knew it was right to look out for the dreary little Maudes, so they moved close together and made room for them. The Maudes didn't cramp them long. When the three boys had eaten the last crumb of cake and licked their spoons, Francie got up and led them to a green slope by the fence, just outside the lighted circle. "Now set down, and watch and see how folks do," she told them. The boys looked to Francie for commands and support. She was really Amos Maude's child, born before he ran away to the Klondike, and it had been rubbed into them that this made a difference.

The Templeton children made their ice-cream linger out, and sat watching the crowd. They were glad to see their mother go to Mr. Rosen's table, and noticed how nicely he placed a chair for her and insisted upon putting a scarf about her shoulders. Their mother was wearing her new dotted Swiss, with many ruffles, all edged with black ribbon, and wide ruffly sleeves. As the twins watched her over their spoons, they thought how much prettier their mother was than any of the other women, and how becoming her new dress was. The children got as much satisfaction as Mrs. Harris out of Victoria's good looks.

Mr. Rosen was well pleased with Mrs. Templeton and her new dress, and with her kindness to the little Maudes. He thought her manner with them just right, — warm, spontaneous, without anything patronizing. He always admired her way with her own children, though Mrs. Rosen thought it too casual. Being a good mother, he believed, was much more a matter of physical poise and richness than of sentimentalizing and reading doctor-books. Tonight he was more talkative than usual, and in his quiet way made Mrs. Templeton feel his real friendliness and admiration. Unfortunately, he made other people feel it, too.

Mrs. Jackson, a neighbour who didn't like the Templetons, had been keeping an eye on Mr. Rosen's table. She was a stout square woman of imperturbable calm, effective in regulating the affairs of the community because she never lost her temper, and could say the most cutting things in calm, even kindly, tones. Her face was smooth and placid as a mask, rather good-humoured, and the fact that one eye had a cast and looked askance made it the more difficult to see through her intentions.

When she had been lingering about the Rosens' table for some time, studying Mr. Rosen's pleasant attentions to Mrs. Templeton, she brought up a trayful of cake.

"You folks are about ready for another helping," she remarked affably.

Mrs. Rosen spoke. "I want some of Grandma Harris's cake. It's a white coconut, Mrs. Jackson."

"How about you, Mrs. Templeton, would you like some of your own cake?"

"Indeed I would," said Mrs. Templeton heartily. "Ma said she had good luck with it. I didn't see it. Vickie brought it over."

Mrs. Jackson deliberately separated the slices on her tray with two forks. "Well," she remarked with a chuckle that really sounded amiable, "I don't know but I'd like my cakes, if I kept somebody in the kitchen to bake them for me."

Mr. Rosen for once spoke quickly. "If I had a cook like Grandma Harris in my kitchen, I'd live in it!" he declared.

Mrs. Jackson smiled. "I don't know as we feel like that, Mrs. Templeton? I tell Mr. Jackson that my idea of coming up in the world would be to forget I had a cook-stove, like Mrs. Templeton. But we can't all be lucky."

Mr. Rosen could not tell how much was malice and

how much was stupidity. What he chiefly detected was self-satisfaction; the craftiness of the coarse-fibred country girl putting catch questions to the teacher. Yes, he decided, the woman was merely showing off, — she regarded it as an accomplishment to make people uncomfortable.

Mrs. Templeton didn't at once take it in. Her training was all to the end that you must give a guest everything you have, even if he happens to be your worst enemy, and that to cause anyone embarrassment is a frightful and humiliating blunder. She felt hurt without knowing just why, but all evening it kept growing clearer to her that this was another of those thrusts from the outside which she couldn't understand. The neighbours were sure to take sides against her, apparently, if they came often to see her mother.

Mr. Rosen tried to distract Mrs. Templeton, but he could feel the poison working. On the way home the children knew something had displeased or hurt their mother. When they went into the house, she told them to go upstairs at once, as she had a headache. She was severe and distant. When Mrs. Harris suggested making her some peppermint tea, Victoria threw up her chin.

"I don't want anybody waiting on me. I just want to

be let alone." And she withdrew without saying good-
night, or "Are you all right, Ma?" as she usually did.

Left alone, Mrs. Harris sighed and began to turn
down her bed. She knew, as well as if she had been at
the social, what kind of thing had happened. Some of
those prying ladies of the Woman's Relief Corps, or the
Woman's Christian Temperance Union, had been intimating to Victoria that her mother was "put upon."
Nothing ever made Victoria cross but criticism. She
was jealous of small attentions paid to Mrs. Harris, because she felt they were paid "behind her back" or "over
her head," in a way that implied reproach to her. Victoria had been a belle in their own town in Tennessee,
but here she was not very popular, no matter how many
pretty dresses she wore, and she couldn't bear it. She
felt as if her mother and Mr. Templeton must be somehow to blame; at least they ought to protect her from
whatever was disagreeable — they always had!

V

MRS. Harris wakened at about four o'clock, as
usual, before the house was stirring, and lay
thinking about their position in this new town. She
didn't know why the neighbours acted so; she was as
much in the dark as Victoria. At home, back in Ten-

nessee, her place in the family was not exceptional, but perfectly regular. Mrs. Harris had replied to Mrs. Rosen, when that lady asked why in the world she didn't break Vickie in to help her in the kitchen: "We are only young once, and trouble comes soon enough." Young girls, in the South, were supposed to be carefree and foolish; the fault Grandmother found in Vickie was that she wasn't foolish enough. When the foolish girl married and began to have children, everything else must give way to that. She must be humoured and given the best of everything, because having children was hard on a woman, and it was the most important thing in the world. In Tennessee every young married woman in good circumstances had an older woman in the house, a mother or mother-in-law or an old aunt, who managed the household economies and directed the help.

That was the great difference; in Tennessee there had been plenty of helpers. There was old Miss Sadie Crummer, who came to the house to spin and sew and mend; old Mrs. Smith, who always arrived to help at butchering- and preserving-time; Lizzie, the coloured girl, who did the washing and who ran in every day to help Mandy. There were plenty more, who came whenever one of Lizzie's barefoot boys ran to fetch them. The hills were full of solitary old women, or women but slightly attached to some household, who were glad to come to Miz' Harris's for good food and a warm bed, and the little present that either Mrs. Harris or Victoria slipped into their carpet-sack when they went away.

To be sure, Mrs. Harris, and the other women of her age who managed their daughter's house, kept in the background; but it was their own background, and they ruled it jealously. They left the front porch and the parlour to the young married couple and their young friends; the old women spent most of their lives in the kitchen and pantries and back dining-room. But there they ordered life to their own taste, entertained their friends, dispensed charity, and heard the troubles of the poor. Moreover, back there it was Grandmother's own house they lived in. Mr. Templeton came of a superior family and had what Grandmother called "blood," but no property. He never so much as mended one of the steps to the front porch without consulting Mrs. Harris. Even "back home," in the aristocracy, there were old women who went on living like young ones, — gave parties and drove out in their carriage and "went North" in the summer. But among the middle-class people and the country-folk, when a woman was a widow and had married daughters, she considered herself an old woman and wore full-gathered black dresses and a black bonnet and became a housekeeper. She accepted this estate unprotestingly, almost gratefully.

The Templetons' troubles began when Mr. Templeton's aunt died and left him a few thousand dollars, and he got the idea of bettering himself. The twins were little then, and he told Mrs. Harris his boys would have a better chance in Colorado — everybody was going West. He went alone first, and got a good position with a mining company in the mountains of southern Colorado. He had been book-keeper in the bank in his home town, had "grown up in the bank," as they said. He was industrious and honourable, and the managers of the mining company liked him, even if they laughed at his polite, soft-spoken manners. He could have held his position indefinitely, and maybe got a promotion. But the altitude of that mountain town was too high for his family. All the children were sick there; Mrs. Templeton was ill most of the time and nearly died when Ronald was born. Hillary Templeton lost his courage and came north to the flat, sunny, semi-arid country between Wray and Cheyenne, to work for an irrigation project. So far, things had not gone well with him. The pinch told on everyone, but most on Grandmother. Here, in Skyline, she had all her accustomed responsibilities, and no helper but Mandy. Mrs. Harris was no longer living in a feudal society, where there were plenty of landless people glad to render service to the more fortunate, but in a snappy little Western democracy, where every man was as good as his neighbour and out to prove it.

Neither Mrs. Harris nor Mrs. Templeton understood just what was the matter; they were hurt and dazed, merely. Victoria knew that here she was censured and criticized, she who had always been so admired and envied! Grandmother knew that these meddlesome "Northerners" said things that made Victoria suspicious and unlike herself; made her unwilling that Mrs. Harris should receive visitors alone, or accept marks of attention that seemed offered in compassion for her state.

These women who belonged to clubs and Relief Corps lived differently, Mrs. Harris knew, but she herself didn't like the way they lived. She believed that somebody ought to be in the parlour, and somebody in the kitchen. She wouldn't for the world have had Victoria go about every morning in a short gingham dress, with bare arms, and a dust-cap on her head to hide the curling-kids, as these brisk housekeepers did. To Mrs. Harris that would have meant real poverty, coming down in the world so far that one could no longer keep up appearances. Her life was hard now, to be sure, since the family went on increasing and Mr. Templeton's means went on decreasing; but she certainly valued respectability above personal comfort, and she could go on a good way yet if they always had a cool pleasant parlour, with Victoria properly dressed to receive visitors. To keep Victoria different from these "ordinary" women meant everything to Mrs. Harris. She realized that Mrs. Rosen managed to be mistress of any situation, either in kitchen or parlour, but that was because she was "foreign." Grandmother perfectly understood that their neighbour had a superior cultivation which made everything she did an exercise of skill. She knew well enough that their own ways of cooking and cleaning were primitive beside Mrs. Rosen's.

If only Mr. Templeton's business affairs would look up, they could rent a larger house, and everything would be better. They might even get a German girl to come in and help, — but now there was no place to put her. Grandmother's own lot could improve only with the family fortunes — any comfort for herself, aside from that of the family, was inconceivable to her; and on the other hand she could have no real unhappiness while the children were well, and good, and fond of her and their mother. That was why it was worth while to get up early in the morning and make her bed neat and draw the red spread smooth. The little boys loved to lie on her lounge and her pillows when they were tired. When they were sick, Ronald and Hughie wanted to be in her lap. They had no physical shrinking from her because she was old. And Victoria was never jealous of the children's wanting to be with her so much; that was a mercy!

Sometimes, in the morning, if her feet ached more than usual, Mrs. Harris felt a little low. (Nobody did anything about broken arches in those days, and the common endurance test of old age was to keep going after every step cost something.) She would hang up her towel with a sigh and go into the kitchen, feeling that it was hard to make a start. But the moment she heard the children running down the uncarpeted back stairs, she forgot to be low. Indeed, she ceased to be an individual, an old woman with aching feet; she became part of a group, became a relationship. She was drunk up into their freshness when they burst in upon her, telling her about their dreams, explaining their troubles with buttons and shoe-laces and underwear shrunk too small. The tired, solitary old woman Grandmother had been at daybreak vanished; suddenly the morning seemed as important to her as it did to the children, and the mornings ahead stretched out sunshiny, important.

VI

THE day after the Methodist social, Blue Boy didn't come for his morning milk; he always had it in a clean saucer on the covered back porch, under the long bench where the tin wash-tubs stood ready for Mrs. Maude. After the children had finished breakfast, Mrs. Harris sent Mandy out to look for the cat.

The girl came back in a minute, her eyes big.

"Law me, Miz' Harris, he's awful sick. He's a-layin' in the straw in the barn. He's swallered a bone, or havin' a fit or somethin'."

Grandmother threw an apron over her head and went out to see for herself. The children went with her. Blue Boy was retching and choking, and his yellow eyes were filled up with rhume.

"Oh, Gram'ma, what's the matter?" the boys cried.

"It's the distemper. How could he have got it?" Her voice was so harsh that Ronald began to cry. "Take Ronald back to the house, Del. He might get bit. I wish I'd kept my word and never had a cat again!"

"Why, Gram'ma!" Albert looked at her. "Won't Blue Boy get well?"

"Not from the distemper, he won't."

"But Gram'ma, can't I run for the veter'nary?"

"You gether up an armful of hay. We'll take him into the coal-house, where I can watch him."

Mrs. Harris waited until the spasm was over, then picked up the limp cat and carried him to the coal-shed that opened off the back porch. Albert piled the hay in one corner — the coal was low, since it was summer — and they spread a piece of old carpet on the hay and made a bed for Blue Boy. "Now you run along with Adelbert. There'll be a lot of work to do on Mr. Holliday's yard, cleaning up after the sociable. Mandy an' me'll watch Blue Boy. I expect he'll sleep for a while."

Albert went away regretfully, but the drayman and some of the Methodist ladies were in Mr. Holliday's yard, packing chairs and tables and ice-cream freezers into the wagon, and the twins forgot the sick cat in their excitement. By noon they had picked up the last paper napkin, raked over the gravel walks where the salt from the freezers had left white patches, and hung the hammock in which Vickie did her studying back in its place. Mr. Holliday paid the boys a dollar a week for keeping up the yard, and they gave the money to their mother — it didn't come amiss in a family where actual cash was so short. She let them keep half the sum Mrs. Rosen paid for her milk every Saturday, and that was more spending money than most boys had. They often made a few extra quarters by cutting grass for other people, or by distributing handbills. Even the disagreeable Mrs. Jackson next door had remarked over the fence to Mrs. Harris: "I do believe Bert and Del are going to be industrious. They must have got it from you, Grandma."

The day came on very hot, and when the twins got back from the Roadmaster's yard, they both lay down on Grandmother's lounge and went to sleep. After dinner they had a rare opportunity; the Roadmaster himself appeared at the front door and invited them to go up to the next town with him on his railroad velocipede. That was great fun: the velocipede always whizzed along so fast on the bright rails, the gasoline engine puffing; and grasshoppers jumped up out of the sagebrush and hit you in the face like sling-shot bullets. Sometimes the wheels cut in two a lazy snake who was sunning himself on the track, and the twins always hoped it was a rattler and felt they had done a good work.

The boys got back from their trip with Mr. Holliday late in the afternoon. The house was cool and quiet. Their mother had taken Ronald and Hughie down town with her, and Vickie was off somewhere. Grandmother was not in her room, and the kitchen was empty. The boys went out to the back porch to pump a drink. The coal-shed door was open, and inside, on a low stool, sat Mrs. Harris beside her cat. Bert and Del didn't stop to get a drink; they felt ashamed that they had gone off for a gay ride and forgotten Blue Boy. They sat down on a big lump of coal beside Mrs. Harris. They would never have known that this miserable rumpled animal was their proud tom. Presently he went off into a spasm and began to froth at the mouth.

"Oh, Gram'ma, can't you do anything?" cried Albert, struggling with his tears. "Blue Boy was such a good cat, — why has he got to suffer?"

"Everything that's alive has got to suffer," said Mrs. Harris. Albert put out his hand and caught her skirt, looking up at her beseechingly, as if to make her unsay that saying, which he only half understood. She patted his hand. She had forgot she was speaking to a little boy.

"Where's Vickie?" Adelbert asked aggrievedly. "Why don't she do something? He's part her cat."

Mrs. Harris sighed. "Vickie's got her head full of things lately; that makes people kind of heartless."

The boys resolved they would never put anything into their heads, then!

Blue Boy's fit passed, and the three sat watching their

pet that no longer knew them. The twins had not seen much suffering; Grandmother had seen a great deal. Back in Tennessee, in her own neighbourhood, she was accounted a famous nurse. When any of the poor mountain people were in great distress, they always sent for Miz' Harris. Many a time she had gone into a house where five or six children were all down with scarlet fever or diphtheria, and done what she could. Many a child and many a woman she had laid out and got ready for the grave. In her primitive community the undertaker made the coffin, — he did nothing more. She had seen so much misery that she wondered herself why it hurt so to see her tom-cat die. She had taken her leave of him, and she got up from her stool. She didn't want the boys to be too much distressed.

"Now you boys must wash and put on clean shirts. Your mother will be home pretty soon. We'll leave Blue Boy; he'll likely be easier in the morning." She knew the cat would die at sundown.

After supper, when Bert looked into the coal-shed and found the cat dead, all the family were sad. Ronald cried miserably, and Hughie cried because Ronald did. Mrs. Templeton herself went out and looked into the shed, and she was sorry, too. Though she didn't like cats, she had been fond of this one.

"Hillary," she told her husband, "when you go down town tonight, tell the Mexican to come and get that cat early in the morning, before the children are up."

The Mexican had a cart and two mules, and he hauled away tin cans and refuse to a gully out in the sage-brush.

Mrs. Harris gave Victoria an indignant glance when she heard this, and turned back to the kitchen. All evening she was gloomy and silent. She refused to read aloud, and the twins took Ronald and went mournfully out to play under the electric light. Later, when they had said good-night to their parents in the parlour and were on their way upstairs, Mrs. Harris followed them into the kitchen, shut the door behind her, and said indignantly:

"Air you two boys going to let that Mexican take Blue Boy and throw him onto some trash-pile?"

The sleepy boys were frightened at the anger and bitterness in her tone. They stood still and looked up at her, while she went on:

"You git up early in the morning, and I'll put him in a sack, and one of you take a spade and go to that crooked old willer tree that grows just where the sand creek turns off the road, and you dig a little grave for Blue Boy, an' bury him right."

They had seldom seen such resentment in their grandmother. Albert's throat choked up, he rubbed the tears away with his fist.

"Yes'm, Gram'ma, we will, we will," he gulped.

VII

O NLY Mrs. Harris saw the boys go out next morning. She slipped a bread-and-butter sandwich into the hand of each, but she said nothing, and they said nothing.

The boys did not get home until their parents were ready to leave the table. Mrs. Templeton made no fuss, but told them to sit down and eat their breakfast. When they had finished, she said commandingly:

"Now you march into my room." That was where she heard explanations and administered punishment. When she whipped them, she did it thoroughly.

She followed them and shut the door.

"Now, what were you boys doing this morning?"

"We went off to bury Blue Boy."

"Why didn't you tell me you were going?"

They looked down at their toes, but said nothing. Their mother studied their mournful faces, and her overbearing expression softened.

"The next time you get up and go off anywhere, you come and tell me beforehand, do you understand?"

"Yes'm."

She opened the door, motioned them out, and went with them into the parlour. "I'm sorry about your cat, boys," she said. "That's why I don't like to have cats around; they're always getting sick and dying. Now run along and play. Maybe you'd like to have a circus in the back yard this afternoon? And we'll all come."

The twins ran out in a joyful frame of mind. Their grandmother had been mistaken; their mother wasn't indifferent about Blue Boy, she was sorry. Now everything was all right, and they could make a circus ring.

They knew their grandmother got put out about strange things, anyhow. A few months ago it was because their mother hadn't asked one of the visiting preachers who came to the church conference to stay with them. There was no place for the preacher to sleep except on the folding lounge in the parlour, and no place for him to wash — he would have been very uncomfortable, and so would all the household. But Mrs. Harris was terribly upset that there should be a conference in the town, and they not keeping a preacher! She was quite bitter about it.

The twins called in the neighbour boys, and they

made a ring in the back yard, around their turning-bar. Their mother came to the show and paid admission, bringing Mrs. Rosen and Grandma Harris. Mrs. Rosen thought if all the children in the neighbourhood were to be howling and running in a circle in the Templetons' back yard, she might as well be there, too, for she would have no peace at home.

After the dog races and the Indian fight were over, Mrs. Templeton took Mrs. Rosen into the house to revive her with cake and lemonade. The parlour was cool and dusky. Mrs. Rosen was glad to get into it after sitting on a wooden bench in the sun. Grandmother stayed in the parlour with them, which was unusual. Mrs. Rosen sat waving a palm-leaf fan, — she felt the heat very much, because she wore her stays so tight — while Victoria went to make the lemonade.

"De circuses are not so good, widout Vickie to manage them, Grandma," she said.

"No'm. The boys complain right smart about losing Vickie from their plays. She's at her books all the time now. I don't know what's got into the child."

"If she wants to go to college, she must prepare herself, Grandma. I am agreeably surprised in her. I didn't think she'd stick to it."

Mrs. Templeton came in with a tray of tumblers and

the glass pitcher all frosted over. Mrs. Rosen wistfully admired her neighbour's tall figure and good carriage; she was wearing no corsets at all today under her flowered organdie afternoon dress, Mrs. Rosen had noticed, and yet she could carry herself so smooth and straight, — after having had so many children, too! Mrs. Rosen was envious, but she gave credit where credit was due.

When Mrs. Templeton brought in the cake, Mrs. Rosen was still talking to Grandmother about Vickie's studying. Mrs. Templeton shrugged carelessly.

"There's such a thing as overdoing it, Mrs. Rosen," she observed as she poured the lemonade. "Vickie's very apt to run to extremes."

"But, my dear lady, she can hardly be too extreme in dis matter. If she is to take a competitive examination with girls from much better schools than ours, she will have to do better than the others, or fail; no two ways about it. We must encourage her."

Mrs. Templeton bridled a little. "I'm sure I don't interfere with her studying, Mrs. Rosen. I don't see where she got this notion, but I let her alone."

Mrs. Rosen accepted a second piece of chocolate cake. "And what do you think about it, Grandma?"

Mrs. Harris smiled politely. "None of our people, or

Mr. Templeton's either, ever went to college. I expect it is all on account of the young gentleman who was here last summer."

Mrs. Rosen laughed and lifted her eyebrows. "Something very personal in Vickie's admiration for Professor Chalmers we think, Grandma? A very sudden interest in de sciences, I should say!"

Mrs. Templeton shrugged. "You're mistaken, Mrs. Rosen. There ain't a particle of romance in Vickie."

"But there are several kinds of romance, Mrs. Templeton. She may not have your kind."

"Yes'm, that's so," said Mrs. Harris in a low, grateful voice. She thought that a hard word Victoria had said of Vickie.

"I didn't see a thing in that Professor Chalmers, myself," Victoria remarked. "He was a gawky kind of fellow, and never had a thing to say in company. Did you think he amounted to much?"

"Oh, widout doubt Doctor Chalmers is a very scholarly man. A great many brilliant scholars are widout de social graces, you know." When Mrs. Rosen, from a much wider experience, corrected her neighbour, she did so somewhat playfully, as if insisting upon something Victoria capriciously chose to ignore.

At this point old Mrs. Harris put her hands on the

arms of the chair in preparation to rise. "If you ladies will excuse me, I think I will go and lie down a little before supper." She rose and went heavily out on her felt soles. She never really lay down in the afternoon, but she dozed in her own black rocker. Mrs. Rosen and Victoria sat chatting about Professor Chalmers and his boys.

Last summer the young professor had come to Skyline with four of his students from the University of Michigan, and had stayed three months, digging for fossils out in the sand-hills. Vickie had spent a great many mornings at their camp. They lived at the town hotel, and drove out to their camp every day in a light spring-wagon. Vickie used to wait for them at the edge of the town, in front of the Roadmaster's house, and when the spring-wagon came rattling along, the boys would call: "There's our girl!" slow the horses, and give her a hand up. They said she was their mascot, and were very jolly with her. They had a splendid summer, — found a great bed of fossil elephant bones, where a whole herd must once have perished. Later on they came upon the bones of a new kind of elephant, scarcely larger than a pig. They were greatly excited about their finds, and so was Vickie. That was why they liked her. It was they who told her about a memorial scholarship at Ann Arbor, which was open to any girl from Colorado.

VIII

I N August Vickie went down to Denver to take her examinations. Mr. Holliday, the Roadmaster, got her a pass, and arranged that she should stay with the family of one of his passenger conductors.

For three days she wrote examination papers along with other contestants, in one of the Denver high schools, proctored by a teacher. Her father had given her five dollars for incidental expenses, and she came home with a box of mineral specimens for the twins, a singing top for Ronald, and a toy burro for Hughie.

Then began days of suspense that stretched into weeks. Vickie went to the post-office every morning, opened her father's combination box, and looked over the letters, long before he got down town, — always hoping there might be a letter from Ann Arbor. The night mail came in at six, and after supper she hurried to the post-office and waited about until the shutter at the general-delivery window was drawn back, a signal that the mail had all been "distributed." While the tedious process of distribution was going on, she usually withdrew from the office, full of joking men and cigar smoke, and walked up and down under the big cotton-wood trees that overhung the side street. When the crowd of men began to come out, then she knew the mail-bags were empty, and she went in to get whatever letters were in the Templeton box and take them home.

After two weeks went by, she grew downhearted. Her young professor, she knew, was in England for his vacation. There would be no one at the University of Michigan who was interested in her fate. Perhaps the fortunate contestant had already been notified of her success. She never asked herself, as she walked up and down under the cottonwoods on those summer nights, what she would do if she didn't get the scholarship. There was no alternative. If she didn't get it, then everything was over.

During the weeks when she lived only to go to the post-office, she managed to cut her finger and get ink into the cut. As a result, she had a badly infected hand and had to carry it in a sling. When she walked her nightly beat under the cottonwoods, it was a kind of comfort to feel that finger throb; it was companionship, made her case more complete.

The strange thing was that one morning a letter came, addressed to Miss Victoria Templeton; in a long envelope such as her father called "legal size," with

Old Mrs. Harris

"University of Michigan" in the upper left-hand corner. When Vickie took it from the box, such a wave of fright and weakness went through her that she could scarcely get out of the post-office. She hid the letter under her striped blazer and went a weak, uncertain trail down the sidewalk under the big trees. Without seeing anything or knowing what road she took, she got to the Roadmaster's green yard and her hammock, where she always felt not on the earth, yet of it.

Three hours later, when Mrs. Rosen was just tasting one of those clear soups upon which the Templetons thought she wasted so much pains and good meat, Vickie walked in at the kitchen door and said in a low but somewhat unnatural voice:

"Mrs. Rosen, I got the scholarship."

Mrs. Rosen looked up at her sharply, then pushed the soup back to a cooler part of the stove.

"What is dis you say, Vickie? You have heard from de University?"

"Yes'm. I got the letter this morning." She produced it from under her blazer.

Mrs. Rosen had been cutting noodles. She took Vickie's face in two hot, plump hands that were still floury, and looked at her intently. "Is dat true, Vickie? No mistake? I am delighted — and surprised! Yes, surprised. Den you will *be* something, you won't just sit on de front porch." She squeezed the girl's round, good-natured cheeks, as if she could mould them into something definite then and there. "Now you must stay for lunch and tell us all about it. Go in and announce yourself to Mr. Rosen."

Mr. Rosen had come home for lunch and was sitting, a book in his hand, in a corner of the darkened front parlour where a flood of yellow sun streamed in under the dark green blind. He smiled his friendly smile at Vickie and waved her to a seat, making her understand that he wanted to finish his paragraph. The dark engraving of the pointed cypresses and the Roman tomb was on the wall just behind him.

Mrs. Rosen came into the back parlour, which was the dining-room, and began taking things out of the silver-drawer to lay a place for their visitor. She spoke to her husband rapidly in German.

He put down his book, came over, and took Vickie's hand.

"Is it true, Vickie? Did you really win the scholarship?"

"Yes, sir."

He stood looking down at her through his kind, remote smile, — a smile in the eyes, that seemed to come up through layers and layers of something — gentle doubts, kindly reservations.

"Why do you want to go to college, Vickie?" he asked playfully.

"To learn," she said with surprise.

"But why do you want to learn? What do you want to do with it?"

"I don't know. Nothing, I guess."

"Then what do you want it for?"

"I don't know. I just want it."

For some reason Vickie's voice broke there. She had been terribly strung up all morning, lying in the hammock with her eyes tight shut. She had not been home at all, she had wanted to take her letter to the Rosens first. And now one of the gentlest men she knew made her choke by something strange and presageful in his voice.

"Then if you want it without any purpose at all, you will not be disappointed." Mr. Rosen wished to distract her and help her to keep back the tears. "Listen: a great man once said: *'Le but n'est rien; le chemin, c'est tout.'* That means: The end is nothing, the road is all. Let me write it down for you and give you your first French lesson."

He went to the desk with its big silver ink-well,

131

where he and his wife wrote so many letters in several languages, and inscribed the sentence on a sheet of purple paper, in his delicately shaded foreign script, signing under it a name: *J. Michelet*. He brought it back and shook it before Vickie's eyes. "There, keep it to remember me by. Slip it into the envelope with your college credentials, — that is a good place for it." From his deliberate smile and the twitch of one eyebrow, Vickie knew he meant her to take it along as an antidote, a corrective for whatever colleges might do to her. But she had always known that Mr. Rosen was wiser than professors.

Mrs. Rosen was frowning, she thought that sentence a bad precept to give any Templeton. Moreover, she always promptly called her husband back to earth when he soared a little; though it was exactly for this transcendental quality of mind that she reverenced him in her heart, and thought him so much finer than any of his successful brothers.

"Luncheon is served," she said in the crisp tone that put people in their places. "And Miss Vickie, you are to eat your tomatoes with an oil dressing, as we do. If you are going off into the world, it is quite time you learn to like things that are everywhere accepted."

Vickie said: "Yes'm," and slipped into the chair Mr.

Rosen had placed for her. Today she didn't care what she ate, though ordinarily she thought a French dressing tasted a good deal like castor oil.

IX

VICKIE was to discover that nothing comes easily in this world. Next day she got a letter from one of the jolly students of Professor Chalmers's party, who was watching over her case in his chief's absence. He told her the scholarship meant admission to the freshman class without further examinations, and two hundred dollars toward her expenses; she would have to bring along about three hundred more to put her through the year.

She took this letter to her father's office. Seated in his revolving desk-chair, Mr. Templeton read it over several times and looked embarrassed.

"I'm sorry, daughter," he said at last, "but really, just now, I couldn't spare that much. Not this year. I expect next year will be better for us."

"But the scholarship is for this year, Father. It wouldn't count next year. I just have to go in September."

"I really ain't got it, daughter." He spoke, oh so kindly! He had lovely manners with his daughter and his wife. "It's just all I can do to keep the store bills paid up. I'm away behind with Mr. Rosen's bill. Couldn't you study here this winter and get along about as fast? It isn't that I wouldn't like to let you have the money if I had it. And with young children, I can't let my life insurance go."

Vickie didn't say anything more. She took her letter and wandered down Main Street with it, leaving young Mr. Templeton to a very bad half-hour.

At dinner Vickie was silent, but everyone could see she had been crying. Mr. Templeton told *Uncle Remus* stories to keep up the family morale and make the giggly twins laugh. Mrs. Templeton glanced covertly at her daughter from time to time. She was sometimes a little afraid of Vickie, who seemed to her to have a hard streak. If it were a love-affair that the girl was crying about, that would be so much more natural — and more hopeful!

At two o'clock Mrs. Templeton went to the Afternoon Euchre Club, the twins were to have another ride with the Roadmaster on his velocipede, the little boys took their nap on their mother's bed. The house was empty and quiet. Vickie felt an aversion for the hammock under the cottonwoods where she had been betrayed into such bright hopes. She lay down on her grandmother's lounge in the cluttered play-room and turned her face to the wall.

When Mrs. Harris came in for her rest and began to wash her face at the tin basin, Vickie got up. She wanted to be alone. Mrs. Harris came over to her while she was still sitting on the edge of the lounge.

"What's the matter, Vickie child?" She put her hand on her grand-daughter's shoulder, but Vickie shrank away. Young misery is like that, sometimes.

"Nothing. Except that I can't go to college after all. Papa can't let me have the money."

Mrs. Harris settled herself on the faded cushions of her rocker. "How much is it? Tell me about it, Vickie. Nobody's around."

Vickie told her what the conditions were, briefly and dryly, as if she were talking to an enemy. Everyone was an enemy; all society was against her. She told her grandmother the facts and then went upstairs, refusing to be comforted.

Mrs. Harris saw her disappear through the kitchen door, and then sat looking at the door, her face grave, her eyes stern and sad. A poor factory-made piece of joiner's work seldom has to bear a look of such intense, accusing sorrow; as if that flimsy pretence of "grained" yellow pine were the door shut against all young aspiration.

X

MRS. Harris had decided to speak to Mr. Templeton, but opportunities for seeing him alone were not frequent. She watched out of the kitchen window, and when she next saw him go into the barn to fork down hay for his horse, she threw an apron over her head and followed him. She waylaid him as he came down from the hayloft.

"Hillary, I want to see you about Vickie. I was wondering if you could lay hand on any of the money you got for the sale of my house back home."

Mr. Templeton was nervous. He began brushing his trousers with a little whisk-broom he kept there, hanging on a nail.

"Why, no'm, Mrs. Harris. I couldn't just conveniently call in any of it right now. You know we had to use part of it to get moved up here from the mines."

"I know. But I thought if there was any left you could get at, we could let Vickie have it. A body'd like to help the child."

"I'd like to, powerful well, Mrs. Harris. I would, indeedy. But I'm afraid I can't manage it right now. The

136

fellers I've loaned to can't pay up this year. Maybe next year — " He was like a little boy trying to escape a scolding, though he had never had a nagging word from Mrs. Harris.

She looked downcast, but said nothing.

"It's all right, Mrs. Harris," he took on his brisk business tone and hung up the brush. "The money's perfectly safe. It's well invested."

Invested; that was a word men always held over women, Mrs. Harris thought, and it always meant they could have none of their own money. She sighed deeply.

"Well, if that's the way it is — " She turned away and went back to the house on her flat heelless slippers, just in time; Victoria was at that moment coming out to the kitchen with Hughie.

"Ma," she said, "can the little boy play out here, while I go down town?"

XI

FOR the next few days Mrs. Harris was very sombre, and she was not well. Several times in the kitchen she was seized with what she called giddy spells, and Mandy had to help her to a chair and give her a little brandy.

"Don't you say nothin', Mandy," she warned the girl. But Mandy knew enough for that.

Mrs. Harris scarcely noticed how her strength was failing, because she had so much on her mind. She was very proud, and she wanted to do something that was hard for her to do. The difficulty was to catch Mrs. Rosen alone.

On the afternoon when Victoria went to her weekly euchre, the old lady beckoned Mandy and told her to run across the alley and fetch Mrs. Rosen for a minute.

Mrs. Rosen was packing her trunk, but she came at once. Grandmother awaited her in her chair in the play-room.

"I take it very kindly of you to come, Mrs. Rosen. I'm afraid it's warm in here. Won't you have a fan?" She extended the palm leaf she was holding.

"Keep it yourself, Grandma. You are not looking very well. Do you feel badly, Grandma Harris?" She took the old lady's hand and looked at her anxiously.

"Oh, no, ma'am! I'm as well as usual. The heat wears on me a little, maybe. Have you seen Vickie lately, Mrs. Rosen?"

"Vickie? No. She hasn't run in for several days. These young people are full of their own affairs, you know."

"I expect she's backward about seeing you, now that she's so discouraged."

"Discouraged? Why, didn't the child get her scholarship after all?"

"Yes'm, she did. But they write her she has to bring more money to help her out; three hundred dollars. Mr. Templeton can't raise it just now. We had so much sickness in that mountain town before we moved up here, he got behind. Pore Vickie's downhearted."

"Oh, that is too bad! I expect you've been fretting over it, and that is why you don't look like yourself. Now what can we do about it?"

Mrs. Harris sighed and shook her head. "Vickie's trying to muster courage to go around to her father's friends and borrow from one and another. But we ain't been here long, — it ain't like we had old friends here. I hate to have the child do it."

Mrs. Rosen looked perplexed. "I'm sure Mr. Rosen would help her. He takes a great interest in Vickie."

"I thought maybe he could see his way to. That's why I sent Mandy to fetch you."

"That was right, Grandma. Now let me think." Mrs. Rosen put up her plump red-brown hand and leaned her chin upon it. "Day after tomorrow I am going to run on to Chicago for my niece's wedding." She saw her old friend's face fall. "Oh, I shan't be gone long; ten days, perhaps. I will speak to Mr. Rosen tonight, and if

Vickie goes to him after I am off his hands, I'm sure he will help her."

Mrs. Harris looked up at her with solemn gratitude. "Vickie ain't the kind of girl would forget anything like that, Mrs. Rosen. Nor I wouldn't forget it."

Mrs. Rosen patted her arm. "Grandma Harris," she exclaimed, "I will just ask Mr. Rosen to do it for you! You know I care more about the old folks than the young. If I take this worry off your mind, I shall go away to the wedding with a light heart. Now dismiss it. I am sure Mr. Rosen can arrange this himself for you, and Vickie won't have to go about to these people here, and our gossipy neighbours will never be the wiser." Mrs. Rosen poured this out in her quick, authoritative tone, converting her *th*'s into *d*'s, as she did when she was excited.

Mrs. Harris's red-brown eyes slowly filled with tears, — Mrs. Rosen had never seen that happen before. But she simply said, with quiet dignity: "Thank you, ma'am. I wouldn't have turned to nobody else."

"That means I am an old friend already, doesn't it, Grandma? And that's what I want to be. I am very jealous where Grandma Harris is concerned!" She lightly kissed the back of the purple-veined hand she had been holding, and ran home to her packing.

Grandma sat looking down at her hand. How easy it was for these foreigners to say what they felt!

XII

MRS. Harris knew she was failing. She was glad to be able to conceal it from Mrs. Rosen when that kind neighbour dashed in to kiss her good-bye on the morning of her departure for Chicago. Mrs. Templeton was, of course, present, and secrets could not be discussed. Mrs. Rosen, in her stiff little brown travelling-hat, her hands tightly gloved in brown kid, could only wink and nod to Grandmother to tell her all was well. Then she went out and climbed into the "hack" bound for the depot, which had stopped for a moment at the Templetons' gate.

Mrs. Harris was thankful that her excitable friend hadn't noticed anything unusual about her looks, and, above all, that she had made no comment. She got through the day, and that evening, thank goodness, Mr. Templeton took his wife to hear a company of strolling players sing *The Chimes of Normandy* at the Opera House. He loved music, and just now he was very eager to distract and amuse Victoria. Grandma sent the twins out to play and went to bed early.

Next morning, when she joined Mandy in the kitchen, Mandy noticed something wrong.

"You set right down, Miz' Harris, an' let me git you some whisky. Deed, ma'am, you look awful porely. You ought to tell Miss Victoria an' let her send for the doctor."

"No, Mandy, I don't want no doctor. I've seen more sickness than ever he has. Doctors can't do no more than linger you out, an' I've always prayed I wouldn't last to be a burden. You git me some whisky in hot water, and pour it on a piece of toast. I feel real empty."

That afternoon when Mrs. Harris was taking her rest, for once she lay down upon her lounge. Vickie came in, tense and excited, and stopped for a moment.

"It's all right, Grandma. Mr. Rosen is going to lend me the money. I won't have to go to anybody else. He won't ask Father to endorse my note, either. He'll just take my name." Vickie rather shouted this news at Mrs. Harris, as if the old lady were deaf, or slow of understanding. She didn't thank her; she didn't know her grandmother was in any way responsible for Mr. Rosen's offer, though at the close of their interview he had said: "We won't speak of our arrangement to anyone but your father. And I want you to mention it to the old lady Harris. I know she has been worrying about you."

Having brusquely announced her news, Vickie hurried away. There was so much to do about getting ready, she didn't know where to begin. She had no trunk and no clothes. Her winter coat, bought two years ago, was so outgrown that she couldn't get into it. All her shoes were run over at the heel and must go to the cobbler. And she had only two weeks in which to do everything! She dashed off.

Mrs. Harris sighed and closed her eyes happily. She thought with modest pride that with people like the Rosens she had always "got along nicely." It was only with the ill-bred and unclassified, like this Mrs. Jackson next door, that she had disagreeable experiences. Such folks, she told herself, had come out of nothing and knew no better. She was afraid this inquisitive woman might find her ailing and come prying round with unwelcome suggestions.

Mrs. Jackson did, indeed, call that very afternoon, with a miserable contribution of veal-loaf as an excuse (all the Templetons hated veal), but Mandy had been forewarned, and she was resourceful. She met Mrs. Jackson at the kitchen door and blocked the way.

"Sh-h-h, ma'am, Miz' Harris is asleep, havin' her

nap. No'm, she ain't porely, she's as usual. But Hughie had the colic last night when Miss Victoria was at the show, an' kep' Miz' Harris awake."

Mrs. Jackson was loathe to turn back. She had really come to find out why Mrs. Rosen drove away in the depot hack yesterday morning. Except at church socials, Mrs. Jackson did not meet people in Mrs. Rosen's set.

The next day, when Mrs. Harris got up and sat on the edge of her bed, her head began to swim, and she lay down again. Mandy peeped into the play-room as soon as she came downstairs, and found the old lady still in bed. She leaned over her and whispered:

"Ain't you feelin' well, Miz' Harris?"

"No, Mandy, I'm right porely," Mrs. Harris admitted.

"You stay where you air, ma'am. I'll git the breakfast fur the chillun, an' take the other breakfast in fur Miss Victoria an' Mr. Templeton." She hurried back to the kitchen, and Mrs. Harris went to sleep.

Immediately after breakfast Vickie dashed off about her own concerns, and the twins went to cut grass while the dew was still on it. When Mandy was taking the other breakfast into the dining-room, Mrs. Templeton came through the play-room.

"What's the matter, Ma? Are you sick?" she asked in an accusing tone.

"No, Victoria, I ain't sick. I had a little giddy spell, and I thought I'd lay still."

"You ought to be more careful what you eat, Ma. If you're going to have another bilious spell, when everything is so upset anyhow, I don't know what I'll do!" Victoria's voice broke. She hurried back into her bedroom, feeling bitterly that there was no place in that house to cry in, no spot where one could be alone, even with misery; that the house and the people in it were choking her to death.

Mrs. Harris sighed and closed her eyes. Things did seem to be upset, though she didn't know just why. Mandy, however, had her suspicions. While she waited on Mr. and Mrs. Templeton at breakfast, narrowly observing their manner toward each other and Victoria's swollen eyes and desperate expression, her suspicions grew stronger.

Instead of going to his office, Mr. Templeton went to the barn and ran out the buggy. Soon he brought out Cleveland, the black horse, with his harness on. Mandy watched from the back window. After he had hitched the horse to the buggy, he came into the kitchen to wash his hands. While he dried them on the roller towel, he said in his most business-like tone:

"I likely won't be back tonight, Mandy. I have to go out to my farm, and I'll hardly get through my business there in time to come home."

Then Mandy was sure. She had been through these times before, and at such a crisis poor Mr. Templeton was always called away on important business. When he had driven out through the alley and up the street past Mrs. Rosen's, Mandy left her dishes and went in to Mrs. Harris. She bent over and whispered low:

"Miz' Harris, I 'spect Miss Victoria's done found out she's goin' to have another baby! It looks that way. She's gone back to bed."

Mrs. Harris lifted a warning finger. "Sh-h-h!"

"Oh yes'm, I won't say nothin'. I never do."

Mrs. Harris tried to face this possibility, but her mind didn't seem strong enough — she dropped off into another doze.

All that morning Mrs. Templeton lay on her bed alone, the room darkened and a handkerchief soaked in camphor tied round her forehead. The twins had taken Ronald off to watch them cut grass, and Hughie played in the kitchen under Mandy's eye.

Now and then Victoria sat upright on the edge of the bed, beat her hands together softly and looked desperately at the ceiling, then about at those frail, confining walls. If only she could meet the situation with violence, fight it, conquer it! But there was nothing for it but stupid animal patience. She would have to go through all that again, and nobody, not even Hillary, wanted another baby, — poor as they were, and in this over-crowded house. Anyhow, she told herself, she was ashamed to have another baby, when she had a daughter old enough to go to college! She was sick of it all; sick of dragging this chain of life that never let her rest and periodically knotted and overpowered her; made her ill and hideous for months, and then dropped another baby into her arms. She had had babies enough; and there ought to be an end to such apprehensions some time before you were old and ugly.

She wanted to run away, back to Tennessee, and lead a free, gay life, as she had when she was first married. She could do a great deal more with freedom than ever Vickie could. She was still young, and she was still handsome; why must she be for ever shut up in a little cluttered house with children and fresh babies and an old woman and a stupid bound girl and a husband who wasn't very successful? Life hadn't brought her what she expected when she married Hillary Templeton; life hadn't used her right. She had tried to keep up appearances, to dress well with very little to do it on, to keep young for her husband and children. She had tried, she had tried! Mrs. Templeton buried her face in the pillow and smothered the sobs that shook the bed.

Hillary Templeton, on his drive out through the sage-brush, up into the farming country that was irrigated from the South Platte, did not feel altogether cheerful, though he whistled and sang to himself on the way. He was sorry Victoria would have to go through another time. It was awkward just now, too, when he was so short of money. But he was naturally a cheerful man, modest in his demands upon fortune, and easily diverted from unpleasant thoughts. Before Cleveland had travelled half the eighteen miles to the farm, his master was already looking forward to a visit with his tenants, an old German couple who were fond of him because he never pushed them in a hard year — so far, all the years had been hard — and he sometimes brought them bananas and such delicacies from town.

Mrs. Heyse would open her best preserves for him, he knew, and kill a chicken, and tonight he would have a clean bed in her spare room. She always put a vase of flowers in his room when he stayed overnight with them, and that pleased him very much. He felt like a youth out there, and forgot all the bills he had somehow to meet, and the loans he had made and couldn't collect. The Heyses kept bees and raised turkeys, and had honeysuckle vines running over the front porch. He loved all those things. Mr. Templeton touched Cleveland with the whip, and as they sped along into the grass country, sang softly:

> "Old Jesse was a gem'man,
> Way down in Tennessee."

XIII

MANDY had to manage the house herself that day, and she was not at all sorry. There wasn't a great deal of variety in her life, and she felt very important taking Mrs. Harris's place, giving the children their dinner, and carrying a plate of milk toast to Mrs. Templeton. She was worried about Mrs. Harris, however, and remarked to the children at noon that she thought somebody ought to "set" with their grandma. Vickie wasn't home for dinner. She had her father's office to herself for the day and was making the most it, writing a long letter to Professor Chalmers. Mr. Rosen had invited her to have dinner with him at the hotel (he boarded there when his wife was away), and that was a great honour.

When Mandy said someone ought to be with the old

lady, Bert and Del offered to take turns. Adelbert went off to rake up the grass they had been cutting all morning, and Albert sat down in the play-room. It seemed to him his grandmother looked pretty sick. He watched her while Mandy gave her toast-water with whisky in it, and thought he would like to make the room look a little nicer. While Mrs. Harris lay with her eyes closed, he hung up the caps and coats lying about, and moved away the big rocking-chair that stood by the head of Grandma's bed. There ought to be a table there, he believed, but the small tables in the house all had something on them. Upstairs, in the room where he and Adelbert and Ronald slept, there was a nice clean wooden cracker-box, on which they sat in the morning to put on their shoes and stockings. He brought this down and stood it on end at the head of Grandma's lounge, and put a clean napkin over the top of it.

She opened her eyes and smiled at him. "Could you git me a tin of fresh water, honey?"

He went to the back porch and pumped till the water ran cold. He gave it to her in a tin cup as she had asked, but he didn't think that was the right way. After she dropped back on the pillow, he fetched a glass tumbler from the cupboard, filled it, and set it on the table he had just manufactured. When Grandmother drew a red cotton handkerchief from under her pillow and wiped the moisture from her face, he ran upstairs again and got one of his Sunday-school handkerchiefs, linen ones, that Mrs. Rosen had given him and Del for Christmas. Having put this in Grandmother's hand and taken away the crumpled red one, he could think of nothing else to do — except to darken the room a little. The windows had no blinds, but flimsy cretonne curtains tied back, — not really tied, but caught back over nails driven into the sill. He loosened them and let them hang down over the bright afternoon sunlight. Then he sat down on the low sawed-off chair and gazed about, thinking that now it looked quite like a sick-room.

It was hard for a little boy to keep still. "Would you like me to read *Joe's Luck* to you, Gram'ma?" he said presently.

"You might, Bertie."

He got the "boy's book" she had been reading aloud to them, and began where she had left off. Mrs. Harris liked to hear his voice, and she liked to look at him when she opened her eyes from time to time. She did not follow the story. In her mind she was repeating a passage from the second part of *Pilgrim's Progress*, which she had read aloud to the children so many times; the passage where Christiana and her band come to the arbour on the Hill of Difficulty: *"Then said Mercy, how sweet is rest to them that labour."*

At about four o'clock Adelbert came home, hot and sweaty from raking. He said he had got in the grass and taken it to their cow, and if Bert was reading, he guessed he'd like to listen. He dragged the wooden rocking-chair up close to Grandma's bed and curled up in it.

Grandmother was perfectly happy. She and the twins were about the same age; they had in common all the realest and truest things. The years between them and her, it seemed to Mrs. Harris, were full of trouble and unimportant. The twins and Ronald and Hughie were important. She opened her eyes.

"Where is Hughie?" she asked.

"I guess he's asleep. Mother took him into her bed."

"And Ronald?"

"He's upstairs with Mandy. There ain't nobody in the kitchen now."

"Then you might git me a fresh drink, Del."

"Yes'm, Gram'ma." He tiptoed out to the pump in his brown canvas sneakers.

When Vickie came home at five o'clock, she went to her mother's room, but the door was locked—a thing she couldn't remember ever happening before. She went into the play-room,—old Mrs. Harris was asleep, with one of the twins on guard, and he held up a warning finger. She went into the kitchen. Mandy was making biscuits, and Ronald was helping her to cut them out.

"What's the matter, Mandy? Where is everybody?"

"You know your papa's away, Miss Vickie; an' your mama's got a headache, an' Miz' Harris has had a bad spell. Maybe I'll just fix supper for you an' the boys in the kitchen, so you won't all have to be runnin' through her room."

"Oh, very well," said Vickie bitterly, and she went upstairs. Wasn't it just like them all to go and get sick, when she had now only two weeks to get ready for school, and no trunk and no clothes or anything? Nobody but Mr. Rosen seemed to take the least interest, "when my whole life hangs by a thread," she told herself fiercely. What were families for, anyway?

After supper Vickie went to her father's office to read; she told Mandy to leave the kitchen door open, and when she got home she would go to bed without disturbing anybody. The twins ran out to play under the electric light with the neighbour boys for a little while, then slipped softly up the back stairs to their room. Mandy came to Mrs. Harris after the house was still.

"Kin I rub your legs fur you, Miz' Harris?"

153

"Thank you, Mandy. And you might get me a clean nightcap out of the press."

Mandy returned with it.

"Lawsie me! But your legs is cold, ma'am!"

"I expect it's about time, Mandy," murmured the old lady. Mandy knelt on the floor and set to work with a will. It brought the sweat out on her, and at last she sat up and wiped her face with the back of her hand.

"I can't seem to git no heat into 'em, Miz' Harris. I got a hot flat-iron on the stove; I'll wrap it in a piece of old blanket and put it to your feet. Why didn't you have the boys tell me you was cold, pore soul?"

Mrs. Harris did not answer. She thought it was probably a cold that neither Mandy nor the flat-iron could do much with. She hadn't nursed so many people back in Tennessee without coming to know certain signs.

After Mandy was gone, she fell to thinking of her blessings. Every night for years, when she said her prayers, she had prayed that she might never have a long sickness or be a burden. She dreaded the heartache and humiliation of being helpless on the hands of people who would be impatient under such a care. And now she felt certain that she was going to die tonight, without troubling anybody.

She was glad Mrs. Rosen was in Chicago. Had she

154

been at home, she would certainly have come in, would have seen that her old neighbour was very sick, and bustled about. Her quick eyes would have found out all Grandmother's little secrets: how hard her bed was, that she had no proper place to wash, and kept her comb in her pocket; that her nightgowns were patched and darned. Mrs. Rosen would have been indignant, and that would have made Victoria cross. She didn't have to see Mrs. Rosen again to know that Mrs. Rosen thought highly of her and admired her—yes, admired her. Those funny little pats and arch pleasantries had meant a great deal to Mrs. Harris.

It was a blessing that Mr. Templeton was away, too. Appearances had to be kept up when there was a man in the house; and he might have taken it into his head to send for the doctor, and stir everybody up. Now everything would be so peaceful. *"The Lord is my shepherd,"* she whispered gratefully. "Yes, Lord, I always spoiled Victoria. She was so much the prettiest. But nobody won't ever be the worse for it: Mr. Templeton will always humour her, and the children love her more than most. They'll always be good to her; she has that way with her."

Grandma fell to remembering the old place at home: what a dashing, high-spirited girl Victoria was, and how proud she had always been of her; how she used to hear her laughing and teasing out in the lilac arbour when Hillary Templeton was courting her. Toward morning all these pleasant reflections faded out. Mrs. Harris felt that she and her bed were softly sinking, through the darkness to a deeper darkness.

Old Mrs. Harris did not really die that night, but she believed she did. Mandy found her unconscious in the morning. Then there was a great stir and bustle; Victoria, and even Vickie, were startled out of their intense self-absorption. Mrs. Harris was hastily carried out of the play-room and laid in Victoria's bed, put into one of Victoria's best nightgowns. Mr. Templeton was sent for, and the doctor was sent for. The inquisitive Mrs. Jackson from next door got into the house at last, — installed herself as nurse, and no one had the courage to say her nay. But Grandmother was out of it all, never knew that she was the object of so much attention and excitement. She died a little while after Mr. Templeton got home.

Thus Mrs. Harris slipped out of the Templetons' story; but Victoria and Vickie had still to go on, to follow the long road that leads through things unguessed at and unforeseeable. When they are old, they will come closer and closer to Grandma Harris. They

156

will think a great deal about her, and remember things they never noticed; and their lot will be more or less like hers. They will regret that they heeded her so little; but they, too, will look into the eager, unseeing eyes of young people and feel themselves alone. They will say to themselves: "I was heartless, because I was young and strong and wanted things so much. But now I know."

New Brunswick, 1931

157

Two Friends

Two Friends

I

EVEN in early youth, when the mind is so eager for the new and untried, while it is still a stranger to faltering and fear, we yet like to think that there are certain unalterable realities, somewhere at the bottom of things. These anchors may be ideas; but more often they are merely pictures, vivid memories, which in some unaccountable and very personal way give us courage. The sea-gulls, that seem so much creatures of the free wind and waves, that are as homeless as the sea (able to rest upon the tides and ride the storm, needing nothing but water and sky), at certain seasons even they go back to something they have known before; to remote islands and lonely ledges that are their breeding-grounds. The restlessness of youth has such retreats, even though it may be ashamed of them.

Long ago, before the invention of the motor-car (which has made more changes in the world than the

War, which indeed produced the particular kind of war that happened just a hundred years after Waterloo), in a little wooden town in a shallow Kansas river valley, there lived two friends. They were "business men," the two most prosperous and influential men in our community, the two men whose affairs took them out into the world to big cities, who had "connections" in St. Joseph and Chicago. In my childhood they represented to me success and power.

R. E. Dillon was of Irish extraction, one of the dark Irish, with glistening jet-black hair and moustache, and thick eyebrows. His skin was very white, bluish on his shaven cheeks and chin. Shaving must have been a difficult process for him, because there were no smooth expanses for the razor to glide over. The bony structure of his face was prominent and unusual; high cheekbones, a bold Roman nose, a chin cut by deep lines, with a hard dimple at the tip, a jutting ridge over his eyes where his curly black eyebrows grew and met. It was a face in many planes, as if the carver had whittled and modelled and indented to see how far he could go. Yet on meeting him what you saw was an imperious head on a rather small, wiry man, a head held conspicuously and proudly erect, with a carriage unmistakably arrogant and consciously superior. Dillon had a musical, vibrating voice, and the changeable grey eye that is peculiarly Irish. His full name, which he never used, was Robert Emmet Dillon, so there must have been a certain feeling somewhere back in his family.

He was the principal banker in our town, and proprietor of the large general store next the bank; he owned farms up in the grass country, and a fine ranch in the green timbered valley of the Caw. He was, according to our standards, a rich man.

His friend, J. H. Trueman, was what we called a big cattleman. Trueman was from Buffalo; his family were old residents there, and he had come West as a young man because he was restless and unconventional in his tastes. He was fully ten years older than Dillon, — in his early fifties, when I knew him; large, heavy, very slow in his movements, not given to exercise. His countenance was as unmistakably American as Dillon's was not, — but American of that period, not of this. He did not belong to the time of efficiency and advertising and progressive methods. For any form of pushing or boosting he had a cold, unqualified contempt. All this was in his face, — heavy, immobile, rather melancholy, not remarkable in any particular. But the moment one looked at him one felt solidity, an entire absence of anything mean or small, easy carelessness, courage, a high sense of honour.

Obscure Destinies

These two men had been friends for ten years before I knew them, and I knew them from the time I was ten until I was thirteen. I saw them as often as I could, because they led more varied lives than the other men in our town; one could look up to them. Dillon, I believe, was the more intelligent. Trueman had, perhaps, a better tradition, more background.

Dillon's bank and general store stood at the corner of Main Street and a cross-street, and on this cross-street, two short blocks away, my family lived. On my way to and from school, and going on the countless errands that I was sent upon day and night, I always passed Dillon's store. Its long, red brick wall, with no windows except high overhead, ran possibly a hundred feet along the sidewalk of the cross-street. The front door and show windows were on Main Street, and the bank was next door. The board sidewalk along that red brick wall was wider than any other piece of walk in town, smoother, better laid, kept in perfect repair; very good to walk on in a community where most things were flimsy. I liked the store and the brick wall and the sidewalk because they were solid and well built, and possibly I admired Dillon and Trueman for much the same reason. They were secure and established. So many of our citizens were nervous little hopper men, trying to get on. Dillon and Trueman had got on; they stood with easy assurance on a deck that was their own.

In the daytime one did not often see them together — each went about his own affairs. But every evening they were both to be found at Dillon's store. The bank, of course, was locked and dark before the sun went down, but the store was always open until ten o'clock; the clerks put in a long day. So did Dillon. He and his store were one. He never acted as salesman, and he kept a cashier in the wire-screened office at the back end of the store; but he was there to be called on. The thrifty Swedes to the north, who were his best customers, usually came to town and did their shopping after dark — they didn't squander daylight hours in farming season. In these evening visits with his customers, and on his drives in his buckboard among the farms, Dillon learned all he needed to know about how much money it was safe to advance a farmer who wanted to feed cattle, or to buy a steam thrasher or build a new barn.

Every evening in winter, when I went to the post-office after supper, I passed through Dillon's store instead of going round it, — for the warmth and cheerfulness, and to catch sight of Mr. Dillon and Mr. Trueman playing checkers in the office behind the wire screening; both seated on high accountant's stools, with the checker-board on the cashier's desk before them. I knew all Dillon's clerks, and if they were not busy, I often lingered about to talk to them; sat on one of the grocery counters and watched the checker-players from a distance. I remember Mr. Dillon's hand used to linger in the air above the board before he made a move; a well-kept hand, white, marked with blue veins and streaks of strong black hair. Trueman's hands rested on his knees under the desk while he considered; he took a checker, set it down, then dropped his hand on his knee again. He seldom made an unnecessary movement with his hands or feet. Each of the men wore a ring on his little finger. Mr. Dillon's was a large diamond solitaire set in a gold claw, Trueman's the head of a Roman soldier cut in onyx and set in pale twisted gold; it had been his father's, I believe.

Exactly at ten o'clock the store closed. Mr. Dillon went home to his wife and family, to his roomy, comfortable house with a garden and orchard and big stables. Mr. Trueman, who had long been a widower, went to his office to begin the day over. He led a double life, and until one or two o'clock in the morning entertained the poker-players of our town. After everything was shut for the night, a queer crowd drifted into Trueman's back office. The company was seldom the same on two successive evenings, but there were three tireless poker-players who always came: the billiard-hall proprietor, with green-gold moustache and eyebrows, and big white teeth; the horse-trader, who smelled of horses; the dandified cashier of the bank that rivalled Dillon's. The gamblers met in Trueman's place because a game that went on there was respectable, was a social game, no matter how much money changed hands. If the horse-trader or the crooked money-lender got over-heated and broke loose a little, a look or a remark from Mr. Trueman would freeze them up. And his remark was always the same:

"Careful of the language around here."

It was never "your" language, but "the" language, — though he certainly intended no pleasantry. Trueman himself was not a lucky poker man; he was never ahead of the game on the whole. He played because he liked it, and he was willing to pay for his amusement. In general he was large and indifferent about money matters, — always carried a few hundred-dollar bills in his inside coat-pocket, and left his coat hanging anywhere, — in his office, in the bank, in the barber shop, in the cattle-sheds behind the freight yard.

Now, R. E. Dillon detested gambling, often dropped a contemptuous word about "poker bugs" before the horse-trader and the billiard-hall man and the cashier of the other bank. But he never made remarks of that sort in Trueman's presence. He was a man who voiced his prejudices fearlessly and cuttingly, but on this and other matters he held his peace before Trueman. His regard for him must have been very strong.

During the winter, usually in March, the two friends always took a trip together, to Kansas City and St. Joseph. When they got ready, they packed their bags and stepped aboard a fast Santa Fé train and went; the Limited was often signalled to stop for them. Their excursions made some of the rest of us feel less shut away and small-townish, just as their fur overcoats and silk shirts did. They were the only men in Singleton who wore silk shirts. The other business men wore white shirts with detachable collars, high and stiff or low and sprawling, which were changed much oftener than the shirts. Neither of my heroes was afraid of laundry bills. They did not wear waistcoats, but went about in their shirt-sleeves in hot weather; their suspenders were chosen with as much care as their neckties and handkerchiefs. Once when a bee stung my hand in the store (a few of them had got into the brown-sugar barrel), Mr. Dillon himself moistened the sting, put baking soda on it, and bound my hand up with his pocket hand-

kerchief. It was of the smoothest linen, and in one corner was a violet square bearing his initials, R. E. D., in
white. There were never any handkerchiefs like that in
my family. I cherished it until it was laundered, and I
returned it with regret.

It was in the spring and summer that one saw Mr.
Dillon and Mr. Trueman at their best. Spring began
early with us, — often the first week of April was hot.
Every evening when he came back to the store after
supper, Dillon had one of his clerks bring two arm-
chairs out to the wide sidewalk that ran beside the red
brick wall, — office chairs of the old-fashioned sort,
with a low round back which formed a half-circle to
enclose the sitter, and spreading legs, the front ones
slightly higher. In those chairs the two friends would
spend the evening. Dillon would sit down and light a
good cigar. In a few moments Mr. Trueman would
come across from Main Street, walking slowly, spa-
ciously, as if he were used to a great deal of room. As he
approached, Mr. Dillon would call out to him:

"Good evening, J. H. Fine weather."

J. H. would take his place in the empty chair.

"Spring in the air," he might remark, if it were April.
Then he would relight a dead cigar which was always in
his hand, — seemed to belong there, like a thumb or
finger.

"I drove up north today to see what the Swedes are doing," Mr. Dillon might begin. "They're the boys to get the early worm. They never let the ground go to sleep. Whatever moisture there is, they get the benefit of it."

"The Swedes are good farmers. I don't sympathize with the way they work their women."

"The women like it, J. H. It's the old-country way; they're accustomed to it, and they like it."

"Maybe. I don't like it," Trueman would reply with something like a grunt.

They talked very much like this all evening; or, rather, Mr. Dillon talked, and Mr. Trueman made an occasional observation. No one could tell just how much Mr. Trueman knew about anything, because he was so consistently silent. Not from diffidence, but from superiority; from a contempt for chatter, and a liking for silence, a taste for it. After they had exchanged a few remarks, he and Dillon often sat in an easy quiet for a long time, watching the passers-by, watching the wagons on the road, watching the stars. Sometimes, very rarely, Mr. Trueman told a long story, and it was sure to be an interesting and unusual one.

But on the whole it was Mr. Dillon who did the talking; he had a wide-awake voice with much variety in it.

Two Friends

Trueman's was thick and low,—his speech was rather indistinct and never changed in pitch or tempo. Even when he swore wickedly at the hands who were loading his cattle into freight cars, it was a mutter, a low, even growl. There was a curious attitude in men of his class and time, that of being rather above speech, as they were above any kind of fussiness or eagerness. But I knew he liked to hear Mr. Dillon talk,—anyone did. Dillon had such a crisp, clear enunciation, and he could say things so neatly. People would take a reprimand from him they wouldn't have taken from anyone else, because he put it so well. His voice was never warm or soft—it had a cool, sparkling quality; but it could be very humorous, very kind and considerate, very teasing and stimulating. Every sentence he uttered was alive, never languid, perfunctory, slovenly, unaccented. When he made a remark, it not only meant something, but sounded like something,—sounded like the thing he meant.

When Mr. Dillon was closeted with a depositor in his private room in the bank, and you could not hear his words through the closed door, his voice told you exactly the degree of esteem in which he held that customer. It was interested, encouraging, deliberative, humorous, satisfied, admiring, cold, critical, haughty, contemptuous, according to the deserts and pretensions of his listener. And one could tell when the person closeted with him was a woman; a farmer's wife, or a woman who was trying to run a little business, or a country girl hunting a situation. There was a difference; something peculiarly kind and encouraging. But if it were a foolish, extravagant woman, or a girl he didn't approve of, oh, then one knew it well enough! The tone was courteous, but cold; relentless as the multiplication table.

All these possibilities of voice made his evening talk in the spring dusk very interesting; interesting for Trueman and for me. I found many pretexts for lingering near them, and they never seemed to mind my hanging about. I was very quiet. I often sat on the edge of the sidewalk with my feet hanging down and played jacks by the hour when there was moonlight. On dark nights I sometimes perched on top of one of the big goods-boxes — we called them "store boxes," — there were usually several of these standing empty on the sidewalk against the red brick wall.

I liked to listen to those two because theirs was the only "conversation" one could hear about the streets. The older men talked of nothing but politics and their business, and the very young men's talk was entirely what they called "josh"; very personal, supposed to be funny, and really not funny at all. It was scarcely speech, but noises, snorts, giggles, yawns, sneezes, with a few abbreviated words and slang expressions which stood for a hundred things. The original Indians of the Kansas plains had more to do with articulate speech than had our promising young men.

To be sure my two aristocrats sometimes discussed politics, and joked each other about the policies and pretensions of their respective parties. Mr. Dillon, of course, was a Democrat, — it was in the very frosty sparkle of his speech, — and Mr. Trueman was a Republican; his rear, as he walked about the town, looked a little like the walking elephant labelled "G. O. P." in *Puck*. But each man seemed to enjoy hearing his party ridiculed, took it as a compliment.

In the spring their talk was usually about weather and planting and pasture and cattle. Mr. Dillon went about the country in his light buckboard a great deal at that season, and he knew what every farmer was doing and what his chances were, just how much he was falling behind or getting ahead.

"I happened to drive by Oscar Ericson's place today, and I saw as nice a lot of calves as you could find anywhere," he would begin, and Ericson's history and his family would be pretty thoroughly discussed before they changed the subject.

Or he might come out with something sharp: "By the way, J. H., I saw an amusing sight today. I turned in at Sandy Bright's place to get water for my horse, and he had a photographer out there taking pictures of his house and barn. It would be more to the point if he had a picture taken of the mortgages he's put on that farm."

Trueman would give a short, mirthless response, more like a cough than a laugh.

Those April nights, when the darkness itself tasted dusty (or, by the special mercy of God, cool and damp), when the smell of burning grass was in the air, and a sudden breeze brought the scent of wild plum blossoms, — those evenings were only a restless preparation for the summer nights, — nights of full liberty and perfect idleness. Then there was no school, and one's family never bothered about where one was. My parents were young and full of life, glad to have the children out of the way. All day long there had been the excitement that intense heat produces in some people, — a mild drunkenness made of sharp contrasts; thirst and cold water, the blazing stretch of Main Street and the cool of the brick stores when one dived into them. By nightfall one was ready to be quiet. My two friends were always in their best form on those moonlit summer nights, and their talk covered a wide range.

I suppose there were moonless nights, and dark ones with but a silver shaving and pale stars in the sky, just as in the spring. But I remember them all as flooded by the rich indolence of a full moon, or a half-moon set in uncertain blue. Then Trueman and Dillon would sit with their coats off and have a supply of fresh handkerchiefs to mop their faces; they were more largely and positively themselves. One could distinguish their features, the stripes on their shirts, the flash of Mr. Dillon's diamond; but their shadows made two dark masses on the white sidewalk. The brick wall behind them, faded almost pink by the burning of successive summers, took on a carnelian hue at night. Across the street, which was merely a dusty road, lay an open space, with a few stunted box-elder trees, where the farmers left their wagons and teams when they came to town. Beyond this space stood a row of frail wooden buildings, due to be pulled down any day; tilted, crazy, with outside stairs going up to rickety second-storey porches that sagged in the middle. They had once been white, but were now grey, with faded blue doors along the wavy upper porches. These abandoned buildings, an eyesore by day, melted together into a curious pile in the moonlight, became an immaterial structure of velvet-white and glossy blackness, with here and there a faint smear of blue door, or a tilted patch of sage-green that had once been a shutter.

The road, just in front of the sidewalk where I sat and played jacks, would be ankle-deep in dust, and seemed to drink up the moonlight like folds of velvet. It drank up sound, too; muffled the wagon-wheels and hoof-beats; lay soft and meek like the last residuum of material things, — the soft bottom resting-place. Nothing in the world, not snow mountains or blue seas, is so beautiful in moonlight as the soft, dry summer roads in a farming country, roads where the white dust falls back from the slow wagon-wheel.

Wonderful things do happen even in the dullest places — in the cornfields and the wheat-fields. Sitting there on the edge of the sidewalk one summer night, my feet hanging in the warm dust, I saw an occultation of Venus. Only the three of us were there. It was a hot night, and the clerks had closed the store and gone home. Mr. Dillon and Mr. Trueman waited on a little while to watch. It was a very blue night, breathless and clear, not the smallest cloud from horizon to horizon. Everything up there overhead seemed as usual, it was the familiar face of a summer-night sky. But presently we saw one bright star moving. Mr. Dillon called to me; told me to watch what was going to happen, as I might never chance to see it again in my lifetime.

That big star certainly got nearer and nearer the moon, — very rapidly, too, until there was not the width of your hand between them — now the width of two fingers — then it passed directly into the moon at about the middle of its girth; absolutely disappeared. The star we had been watching was gone. We waited, I do not know how long, but it seemed to me about fifteen minutes. Then we saw a bright wart on the other edge of the moon, but for a second only, — the machinery up there worked fast. While the two men were exclaiming and telling me to look, the planet swung clear of the golden disk, a rift of blue came between them and widened very fast. The planet did not seem to move, but that inky blue space between it and the moon seemed to spread. The thing was over.

My friends stayed on long past their usual time and talked about eclipses and such matters.

"Let me see," Mr. Trueman remarked slowly, "they reckon the moon's about two hundred and fifty thousand miles away from us. I wonder how far that star is."

"I don't know, J. H., and I really don't much care.

When we can get the tramps off the railroad, and manage to run this town with one fancy house instead of two, and have a Federal Government that is as honest as a good banking business, then it will be plenty of time to turn our attention to the stars."

Mr. Trueman chuckled and took his cigar from between his teeth. "Maybe the stars will throw some light on all that, if we get the run of them," he said humorously. Then he added: "Mustn't be a reformer, R. E. Nothing in it. That's the only time you ever get off on the wrong foot. Life is what it always has been, always will be. No use to make a fuss." He got up, said: "Good-night, R. E.," said good-night to me, too, because this had been an unusual occasion, and went down the sidewalk with his wide, sailor-like tread, as if he were walking the deck of his own ship.

When Dillon and Trueman went to St. Joseph, or, as we called it, St. Joe, they stopped at the same hotel, but their diversions were very dissimilar. Mr. Dillon was a family man and a good Catholic; he behaved in St. Joe very much as if he were at home. His sister was Mother Superior of a convent there, and he went to see her often. The nuns made much of him, and he enjoyed their admiration and all the ceremony with which they entertained him. When his two daughters were going to the convent school, he used to give theatre parties for them, inviting all their friends.

Mr. Trueman's way of amusing himself must have tried his friend's patience — Dillon liked to regulate other people's affairs if they needed it. Mr. Trueman had a lot of poker-playing friends among the commission men in St. Joe, and he sometimes dropped a good deal of money. He was supposed to have rather questionable women friends there, too. The grasshopper men of our town used to say that Trueman was financial adviser to a woman who ran a celebrated sporting house. Mary Trent, her name was. She must have been a very unusual woman; she had credit with all the banks, and never got into any sort of trouble. She had formerly been head mistress of a girls' finishing school and knew how to manage young women. It was probably a fact that Trueman knew her and found her interesting, as did many another sound business man of that time. Mr. Dillon must have shut his ears to these rumours, — a measure of the great value he put on Trueman's companionship.

Though they did not see much of each other on these trips, they immensely enjoyed taking them together. They often dined together at the end of the day, and afterwards went to the theatre. They both loved the theatre; not this play or that actor, but the theatre, — whether they saw *Hamlet* or *Pinafore*. It was an age of good acting, and the drama held a more dignified position in the world than it holds today.

After Dillon and Trueman had come home from the city, they used sometimes to talk over the plays they had seen, recalling the great scenes and fine effects. Occasionally an item in the Kansas City *Star* would turn their talk to the stage.

"J. H., I see by the paper that Edwin Booth is very sick," Mr. Dillon announced one evening as Trueman came up to take the empty chair.

"Yes, I noticed." Trueman sat down and lit his dead cigar. "He's not a young man any more." A long pause. Dillon always seemed to know when the pause would be followed by a remark, and waited for it. "The first time I saw Edwin Booth was in Buffalo. It was in *Richard the Second*, and it made a great impression on me at the time." Another pause. "I don't know that I'd care to see him in that play again. I like tragedy, but that play's a little too tragic. Something very black about it. I think I prefer *Hamlet*."

They had seen Mary Anderson in St. Louis once, and talked of it for years afterwards. Mr. Dillon was very proud of her because she was a Catholic girl, and called

180

her "our Mary." It was curious that a third person, who had never seen these actors or read the plays, could get so much of the essence of both from the comments of two business men who used none of the language in which such things are usually discussed, who merely reminded each other of moments here and there in the action. But they saw the play over again as they talked of it, and perhaps whatever is seen by the narrator as he speaks is sensed by the listener, quite irrespective of words. This transference of experience went further: in some way the lives of those two men came across to me as they talked, the strong, bracing reality of successful, large-minded men who had made their way in the world when business was still a personal adventure.

II

M R. Dillon went to Chicago once a year to buy goods for his store. Trueman would usually accompany him as far as St. Joe, but no farther. He dismissed Chicago as "too big." He didn't like to be one of the crowd, didn't feel at home in a city where he wasn't recognized as J. H. Trueman.

It was one of these trips to Chicago that brought about the end—for me and for them; a stupid, senseless, commonplace end.

Being a Democrat, already somewhat "tainted" by the free-silver agitation, one spring Dillon delayed his visit to Chicago in order to be there for the Democratic Convention — it was the Convention that first nominated Bryan.

On the night after his return from Chicago, Mr. Dillon was seated in his chair on the sidewalk, surrounded by a group of men who wanted to hear all about the nomination of a man from a neighbour State. Mr. Trueman came across the street in his leisurely way, greeted Dillon, and asked him how he had found Chicago, — whether he had had a good trip.

Mr. Dillon must have been annoyed because Trueman didn't mention the Convention. He threw back his head rather haughtily. "Well, J. H., since I saw you last, we've found a great leader in this country, and a great orator." There was a frosty sparkle in his voice that presupposed opposition, — like the feint of a boxer getting ready.

"Great windbag!" muttered Trueman. He sat down in his chair, but I noticed that he did not settle himself and cross his legs as usual.

Mr. Dillon gave an artificial laugh. "It's nothing against a man to be a fine orator. All the great leaders

182

have been eloquent. This Convention was a memorable occasion; it gave the Democratic party a rebirth."

"Gave it a black eye, and a blind spot, I'd say!" commented Trueman. He didn't raise his voice, but he spoke with more heat than I had ever heard from him. After a moment he added: "I guess Grover Cleveland must be a sick man; must feel like he'd taken a lot of trouble for nothing."

Mr. Dillon ignored these thrusts and went on telling the group around him about the Convention, but there was a special nimbleness and exactness in his tongue, a chill politeness in his voice that meant anger. Presently he turned again to Mr. Trueman, as if he could now trust himself:

"It was one of the great speeches of history, J. H.; our grandchildren will have to study it in school, as we did Patrick Henry's."

"Glad I haven't got any grandchildren, if they'd be brought up on that sort of tall talk," said Mr. Trueman. "Sounds like a schoolboy had written it. Absolutely nothing back of it but an unsound theory."

Mr. Dillon's laugh made me shiver; it was like a thin glitter of danger. He arched his curly eyebrows provokingly.

"We'll have four years of currency reform, anyhow.

183

By the end of that time, you old dyed-in-the-wool Republicans will be thinking differently. The under dog is going to have a chance."

Mr. Trueman shifted in his chair. "That's no way for a banker to talk." He spoke very low. "The Democrats will have a long time to be sorry they ever turned Pops. No use talking to you while your Irish is up. I'll wait till you cool off." He rose and walked away, less deliberately than usual, and Mr. Dillon, watching his retreating figure, laughed haughtily and disagreeably. He asked the grain-elevator man to take the vacated chair. The group about him grew, and he sat expounding the reforms proposed by the Democratic candidate until a late hour.

For the first time in my life I listened with breathless interest to a political discussion. Whoever Mr. Dillon failed to convince, he convinced me. I grasped it at once: that gold had been responsible for most of the miseries and inequalities of the world; that it had always been the club the rich and cunning held over the poor; and that "the free and unlimited coinage of silver" would remedy all this. Dillon declared that young Mr. Bryan had looked like the patriots of old when he faced and challenged high finance with: "You shall not press down upon the brow of labour this crown of thorns; you shall not crucify mankind upon a cross of gold." I thought that magnificent; I thought the cornfields would show them a thing or two, back there!

R. E. Dillon had never taken an aggressive part in politics. But from that night on, the Democratic candidate and the free-silver plank were the subject of his talks with his customers and depositors. He drove about the country convincing the farmers, went to the neighbouring towns to use his influence with the merchants, organized the Bryan Club and the Bryan Ladies' Quartette in our county, contributed largely to the campaign fund. This was all a new line of conduct for Mr. Dillon, and it sat unsteadily on him. Even his voice became unnatural; there was a sting of come-back in it. His new character made him more like other people and took away from his special personal quality. I wonder whether it was not Trueman, more than Bryan, who put such an edge on him.

While all these things were going on, Trueman kept to his own office. He came to Dillon's bank on business, but he did not "come back to the sidewalk," as I put it to myself. He waited and said nothing, but he looked grim. After a month or so, when he saw that this thing was not going to blow over, when he heard how Dillon had been talking to representative men all over the county, and saw the figure he had put down for the campaign fund, then Trueman remarked to some of his friends that a banker had no business to commit himself to a scatter-brained financial policy which would destroy credit.

The next morning Mr. Trueman went to the bank across the street, the rival of Dillon's, and wrote a cheque on Dillon's bank "for the amount of my balance." He wasn't the sort of man who would ever know what his balance was, he merely kept it big enough to cover emergencies. That afternoon the Merchants' National took the cheque over to Dillon on its collecting rounds, and by night the word was all over town that Trueman had changed his bank. After this there would be no going back, people said. To change your bank was one of the most final things you could do. The little, unsuccessful men were pleased, as they always are at the destruction of anything strong and fine.

All through the summer and the autumn of that campaign Mr. Dillon was away a great deal. When he was at home, he took his evening airing on the sidewalk, and there was always a group of men about him, talking of the coming election; that was the most exciting presidential campaign people could remember. I often passed this group on my way to the post-office, but there was no temptation to linger now. Mr. Dillon seemed like another man, and my zeal to free humanity from the cross of gold had cooled. Mr. Trueman I seldom saw. When he passed me on the street, he nodded kindly.

The election and Bryan's defeat did nothing to soften Dillon. He had been sure of a Democratic victory. I believe he felt almost as if Trueman were responsible for the triumph of Hanna and McKinley. At least he knew that Trueman was exceedingly well satisfied, and that was bitter to him. He seemed to me sarcastic and sharp all the time now.

I don't believe self-interest would ever have made a breach between Dillon and Trueman. Neither would have taken advantage of the other. If a combination of circumstances had made it necessary that one or the other should take a loss in money or prestige, I think Trueman would have pocketed the loss. That was his way. It was his code, moreover. A gentleman pocketed his gains mechanically, in the day's routine; but he pocketed losses punctiliously, with a sharp, if bitter, relish. I believe now, as I believed then, that this was a quarrel of "principle." Trueman looked down on anyone who could take the reasoning of the Populist party seriously. He was a perfectly direct man, and he showed his contempt. That was enough. It lost me my special pleasure of summer nights: the old stories of the early West that sometimes came to the surface; the minute biographies of the farming people; the clear, detailed, illuminating accounts of all that went on in the great crop-growing, cattle-feeding world; and the silence, — the strong, rich, outflowing silence between two friends, that was as full and satisfying as the moonlight. I was never to know its like again.

After that rupture nothing went well with either of my two great men. Things were out of true, the equilibrium was gone. Formerly, when they used to sit in their old places on the sidewalk, two black figures with patches of shadow below, they seemed like two bodies held steady by some law of balance, an unconscious relation like that between the earth and the moon. It was this mathematical harmony which gave a third person pleasure.

Before the next presidential campaign came round, Mr. Dillon died (a young man still) very suddenly, of pneumonia. We didn't know that he was seriously ill until one of his clerks came running to our house to tell us he was dead. The same clerk, half out of his wits — it looked like the end of the world to him — ran on to tell Mr. Trueman.

Mr. Trueman thanked him. He called his confidential man, and told him to order flowers from Kansas City. Then he went to his house, informed his housekeeper that he was going away on business, and packed his bag. That same night he boarded the Santa Fé Limited and didn't stop until he was in San Francisco. He was gone all spring. His confidential clerk wrote him letters every week about the business and the new calves, and got telegrams in reply. Trueman never wrote letters.

When Mr. Trueman at last came home, he stayed only a few months. He sold out everything he owned to a stranger from Kansas City; his feeding ranch, his barns and sheds, his house and town lots. It was a terrible blow to me; now only the common, everyday people would be left. I used to walk mournfully up and down before his office while all these deeds were being signed,—there were usually lawyers and notaries inside. But once, when he happened to be alone, he called me in, asked me how old I was now, and how far along I had got in school. His face and voice were more than kind, but he seemed absent-minded, as if he were trying to recall something. Presently he took from his watch-chain a red seal I had always admired, reached for my hand, and dropped the piece of carnelian into my palm.

"For a keepsake," he said evasively.

When the transfer of his property was completed, Mr. Trueman left us for good. He spent the rest of his life among the golden hills of San Francisco. He moved into the Saint Francis Hotel when it was first built, and had an office in a high building at the top of what is now Powell Street. There he read his letters in the morning and played poker at night. I've heard a man whose offices were next his tell how Trueman used to sit tilted back in his desk chair, a half-consumed cigar in his mouth, morning after morning, apparently doing nothing, watching the Bay and the ferry-boats, across a line of wind-racked eucalyptus trees. He died at the Saint Francis about nine years after he left our part of the world.

The breaking-up of that friendship between two men who scarcely noticed my existence was a real loss to me, and has ever since been a regret. More than once, in Southern countries where there is a smell of dust and dryness in the air and the nights are intense, I have come upon a stretch of dusty white road drinking up the moonlight beside a blind wall, and have felt a sudden sadness. Perhaps it was not until the next morning that I knew why, — and then only because I had dreamed of

Two Friends

Mr. Dillon or Mr. Trueman in my sleep. When that old scar is occasionally touched by chance, it rouses the old uneasiness; the feeling of something broken that could so easily have been mended; of something delightful that was senselessly wasted, of a truth that was accidentally distorted — one of the truths we want to keep.

Pasadena, 1931

Acknowledgments

THE TEXTUAL EDITING OF *Obscure Destinies* is the result of contributions from many members of the Cather Edition staff, among whom we wish to acknowledge especially Kathleen Danker and Erin Marcus. Numerous graduate students contributed to the project, especially Deborah Cumberland, Deborah Forssman, Susan Kelly, Emily Levine, Susan Moss, Kelly Olson, Michael Radelich, and Deborah Seivert.

We are deeply grateful to Helen Cather Southwick, who provided us with a copy of the late typescript of "Two Friends," and to a collector who wishes to remain anonymous, who provided a copy of the typescript of "Old Mrs. Harris" and a copy of an early typescript of "Two Friends." Our knowledge of Cather's writing and revision processes has been greatly enlarged by their generous willingness to allow us to use these materials.

Consultations early in the project were helpful at different stages in the preparation of this edition. In *Willa Cather: A Bibliography* (Lincoln: U of Nebraska P, 1982), Joan Crane provided an authoritative starting place for our identification and assembly of basic materials, then in correspondence was unfailingly generous with her expertise. The late Fredson Bowers (University of Virginia) advised us about the steps necessary to organize the project. As editor of the Lewis and Clark journals, Gary Moulton (University of Nebraska–Lincoln) generously provided expertise and encouragement. David J. Nordloh (Indiana University) provided invaluable advice as we established policies and procedures and wrote our editorial manual. Conversations with Richard Rust (University of North Carolina–Chapel Hill) were helpful in refining procedures concerning variants. Then James L. W. West III (Pennsylvania State University) brought knowledge of publishing history as well as editorial practices to his inspection of our materials on behalf of the Committee on Scholarly Editions.

In the preparation of the apparatus, Deborah Cumberland, Deborah Forssman, Heather Hiatt, Susan Kelly, Deborah Seivert, and Chris Wolack provided important assistance in assembling materials for the historical essay and explanatory notes. Helen Cather Southwick and Beverly Cooper kindly shared letters dealing with revisions in the text. Mrs. Southwick also assisted us in the interpretation of handwriting on the typescripts. Professor Herbert Johnson (Rochester Institute of Technology) generously shared his knowledge of printing history and technique.

We appreciate the assistance of Michelle Fagan and Lynn R. Beideck-Porn, Archives and Special Collections of Love

Library, University of Nebraska–Lincoln; Patricia Phillips, director, Willa Cather Pioneer Memorial and Educational Foundation, Red Cloud; Anne Billesbach, first at the Cather Historical Center, Red Cloud, and later at the Nebraska State Historical Society, Lincoln; and John Lindall, formerly of the Cather Historical Center. And, we wish to acknowledge our indebtedness to the late Mildred R. Bennett, whose work as founder and president of the Willa Cather Pioneer Memorial and Educational Foundation ensured that Cather-related materials in Webster County would be preserved, and whose knowledge guided us through those materials.

We relied upon many people who generously contributed their specialized knowledge: Paul A. Olson, for his expertise in plains culture; Kay Young, for her knowledge of plains flora; Andrea Pinto Lebowitz, for the further identification of flora; and Paul Johnsgard, for his knowledge of birds of the Great Plains.

We are grateful to the staffs of Love Library, University of Nebraska–Lincoln; the Nebraska State Historical Society, Lincoln; the Heritage Room, Bennett Martin Public Library, Lincoln; the Harry Ransom Humanities Research Center, University of Texas at Austin; Houghton Library, Harvard University; the Newberry Library, Chicago. Of special importance were the collections of Bernice Slote and Virginia Faulkner and of J. Robert Sullivan, Archives and Special Collections of Love Library, University of Nebraska–Lincoln. We acknowledge with thanks the Harry Ransom Humanities Research Center, University of Texas at Austin, for permission to quote from the papers of Alfred A. Knopf.

For their administrative support at the University of Nebraska–Lincoln, we thank Gerry Meisels and John G. Peters, formerly deans of the College of Arts and Sciences; Brian L. Foster, dean of the College of Arts and Sciences; John Yost, formerly vice chancellor for research; and John R. Wunder, formerly director of the Center for Great Plains Studies. We are especially grateful to Stephen Hilliard and Linda Ray Pratt, who as chairs of the Department of English, provided both departmental support and personal encouragement for the Cather Edition.

For funding during our initial year on the project we are grateful to the Woods Charitable Fund. For research grants during subsequent years we thank the Nebraska Council for the Humanities and, at the University of Nebraska–Lincoln, the Research Council, the College of Arts and Sciences, the Office of the Vice Chancellor for Research, and the Department of English.

The preparation of this volume was made possible in part by a grant from the National Endowment for the Humanities, an independent federal agency.

Historical Apparatus

Historical Essay

THE dustjacket of Willa Cather's new book in 1932, *Obscure Destinies*, announced "Three New Stories of the West," heralding her return to what many readers thought of as "her" territory — the Great Plains — from forays into Canada in *Shadows on the Rock* (1931) and the Southwest in *Death Comes for the Archbishop* (1927). The stories in this new book also reflected her return to the well of memory that had inspired the books that made her reputation: *O Pioneers!*, *The Song of the Lark*, *My Ántonia*, *One of Ours*, and *A Lost Lady*.

The publication of *Obscure Destinies* also marked the end of the most extraordinarily productive and successful decade of Cather's career. In those ten years she published six novels, won the 1923 Pulitzer Prize and other literary medals, received honorary degrees from important universities, achieved bestsellerdom, sold a novel to the movies, and attained financial security. It was a decade in which she was not only sought after but accessible: she gave interviews and lectures and published essays and letters discussing her theories and methods of writing.[1] However, in the remaining four-

199

teen years of her life, as ill health overtook her and she with-drew from the world, she would publish only two novels (*Lucy Gayheart* and *Sapphira and the Slave Girl*) and a collection of essays, mostly from earlier years (*Not Under Forty*).[2] *Obscure Destinies*, then, gives the reader the work of Cather at her peak.

Genesis and Composition

Not long after the publication of *Obscure Destinies*, Cather wrote a friend that deaths came pouring down after a person has turned fifty, adding that when they both were young, people didn't die (WC to Zoë Akins, 21 November 1932). Cather turned fifty in 1923.[3] Her father's sudden death in 1928 and the slow approach of death to her mother, who was stricken with paralysis in late 1928 and died in 1931, forced her to confront the loss of those who were closest to her. In the decade preceding *Obscure Destinies*, many people who formed the background of Cather's life also died: Cather's Aunt Franc, Frances Smith Cather, prototype for Mrs. Wheeler in *One of Ours*, in 1922; Marjorie Anderson, a prototype for Marty in the poem "Poor Marty" as well as for Mandy in "Old Mrs. Harris," in October 1924; Cather's aunt, Sarah Boak Andrews, in April 1925; her cousin Frank Cather in December 1927. Another cousin, Kyd Clutter, died in March 1928, just before Charles Cather (in fact, a local newspaper speculated that Charles Cather's death was hastened by the shock of hearing this news).[4]

As Cather wrote in a letter of condolence, these disappearances impoverished those left behind (wc to Dorothy Canfield Fisher, 30 September 1930). Not surprisingly, the works of this richest and most productive decade of her life reveal her characters facing change, loss, and death.

Cather was reluctant to discuss works in progress, nor did she later write of her inspiration and aims for this book, as she did for some of her others.[5] An account of the writing of *Obscure Destinies* is also obscured by the fact that Cather was occupied with the writing and publication of *Shadows on the Rock* during the time she wrote these stories.

Nonetheless, the impetus for the first story, "Neighbour Rosicky," seems to have been the death of her father, Charles F. Cather, on 3 March 1928. This was the first loss of someone from Cather's immediate family circle, perhaps the first to affect her deeply. Friends later told of how Cather paced back and forth between the house and the church on the day of the funeral, wringing her hands (Bennett 28). Years later Cather wrote Zoë Akins of arriving at Red Cloud at three in the morning; she spent several hours alone with the body as the dawn came, touching it with light and filling her with peace (wc to za, 7 June 1941). These are the emotions — a sense of peace and of a life completed — that give "Neighbour Rosicky" much of its power and beauty.

Cather did not write immediately or directly of her father's death: the pain, as well as the peace, were probably too close. When she did come to write "Neighbour Rosicky," she distanced herself further by using as her subject the death, two years earlier, of John Pavelka, husband of her old friend Anna Sadilek Pavelka, model for Ántonia. After her father's death Cather stayed alone in Red Cloud for nearly two months while her mother went to California to visit Cather's brother Douglas. This stay gave her a rare opportunity to immerse herself once again in the physical world of Webster County as well as in her memories. She wrote Blanche Knopf that she had been very tired and found Red Cloud a good place to rest (wc to bk, 13 April 1928). When she arrived back in New York in early May, she still felt exhausted, declaring that she had done no writing for the past six months and would probably do none for the next six months (wc to Mary Austin, 9 May 1928). However, the dateline "New York, 1928" suggests that she at least began the story at this time.

After accepting an honorary degree from Columbia University, Cather left for her new summer home on the island of Grand Manan in New Brunswick, Canada, in late June 1928. On the journey the illness of Edith Lewis, who was accompanying her, caused an unexpected stay in the city of Quebec, which Cather had never seen before. Quebec enchanted her and inspired her to write the story that would become *Shadows on the Rock*. However, seventeenth-century Quebec was an unfamiliar locale and research would be required; her previous historical novel, *Death Comes for the Archbishop* (1927), had been set in the Southwest, a region whose landscape and culture Cather had known for many years. Unable to begin on this project in the remoteness of

Grand Manan, Cather turned instead to a world she could summon up at will, that of her memories. One result was a story, "Double Birthday," set in Pittsburgh, where she had lived from 1896 to 1906, and drawing also on memories of people she had known while attending the University of Nebraska (Woodress 417). Cather returned to Quebec City in October for a short time, then again for several weeks in November (wc to Professor Goodman [28 October 1928] and wc to BK, rec'd 29 October 1928). "Neighbour Rosicky," if it had not been finished in May or June, was probably completed in the few weeks Cather spent in New York at the end of the year, although it would not be published for another year and a half.

The beginnings of the idea of "Old Mrs. Harris," which is datelined "New Brunswick, 1931," may be traced to early December 1928, when Cather's mother, still in California with Douglas, suffered a severe stroke. Cather, delayed by illness herself, went to Long Beach to stay with her mother in February 1929. Her mother's condition shook her deeply. As she wrote Blanche Knopf, Mrs. Cather was partially paralyzed and unable to speak, yet her forceful personality remained intact, imprisoned in the broken-down body, dependent on her nurses and her children (wc to BK, rec'd 19 March 1929). Such a situation may well have set Cather to reflecting on aging and the nature of the relationships between mothers and daughters.[6]

A specific catalyst for "Two Friends" is more difficult to discern than for the other stories. However, Cather's concerns at this time were with memory, both cultural and personal, and with the idea of the rock, some anchor or "unalterable realit[y], somewhere at the bottom of things" (161). The specific memories she uses may have been sparked by reminiscences among herself and her siblings — Douglas lived in Long Beach and Elsie was sometimes visiting at the same time as Cather — and presumably other visitors to Mrs. Cather over the next three years. A number of Webster County people had retired to southern California; their shared memories of the people and events of Red Cloud's past would have been a likely topic of conversation.[7] These conversations might also have aroused memories that led to one of Cather's longest public autobiographical writings, the letter published in the *Omaha World-Herald* as "Willa Cather Mourns Old Opera House" (27 October 1929), which describes her reactions to the theatrical events of her childhood. These memories parallel the memories of the two theater-going protagonists of "Two Friends," who also felt the thrill of the live stage and were able to transmit it to the story's narrator.

With memories and feelings aroused by this contact with family and old acquaintances, Cather left California in June 1929. After stopping at Yale University for another honorary degree, she returned to Grand Manan to work on *Shadows on the Rock*. In August the Knopfs forwarded a request from the *Ladies' Home Journal* for a story; Cather responded rather testily that she didn't write to order, had nothing on hand, and moreover was busy with her new book (wc to bk, 16

August 1929). This suggests that "Neighbour Rosicky" had already been sold to the *Woman's Home Companion*.[8]

Shadows on the Rock absorbed Cather's attention at the end of the year; she was back and forth to Quebec from November into January. In February and March of 1930 she visited her mother in California. "Neighbour Rosicky" was published in April and May of 1930 as Cather prepared to sail to Europe, where she stayed with her old friend Isabelle Mc-Clung Hambourg and continued her researches for *Shadows on the Rock*. It is unlikely that Cather worked on anything during this trip: she had earlier found that it was difficult for her to write in Europe (Bohlke 84). In September she returned home via Quebec, making another stay there. Once back in New York she worked steadily on *Shadows on the Rock*, finishing it just after Christmas 1930.

With page proofs for the new book in hand, Cather returned to California in March 1931. As she crossed Kansas on the Santa Fé, through the area that would become the setting of "Two Friends," she wrote her friend Irene Miner Weisz about the relationships of mothers and daughters, regretting her own self-absorption and the way she had taken her parents for granted (WC to IMW, 12 March 1931). Here some of the themes of "Old Mrs. Harris" are clearly "teasing her mind," to use the phrase Cather had borrowed from Sarah Orne Jewett.

After a brief visit with her mother in Pasadena, Cather went north to receive an honorary degree at Berkeley in March. She stayed several weeks in San Francisco, renewing her acquaintance with the Menuhins, whom she had met in Paris in 1930. She liked San Francisco, feeling it was a city that still had individuality, and even half-considered coming there to live.[9] Her liking for San Francisco and her dislike of the Los Angeles area probably influenced her choice of Trueman's place of exile in "Two Friends."

Another sign that Cather was playing with the themes and perhaps the characters of "Old Mrs. Harris" at this time is shown in the poem "Poor Marty," published in the May 1931 *Atlantic Monthly*, her first published poem since those added to the 1923 edition of *April Twilights*. Marty, inspired by the Cather family servant Marjorie (Margie) Anderson, is akin to Mandy of "Old Mrs. Harris" in her simplicity, poverty, and humble goodness.

During this spring, busy as she was with the proofing of *Shadows on the Rock*, Cather also found time to write an essay for a *Colophon* series, "My First Novel." Cather's contribution, which appeared in the June 1931 issue, was "My First Novels (There Were Two)." In this essay Cather describes her false start, the Jamesian *Alexander's Bridge* (1912), which dealt with well-to-do Boston and trans-Atlantic society; *O Pioneers!*, she said, was her true first novel, the one in which she had discovered her own subject and voice.

It seems likely that "Two Friends," datelined "Pasadena, 1931," was finished during this, Cather's last stay in California. She kept it with her for the time being, neither sending it to the Knopfs nor attempting, apparently, to sell it to a magazine. Possibly *Obscure Destinies* was already taking shape in her mind. On the way back to New York, she stopped in Kearney, Nebraska, to see her brother James and his family. In one of the last interviews with a reporter she ever gave, she disclosed that she had written some short stories and that "Neighbour Rosicky" would "come out in a collection of short stories soon" (*Kearney Hub*, 2 June 1931; rpt. *Commercial Advertiser* [Red Cloud], 3 June 1931).

Once Cather was back in New York, there was little time for writing before she went to Princeton in mid-June to receive still another honorary degree. In early July she and her companion Edith Lewis went to Grand Manan to open the cottage and receive visits from two of Cather's nieces. She admitted to the Knopfs that she had been out walking rather than working. The first of August marked the publication of *Shadows on the Rock*, the close of that chapter in her life. She must have been hard at work on "Old Mrs. Harris" in August; meanwhile, *Shadows on the Rock* became a bestseller, Louise Bogan's profile of her life and work appeared in the *New Yorker* (8 August 1931), and her picture — a bad one, she commented in a letter to her mother (10 August 1931) — appeared on the cover of *Time*.

Cather's mother died at the end of August. Unable to reach Red Cloud in time for the funeral — a ferryboat called at the island only twice a week — Cather stayed at Grand Manan and finished her final tribute to her mother. In early September she sent two stories to Alfred Knopf, asking him to read them "as a favor" (Knopf, Memoirs). The stories were "Two Friends" and "Old Mrs. Harris."

Materials and Models

The materials of these stories are drawn from some of the deepest and most intimate memories of Cather's childhood and family life in Red Cloud; from her memories of the relatively public life of Webster County people in the 1880s and 1890s; and from her knowledge of their ongoing lives. The first story, "Neighbour Rosicky," is the only one with a setting contemporary with its writing (although it in turn draws on Rosicky's memories). The character of Rosicky (pronounced Ro-*sis*-ky) was based in part on John Pavelka, a Webster County farmer of Czech descent who was the husband of Cather's girlhood friend Anna Sadilek, prototype for both Ántonia Shimerda and Mary Rosicky. Cather probably became acquainted with Pavelka about 1916, when she, like Jim Burden visiting Ántonia, came to visit Anna after many years of absence.

As the jacket copy pointed out to the first readers of *Obscure Destinies*, the character of Anton Cuzak in *My Ántonia* bears many similarities to that of Rosicky. In the earlier novel the Cuzak/Rosicky character is seen as a bit of an oddity, the city man tied to the farm by virtue of Ántonia's destiny, a little surprised at himself as the father of all those children. Neighbour Rosicky is the center of his story, at ease in the home where he can cook breakfast and mend clothing with the same dexterity with which he shells corn and mows hay. He is a true lover of the land which he works so hard to pass on to his sons. Like Rosicky and Cuzak, Pavelka had worked for others many years before finding his home and

208

his independence on a Nebraska farm. Although both men were apprenticed to tailors, the harrowing early experiences of life in great cities that Rosicky reveals to Polly and his children were probably not Pavelka's: he had come to the United States with his parents after being drafted into the Austrian army. Cather may well have heard similar stories about or from other immigrants. And, when she visited Webster County in July 1926, she may have heard from Anna Pavelka how John Pavelka died while mending overalls, just as Rosicky does.[10]

Although Cather drew on her own memories and background for the subject of "Neighbour Rosicky," perhaps the memory of her friend and mentor, Sarah Orne Jewett, influenced the form. This story resembles Jewett's quietly beautiful stories and sketches of simple New England people, rooted to their land and homes, more than anything else Cather wrote. Cather had edited a collection of Jewett's stories in 1924; her preface had praised Jewett's ability to make beauty out of humble materials.

"Old Mrs. Harris" is densely populated with the people and places of Cather's childhood years in Red Cloud. It is one of her most concentratedly autobiographical stories. Cather was born in the home of her mother's mother, Rachel Seibert Boak (1816–93), a prototype for Rachel Blake in *Sapphira and the Slave Girl* as well as for Mrs. Harris. Mrs. Boak was born in Berkeley County, Virginia.[11] She bore nine children, five of whom died young, including one son who died while serving in the Confederate army. Cather's mother, Mary Virginia (Jenny), who was born in 1852, was probably the youngest of the surviving children. Although Mrs. Boak's eldest daughter, Sarah, was settled in Virginia with her family, it is a measure of the mother's devotion to this youngest child that Mrs. Boak chose to sell her home and go to the wilds of Nebraska when Charles Cather moved his family to Webster County in 1883.[12]

Mrs. Boak's life in Nebraska was, like Mrs. Harris's, one of unobtrusive usefulness. Jenny Cather was often ill or pregnant; much of the management of the household as well as of the children fell to Mrs. Boak. The Cather family lived for almost two years on a farm in Webster County; as the country schools were in session only three months of the year, much of the children's education came from Mrs. Boak. The Bible and *Pilgrim's Progress* were two of the main texts; Cather later said she read *Pilgrim's Progress* eight times in one winter (Bohlke 3, 129). In the evenings the family read aloud from Shakespeare and the standard nineteenth-century novelists. When the Cathers moved to Red Cloud early in 1885, the little passageway room between the kitchen and dining room was allotted to Mrs. Boak (see illustration 10).

In late May of 1893 Mrs. Boak fell ill, so seriously that the family sent for Willa to come home from the University of Nebraska before the term was over. Willa reported in a letter to a university friend that her grandmother was much better, although still very weak (WC to Mariel Gere, 1 June 1893). Ten days later Mrs. Boak was dead.

An obituary, unusually long for someone so obscure, appeared in the *Red Cloud Chief*, clearly written by someone close to the Cather family:

> Grand-ma Boak was unselfish. . . . Generous to all, she reserved close intimacy for those whom she loved, and them she loved as few women are capable of loving. It was not her nature to stint or bargain with her favor. She gave all and gave freely. She would at any time have given her heart's treasure to gratify the lightest desire of one she loved. . . . Many as were grand-ma's friends, it is among the children that we find those who knew her best while she lived and sorrow most deeply at her death. . . . [T]ime could not take from her that sweet simplicity of heart which enables age [to] sympathize with child-hood. . . . Rest is indeed rest after a life of such untiring activity as hers has been.
>
> . . . [With] a long sigh of life that was tired, . . . Grand-ma Boak had passed beyond the reach of human aid or human tenderness; had solved the great mystery; knew as the aching hearts about her could not know, the purpose, the aim and the end of that love and faithfulness which counts neither pain nor cost, which empties out its richness like water, yet is ever greater by the giving. (16 June 1893)

When, at the end of the story, Cather writes of the heartlessness of youth, she may have been thinking of herself, superficially at least not much affected by her grandmother's death: by the end of that June young Willa was inviting the Gere girls to visit and announcing her own recovery from a prolonged illness caused by eating too much banana ice cream (wc to Mariel, "Ned," and Frances Gere, 30 June 1893). The story of old Mrs. Harris itself is evidence of how Cather, like Victoria and Vickie, came to "think a great deal about [Grandma Harris], and remember things they never noticed; and . . . regret that they heeded her so little" (157).

The same passage adds, "and their lot will be more or less like hers" (157). Victoria Templeton probably never could have imagined her fate might be like her mother's. Mary Virginia Boak Cather (1852–1931), like Victoria Templeton, was a southern lady, handsome and always beautifully dressed, with high standards of both decorum and hospitality. A seemingly haughty woman, Virginia Cather could be generous as well as jealous.[13] In some respects her fate was the one that Mrs. Harris had most dreaded: that of a helpless dependent through a long illness. But even as an invalid, Virginia Cather commanded the obedience and devotion of her family.

Cather's own relationship with her mother was a complex one, as biographers have demonstrated; mother and daughter were very different in their tastes and aspirations. However, Mrs. Cather (sharing this trait with Mrs. Kronborg in *The Song of the Lark*) allowed her children considerable mental and physical independence within the framework of her household rules. Vickie's independence (or isolation) from her mother is shown indirectly in the story: the only time Victoria and Vickie Templeton are together, however briefly, is in the scene where Victoria tells Vickie and the twins to let the Maude children sit with them at the ice cream social.

By most accounts, Cather was devoted to her father, a model in some respects for the gentle, courteous Hillary Templeton. Charles Cather (1848–1928) came from a Virginia family of Union rather than Confederate sympathies; in the early 1870s, as a young man before his marriage, he traveled extensively in the West and Southwest when it was still wild. Like Templeton, Cather had extensive landholdings; like many others, he suffered financially during the general depression of the 1890s. But unlike Templeton, Charles Cather seems to have been a leader of the community: he was elected many times to the city council, the county board of commissioners, and the school board, and he served a term as mayor of Red Cloud. The newspaper account of his death noted that "He was unusually well informed on any question that might arise, and his opinions on any matter were always listened to with respect" (*Webster County Argus*, 8 March 1928).

Vickie Templeton has, of course, many qualities in common with Cather herself as a girl. Like many adolescents, both the character and her creator loved and at the same time felt alienated from their families and from the small towns in which they lived. Both were intent on learning for reasons inexplicable to themselves and most others, and both experienced financial difficulties in their pursuit of an education.

Bennett reports that the money for Cather's first year at the university was borrowed from a business associate of Charles Cather (233). Cather was not, however, simply portraying herself. Vickie is a more conventional character than the young Cather: whereas Willa wore a boyish haircut, was interested in taxidermy and vivisection, and wanted to be a surgeon, Vickie wears her hair in a braid and reads.

Marjorie Anderson (1854–1924), a prototype for the simple Mandy, was, after Mrs. Boak, the other mainstay of the Cather household. Margie, as she was called, was one of fifteen children of Mary Anderson, a neighbor of the Cathers in Virginia who inspired the character of Mandy Ringer in *Sapphira and the Slave Girl*. Margie worked in the Charles Cather family as a nursemaid and helper; when the Cathers came west they brought Margie and her brother Enoch with them. Shortly thereafter, Margie married another transplanted Virginian, a man named O'Leary, but the marriage did not last long; the man disappeared and Margie came back to the Cathers for the rest of her life. She feared that he might come back for her, and became afraid of being seen by people outside the family — a tendency that gave rise to rumors that the Cathers were hiding her (*Argus*, 30 October 1924).

Mrs. Rosen's prototype, Fannie Meyer Wiener (1852–93), was born in France; according to Bennett, it was she who introduced Cather to French literature (119).[14] After Mrs. Wiener joined her husband in Red Cloud in January 1884, she became a member of the best social circles of the town.

She was instrumental in the founding of the Red Cloud Be-
nevolent Society, which gave aid to the poor: friction between the church ladies' auxiliaries had made them ineffec-
tive. Like Mrs. Rosen, Fanny Wiener was childless; she often
had nieces and nephews (like the Sammy of the story) stay
with her, sometimes for long periods of time, and she often
visited her relatives in Chicago. Although Mrs. Rosen's
health is not an issue in the story, Mrs. Wiener became very
ill early in 1893. Although Cather wrote Mariel Gere that
Mrs. Wiener was much better (wc to MG, 30 June 1893), she
died in early September 1893.

Charles F. Wiener (1846–1911), the prototype of Mr.
Rosen, was born in Bohemia and brought to the United
States — probably to New York — as a child. He served in the
merchant marine during the Civil War and came to Red
Cloud in December 1883 to establish a quality men's clothing business. This was located in a brick store he had built
three doors north of the Miner Bros. general store; the second story was fitted up as an apartment for himself and his
wife. The Wieners moved into this apartment in October
1885, so they were near neighbors of the Cathers for only a
short time, but the families continued to be friends. Reports
of parties and other outings in the local newspapers show
that the Wieners and the Cathers moved in the same social
circles. An early letter of Cather's tells of Mr. Wiener taking
her driving (wc to MG, 16 June 1894), and he let her use his
apartment for a dancing-party she gave in January 1896.

Wiener was, from all the evidence available through the

newspapers, a very successful businessman. He brought new methods of advertising and publicity to Red Cloud; his men's clothing store was known throughout the Republican River valley, and he established a branch store in Wymore. His clerks became the next generation of business leaders in Red Cloud in the early twentieth century. Wiener was elected to offices in the various lodges and fraternal organizations of Red Cloud and in the local post of the Grand Army of the Republic. His leadership in the town was acknowledged when he was elected mayor in 1893; when Silas Garber's Farmers and Merchants Bank failed in June 1893, Wiener was chosen to hold the deeds that the stockholders gave as security to repay the depositors. Then in 1897, a brother in New York City died, leaving his business to Charles Wiener. Wiener sold his business (although he retained an interest in it for several years) and his belongings (including a number of bookcases which held the library that had been so important to the young Cather) and left for New York.

All this seems somewhat at variance with the picture in this story of Mr. Rosen as the dreamy, somewhat unsuccessful businessman. Cather said that her characters were, with only one or two exceptions, combinations of several actual people (Bohlke 45). This may have been a defensive statement to deflect criticism of her use of the people she knew, but it may be the case here. Another scholar-businessman to whom Cather was attached, and whom she may also have had in mind when creating Mr. Rosen, was William Ducker (1835–93), an Englishman who worked in various dry goods stores, where he could be found reading Homer over the counter (Brown and Edel 34). He taught Cather Latin and Greek and encouraged her interest in science. Ducker also died in that summer of 1893, just two months after Mrs. Boak and a month before Mrs. Wiener.

"Two Friends," unlike "Old Mrs. Harris" with its rich cast of characters, is a story that subordinates all else to highlighting the two central characters and their relationship to the narrator and to each other.[15] The pictures of Mr. Dillon and Mr. Trueman were not meant to be portraits of the actual men but an impression of the effect that both men had on her as a child, as Cather wrote Carrie Miner Sherwood, the daughter of one of the prototypes (4 July 1932). Other characters, including the narrator, are not even named. A few words about the lives of both these men may help to distinguish Cather's impression from the reality on which she drew.

Cather probably first learned of J. L. Miner, prototype for R. E. Dillon, soon after her family came to Webster County in 1883.[16] James Louis Miner was born in Somerset, Ohio, in 1847. Orphaned at an early age, he was reared by a brother, Hugh Miner, who was fifteen years his senior. The brothers moved to Waukon, Iowa, where James Miner met and married Julia Erickson in 1868. In February 1878 the Miner brothers bought a frame building on the corner of Third and Webster Streets in Red Cloud, where two of their sisters had pioneered, and in April opened a general store. The business prospered, becoming the leading retail establishment in the

Republican River valley area; by 1881 Miner was going to Chicago to buy his goods, and in 1883 the brothers built the first brick store building in Red Cloud.

J. L. Miner soon became important in the affairs of the town; he was one of the village trustees in 1879 and one of the first city councilmen when Red Cloud became a city in 1885. He was also on the board of the First National Bank of Red Cloud and was president of the first Retail Merchants Association. He was active in various enterprises that were formed to prospect for coal, to bring new railroads and factories to town, and to improve the bridges and roads. His position is the more remarkable in that he was always a Democrat in a fiercely Republican town. He was one of the backers of a short-lived Democratic newspaper in Red Cloud, the *Helmet* (no copies of which are known to have survived). When Democrat Grover Cleveland was elected in 1884, the leading Republican newspaper reported that Miner was celebrating by wearing a rooster (then the symbol of the Democratic Party) on his silk hat (*Red Cloud Chief*, 5 December 1884). As the Populist Party gained power in the 1890s, Miner was mentioned as a Populist candidate for county office (*Argus*, 10 August 1894). He was also one of the mainstays of the Catholic church in Red Cloud, at a time when Catholicism was viewed with suspicion and hostility by many Protestant denominations.

Like his fictional counterpart, Miner was a landowner as well as a merchant. He had bought a farm when he first came to town, and in 1884 he bought 700 acres of bottomland near the river west of town and went into cattle ranching, shipping his cattle annually to Chicago or Kansas City. Like Dillon, Miner was also a banker. After the last Red Cloud bank closed in the panic year of 1893, Miner opened a new bank, the significantly named People's Bank, located in the rear of his store (see illustration 22).

It is not clear from the newspaper records whether Miner was actually at the Democratic convention that nominated William Jennings Bryan for president, but he returned from Illinois shortly afterwards. The *Webster County Argus* observed that "In politics [Miner] was generally a democrat or a populist. He was a very warm admirer of Mr. Bryan and very zealous in his support of that gentleman" (26 May 1905). However, Cather had left Red Cloud for Pittsburgh in late June of 1896 and so could not have observed firsthand his activities and those of the Webster County Bryan Clubs and the Bryan Ladies Quartette.

Dillon's death is more sudden and dramatic than Miner's. Instead of dying suddenly before the presidential campaign of 1900, as Dillon does, Miner was taken ill in January of 1905 and at first appeared to be recovering; in mid-May the *Argus* reported that he had gone to Excelsior Springs, Arkansas, to recover from a severe attack of Bright's disease. He died there 24 May 1905.

Obituaries and eulogies are not always the most reliable accounts of character, but those for J. L. Miner give views by some of his contemporaries of a man very similar to Cather's Mr. Dillon. "He was not a man to yield himself to the softer affections of friendship, but when he did become a friend to a man, it meant very much to the man he befriended. There are very few who, once having come within the circle of the more intimate relations with him willingly withdrew from the intimacy" (*Argus*, 26 May 1905). But "naturally a man like Mr. Miner created antagonisms. It is useless to ask of a strong positive aggressive personality that, in his onward course, it shall be always considerate of those whose chief occupation in life seems to be to stand in the way" (*Argus*, 2 June 1905). In his private life "Mr. Miner's generosity to the needy people of the town was taken for granted. While it was never learned from his lips, the extent of his liberality is gratefully remembered by many recipients" (2 June 1905). He was "a man exceptionally free from vice; of irreproachable morals, and was strenuously devoted to his ideas of right and wrong" (26 May 1905).

Although William Newman (W. N.) Richardson, the model for J. H. Trueman, was also a prominent citizen of Red Cloud — perhaps its wealthiest citizen — he was not so actively involved in the political and social life of the town, so there are fewer records of him in its newspapers. He was born near Buffalo, New York, in 1839, and moved with his family to Warren, Illinois, as a boy. After his return from service with the Union army during the Civil War, he married Charlotte Chapman. They came to Webster County with their four-year-old daughter, Winifred, in 1872; she was later sent to a boarding school in St. Joseph, Missouri, as were the fictional Dillon's daughters.[17] Richardson soon became a partner with Captain Silas Garber, founder of Red Cloud, in the Garber Bros. store and also went into stock-raising on a large scale; he built his own stockyard on his five-acre residential property at Second and Webster Streets. The Cather family came to Webster County in 1883, the same year that Richardson's wife died, so it is likely that Cather knew him or knew of him first when he was, like Trueman, a widower. However, Richardson did not remain a widower, as Trueman did; he married Bessie Tangil on 12 February 1886 and had three more daughters. By the spring of 1885 the Cather family had moved to Red Cloud, and the young Willa Cather could observe Richardson and Miner firsthand.

Richardson did indeed operate on a grander scale than others in Red Cloud. His name occurs most often in the local newspapers in connection with the numbers of carloads of stock he was shipping to Chicago — sixty carloads in June 1885. It was said he paid $30,000 in freight charges to ship his livestock in 1884, more than anyone else in the entire state (*Commercial Advertiser* [Red Cloud], 22 February 1934). One pioneer, U. G. Knight, recalled that several times Richardson shipped cattle directly to England (*Commercial Advertiser*, 2 March 1931). His right-hand man for many years was Samuel Temple; it is possible that Cather had Temple in mind when she wrote of Trueman's "confidential man" (189).

Richardson was a Republican, like most Union veterans, but he does not seem to have been active in political affairs. The kinds of informal talks and visits described in the story were not likely to be written up in the local news columns, and, not surprisingly, the Red Cloud papers record neither a friendship nor a split between Miner and Richardson. The closest hint of a division between them occurs in two items in the *Webster County Argus*: on 21 August 1896 the paper reported that J. L. Miner was back from Chicago saying that Bryan was doing well in Illinois. The next week the paper announced that W. N. Richardson was back from Chicago saying that Illinois was for McKinley (28 August 1896). Sources within the Miner family gave a different account, according to John March: their differences concerned business, not politics, and came to a head when Miner encouraged farmers to fatten their cattle for market themselves rather than selling cattle to cattle-feeders like Richardson (776).

Unlike the fictional Trueman, Richardson had many family ties to Red Cloud, and although he talked about leaving, even putting his property up for sale on several occasions, he never pulled up stakes in the way Trueman does. He moved into a new house at Sixth and Walnut Streets in 1909 and died 16 August 1914, nine years after the death of J. L. Miner. The assessment of his character in the obituary rings remarkably true to Cather's description of Trueman: "Had he been possessed of saving, miserly qualities he might have accumulated an immense fortune. But he despised niggardliness, meanness, littleness. He was a man of large outlook, large affairs — and he chose to live as one who did big things. He lived generously, liberally, contented if he kept his word good, his debts paid, his obligations fulfilled, and secured a suitable provision for his family" (*Argus*, 20 August 1914).

Cather's re-creation of the larger-than-life effect of the two friends rang true to others. U. G. Knight, who had been a businessman in Red Cloud in the 1890s and became a chronicler of the early days of Webster County, wrote that Cather "most effectually portrays two of Red Cloud's most prominent men of the past. Anyone as well acquainted with these men as all residents of other days there can place them in an instant. Even the store building where one of them did business and the office of the other is as vivid as the sun." The story felt so true to Knight that he was willing to take Cather's word for things he did not himself remember: "I do not recall that these two old cronies played checkers so much but probably they did" (*Commercial Advertiser*, 7 December 1932).

First Publications

Magazine publication was an important source of supplemental income for Cather. She had serialized her novels regularly since 1923 despite a dislike for the serial format that distorted her form and thus her meanings.[18] She had become a sought-after writer by this time; Knopf records that Harry Payne Burton, about to become the editor of *Cosmopolitan*, said he would "gladly" pay $25,000 for a 22,000-word story from Cather — this in September 1931 (Knopf, Memoirs).[19]

The few short stories Cather wrote in the 1920s seem to have been quickly placed: "Uncle Valentine" appeared in the *Woman's Home Companion* (February and March 1925) and

"Double Birthday" was published by the *Forum* in February 1929 (Woodress 359, 417). "Two Friends" and "Old Mrs. Harris" were both sold within a month after Knopf received them. However, "Neighbour Rosicky" was an unusual case. Nearly two years elapsed between its probable completion in spring 1928 and its first publication in two parts in the *Woman's Home Companion* for April and May 1930. It seems unlikely that Cather would have had difficulty in selling it or that a magazine would have long delayed publication of a story by the author of the currently bestselling *Death Comes for the Archbishop*. The extant correspondence gives no hint as to what plans she may have had for the story. In the absence of evidence from Cather or her close associates, it may be conjectured that Cather kept the story by her because her feelings were so deeply involved in it.

By 1 October 1931, the *Woman's Home Companion* had also bought "Two Friends," bringing it out in July 1932.[20] They paid $3,500 for it; Knopf noted in his memoirs that magazine prices had come down because of the depression. The $15,000 price paid for "Old Mrs. Harris" in mid-September 1931, however, would have been sizable at any time. The purchaser was the *Ladies' Home Journal*, then under the editorship of Loring A. Shuler. The three-part story appeared in September, October, and November of 1932 — after book publication, which was unusual for a first-run serial. Its magazine title, "Three Women," may have been Cather's own, stressing as it does continuity of the lives within the story. Alternatively, the title may have been suggested by the editors to make the story seem new to readers who might have heard of the book or to make the story more attractive to casual readers who might think a story about an obscure old woman would not be interesting.

Between the time the stories were sold to the magazines and their publication in book form, Cather revised each extensively; the differences between the serials and the Knopf texts show Cather's ongoing involvement with her stories. (These revisions are analyzed in detail in the Textual Essay.) She intensified each story's particular feeling even as she pursued her customary concerns for economy, clarity, vividness of expression, and the honing of character. Phrases that echoed those in another story too closely were revised. In the case of "Old Mrs. Harris," a number of long and significant passages appear for the first time in the Knopf text.

Obscure Destinies was published on 1 August 1932 by Knopf in a first trade printing of 25,000 copies. This was a large print run for a short story collection, but it is consistent with the first printings of her two previous books. Cather was a bestselling author by this time, and the print run reflects Knopf's confidence in Cather's popularity.[21] It was Cather's first collection of short stories since her earliest Knopf publication, *Youth and the Bright Medusa* (1920), and she seems to have planned for publication of these three stories as a whole.[22] She ignored "Uncle Valentine" and "Double Birthday," both strong stories that had not yet appeared in book form, and placed "Old Mrs. Harris" as the centerpiece between "Neighbour Rosicky" and "Two Friends." ("Old Mrs. Harris" is approximately the length of *My Mortal Enemy* [1926] and could also have been published alone, if Cather had wished; depression-era economics may have been a deterrent.)

It is unclear when the title of the book, which now seems so inevitable, was decided upon. Cather's title, drawn from Thomas Gray's "Elegy Written in a Country Churchyard," suggests both her subjects and her themes: "their homely joys and destinies obscure." Many of Cather's earlier stories had focused on extraordinary individuals, often recognized by the world at large — successful farmers, famous artists or opera singers, distinguished professors, archbishops. Even Gray laments more over the potentially great souls than the ordinary ones: the "mute inglorious Milton" or "guiltless" Cromwell who might be buried there, all his talents and destinies frustrated by poverty and lack of opportunity, shut away even in death in "his narrow cell." In this book Cather takes for her subjects the truly obscure, the seemingly failed, and shows the "homely joys" that help to redeem their lives — the kolaches and footrubs and conversations. Rosicky reflects on the comfort of being at rest among friends and neighbors, close to his home fields; Mrs. Harris takes pleasure in the love of her grandchildren and is thankful not to be a burden. The young observer of the two friends is the only one who feels the same kind of regret and lament for wasted lives as the speaker in Gray's poem.

Early Reception

The *New York Times Book Review* heralded "The Return of Willa Cather" in the front-page headline of its review of *Obscure Destinies*. The reviewer noted Cather's return to the western setting of her earlier books and to her memories as a source. Many other reviewers employed the same theme, although they disagreed on how the return would affect her art. Henry Seidel Canby noted that "this is the West of Miss Cather's early novels . . . and into it her imagination plunges deep for recollections of great souls that make a contrast and a salvation" (*Saturday Review of Literature*, 6 August 1932, 29). John Chamberlain said it was "better for the tensile strength of her art" that Cather should return to the West for her subject (*New York Times Book Review*, 31 July 1932, 1). But Archer Winsten suggested that the return was a dead end; although no one could describe the West so well as Cather, "our first raptures gone, they will return only when she begins discovering again" (*Bookman*, October 1932, 649). And Margaret Cheney Dawson feared that "now something is lacking, . . . some intensity of feeling which once raised characters rather like these to an importance the new portraits do not attain" (*New York Herald Tribune Books*, 31 July 1932).

Almost all agreed in praising — or taking for granted — Cather's artistry, especially in her depiction of character. "It is remarkable how easily and surely . . . Miss Cather builds up these stories, without one trick, without one undue emphasis, with every significant detail," as Canby said (*Saturday*

Review of Literature, 6 August 1932, 29). Another reviewer spoke of Cather's ability to select the right detail "to give the whole an effect of the expansiveness of nature, and at the same time to communicate the sense of a creative impulse ruling the design" (*Yale Review*, September 1932, viii). Lewis Mumford spoke of her "tender understanding of the humbler levels of consciousness which betrays the genuine novelist" (*Atlantic Monthly*, December 1932, 766), while another reviewer noted Cather's "versatility, her deep, broad wisdom and her sympathetic understanding of human values" (*Catholic World*, November 1932, 246). But Hazel Hawthorne, writing in the *New Republic*, felt Cather had pared too much away: "Her work, to be sure, has the strong purity of bare rock, but sometimes one wishes for more, for the subtler interest of plant and branch and foliage" (10 August 1932, 350).

Political differences between Cather and some of her reviewers were beginning to affect her reputation, at least on the literary scene, as some reviewers praised or castigated her as her subject matter did or did not fit their political agenda. The *Omaha World-Herald* reviewer praised "Neighbour Rosicky" for showing the kind of self-reliant spirit that "needed no subsidies, no federal Santa Claus, but [that] did demand a square deal" (7 August 1932, 4E). But John Chamberlain thought Rosicky's beliefs about the independence of the small farmer "would have been news to the oppressed" mortgaged farmers "who have looked in vain to the Farm Board" (*New York Times Book Review*, 31 July 1932, 1). And

Clifton Fadiman, writing in the *Nation*, deplored Cather's "misted memories" of the West: "The old West had its humble peasants, its kindly small-town bankers; but for the most part it was the joint creation of masters and slaves" (3 August 1932).

Reviewers generally commended "Neighbour Rosicky," although most saw its protagonist as a simple peasant type whose outstanding characteristic was his love of the land. Winsten said, "simply as a story, [it] stands forth as the best[,] . . . as 'complete and beautiful' as Rosicky's life seemed to Doctor Ed" (*Bookman*, October 1932, 649). Fadiman praised it faintly as "an idyll of quiet sentiment" but warned that the reader should not look to Cather for "a large, true, realistic picture of the time." On the other hand, the *Omaha World-Herald* endorsed the realism of the story by proclaiming that Nebraska had "thousands of Rosickys," who "asked only for the opportunity to work and save in peace" (7 August 1932, 4E). On another battlefront, Howard Mumford Jones, while he called the story "a charming genre picture . . . , gentle and penetrating and beautiful," seems also to have seen it as a tragedy in which Cather observes with "cruel precision . . . the damage women do"; Rosicky dies, he says, "in an effort to create happiness for a city-bred daughter-in-law," just as Mrs. Harris "sacrifices" herself for her belle of a daughter (*Virginia Quarterly Review*, September 1932, 592).

"Old Mrs. Harris" was often seen as the best of the three stories. A notice in *Harper's* called it the most important, one that showed a rare understanding of women (August 1932).

Helen McAfee in the *Yale Review*, which considered the story more a novel than a long short story, showed her perception of Cather's artistry: the method of presenting "homely details closely observed" in less skilled hands "has yielded some of our bulkiest and redundant modern novels," but Cather's story "is a model of compactness and lucidity. In its hundred pages, never crowded, never hurried, there seems scarcely a line to take away. Equally, I think, there is nothing that need be added to them" (September 1932, viii). Other reviewers seem to have been looking for (and sometimes finding) quite different things in the story. John Chamberlain, writing in the *New York Times Book Review*, called the story "a genuine work of art," not because of Vickie or Victoria or even Mrs. Harris but because of its "subtle dissection of any American town in which 'infinitely repellant particles' from all over the map have met and mingled and worked out a temporary adjustment. It is a more brooding 'Main Street' in petto" (31 July 1932). Fadiman and Archer Winsten were among the few who thought the story needed fuller treatment: Winsten called it the "first section of an unfinished novel," with important characters left hanging in mid-air (*Bookman* 649).

Not surprisingly, the most penetrating and sympathetic review was that of Dorothy Canfield Fisher, fellow novelist and friend from Cather's university days: " 'Old Mrs. Harris' is a creation of pure unexpected beauty. The worn-out old drudge . . . looks out at the reader from her 'hideous cluttered room,' with the reposeful classic dignity of the finest of Rembrandt's portraits of life-worn old women. . . . There is mighty stuff in this story, handled with marvelous tact and restraint. . . . [W]hen the battered old heroine lies down on her wretched bed to die, we are beyond tears, on our knees beside her, stricken into silent awe by her unconscious majesty."[23]

Many reviewers dismissed "Two Friends," as did Howard Mumford Jones, who called it a "slight essay." Fadiman thought it an "anecdote" spun out for forty pages; John Chamberlain thought it a fine evocation of the past but said that the political turn of the plot was superficial and unprepared for (he also noted that Dillon misquotes Bryan). Archer Winsten, too, called the politics "perfunctory." However, Margaret Cheney Dawson, writing in the *New York Herald Tribune*, said "although it is by far the shortest and least substantial, it has some claim to be called the best" (31 July 1932, 3). The other two stories, she thought, were touching but forgettable, lacking some "intensity of feeling" that Cather's earlier works possessed. But "Two Friends," she said, "makes you feel . . . that you have perceived one of the subtler implications of a commonplace fact."

Clearly, many reviewers read what they wanted to in Cather; her popularity and her reputation made her a target for those who wanted literature to be at the service of the social sciences. Because Cather did not write exposés, they felt she must be writing sentimentally; if her characters were not underdogs and victims, they could not be real. Henry Seidel Canby, however, had the breadth to see that the stories contain "all the elements of that country of disillusion which the sociological novelists have made wearisomely familiar"; that Cather was "never flattering, never ignorant of cruelty, ugliness, disappointment, never afraid of humor . . . nor of beauty. . . . And this is perhaps why, in an unsentimental period, she can make great souls" (*Saturday Review of Literature*, 6 August 1932, 29).

"Neighbour Rosicky" is one of Cather's best-known stories, in part perhaps because she and her estate frequently allowed it to be anthologized.[24] Cather herself, when she sent her two new stories to Alfred Knopf to read in 1931, felt that "Two Friends" was the best story she had ever written ("Miss Cather" 214). By the time the book was published, however, she had come to appreciate "Old Mrs. Harris" more, calling it the best of the three stories by far (wc to Zoë Akins, 16 September 1932) but wondering how it would appeal to people who didn't know Southerners. A few years later, however, when she sent a copy of *Obscure Destinies* to a friend (wc to Mrs. Mellen, [late December 1935]), Cather expressed her satisfaction with the second story, adding that simplicity is always hardest to achieve.

Notes

1. See L. Brent Bohlke, *Willa Cather in Person*, for an account of Cather's activities and for reprints of interviews, lecture reports, and public letters.
2. See James L. Woodress, *Willa Cather: A Literary Life*, for an account of the causes of this withdrawal.

3. By her official reckoning, however, Cather did not turn fifty until 1926; on the advice of S. S. McClure in the early years of the century, she had changed her birth date from 1873 to 1875, then 1876 (Brown and Edel 17).

4. Cather also suffered the loss of many friends from her childhood and university days. Among these were Max Westermann, one of the family that inspired the Ehrlichs in *One of Ours*, and a friend with whom she often stayed in Lincoln, who died in September 1924; Matilda Larson Brodstone, who died in November 1924, one of the immigrant women whom Cather admired and mother of a high school friend, Evelyn Brodstone Vestey; Mrs. Stephen Pound, the mother of Cather's college friend Louise Pound, who died in December 1928; Dr. Julius Tyndale, friend and mentor from her college days, and a prototype for the elder Albert Englehardt in "Double Birthday," who died in June 1929; Herbert Bates, a teacher from her university days and a prototype for Gaston Cleric in *My Ántonia*, who died in 1929; Flavia Canfield, who died in August 1930, a prototype for the protagonist of "Flavia and Her Artists" and the mother of Cather's friend Dorothy Canfield Fisher. Cather was not equally close to all these people, of course, but some of them, notably Dr. Tyndale, were probably closer to her than some of her relatives were.

5. For example, Cather wrote a letter to the editor of *Commonweal* (27 November 1927) discussing *Death Comes for the Archbishop*; a brief essay in *Colophon* (June 1931), "My First Novels (There Were Two)," about *Alexander's Bridge* and *O Pioneers!*; a letter to Governor Wilbur Cross, published in the *Saturday Review of Literature* (17 October 1931), about *Shadows on the Rock*; and a letter to *The News Letter of the College English Association* (Octo-

ber 1940) on *The Professor's House*. These have been reprinted in
Willa Cather on Writing: Critical Studies on Writing as an Art
(New York: Knopf, 1949).

6. The relationships of fathers or father-figures and daughters are
important in much of Cather's fiction: Alexandra and Ántonia
and their fathers, Godfrey St. Peter and his daughters, Myra
Driscoll and her uncle, Euclide Auclair and Cécile, and later
Lucy Gayheart and her father. *The Song of the Lark* is unusual in
Cather's earlier fiction in its treatment of the relationship between Thea Kronborg and her mother.

7. Mrs. Winifred Richardson Garber, eldest daughter of W. N.
Richardson, the model for J. H. Trueman, was living in California at this time, and Cather's sister Elsie kept in at least occasional touch with them (Elsie Cather to Carrie Miner Sherwood, 14 August 1931). Even a distant acquaintance from Cather's newspaper days in Lincoln, Dr. Bixby, called on the Cather
family in Long Beach (*Nebraska State Journal*, 31 January 1929).

8. Although the Knopfs often acted as Cather's agents in placing
stories — they offered *One of Ours* and *A Lost Lady* for serialization and would sell "Old Mrs. Harris" and "Two Friends" —
Paul Reynolds had acted as her agent since 1916; he had placed
Death Comes for the Archbishop in 1926. Cather may have also
sold pieces on her own; she wrote Reynolds that she had sent
"Neighbour Rosicky" to Gertrude Lane at *Woman's Home Companion* as a result of a phone call (wc to pr, 25 March 1930).
Before her poem "Poor Marty" appeared in the *Atlantic*, Cather
wrote the Knopfs to watch for it; apparently they had had nothing to do with its sale (wc to bk, 28 April 1931). Knopf's memoirs give no indication that his firm had anything to do with the
sale of "Neighbour Rosicky."

9. By this time Cather had been living in "temporary" quarters in the Grosvenor Hotel for nearly four years, since being forced by construction to move from her Bank Street apartment.

10. This detail of Pavelka's death was reported in the *Bladen [Nebr.] Enterprise*, 7 May 1926. Although it is possible that Cather saw it on a later visit to Webster County, it seems more likely that she heard it from a member of the Pavelka family. Cather subscribed to a Red Cloud paper for many years, but there are no indications that she subscribed to any of the papers from the smaller towns in Webster County.

11. Little is known of Mrs. Boak's early life except that she married very young, in 1830; if *Sapphira and the Slave Girl* is biographical, Rachel may have married partly in order to escape from her mother, Rhuhamah Seibert, who probably suggested Sapphira. Rachel's husband, William Lee Boak (1805–54), was elected to the Virginia House of Delegates three times; in 1845 he went to Washington, D.C., as an official of the Department of the Interior (Brown and Edel 14). After her husband's death, Mrs. Boak moved back to Frederick County, Virginia, where her father left her a house, Cather's birthplace. Although Mrs. Harris never appears to think about her late husband, Mrs. Boak's obituary, evidently written by a close family member, noted that as she was dying, her "desire . . . to meet the husband of her youth . . . seemed to grow with her weakness" (*Red Cloud Chief*, 16 June 1893).

12. Three of Sarah's children accompanied the extended Cather family to Nebraska: Elizabeth Seymour, who lived with the Charles Cather family from 1883 to 1904, does not appear in "Old Mrs. Harris," although she is said to be a model for Tillie

in *The Song of the Lark*; Nan and Will Andrews came west with the George Cather family.

13. Lonnie Pierson Dunbier records that Lyra Garber and a friend used to tease Mrs. Cather's jealousy by flirting with Mr. Cather at the gate ("Silas and Lyra Garber: A Nebraska Story," master's thesis, University of Nebraska, 1977); Woodress says Cather told a friend that she dared not go back to Red Cloud while her mother was in California for fear of upsetting her (435).

14. Mrs. Wiener's early life is obscure, but her family probably settled in Pittsburgh after coming to the United States: her father died in Pennsylvania in 1890; a few months later a nephew came from Pittsburgh to work in Charles Wiener's store (*Red Cloud Republican*, 15 March 1890, 30 May 1890). Others of her family came farther west, some to Chicago and others to Council Bluffs, Iowa.

15. "Two Friends," by its very title, suggests an antecedent in a story of Turgenev's, "The Two Friends" (1853). Cather knew and admired Turgenev's work from her college days, as references to him in her early reviews show. The most compelling parallel is in the conversations between the friends. "Then conversation began — leisurely conversation with rests and pauses. They talked about the weather, about the preceding day, about field labors and the price of grain; they also talked about the landed gentry of the vicinity, male and female" (*First Love and Other Stories* 257). Turgenev, like Cather, leaves the reader to reflect on how relationships can be destroyed by trivial causes; Cather's story, less satiric and less sensational than Turgenev's, is bleaker: Piotr gains a wife and a comforting memory, but the characters in Cather's story lose something that was precious to them all.

236

16. Carrie Miner Sherwood recalled her first sight of the young Willa, sitting on a shelf at the Miner Bros. store while being fitted for a pair of shoes by Carrie's father (wcpm *Newsletter*).

17. Winifred Richardson married William Seward Garber, son of Governor Silas Garber by his first wife. Silas Garber and his second wife Lyra were prototypes for the Forresters in *A Lost Lady*. Winifred Richardson Garber's daughters, who were interviewed by Lonnie Pierson Dunbier in the 1970s, felt their mother might have been a prototype for the character of Winifred Bartley in *Alexander's Bridge*.

18. *A Lost Lady* appeared in the *Century* (April–June 1923); *The Professor's House* appeared in nine weekly issues of *Collier's* (June–August 1925); *My Mortal Enemy* appeared in *McCall's* (March 1926); *Death Comes for the Archbishop* appeared in six issues of *Forum* (January–June 1927); and *Lucy Gayheart* would appear in *Woman's Home Companion* (March–July 1935). See Crane (252). Knopf had offered *One of Ours* (1922) to various magazines, including the *Saturday Evening Post*, but found no takers. See the Textual Essay, p. 357–58, for a discussion of the distortions involved in serial publication.

19. Knopf received "Old Mrs. Harris" at about the same time as Burton made his proposal, which may have been more of an invitation than an actual offer. The story is roughly 20,000 words in the Knopf edition, somewhat less in its serial version; it would seem to have been just what Burton wanted, but Knopf does not explain why nothing came of it.

20. Gertrude B. Lane was its editor, one whose judgment Cather respected. Lane had published "Uncle Valentine" in February and March 1925. When Cather offered Lane "The Old Beauty" in the winter of 1936–37, however, Lane was unenthusiastic,

although she was willing to publish the story. Cather withdrew the story and it remained in manuscript until after her death.

21. Blanche Knopf wrote Cather, "I have never before read anything that got right inside me as that did," and praised her ability to depict characters "in such a way that they become a good deal more real than the landscape outside the window or the person sitting across the table" (BK to WC, 10 September 1931).

22. See her statement in the Kearney interview, p. 207, above.

23. *Book of the Month Club News*, August 1932; reprinted as an advertisement by Knopf in the *New York Times Book Review*, 28 August 1932. Although *Obscure Destinies* was not the club's main selection, as *Shadows on the Rock* had been in 1931, it was an alternate.

24. See Crane (248–49). Only "A Wagner Matinée," "The Sculptor's Funeral," and "Paul's Case" equal or exceed "Neighbour Rosicky" in number of reprints and anthologizations.

Works Cited

Bixby, W. Letter to the editor. *Nebraska State Journal*, 31 January 1929, 4.

Bladen [Nebr.] Enterprise. Obituary of John Pavelka. 7 May 1926.

Bohlke, Brent L., ed. *Willa Cather in Person: Interviews, Speeches, and Letters*. Lincoln: U of Nebraska P, 1986.

Brown, E. K., and Leon Edel. *Willa Cather: A Critical Biography*. New York: Knopf, 1953.

Canby, Henry Seidel. "This is Humanism." *Saturday Review of Literature*, 6 August 1932, 649.

Cather, Willa. Letters to Zoë Akins. Huntington Library, San Marino, California.

——. Letter to Mary Austin. 9 May 1928. Huntington Library, San Marino, California.

——. Letter to Virginia Boak Cather. Willa Cather Pioneer Memorial and Educational Foundation, Red Cloud.

——. Letters to Dorothy Canfield Fisher. Bailey Howe Library, University of Vermont.

——. Letters to Mariel Gere. Gere Collection. Nebraska State Historical Society, Lincoln.

——. Letters to Blanche Knopf. Knopf Collection. Harry Ransom Humanities Research Center, University of Texas at Austin.

——. Letter to Mrs. Mellen. [late December 1935]. Willa Cather Pioneer Memorial and Educational Foundation, Red Cloud.

——. Letter to Carrie Miner Sherwood. 4 July 1932. Willa Cather Pioneer Memorial and Educational Foundation, Red Cloud.

——. Letter to Paul R. Reynolds. 25 March 1930. Butler Library, Columbia University.

Chamberlain, John. "The Return of Willa Cather." *New York Times Book Review*, 31 July 1932, 1.

Crane, Joan. *Willa Cather: A Bibliography*. Lincoln: U of Nebraska P, 1982.

Dawson, Margaret Cheyney. "Miss Cather's New Portraits." *New York Herald Tribune Books*, 31 July 1932, 3.

Dunbier, Lonnie Pierson. "Silas and Lyra Garber: A Nebraska Story." Master's thesis. University of Nebraska, 1977.

Fadiman, Clifton. "Misted Memories." *Nation*, 3 August 1932, 107.

Fisher, Dorothy Canfield. *Book of the Month Club News*, August 1932; rpt. *New York Times Book Review*, 28 August 1932 (advertisement).

239

Hawthorne, Hazel. "Willa Cather's Homeland." *New Republic*, 10 August 1932, 350.

Jones, Howard Mumford. "Battalions of Women." *Virginia Quarterly Review*, September 1932, 592.

Knight, U. G. Letter to the editor. *Commercial Advertiser* (Red Cloud, Nebr.), 7 December 1932.

Knopf, Alfred A. Memoirs. Typescript. Knopf Collection, Harry Ransom Humanities Research Center, University of Texas at Austin.

——. "Miss Cather." *The Art of Willa Cather*. Ed. Bernice Slote and Virginia Faulkner. Lincoln: U of Nebraska P, 1974.

March, John. *A Reader's Companion to the Fiction of Willa Cather*. Ed. Marilyn Arnold with Debra Lynn Thornton. Westport, Conn.: Greenwood, 1993.

McAfee, Helen. "The Library of the Quarter: Outstanding Novels." *Yale Review* n.s. 22 (autumn 1932): vii–viii.

Mumford, Lewis. Review of *Obscure Destinies*. *Atlantic Monthly*, December 1932, 766.

Omaha World-Herald. Review. 7 August 1932, 4E.

Red Cloud [Nebr.] Chief. Lincoln, Nebraska State Historical Society.

Republican (Red Cloud, Nebr.). 15 March 1890. Lincoln, Nebraska State Historical Society.

Review of *Obscure Destinies*. *Catholic World* 136 (November 1932): 246–47.

Sherwood, Carrie Miner. Reminiscences. Willa Cather Pioneer Memorial and Educational Foundation *Newsletter* XIV, 2 (fall 1970): 1.

Thomas, Elmer A. *80 Years in Webster County*. Hastings, Nebr.: n.p., 1953.

Webster County [Nebr.] Argus. Lincoln, Nebraska State Historical Society.

Winsten, Archer. Review of *Obscure Destinies*. *Bookman* 75 (October 1932): 648–49.

Woodress, James. *Willa Cather: A Literary Life*. Lincoln: U of Nebraska P, 1987.

Illustrations

"Neighbor Rosicky"

1. John and Anna Pavelka, c. 1920. Courtesy of the Willa Cather Memorial and Educational Foundation (WCPM) and the Nebraska State Historical Society.

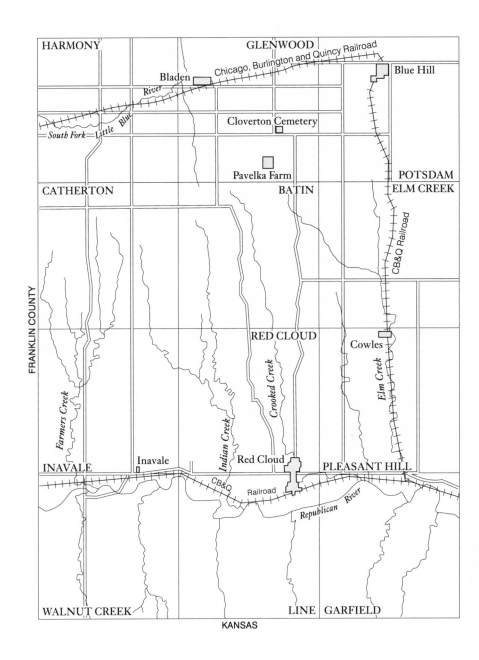

HARMONY

GLENWOOD

Chicago, Burlington and Quincy Railroad

Bladen

Blue Hill

River

Cloverton Cemetery

South Fork — Little Blue

Pavelka Farm

POTSDAM

CATHERTON

BATIN

ELM CREEK

CB&Q Railroad

FRANKLIN COUNTY

RED CLOUD

Cowles

Elm Creek

Farmers Creek

Indian Creek

Crooked Creek

INAVALE

Inavale

Red Cloud

PLEASANT HILL

CB&Q   Railroad

Republican River

WALNUT CREEK

LINE GARFIELD

KANSAS

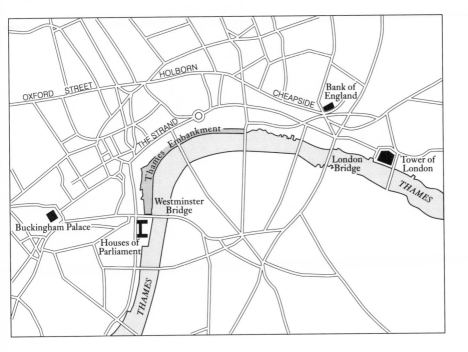

2. Left: Part of Webster County,
1900, showing Bladen, Blue Hill,
the Pavelka farm, Cloverton
cemetery, and Red Cloud.

3. Above: Central London in
1900, showing the Embankment,
The Strand, Oxford Street, and
Cheapside. Based on *Pictorial and
Descriptive Guide to London* (1900).

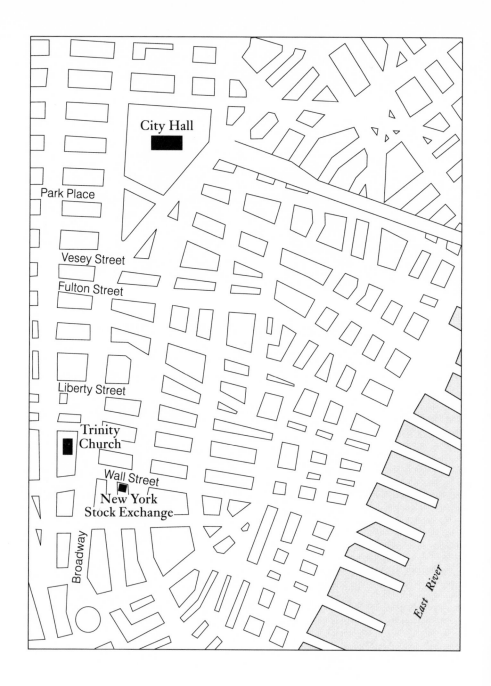

City Hall

Park Place

Vesey Street

Fulton Street

Liberty Street

Trinity
Church

Wall Street

New York
Stock Exchange

Broadway

East River

4. Left: Lower Manhattan, showing
Broadway, Park Place, Vesey Street,
Liberty Street, Trinity Church, and
Wall Street.

5. Above: Cloverton cemetery, date
unknown. Courtesy of the WCPM
and the Nebraska State Historical
Society.

Willa Roberts
Managing Editor

Woman's Home ~ Companion ~

Henry B. Quinan
Art Director

Volume LVII   *Edited by Gertrude b. Lane*   *Number 4*

APRIL 1930

ILLUSTRATED BY
MAURICE L. BOWER

"You go an' fix yourself up, Polly, an' I'll leave everything nice fur you"

Neighbor Rosicky

By
WILLA CATHER

WHEN Dr. Burleigh told neighbor Rosicky he had a bad heart, Rosicky protested.

"So? No, I guess my heart was always pretty good. I got a little asthma, maybe. Just a awful short breath when I was pitchin' hay last summer."

"Well now, Rosicky, if you know more about it than I do, what did you come to me for? It's your heart that makes you short of breath, I tell you. You're sixty-five years old, and you've always worked hard and your heart's tired. You've got to be careful from now on and you can't do heavy work any more. You've got five boys at home to do it for you, and you'll have to look on for a while."

The old farmer looked up at the doctor with a gleam of amusement in his queer triangular-shaped eyes. His eyes were large and lively, but the lids were caught up in the middle in a curious way so that they formed a triangle. He did not look like a sick man. His brown face was creased but not wrinkled, he had a ruddy color in his smooth-shaven cheeks and in his lips, under his long brown mustache. His hair was thin and ragged around his ears but very little gray. His forehead, naturally high and crossed by deep parallel lines, now ran all the way up to his pointed crown. Rosicky's face had the habit of looking interested, suggested a contented disposition and a reflective quality that was gay rather than grave. This gave him a certain detachment, the easy manner of an onlooker and observer.

"Well, I guess you ain't got no pills fur a bad heart, Dr. Ed. I guess the only thing is fur me to git me a new one."

Dr. Burleigh swung round in his desk chair and frowned at the old farmer. "I think if I were you I'd take a little care of the old one, Rosicky."

Rosicky shrugged. "Maybe I don't know how. I expect you mean fur me not to drink my coffee no more."

"I wouldn't, in your place. But you'll do as you choose about that. I've never yet been able to separate a Bohemian from his coffee or his pipe. I've quit trying. But the sure thing is you've got to cut out farm work. You can feed the stock and do chores about the barn, but you can't do anything in the fields that makes you short of breath."

"How about shelling corn?"

"Of course not!"

Rosicky considered with puckered brows.

"I can't make my heart go no longer'n it wants to, can I, Dr. Ed?"

"I think it's good for five or six years yet, maybe more, if you'll take the strain off it. Sit around the house and help Mary. If I had a good wife like yours, I'd want to stay around the house."

His patient chuckled. "It ain't no place for a man. I don't like no old man hanging round the kitchen too much. An' my wife, she's a awful hard worker her own self."

"That's it; you can help her a little. My lord, Rosicky, you are one of the few men I know who has a family he can get some comfort out of; happy dispositions, never quarrel among themselves, and treat you right. I want to see you live a few years and enjoy them."

"Oh, they're good kids, all right," Rosicky admitted.

The doctor wrote him a prescription and asked him how his oldest son, Rudolph, who had married in the spring, was getting on. He had struck out for himself on rented land. "And how's Polly? I was afraid Mary mightn't like an American daughter-in-law, but it seems to be working out all right."

"Yes, she's a fine girl. Dat widder woman bring her daughters up very nice. Polly got lots of spunk, an' she got some style too. Da's nice, fur young people, to have some style." Rosicky inclined his head gal-

7

"Old Mrs. Harris"

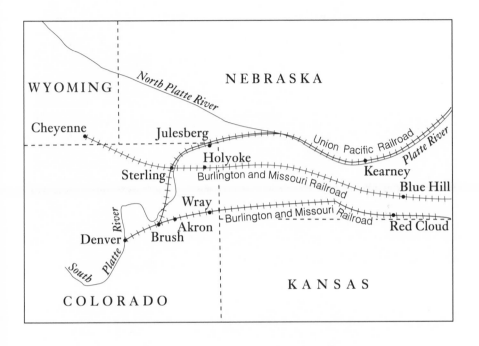

7. Northeastern Colorado, southeastern Wyoming, and western Nebraska, showing Denver, Cheyenne, Wray, the North and South Platte Rivers, and the Burlington Railroad lines, c. 1900.

8. Above: Cather house at Third Avenue and Cedar Street, c. 1900. Courtesy of the WCPM and Nebraska State Historical Society.

9. Left: Rachel Seibert Boak (Mrs. Harris), date unknown. Courtesy of the WCPM and the Nebraska State Historical Society.

10. Right: Plan of the Cather house.

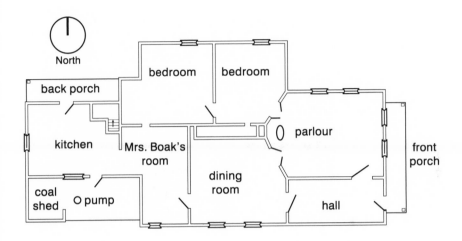

North

back porch

bedroom

bedroom

parlour

front porch

kitchen

Mrs. Boak's room

coal shed

O pump

dining room

hall

11. Left: Roscoe and Douglas Cather ("Albert and Adelbert"), mid-1880s. Courtesy of the WCPM and the Nebraska State Historical Society.

12. Below: Virginia (Jennie) Boak Cather, c. 1900. Courtesy of the WCPM and the Nebraska State Historical Society.

13. Above left: Boys playing in Red Cloud, early twentieth century. The Cather house is behind the telephone pole. Courtesy of the Nebraska State Historical Society.

14. Left: Mrs. Boak's house in Back Creek, Virginia, c. 1900. Courtesy of the WCPM and the Nebraska State Historical Society.

15. Above: James Cather as a baby, c. 1887. Courtesy of the WCPM and the Nebraska State Historical Society.

16. Above: Charles Wiener, 1890s. Courtesy
of the WCPM and the Nebraska State Historical
Society.

17. Right: Page from the September 1932 *Ladies'
Home Journal* serialization of "Three Women"
("Old Mrs. Harris"), with illustration by Frederic
A. Anderson.

THE PRICE of the HOME JOURNAL

PUBLISHED once a month. 10c the copy. By subscription. To the United States and Possessions, and Newfoundland and Labrador, $1.00 the year; $2.00 for 2 years; $3.00 for 3 years.

To Canada, $1.50 the year; $2.75 for 2 years; $3.75 for 3 years (including proper tax).

Remit by Post Office or Express Money Order, Check or by Draft payable in United States or Canadian Funds.

To Argentina, Bolivia, Brazil, Chile, Colombia, Costa Rica, Cuba, Dominican Republic, Ecuador, Guatemala, Haiti, Mexico, Nicaragua, Panama, Paraguay, Peru, Republic of Honduras, Salvador, Spain, Uruguay and Venezuela, $1.50 the year. To other countries, $4.00 the year.

Remittances to be by Postal or Express Money Order or by Draft payable in United States Funds.

LADIES' HOME JOURNAL
(THE HOME JOURNAL)

THE FAMILY MAGAZINE OF AMERICA

Registered in the United States Patent Office and in Foreign Countries

PUBLISHED ON THE SECOND THURSDAY OF THE MONTH PRECEDING ITS DATE BY

THE CURTIS PUBLISHING COMPANY

INDEPENDENCE SQUARE
PHILADELPHIA, PENNSYLVANIA

CYRUS H. K. CURTIS, President
GEORGE H. LORIMER, First Vice-President
JOHN B. WILLIAMS, Second Vice-President
WALTER D. FULLER
Issued Vice-President and Secretary
PHILIP S. COLLINS
Second Vice-President and Treasurer
FRED A. HEALY
Issued Vice-President and Advertising Director

LORING A. SCHULER, Editor

CHULA C. SHERLOCK, STUART O. BLYTHE, RICHARD H. MYERS, LILA RALPH, J. HAROLD HAWKINS, LOIS PALMER, ELIZABETH WOODWARD, CATHARINE OGLESBY, —Associate Editors

Copyright, 1932 (under mark registered), by The Curtis Publishing Company, in the United States and Great Britain, London Offices, 6, Henrietta Street, Covent Garden, W. C. All rights reserved. Entered as second-class matter May 6, 1911, at the Post Office at Philadelphia, Pa., under Act of March 3, 1879. Additional entry at Columbus, O., Chicago, Ill., Indianapolis, Ind., San Francisco, Cal., Seattle, Wash., Houston, Tex., Des Moines, Ia., Los Angeles, Cal., St. Louis, Mo., Saginaw, Mich., Milwaukee, Wis., St. Paul, Minn., Kansas City, Mo., Savannah, Ga., Denver, Colo., Portland, Ore., Louisville, Ky., Omaha, Neb., Ogden, Utah, Jacksonville, Fla., New Orleans, La., Portland, Me.

GRANDMOTHER LOVED TO READ, ANYTHING, THE BIBLE OR THE STORY IN THE PAPER. SHE PUT ON HER SPECTACLES AND BEGAN "TOM SAWYER"

Three Women ❧ ❧ By WILLA CATHER

Illustrated by Frederic A. Anderson

MRS. DAVID ROSEN, her cross-stitch in her hand, sat looking out of the window across her own green lawn to the ragged, sunburned back yard of her neighbors on the right. Occasionally she glanced anxiously over her shoulder toward her shining kitchen, with a black-and-white linoleum floor in big squares, like a marble pavement.

"Will dat woman never go?" she muttered impatiently, just under her breath. She spoke with a slight accent—it affected only her *th's*, and occasionally the letter *r*—but people in Skyline thought this unfortunate in a woman whose superiority they recognized.

Mrs. Rosen ran out to move the sprinkler to another spot on the lawn, and in doing so she saw what she had been waiting to see. From the house next door a tall, handsome woman emerged, dressed in white broadcloth and a hat with white lilacs; she carried a sunshade and walked with a free, energetic step, as if she were going out on a pleasant errand. Mrs. Rosen darted quickly back into the house, lest her neighbor should hail her and stop to talk. She herself was in

Copyright, 1932, by Willa Cather.

her kitchen homework dress, a crisp blue chambray which fitted smoothly over her tightly corseted figure, and her lustrous black hair was done in two smooth braids, wound flat at the back of her head, like a braided rug. She did not stop for a hat—her dark, ruddy, salmon-tinted skin had little to fear from the sun. She opened the half-closed oven door and took out a symmetrically braided coffee cake, beautifully browned, delicately peppered over with poppy seeds, with sugary margins about the twists. On the kitchen table a tiny stood ready with cups and saucers. She wrapped the cake in a napkin, snatched up a little French coffeepot with a black wooden handle, and ran across her green lawn, through the alleyway and the sandy, unkept yard next door, and entered her neighbor's house by the kitchen.

The kitchen was hot and empty, full of the untempered afternoon sun. A door stood open into the next room; a cluttered, hideous room, yet somehow homy. There, beside a goods box covered with figured oilcloth, stood an old woman in a brown calico dress, washing her hot face and neck at a tin basin. She stood in an attitude of profound weariness. She started guiltily as the visitor entered.

"Don't let me disturb you, grandma," called Mrs. Rosen. "I always have my coffee at dis time in the afternoon. I was just about to sit down to it when I thought, 'I will run over and see if Grandma Harris won't take a cup with me.' I hate to drink my coffee alone."

Grandma looked troubled—at a loss. She folded her towel and concealed it behind a curtain hung across the corner of the room to make a poor sort of closet. The old lady was always composed in manner, but it was clear that she felt embarrassment.

"Thank you, Mrs. Rosen. What a pity Victoria just this minute went down town."

"But dis time I came to see you yourself, grandma. Don't let me disturb you. Sit down there in your own rocker, and I will put my tray on dis little chair between us, so."

Mrs. Harris sat down in her black wooden rocking-chair with curved arms and a faded cretonne pillow on the wooden seat. It stood in the corner beside a narrow lounge with spindle frame. She looked on silently while Mrs. Rosen

(Continued on Page 70)

3

34

~~her head". Whenever she 'bridled ' or withdrew herself, something of that kind had occurred.~~

~~Mrs. Harris got into bed, said our Father and The Lord is my Shepherd, and went to sleep lying gratefully on her back and snoring comfortably.~~

V

Mrs. Harris

~~She~~ wakened at about four oclock, as usual, and thought about ~~the~~ their position in this new town, ~~situation over~~ (before the house was aza stirring). She didn't know why the neighbors acted so; she was as much in the dark as Victoria. At home, back in Tennessee, her place in the family ~~position~~ was not exceptional but ~~traditionally correct~~ perfectly regular. As Mrs. Harris had told Mrs Rosen, when that lady asked why in the world she didn't break Vickie in to help her in the kitchen, "We are only young once, and trouble comes soon enough." Young girls, in the South ~~Tennessee~~, were supposed to be care-free and foolish; the fault Grandmother's ~~only criticism of~~ found in Vickie was that she wasn't foolish enough. When the foolish girl married and began to have ~~bear~~ children, everything else must give way to that. She must be humored and given the best of everything, because having children was hard on a woman, and it was the most important thing in the world. In Tennessee every young married woman in good circumstances had an old woman in the house, a mother or mother-in-law or an old aunt, who managed the household economies and directed the helpers ~~working women, working with them.~~ That was the great difference; in Tennessee there had been ~~were~~ plenty of helpers. There was old Miss Sadie Crummer, ~~Grubb~~ who came to the house to spin and sew and mend; old Mrs. Smith, who always arrived to help at butchering and preserving time; Lizzie, the colored girl, who ~~came to do~~ did the washing and who ran in every day to help Mandy. There were plenty more who came whenever one of Lizzie's barefoot boys ran to fetch them. The hills were full of solitary old women, or women who were but slightly attached

18. Typescript page with corrections in the hands of Cather and her companion, Edith Lewis.

"Two Friends"

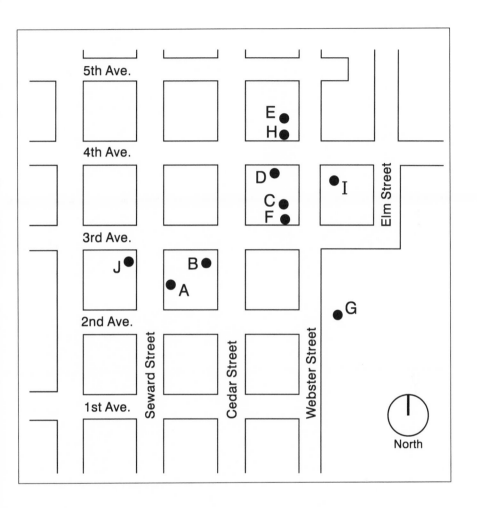

19. Downtown Red Cloud, c. 1900. "Old Mrs. Harris": A, Wiener house; B, Cather house; C, Wiener store; D, post office; E, Opera House. "Two Friends": F, Miner Bros. store and bank; G, Richardson house; H, State Bank of Red Cloud; I, Farmers and Merchants Bank; J, Miner house.

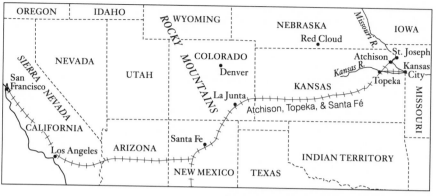

20. Part of the Santa Fé railroad system, 1890. The Kansas (Caw) River and a main line of the Santa Fé run together between Topeka and Kansas City.

21. Exterior of Miner Bros. store and bank, c. 1893–1900. Cather's initials are carved in the long south-facing brick wall. The bank was at the rear. Courtesy of the WCPM and the Nebraska State Historical Society.

22. Interior of People's Bank, with James L. Miner at counter, c. 1902–1905. Courtesy of the WCPM and the Nebraska State Historical Society.

Even in early youth, when the mind is so eager for the new and untried strange, while it is still a stranger to faltering and fear, we yet like to feel that there are certain unalterable ~~facts~~, some- rea~~feelings~~ where at the bottom of things, a sure foundation. ~~Sometimes~~ these anchors ~~are~~ may be ideas, but more often they are merely pictures, vivid memories which are in themselves ideas or ideals. They may be very homely; the only thing we can say of them is that in some ~~curious~~ unaccountable and very personal way, they ~~satisfy~~ fortify us. The sea gulls that seem so much creatures of the free wind and waves, that are as homeless as the sea, able to rest upon the ~~waves~~ tides and ride the storm, need- ing nothing but water and sky, at certain seasons they ~~xxxxx~~ even go go back to something they have know before; to islands that are their breeding grounds, to lonely ledges where they creep ~~into~~ ~~well-known holes and caves,~~ into mere fissures and cracks in the rock. The restlessness of youth has such retreats, even though it may be ashamed of them.

Long ago, before the invention of the motor-car, (which has made more changes in the world than the war, which indeed produced the particular 1 kind of war that happened just a hundred years after Waterloo) in a little wooden town in a shallow Kansas, river valley of Central Kansas, there lived two friends. They were "business men", the two most prosperous and influential men in our com- munity, the two men whose affairs took them out into the world to big cities, who had ~~business~~ connections in Saint Joseph and Chicago. In my childhood they represented to me success and power ✗

23. Typescript of first page, version 1, with revisions in Cather's hand.

TWO FRIENDS

~~I~~
~~Helen Cather~~

Even in early youth, when the mind is so eager for the
new and untried, while it is still a stranger to faltering and
fear, we yet like to think that there are certain unalterable
realities, somewhere at the bottom of things.   These anchors
may be ideas; but more often they are merely pictures, vivid
memories, ~~which are in themselves ideas or ideals.~~   ~~They may be~~
~~very homely; The only thing we can say of them is that~~ which in some
unaccountable and very personal way, *give us courage* ~~they fortify us.~~   The sea=
gulls, ~~that~~ *which that* (seem so much creatures of the free wind and waves,
~~that~~ *which that* (are as homeless as the sea (able to rest upon the tides and
ride the storm, needing nothing but water and sky,)) at certain
seasons even they go back to something they have known before; to
remote islands ~~that are their breeding grounds,~~ *and* to lonely ledges *that are*
their breeding-grounds. ~~they creep into mere fissures and cracks in the rock,~~   The
restlessness of youth has such retreats, even though it may be
ashamed of them.

Long ago, before the invention of the motor-car (which
has made more changes in the world than the War, which indeed
produced the particular kind of war that happened just a hundred
years after Waterloo), in a little wooden town in a shallow
Kansas river valley, there lived two friends.   They were
"business men", the two most prosperous and influential men in
our community, the two men whose affairs took them out into the
world to big cities, who had "connections" in ~~Saint~~ St. Joseph and
Chicago.   In my childhood they represented to me success and

24. Typescript of first page, version 2, with corrections in Lewis's hand. Courtesy
of Helen Cather Southwick.

Woman's Home C**ompanion**

Edited by Gertrude B. Lane

WILLA ROBERTS
Managing Editor

HENRY B. QUINAN
Art Director

Vol. LIX   No. 7   JULY 1932

Two Friends

WILLA CATHER

ILLUSTRATOR: WALTER EVERETT

Mr. Dillon called to me, told me to watch what was going to happen

EVEN IN early youth when the mind is so eager for the new and untried, while it is still a stranger to faltering and fear, we yet like to think that there are certain unalterable realities somewhere at the bottom of things. These anchors may be ideas; but more often they are merely pictures, vivid memories, which in some unaccountable and very personal way give us courage. The sea gulls, that seem so much creatures of the free wind and waves, that are as homeless as the sea (able to rest upon the tides and ride the storm, needing nothing but water and sky), at certain seasons even they go back to something they have known before; to remote islands and lonely ledges that are their breeding grounds. The restlessness of youth has such retreats, even though it may be ashamed of them.

LONG AGO, before the invention of the motor car, in a little wooden town in a shallow Kansas river valley, there lived two friends. They were business men, the two most prosperous and influential men in our community, the two men whose affairs took them out into the world to big cities, who had connections in St. Joseph and Chicago. In my childhood they represented to me success and power.

R. E. Dillon was of Irish extraction, one of the dark Irish, with glistening jet-black hair and mustache, and thick eyebrows. His skin was very white, bluish on his shaven cheeks and chin. Shaving must have been a difficult process for him, because there were no smooth expanses for the razor to glide over. The bony structure of his face was prominent and unusual; high cheekbones, a bold Roman nose, a chin cut by deep lines, with a hard dimple at the tip, a jutting ridge over his eyes where his curly black eyebrows grew and met. It was a face in many planes, as if the carver had whirled and modeled and indented to see how far he could go. Yet on meeting him what you saw was an imperious head on a rather small wiry man, a head held conspicuously and proudly erect, and consciously superior. Dillon had a musical vibrating voice and the changeable gray eye that is peculiarly Irish. His full name, which he never used, was Robert Emmet Dillon; so there must have been a certain feeling somewhere back in his family.

He was the principal banker in our town and proprietor of the large general store next the bank; he owned farms up in the grass country and a fine ranch in the green timbered valley of the Kaw. He was, according to our standards, a rich man.

His friend, J. H. Trueman, was what we called a big cattleman. Trueman was from Buffalo; his family were old residents there, and he had come West as a young man because he was restless and unconventional in his

tastes. He was fully ten years older than Dillon, in his early fifties when I knew him; large, heavy, very slow in his movements, not given to exercise. His countenance was as unmistakably American as Dillon's was not—but American of that period, not of this. He did not belong to the time of efficiency and advertising and progressive methods. For any form of pushing or boosting he had a cold, unqualified contempt. All this was in his face—heavy, immobile, rather melancholy, not remarkable in any particular. But the moment one looked at him one felt solidity, an entire absence of anything mean or small, easy carelessness, courage, a high sense of honor.

These two men had been friends for ten years before I knew them, and I knew them from the time I was ten until I was thirteen. I saw them as often as I could, because they led more varied lives than the other men in our town; one could look up to them. Dillon, I believe, was the more intelligent. Trueman had, perhaps, a better tradition, more background.

Dillon's bank and general store stood at the corner of Main Street and a cross street, and on this cross street, two short blocks away, my family lived. On my way to and from school, and going on the countless errands that I was sent upon day and night; I always passed Dillon's store. Its long red brick wall, with no windows except high overhead, ran possibly a hundred feet along the sidewalk of the cross street. The front

door and show windows were on Main Street, and the bank was next door. The board sidewalk along that red brick wall was wider than any other piece of walk in town, smoother, better laid, kept in perfect repair; very good to walk on in a community where most things were flimsy. I liked the store and the brick wall and the sidewalk because they were solid and well built, and possibly I admired Dillon and Trueman for much the same reason. They were secure and established. So many of our citizens were nervous little grasshopper-men, trying to get on. Dillon and Trueman had got on; they stood with easy assurance on a deck that was their own.

IN THE daytime one did not often see them together —each went about his own affairs. But every evening they were both to be found at Dillon's store. The bank, of course, was locked and dark before the sun went down, but the store was always open until ten o'clock; the clerks put in a long day. So did Dillon. He and his store were one. He never acted as salesman, and he kept a cashier in the wire-screened office at the back end of the store; but he was there to be called on. The thrifty Swedes to the north, who were his best customers, usually came to town and did their shopping after dark—they didn't squander daylight hours in farming season. In these evening visits with his customers and on his drives in his backboard among the farms, Dillon

25. Page from the *Woman's Home Companion* serialization of "Two Friends" (July 1932), with illustration by Walter Everett. Cather disliked Everett's depiction of the two men.

Explanatory Notes

THE explanatory notes are designed to assist the reader
in understanding the text by providing information on
persons, places, historical events, literary allusions, and specialized terminology that is not readily available elsewhere
such as in a standard desk dictionary or one-volume en-
cyclopedic reference. Regional, occupational, religious, and
other specialized terms are explained when more information is needed than can be found in desk references. Prototypes for characters have been suggested when they are
likely on the basis of Cather's own comments or on contemporary evidence. Cather often refers to well-known people
by their real names; because many of these have become
obscure to modern readers, they have been briefly identified.
Cather also used both real and fictional place-names; the
notes identify both and give the likely prototype for the fictional names, when known. Brief backgrounds for historical
events are also included; if Cather diverges from the facts as
understood by modern historians, that will be noted. Sources
of quotations are provided, as well as the complete original

quotation if different from that in the text, and a translation if necessary.

Information on prototypes of people in the stories is based primarily on the United States Censuses of 1880, 1900, and 1920 for Webster County, Nebraska; the Nebraska State Census of 1885; and Webster County newspapers of the 1880s through the 1920s, such as the *Red Cloud Chief*, the *Webster County Argus*, and the *Bladen Enterprise*. Mildred Bennett's *The World of Willa Cather* (Lincoln: U of Nebraska P, 1961) and Elmer Thomas's *Eighty Years in Webster County* (Hastings, Nebr.: n.p., 1953) were helpful, as was John March and Marilyn Arnold's *A Reader's Companion to the Fiction of Willa Cather* (Westport, Conn.: Greenwood, 1993). Augustus Koch's 1881 bird's-eye view of Red Cloud and the Sanborn Fire Insurance maps of 1886 and 1892, the 1923 plat book of Webster County, and Mabel Cooper-Skjelver's *Webster County: Visions of the Past* (n.p., n.d.), were useful for the geography of Webster County (the basis for the setting of all three stories, despite the ostensible locations in Colorado and Kansas).

Cather uses common names for her references to local flora and fauna; these have been glossed with the botanical names and brief descriptions of the most likely species for the setting. Botanical information for Webster County was derived first from the early biologists who surveyed Nebraska. These include Charles E. Bessey, *Preliminary Report on the Native Trees and Shrubs of Nebraska* 4, art. no. 4 (Lincoln, College of Agriculture Experiment Station, n.d.); Niels F.

Petersen, *Flora of Nebraska: a List of Conifers and Flowering Plants of the State with Keys for Their Determination* (Lincoln: privately printed, c. 1912); Raymond Pool, *Handbook of Nebraska Trees* (1919; 3d ed., Lincoln: University of Nebraska Conservation and Survey Division, 1951); John M. Winter, *An Analysis of the Flowering Plants of Nebraska with Keys to the Families, Genera, and Species, with Notes Concerning Their Occurrence, Range, and Frequency within the State* (Lincoln: Nebraska Conservation and Survey Division, 1936). Nomenclature and other information was cross-checked with current authorities such as Lauren Brown, *Grasslands*, Audubon Society Nature Guide (New York: Knopf, 1985); Robert Lommasson, *Nebraska Wildflowers* (Lincoln: U of Nebraska P, 1973); Nebraska Statewide Arboretum, *Common and Scientific Names of Nebraska Plants: Native and Introduced*, Publication No. 101 (Lincoln: Nebraska Statewide Arboretum, n.d.); and Theodore Van Bruggen, *Wildflowers, Grasses, and Other Plants of the Northern Plains and Black Hills* (Interior, S. Dak.: Badlands Natural History Association, 1983).

"Neighbour Rosicky"

Doctor Burleigh: After Cather went to Pittsburgh in 1896, she was   7
introduced to a Dr. William Burleigh; she repeated his name several times, then said she was going to use it in a story some time (Kathleen D. Byrne and Richard C. Snyder, *Chrysalis: Willa Cather in Pittsburgh, 1896–1906* [Pittsburgh: Historical Society of Western Pennsylvania, 1980], 24).

7   Rosicky: John Pavelka (1859–1926) served as the prototype for Rosicky and for Anton Cuzak in *My Ántonia*; he was the husband of Anna Sadilek Pavelka, prototype for Ántonia. Like Rosicky, Pavelka was apprenticed to a tailor in his youth; however, he came to the United States with his parents and spent fourteen years at a lumber mill in California before coming to Nebraska in the mid-1890s.

    Cather may have borrowed the name from John Rosicky (1845–1910) of Omaha, one of the best-known Czechs in Nebraska when Cather was growing up. Through his Czech-language newspapers he did much to encourage Czech immigration to the state. His daughter, Rose Rosicky, wrote *A History of Czechs (Bohemians) in Nebraska* (Omaha: Czech Historical Society of Nebraska, 1929), which Cather praised.

9   shelling corn: Various machines were invented in the nineteenth century to strip the corn kernels from the cob; turning the crank that operated the machine was hard work.

9   Mary: The character of Mary is based on that of Anna Sadilek Pavelka, the prototype for Ántonia.

9   Rudolph: The eldest son of John and Anna Pavelka was Hugo Pavelka (1899–1971). Cather took special interest in his career as a farmer (Bennett 51). In *My Ántonia*, the eldest son of Anton and Ántonia Cuzak is also called Rudolph.

9   Polly: Etta J. Alberts of Blue Hill, Nebraska, married Hugo Pavelka on 21 October 1925.

10   hay-rake: Horse-drawn steel dump rakes were common by the 1920s; a lever near the operator's foot lifted the teeth of the rake, dumping the mown hay in a pile or in a continuous windrow, depending on the type of rake.

desk-telephone: These telephones operated in much the same way   10
as the wall-mounted types; however, the transmitter was mounted
on a pedestal stand; the receiver was a separate piece held to the ear.
"French" telephones, with speaker and receiver in one unit, were
coming into use in 1928, about the time this story was written.

plush cap and corduroy jacket with a sheepskin collar: Rosicky is   10
wearing his winter working clothes rather than dressing up in a suit
for coming to town; similar caps and jackets are still worn.

Tom Marshall's: Comfortless modern farm homes like this were   10
depicted in *One of Ours* (1922). In *My Ántonia* one of the town
families is named Marshall.

buggy: Buggies were inexpensive and lightweight, making them   11
easy for a single horse to pull over rough or wet ground or, as here,
through snow. They were much used by doctors and others who
traveled on business.

Josephine: There were four daughters in the Pavelka family; the   12
youngest, Elizabeth, was called Nina in *My Ántonia*. The three
elder daughters were married at the time of John Pavelka's death.

What do people go to Omaha for?: Omaha, the largest city in   13
Nebraska, had a number of large hospitals and the University of
Nebraska Medical School.

geraniums: The common geranium, *Pelargonium hortorum*, has   15
bright red flowers, although there are varieties with blossoms in
white or shades of pink. They grow well as houseplants and were
very popular in the early and late nineteenth century; in the 1920s
they were considered somewhat old-fashioned.

16   farm-implement store: James Peterson's farm-implement store in Red Cloud was at the southwest corner of Third and Webster Streets, across the street from the old Miner Bros. general store, owned by R. W. Weesner in the 1920s.

16   plucked eyebrows: In the nineteenth century eyebrows were left in their natural state, although an arched shape was admired; plucking with tweezers to achieve a delicate line became common by the 1920s, and eyebrow-penciling devices were used to fill in the line, or in some cases, to produce new and completely artificial brows, like those of film star Marlene Dietrich.

18   the graveyard: John and Anna Pavelka are buried in the Cloverton cemetery (see illustrations 2, 5) in the countryside north of their farm. Cather has changed the distances; the cemetery is about thirteen miles north of Red Cloud, and four and a half miles southeast of Bladen and southwest of Blue Hill, the possible prototypes for the unnamed town where Rosicky visits the doctor.

19   long red grass: The big bluestem, *Andropogon gerardii*, is a native grass that turns reddish after frost; its seed stalks reach three to eight feet in height.

19   evergreens: The eastern red cedar, *Juniperus virginiana*, is most likely, as it is one of the three evergreen, coniferous trees native to Nebraska. Evergreen trees are traditionally planted in cemeteries as a symbol of immortality.

19   mowing-machine: Horse-drawn machines for mowing hay had a seat for the driver between the two wheels; the toothed cutting bar or bars that extended to the side could be as little as four feet wide or as much as eight feet. Devices to throw the hay into windrows could be attached to the cutter bars.

John: Clement was the youngest Pavelka boy; in *My Ántonia* the   20
youngest boy is called Jan, the Czech equivalent of John.

kolache: Kolaches, round sweet rolls with fruit, poppyseed, or cot-   20
tage cheese fillings, are a characteristic Czech pastry. When Jim
comes to visit Ántonia's farm in *My Ántonia*, she makes kolaches,
and one of the boys assumes Jim won't know what they are.

the thickened nail of his right thumb told the story of his past: 21
Rosicky, like his prototype John Pavelka, had been a tailor in his
youth.

buggy-rake: A team of horses pulled a four-wheeled apparatus with   22
a seat for the driver behind the rake bar which gathered up the
mown hay with its long curved teeth; a foot-activated lever raised
the teeth, allowing the hay to be dumped in a pile behind the
machine, to be loaded later. When mechanical loaders were used,
which needed to have the hay laid in long windrows for best efficiency, side-delivery rakes pushed the hay in a continuous line at
the side.

creamery agent: Many small towns supported creameries, which   24
bought raw milk from the farmers and made butter for local and
regional markets; creameries also sold cream and milk locally. Farmers might deliver the milk, or the agent, whose job it was to induce
farmers to contract their milk to the creamery, might pick it up.

the Fasslers: The Fassler brothers, Chris, John, Henry, Jacob, and   24
Phillip, were early residents of the Glenwood and Potsdam pre-
cincts of Webster County. By 1900 Chris and Phillip Fassler owned
nearly a section of land about two miles north of the Pavelka land in
Glenwood township. Chris Fassler served as county treasurer in the
early 1890s; he was childless, but his brothers had families of two to
seven children.

25   Bohemian papers: A number of Czech-language periodicals were available in Nebraska, including John Rosicky's *Pokrok zapadu* (The Progress of the West), founded in 1871 by Edward Rosewater; Rosicky's *Hospodar* (The Farmer), founded in 1891; *Narodni pokruk* (National Progress) founded in 1921, all published in Omaha. Other Czech communities had local papers, generally shorter-lived than the Omaha papers; weekly Czech papers were also published in Chicago.

25   Cheapside: When Cather visited London on her first trip in 1902, she stayed at a small hotel near Cheapside, an ancient street of shops in the City of London. She wrote of the area: "If the street life . . . of the common but so-called respectable part of the town, is in any city more gloomy, more ugly, more grimy, more cruel than in London, I certainly don't care to see it" (William M. Curtin, *The World and the Parish: Willa Cather's Articles and Reviews 1893–1902* [Lincoln: U of Nebraska P, 1970], 907).

26   Castle Garden: From 1855 to 1892, immigrants landing in New York City, the busiest port of entry, were taken by ferry to Castle Garden on the southwest end of Manhattan Island. It had been built as a fort in 1807, then converted to an amusement center before the state took it over for the first immigrant landing port in the country. There the new arrivals could change their money, buy food, wash in free hot water, buy railroad tickets, and obtain information about housing and jobs. In 1891 the federal government took the responsibility for receiving and regulating immigrants, and Ellis Island, a larger site, replaced Castle Garden.

26   Vesey Street: An east–west street in lower Manhattan, between Broadway and the Hudson River.

the Washington Market: Founded in 1812, this block-square mar-   26
ketplace was bounded by Fulton, Vesey, West, and Washington
Streets.

rich German housewives up-town: As some German-Americans   27
prospered in New York City in the 1860s through the 1880s, they
left the Kleindeutschland, a large area of downtown New York
settled almost exclusively by Germans, for the new fashionable dis-
tricts to the north (uptown).

Park Place: This street, named for the City Hall Park at its east end,   28
connects Broadway with West Street.

lilac hedge: *Syringa vulgaris*, the common lilac, has fragrant lav-   28
ender, purple, or white blossoms in May.

Trinity churchyard: Trinity parish was chartered in 1697; Queen   28
Anne gave it a grant of land west of Broadway in 1705. The present
building is a brownstone neo-Gothic church built in 1846 at Broadway and Wall Street; its spires made it the tallest building in New
York for much of the nineteenth century. The two-and-a-half-acre
graveyard is on the church's south side.

Wall Street, Liberty Street, Broadway: Wall Street, then as now,   28
was the center of New York finance and the location of the New
York Stock Exchange. Broadway runs roughly north and south,
past Trinity church and City Hall; Liberty Street runs east and west
a few blocks north of Wall Street. See illustration 4.

Bohemian athletic societies: The most important athletic societies   30
in Czechoslovakia, and in Czech communities in America, were the
Sokol gymnastic societies; large conventions were held every four
years.

31 the moving-picture show: Red Cloud's first movie theater, the Tepee, opened in 1910. After Besse Auditorium opened in 1921, movies were shown there, including the premiere of *A Lost Lady* in 1925. Bladen and Blue Hill also had movie theaters after 1913.

32 shingled yellow hair: This very short haircut became popular for young women in the 1920s; the hair was cut like a man's, cropped close to the back of the head, so that the ends of the hairs are exposed, like the shingles of a roof.

35 crop failure all over the county: The dry years, which led to crop failures and started the Great Depression early for farmers, began in Nebraska in 1924.

36 factory job in Omaha. . . . take him back at the stockyards: Omaha, a major railway terminus, had large stockyards and several meatpacking plants where many immigrants worked.

38 Jerusalem cherry trees: The Jerusalem or winter cherry (*Solanum pseudo capsicum*) is a name for several plants of the nightshade family. Grown as houseplants in the Midwest, they have red fruits that ripen in winter.

38 the Embankment: The Albert Embankment, running for nearly a mile south of the Lambeth bridge on the east bank of the Thames, and the Victoria Embankment, running along the north side of the Thames between the Westminster and Blackfriars bridges, were completed in 1870. The river walls made it possible to reclaim marshland for the underground railroad, a surface road, and open land laid out as public gardens. In 1902 Cather wrote, "The beautiful river front on the east side of the Thames called the Albert Embankment . . . is night and day thronged with drunken, homeless men and women who alternately claw each other with their

278

nails and give each other a chew of tobacco" (*The World and the Parish* 908).

horsehair sofa: Hair from the tails and manes of horses, mixed with   39
wool or linen, made a very durable upholstery fabric that was much
used in the nineteenth century; it was usually black.

packing house: Rudolph probably means one of the meatpacking   41
houses in South Omaha (see p. 36); established in the 1880s with
companies such as Swift and Cudahy, South Omaha quickly became one of the largest livestock market and meatpacking centers
in the country. The stockyards and packers employed many first
and second generation immigrants.

that terrible hot wind: Crop-damaging hot winds struck Webster   41
County in July 1913, a date consistent with the 1920s setting of the
story and with the reference to "fifteen years since that time" (44).
Cather's own experience with such a wind came on 26 July 1894, a
landmark day; she wrote of it in 1900 in "The Hottest Day I Ever
Spent" (reprinted in *The World and the Parish* 778–82), and there
are other references to it in her fiction. A hot south wind turned
green corn to shriveled dry stalks in a matter of hours. The *Webster
County Argus* wrote, "The simoon of last Thursday will long be
remembered. Like a besom of destruction it swept across the
country . . . about destroying every vestige of corn" (1 August
1894). A contemporary of Cather's, writing as the drought of the
1930s began to settle in, called the wind of 1894 "the most appall-
ing calamity that has ever happened in this country" (*Commercial
Advertiser* [Red Cloud], 10 August 1931).

we didn't have alfalfa yet: Alfalfa (*Medicago sativa*), also known as   41
lucerne, is a legume with a long taproot that reaches deep for sub-
soil moisture. It was not widely grown until the droughts of the

279

1890s compelled farmers to look for drought-resistant crops. In *O Pioneers!* Alexandra called it "the salvation of this country" (154).

41   plum preserves: *Prunus americana*, one of the species of wild plums native to Nebraska, is the most likely source of fruit for preserves at the time of the story. Technically a small tree, it sprouts from the roots, forming dense thickets along stream banks, in pastures, and along fencerows. The white flowers in early April give way to sweet, juicy red or purple fruits in August.

42   box-elder trees: Box elders (*Acer negundo*) were frequently planted in Nebraska, especially in windbreaks, because they are tough and can survive the dry summers and harsh winters with little care. Although Cather did not particularly like box elders, referring to them once as travesties of trees, she appreciated their value for the pioneers.

43   mulberry hedge: Mulberry trees sprout profusely when cut, making them adaptable for hedge use. *Morus rubra*, the red mulberry tree, is native to the eastern border of the state, where it grows fifteen to thirty feet tall. It grows rapidly; the fruit is edible and the wood may be used for fenceposts. *Morus alba*, known both as white mulberry and black mulberry, is a hardy, spreading tree introduced from Asia; it has become naturalized in the eastern United States. A section of *O Pioneers!* is called "The White Mulberry Tree."

43   linden trees: Although there are European varieties, it is likely that the ones on the Rosicky farm were *Tilia americana*, native to rich, moist soils such as the river bottoms of the Blue River in southern Nebraska. They are adaptable trees, growing quickly to as much as sixty feet. The fragrant flowers are attractive to bees. In *O Pioneers!* Marie Shabata refers to a Czech belief that lindens are a lucky tree (139).

wild-grape wine: Several species of grapes are native to Nebraska,   43
including *Vitis aestivalis*, *V. riparia*, and *V. vulpina*.

the Strand . . . New Oxford Street: The Strand, just north of the   47
Thames, is part of one of the major thoroughfares through London; it runs seven-eighths of a mile from Charing Cross to Temple
Bar and was known for its theaters, offices, and shops. New Oxford
Street, north of the Strand, is a short section of another major
thoroughfare, constructed to straighten the line of the road between Oxford Street on the west and Holborn on the east. In her
letter from London in 1902, Cather wrote of spending "morning
after morning on High Holborn or the Strand" (*The World and the
Parish* 907), watching people pass. She also commented on the
courtesy and good nature of the shop girls of Oxford Street and
Bond Street (908).

not like de Austrians: In the nineteenth century the area known as   47
Bohemia was part of the Austro-Hungarian Empire; Austrians in
the ruling classes would have spoken Czech with an accent.

ten shillings: At the average exchange rate of the time, ten shillings   48
would have been worth $2.50 — a good day's wages for a moderately
skilled man.

Covent Garden: Beginning in the early seventeenth century, a mar-   48
ket was held in what was originally the garden of the convent of St.
Peter's, north of Charing Cross. The wholesale market, famous for
its flowers, fruits, and vegetables, was held very early on Tuesday,
Thursday, and Saturday mornings.

wheat: Corn was the main crop in Webster County when Cather   50
was growing up; traditional varieties of spring-planted wheat were
unsuited to the climate. Toward the end of the century winter

wheat was introduced; planted in the fall, it received moisture from the snowfall, usually more reliable in Webster County than summer rain, and ripened early in the summer.

50   ploughed up and planted over again. . . . It had happened before: The *Red Cloud Chief*, 5 April 1917, urged farmers to plow up drought-damaged wheat immediately and replant.

52   the organized industries that see one out of the world in big cities: The *Woman's Home Companion* version of the story specified these industries as "doctors, hospitals, undertakers" (92). Only those who could not afford nursing in their homes went to municipal hospitals when they were ill.

52   Mr. Haycock: Although Cather may not have had a particular undertaker in mind, members of the Amack family were undertakers in Red Cloud for many years.

53   sulky plough: A horse-drawn plow that allowed the plowman to sit while guiding the horses, instead of walking behind, was patented in 1856. Sulky plows (mentioned also in *My Ántonia*) had three wheels, two to run in the furrow and a larger one on the unplowed ground. The wheel frame supported the metal seat for the driver, and foot levers made it possible to lift the plow bottom for ease in turning corners.

53   Russian thistles: This annual weed, *Salsola kali tenuifolia*, which was formerly known as *Salsola pestifer*, is thought to have come to the United States from Russia in the 1870s. It became naturalized quickly and became a serious pest in the plains states, appearing in Webster County by 1894. The plant forms a bushy globe three to four feet high; when it dries the stem breaks and the plant is blown about by the wind (hence the common name tumbleweed), scattering its many seeds over long distances.

282

"Old Mrs. Harris"

Mrs. David Rosen: See the Historical Essay (214) for an account of   65
Fanny Wiener, a prototype for Mrs. Rosen. Cather may have based
the name on that of the Rosenthal Bros., clothiers in Red Cloud
before the Wieners came.

linoleum floor: Linoleum was invented in the mid–nineteenth cen-   65
tury. It was valued for its ability to withstand grease and water,
unlike wood floors, which were much commoner.

Skyline: Cather indicates the setting of the story generally as the   65
area "between Wray and Cheyenne" (111), that is, in northeastern
Colorado and southeastern Wyoming; the references to the sand-
hills (101) and the irrigated farmland near the river (148) indicate
that Skyline is set on the Burlington Railroad east of Sterling, Colorado. The fictional Moonstone, Colorado, in *The Song of the Lark*
(1915) is set in this area also. Both towns are based on Cather's
memories of life in Red Cloud, Nebraska, where she lived from
1885 to 1896. The surviving typescript shows that the town was at
first called Topaz Valley.

sprinkler: Red Cloud installed city waterworks in the late 1880s; the   65
supply was of somewhat uncertain quality and quantity for many
years. The hours in which sprinklers could be run were restricted to
early morning and evening; there were many complaints in the
newspapers about people who left their sprinklers on all night, thus
draining the standpipe.

French coffee-pot: The finely ground coffee was placed in the up-   66
per chamber of the coffeepot, and boiling water from the stove was
poured over it, percolating through to the storage chamber. In *My
Ántonia*, Mr. Harling, the wealthy grain merchant, keeps a French

283

coffeepot in his room so that his wife can make coffee for him at any time of night (179).

66 an old woman: The character of Mrs. Harris was based on that of Cather's grandmother, Rachel Seibert Boak (1816–93), her mother's mother (see illustration 9). When the Charles and Virginia Cather family moved to Nebraska, Mrs. Boak accompanied them and lived with the family until her death. Mrs. Boak was also the model for Rachel in Cather's *Sapphira and the Slave Girl* (1940).

66 brown calico dress: Calico, cotton fabric usually printed with small overall floral or geometric motifs, was one of the cheapest fabrics available; Red Cloud dry goods stores sold it for three to five cents a yard. Brown was an unfashionable color and Mrs. Harris's full-gathered skirt (see p. 72) is nearly thirty years out of fashion by the 1890s. In contrast, Mrs. Harris's daughter wears stylish clothing of broadcloth, challis, and organdy, fashionable fabrics that cost more than ten times as much as calico.

67 Grandma: When Cather was growing up in Red Cloud in the 1880s, it was not unusual for people to bestow the courtesy titles of aunt or uncle or as here, grandma, on older people for whom they felt affection; such titles were even used in the Red Cloud newspapers.

68 Victoria: Victoria (Mrs. Hillary Templeton) is based in part on Cather's mother, Mary Virginia Boak Cather (1850–1931). She was remembered as a handsome, imperious woman. See illustration 12.

71 old home in Tennessee: Cather was born in Mrs. Boak's house in Back Creek Valley, Virginia (see illustration 14). Southerners were unusual in the northern plains states; when they moved west they were more likely to settle in Kansas, Oklahoma, or Texas. Apart

284

from the Virginians who followed Cather's uncle, George P. Cather, to northwestern Webster County (the area was known as New Virginia), there were few southerners in Webster County.

Maltese cat: These cats are known for their short, thick, blue fur;   72 some have white spots on their chests. Their origins are unclear; blue cats, very popular in late-nineteenth-century America, have been called Maltese, Spanish, American, or Russian cats at various times.

Vickie: Victoria Templeton's daughter has some qualities in com-   72 mon with Cather herself, particularly her desire to learn and to seek higher education. Like Vickie, Cather did not much resemble her stylish, Southern-belle mother.

Miss Sadie Crummer: At one point the surviving typescript refers   73 to Sadie Grubb, whose last name is revised to Crummer. Grubb was the name of a neighbor family in Virginia, some of whom also came to Webster County, settling in the Catherton area, so Cather may have had a real person in mind.

my husband's store: Charles Wiener's store, the Golden Eagle   74 Clothing Store, was a men's clothing store on the west side of Webster Street between Third and Fourth Avenues, three doors north of the Miner Bros. store. See illustration 19.

the baby . . . Hughie: No member of Willa Cather's family can be   74 identified as an exact prototype for Hughie, who is more than two years old when the story opens (see p. 95). Her sister Elsie was born in January 1890, the year Cather left for the university. Her brother John (Jack) was born in 1892. However, James Cather, born in December 1886, would have been a baby fairly early in the Wiener's acquaintance with the Cathers.

74 Mr. Holliday's: The Burlington Railroad's roadmaster in Red Cloud while Cather was growing up was E. F. Highland. One of the most popular men in town, he was a good friend of the Wieners and came back to visit them often after his transfer to Holyoke, Colorado, in early 1890. He may have helped Douglas Cather obtain a position with the railroad in the Sterling-Holyoke area in 1897. In parts of the surviving typescript the roadmaster's name is given as Mr. Thomas, corrected to Holliday; Thomas was the name of a prominent Webster County family.

74 the twins: These boys were probably based on Cather's brothers Roscoe (1877–1945) and Douglas, or Douglass, as Cather preferred to spell it, (1879–1938). Both were very close to Cather throughout their lives. See illustration 11, where they are dressed virtually as twins. In the magazine edition, the twins are said to be twelve years old instead of ten, as here.

74 Ronald: There is no exact prototype in Cather's family; her brother James (1886–1966) would have been closest to kindergarten age at the time Cather was preparing for the university in 1890.

75 velocipedes: Various two- and three-wheeled foot-propelled vehicles, including forerunners of the bicycle and tricycle, were called velocipedes; the pedals attached directly to the front axle. The 1897 Sears Roebuck catalog sold them as cheap alternatives to bicycles, which cost ten times as much.

75 Mr. Rosen: See the discussion of Charles Wiener, the prototype for Mr. Rosen, on p. 215 of the Historical Essay.

75 Mandy, the bound girl: In the eighteenth and early nineteenth centuries in America, orphan children were put in families as servants, bound to work for their room and board until they were eighteen.

286

The practice became obsolete by the middle of the nineteenth century; it is highly unlikely that Mandy was legally bound to the Templeton family, whatever the emotional and economic bonds. See the discussion of Marjorie Anderson in the Historical Essay (214) for information on Mandy's prototype.

arc lights: A bright light is produced by sending an electric current 76 across the gap between two conductors. Although Sir Humphry Davy constructed the first arc lamp in 1807, arc lighting did not become practical for streetlights until the late 1870s. Sixteen arc lights were placed on streets, mainly in the downtown area of Red Cloud, in July 1887, and became operational by 8 September 1887. One of the street lights was at Third and Seward, just west of the Cather house. A separate system provided incandescent lights for interiors by December 1888.

Tom Sawyer: The Adventures of Tom Sawyer, by Mark Twain, was 76 published in 1876.

continued story in the Chicago weekly paper: One such paper, the 76 *Chicago Weekly Record*, usually contained one long serial story by authors such as H. Rider Haggard, Miss Braddon, and many now-forgotten writers; several short stories; many columns full of quasi-true stories, anecdotes, and jokes; a few news stories; a financial page; and columns on fashion, household hints, society news, and so forth. A subscription to the sixteen-page paper cost a dollar a year.

brass "safety lamp": Early fluid-burning lamps were liable to ex- 76 plode when flammable gasses accumulated within partially empty bowls. Many kinds of so-called safety lamps were devised; the most successful were based on Sir Humphry Davy's observation that wire gauze could help prevent the transmission of flame. Safety lamps enclosed the wick in a cylinder of wire mesh extending to the bottom of the bowl; the bowls, and consequently the lamps, were small to prevent gasses from accumulating in large quantities. Lamps were made of glass and a variety of metals such as pewter, tin, and brass.

76 old-fashioned silver-rimmed spectacles: A few silver-framed spectacles were still being sold in the Montgomery Ward catalog of 1895; they were considerably more expensive than most of the commoner steel- or nickel-framed types. Silver frames, being soft, were easily bent out of shape.

78 Vickie's room: Like Vickie's, Cather's childhood bedroom was an enclosed area of the attic; Cather drew upon her memories of it also for Thea's room in *The Song of the Lark* and for Leslie's room in "The Best Years."

79 your feet an' legs is swelled: Edema (swelling) of the legs and ankles can be a symptom of a number of serious diseases. Congestive heart failure, a result of a weakened heart's inability to pump sufficient blood to the lungs and other parts of the body, can cause such swelling, as well as the dizziness and faintness Mrs. Harris also experiences (137). Bright's disease of the kidneys is another possible cause of such symptoms. It also can cause nausea, loss of appetite, and chills and fever.

80 "*The Lord is my shepherd*": Psalm 23.1

80 a young nephew from Chicago: Many young relatives stayed with the Wieners, including two nieces from Chicago, Pauline and Selma Meyer, and two nephews from New York, Adam and Alfred Wiener.

had eight children: Mrs. Boak's obituary reported that she had had   81
nine children, four of whom survived her: sons in Virginia and
Florida, daughters in Virginia and Nebraska. One son, William
Seibert, died fighting for the Confederacy in the Civil War.

her lemon tree, in a tub on the front porch: *Citrus limonia*, native to   82
the Mediterranean area, forms a small tree with fragrant blossoms
and fruit at all times of the year in warm climates. It is very suscepti-
ble to frost; Mrs. Harris grew it in a tub so that it could be taken
inside during the colder months.

black bonnet with a long crepe veil: The bonnet and crepe veil were   84
part of nineteenth-century widows' mourning apparel. A year was
the prescribed period of deep mourning for a spouse, but some
women wore mourning for the rest of their lives.

Decoration Day exercises: May 30 was set aside to honor the Union   84
veterans of the Civil War. In Red Cloud the exercises, as Cather
referred to them in an 1889 letter, usually consisted of a parade of
veterans and officials to the cemetery, with private citizens following in carriages; music; speeches; and the decoration of soldiers'
graves with flowers. These ceremonies were followed by a proces-
sion to the opera house or a church for more music and speeches.

young Mr. Templeton: See the Historical Essay (213) for a discus-   86
sion of Cather's father, Charles Cather, who had some qualities in
common with Mr. Templeton.

the Waverley Novels in German: The great success of Walter   87
Scott's historical romance, *Waverley* (1814), led to his subsequent
novels being later grouped under that name. Scott's complete works
were translated into German in 1826–29, in 1850, and in 1861–69.

87 Coleridge's translation of Schiller's *Wallenstein*: Samuel Taylor Coleridge's translation of the third part of Friedrich Johann Christoph von Schiller's (1759–1805) historical tragedy *The Death of Wallenstein* appeared in 1800, the same year it was published in Germany. The play deals with the career of Albrecht Eusebius von Wallenstein (1583–1634), an Austrian general who was murdered by his officers because they believed he was going over to the enemy in the Thirty Years War.

    While at the university, Cather wrote Louise Pound about rereading *Wallenstein*, which was a favorite of Louise's, and enclosed her own translation of part of a scene; this was before she had begun formal study of German (wc to Louise Pound, 25 June [1893]).

87 Raphael's *Hours*: The painting referred to may be *The Hours of the Day and Night*, an allegorical piece based on classical models which was attributed to Raphaello Sanzio (1483–1520) by many early nineteenth-century critics; it may be by his pupils or assistants.

88 the crops were burned up: This may be another reference to the summer of 1894; see note for p. 41.

88 sand-hills to the south: An area of sandhills (grass-covered dunes left after the vanishing of a great inland sea) lies between Holyoke and Wray, Colorado (see illustration 7).

89 *Wilhelm Meister*: Johann Wolfgang von Goethe (1749–1832) wrote this novel in two parts; *Wilhelm Meister's Apprenticeship* (1795–96) describes the disillusionment of a young man; *Wilhelm Meister's Travels* (1829) completes the story of his education. Both were translated into English by Thomas Carlyle. Much of Book V of the *Apprenticeship* concerns the production of Hamlet by the theatrical troupe to which Wilhelm belongs and discussions of how the roles should be played. *Wilhelm Meister* is named as one of the books that Niel Herbert reads in *A Lost Lady* (1923).

Faust: The story of the German conjurer, Johann Fausten (1488–   90
1541) was the subject of dramas by Christopher Marlowe (c. 1588)
and by Goethe (1808, 1832), as well as of many operas, the most
famous being that by Gounod (1859). The devil, Mephistopheles,
or Mephisto in some translations, attempts to win Faust's soul; his
efforts culminate in Faust's seduction of Gretchen (Marguerite in
the opera) and her death.

Dies Irae hymn: Toward the end of Part I of Goethe's *Faust*, Gret-   90
chen is in the Cathedral while a requiem Mass, of which this hymn is
a part, is taking place. The words, which are based on a prophecy of a
day of wrath and destruction (Zeph. 1.15), are attributed to Thomas
of Celano (c. 1200–55), the biographer of Saint Francis of Assisi.
The first verse of the eighteen-verse hymn reads:

> Dies irae, dies illa,
> Solvet saeclum in favilla,
> Teste David cum Sibylla.

David and the Sibyl: A number of the psalms attributed to David,   90
Israel's greatest king, foretell a coming judgment in words similar
to those of the hymn: "He will crush kings on the day of his wrath. /
He will judge the nations, heaping up the dead" (Ps. 110.5–6). The
Sibyls were priestesses of Apollo; in the Middle Ages their oracular
sayings were believed to have prophesied the life of Jesus. Twelve
were given names and associated with specific events; Cuman is
probably the one referred to in the *Dies Irae*, because she foretold a
Last Judgment.

still wore in a single braid: When a girl was considered to be grown   91
up, which might be as early as the age of sixteen, her status was
signified by pinning her long hair up close to her head. Cather
herself defied these conventions and wore her hair boyishly short
until after her freshman year at the university.

93   a cloak of the sleeveless dolman type: Dolman wraps had no separately cut sleeves seamed to the garment; instead, the arm covering was cut as an extension of the bodice.

93   *Rigoletto*: Rigoletto is the court jester in the opera of that name by Giuseppe Verdi (1813–1901), which was first produced in Venice in 1851 and quickly became one of the standard operas; the libretto was based on Victor Hugo's *Le roi s'amuse* (1832). Mr. Rosen's reference is probably to the traditional parti-colored costume of jesters, which he implicitly compares to the alternate gray and white furs of Mrs. Rosen's cloak.

95   at the extreme north end of town: The fashionable part of Red Cloud was on the north; the socio-geographical distinctions are described in *Lucy Gayheart*, where the north part of the town is called "Quality Street."

96   a hot toddy: Although recipes varied, a hot toddy was basically composed of whiskey or other spirits, mixed with very hot water and sweetened with sugar. The hot water probably accounts for the "smoking goblets" of the toddies on p. 98.

96   hard-coal burner: Heating stoves, which usually were placed in the parlor or sitting room, were made to burn hard or soft coal, wood, or even straw or corncobs. They were generally cylindrical in form, raised on four legs, and often had foot rails on two sides. All but the very cheapest had nickel-plated trim.

96–97   Brussels carpet: These machine-woven carpets often featured large, naturalistic floral designs in shaded colorations; they were relatively cheap and very durable. Woven in wide widths, they could be seamed together for wall-to-wall carpeting; the busy designs helped hide the seams.

292

"Hagar and Ishmael in the Wilderness": Ishmael was the son of Abraham by his wife's handmaid, Hagar. When Sarah, Abraham's wife, finally bore a son (Isaac), she asked Abraham to drive Hagar and Ishmael out into the wilderness (Gen. 11–12; 21.9–21). Paintings on religious subjects, such as this one by Paolo Veronese (1528–88), were frequently reproduced for home decoration. 97

"The Light of the World": This popular painting (1854) by William Holman Hunt (1827–1910), one of the most successful of the Pre-Raphaelite artists, depicts Christ with a lantern, knocking at a door. Hunt specialized in depictions of biblical scenes, which were very popular and much reproduced in the nineteenth century. The title comes from Matthew 5.16: "Ye are the light of the world." 97

cottonwood trees: Both *Populus sargentii*, the plains cottonwood, and *Populus deltoides occidentalis*, the eastern cottonwood, are natives that grow rapidly into large trees even in the harsh conditions of the plains. The name comes from the cotton-like tufts of down at the base of the seeds. Cather was fond of cottonwoods and was distressed when later generations began cutting down the ones treasured by the pioneers. 99

the Roadmaster: The division roadmasters of a railroad were responsible for the construction and maintenance of their section of track— usually about 100 miles of single track, fewer on heavily traveled routes— and supervision of all the workmen. Red Cloud's roadmaster in the late 1880s was E. F. Highland (see note on Mr. Holliday, p. 74). 99

to turn on the sprinkler at the right hours: Watering was allowed for two hours in the evening and two hours in the early morning, although it appears from the newspapers that these restrictions were often ignored. 99

293

100   they didn't have city water . . . (it was expensive): The water rates set in 1887, when municipal waterworks were put in, made a charge of $6.00 a year for houses with fewer than eight rooms. Taps for lawn sprinklers were $2.00 a year for the first twenty-five-foot lot, and $1.00 for each additional lot (*Argus*, 8 September 1887). The yard of the Cathers' house included several lots.

100   iron hoops: Hoops, circles of wood or iron, were popular children's playthings; the object was to keep the hoop rolling upright, pushing or guiding it by hand or with a stick.

100   a deep ragged ditch: In the summer of 1887 the Cather children and their playmates, the Miner children, constructed a play town, Sandy Point, made of packing boxes in the Cather yard; one of the first projects was building a bridge over the ditch in the Cather yard so that Margie Miner's wagon could be brought across. Cather's brothers, Douglas and Roscoe, were the builders (Bennett 172-73).

101   Cheyenne: A Burlington Railroad line reached Cheyenne, the capital of Wyoming, in 1887, via Holyoke and Sterling, Colorado; Cheyenne was an important city on the original Union Pacific line also.

102   the Adirondacks in summer: The Adirondack mountain region of northern New York state, west of Lake Champlain, had become a favorite summer resort area by the mid-nineteenth century. Although much of the area was, and is, wilderness, hotels were built on the chain of lakes that runs through the center, and summer "camps" were built by the wealthy.

102   the poor Maude children: No prototype has been found for this family.

Klondike: Gold was discovered in the remote Klondike River area 104
of Canada's Yukon Territory in August 1896; the great rush began
in 1897. The allusion suggests that Cather is setting the story in the
early twentieth century, although nothing else conflicts with the
early 1890s, Cather's own growing-up years. Cather introduced the
Klondike gold rush in *My Ántonia* also, with the story of Tiny
Soderball, who made her fortune there.

how much prettier their mother was: Dr. Elmer A. Thomas, a con- 105
temporary of Cather's in Red Cloud, wrote that it was said "the
Cather children boasted of their mother being the 'only lady in
town,' in that she had servants to do all her work. This made us
curious to see the mother, and sure enough, her toilet and dress
along with a haughty air, substantiated in our minds this alleged
superiority complex"; he added that years later he found Mrs.
Cather to be "underneath that haughty attitude, quite human and
very likeable" (*80 Years in Webster County* [Hastings, Nebr.: n.p.,
1953], 112).

Mrs. Jackson, a neighbor: No prototype has been identified; how- 105
ever, Mrs. Jackson shares some characteristics with Mrs. Livery
Johnson in *The Song of the Lark*, who is identified by John March as
being based on Mrs. George Gates, a wctu member whose husband kept a livery stable. The Cathers' next-door neighbors (see p.
143) in the 1880s and 1890s were the M. B. McNitts.

Woman's Relief Corps: The women's auxiliary (founded 1881) of 108
the Grand Army of the Republic was composed of the wives, widows, and mothers of Union veterans of the Civil War. It raised
money to give aid (relief) to needy veterans and their families, and
to promote patriotism. The Red Cloud chapter was installed in
May 1884; Mrs. Antoinette McNitt, the Cathers' next-door neighbor, was elected first vice president.

108   Woman's Christian Temperance Union: This national organiza-
       tion was founded in 1874 to work for the abolition of alcohol sales.
       It became the largest women's group in the country: by 1892 it and
       its auxiliaries had over 200,000 dues-paying members, who were
       mostly Protestant and middle class (Ruth Bordin, *Women and Tem-
       perance: The Quest for Power and Liberty 1873–1900* [Philadelphia:
       Temple U P, 1981]).

109   butchering- and preserving-time: Preserving time began in sum-
       mer, as fruits and vegetables ripened ready for canning, drying, or
       making pickles and jams; butchering time was usually late fall, when
       cooler weather would help to keep meat from spoiling as it was
       being dried, smoked, or otherwise preserved. Of course, an animal
       might be butchered for immediate use at any time of year.

111   a mining company in the mountains of southern Colorado: The
       mining towns of southern Colorado, although less well known than
       those in the central part of the state, produced gold and silver from
       the late 1860s on. Before his marriage in 1872, Cather's father,
       Charles, went West and traveled extensively in Colorado and New
       Mexico. This period in the Templeton family's life corresponds
       roughly with the two years the Cather family spent on the farm in
       northwestern Webster County.

111   nearly died when Ronald was born: Mildred Bennett, in "The
       Childhood Worlds of Willa Cather" (*Great Plains Quarterly* 2 [fall
       1982]: 206), reported that Mrs. Cather lost a baby and was very ill in
       the summer of 1883, not long after the family moved from Virginia
       to the farm in northern Webster County. The county newspapers
       reported that Mrs. Cather was an invalid in the summer of 1884.
       Her health may have played a part in the decision to move to Red
       Cloud, where medical help was readily available. Willa Cather her-

296

self was said to have contracted an illness similar to polio while living there. See L. Brent Bohlke, *Willa Cather in Person* (Lincoln: U of Nebraska P, 1986), 129.

between Wray and Cheyenne: Wray, near the Colorado-Nebraska   111
border, is on the main line of the Burlington Railroad to Denver; another Burlington line farther north ran through Sterling, Colorado, to Cheyenne in southeastern Wyoming. Cather visited her brother Douglas when he worked for the Burlington in Sterling in 1897 and in Cheyenne after 1898. Her stories "The Affair at Grover Station" (1900) and "A Death in the Desert" (1903) are set in Wyoming. Another brother, James, later had a store in Holyoke, Colorado.

curling-kids: In the days before permanent waves, locks of hair   112
were wound on flexible wires encased in tubes of kid leather; when the hair was wound, the ends of the wires were bent back to hold the curler in place.

broken arches: Fallen arches, sometimes referred to as flat feet, are   114
caused by weakening of foot muscles and lengthening of the ligaments that support the arch; the condition sometimes occurs in those who are forced to stand for long periods of time. Means of treatment in the twentieth century have included arch supports in shoes, casts to force the foot back into shape, exercises, and surgery.

the distemper: Feline infectious panleucopenia is a highly con-   115
tagious viral disease of cats; the virus destroys white blood cells quickly. Death may be due to dehydration from vomiting and diarrhea or from secondary infections. Untreated, cats often die. Vaccination and antibiotics are now used to prevent or treat the disease.

117   railroad velocipede: The railroad velocipedes pictured in such sources as Marshall Kirkman's *The Science of Railways* (1896) were three-wheeled vehicles meant to carry only one person; however, the illustration of a track inspection car in the same text shows a four-wheeled vehicle with a seat in front of an open platform, which could easily have carried three people. Frequent inspection of the track was one of the roadmaster's duties.

117   grasshoppers: Many species of grasshoppers (locusts) are common to both Colorado and Nebraska; members of species of *Melanoplus* and *Dissosteira* are especially abundant. A 1905 text describes the Carolina locust (*Dissosteira carolina*) as the "light brown species seen so frequently along dusty roads." See Leland O. Howard, *The Insect Book* (New York: Doubleday, 1901), 333.

117   rattler: Prairie rattlesnakes (*Crotalus viridis viridis*), which can grow to thirty-eight inches long, were one of the hazards of life on the western plains. *My Ántonia* has an account of the killing of a rattlesnake in Book I, chapter 7.

119   scarlet fever: So-called from the red rash that commonly affects the face and body, this disease was frequently fatal.

119   diphtheria: Fatal in nearly half the number of cases in the late nineteenth century, this contagious disease damages the heart and central nervous system and is often characterized by the buildup of a false membrane lining of the throat that can cause suffocation. There was little effective treatment.

120   the Mexican: Although there are no persons of Mexican birth recorded in the 1885 state census of Red Cloud, Cather recalled a singer who was to become a prototype of Spanish Johnny in *The Song of the Lark* (wc to S. S. McClure, 1 February 1915); the Colo-

rado towns in which Cather visited her brother Douglas would have been more likely than Red Cloud to have had Mexican-American communities.

crooked old willer tree: Although many species of willows grow in moist areas along stream beds in Nebraska and eastern Colorado, the reference to the crooked trunk of this tree suggests the native black willow, *Salix nigra*, which often has a short, bent trunk in contrast to the smoother, more upright growth of many of the other common willows. The black willow grows from twenty to forty feet tall and has dark brown or black bark. Willows, especially the weeping varieties with pendulous branches, are a traditional symbol of grief. **120**

the sand creek: Streams and rivers with sandy bottoms were part of Cather's imaginative landscape; the fictional Sand River Valley is part of the setting of "The Bohemian Girl"; the fictional Sandtown, Nebraska, and Sand City, Kansas, are the settings of other early stories, "The Enchanted Bluff" and "The Sculptor's Funeral," respectively. A sandy creek divides Captain Forrester's place from the town in *A Lost Lady*, and another sandy creek is mentioned in *One of Ours*. **120**

the church conference: Mrs. Boak and the Cather family were Baptists when Cather was growing up. Ministers from the Republican Valley Baptist Association met in Red Cloud in September 1888; visiting ministers usually stayed in private homes to minimize expenses. **122**

Professor Chalmers: No prototype has been identified; however, when Cather was at the University of Nebraska in the early 1890s, she would have known of E. H. Barbour, professor of geology, who led students on geological expeditions to western Nebraska and **125**

299

South Dakota in the summers. Notable collections of fossils were brought to the state museum on campus.

126 the University of Michigan: Founded in 1817 at Ann Arbor, Michigan, this institution became one of the leading public universities of the West. Cather received an honorary degree from the University of Michigan in 1924.

126 light spring-wagon: These light, open wagons were characterized by springs beneath the box; each of the two to four movable seat boards in the box could accommodate two people, making spring wagons an inexpensive means of transporting groups of people.

127 went down to Denver: Vickie would have traveled west to Sterling, then southwest to Denver, the capital of Colorado.

127 a singing top: A hollow metal top with small slits in it will make a humming or singing sound as it spins.

128 walked up and down under the big cottonwood trees: Similarly, in *The Song of the Lark*, Thea paces under the cottonwood trees outside the post office while she awaits the mail from Chicago (Book II, chapter ix).

129 striped blazer: This style was borrowed from men's sports clothes of the time; a picture of Cather and her friend Louise Pound in the early 1890s shows Pound in a striped jacket and Cather in a checked one.

129 clear soups: Probably a bouillon or consommé, both of which involve simmering meat and meaty bones with water, herbs, and seasoning vegetables such as onions for several hours; these ingredients are strained out and the broth is cooled to remove the fat, then clarified with egg whites.

'Le but n'est rien . . .': John March points out that Cather also used   131
this quotation in a 1925 interview (see Bohlke 76) and in her essay
on Thomas Mann. The exact source has not been found.

J. Michelet: The multivolume *Histoire de France*, by Jules Michelet   132
(1798–1874), published 1833–43, is a famous example of Romantic
narrative history.

Uncle Remus stories: Joel Chandler Harris (1848–1908) published   134
Uncle Remus His Songs and His Sayings: The Folklore of the Old Planta-
tion in 1881, *Nights with Uncle Remus* in 1883, and other books.
Harris retells African-American folktales in dialect, in the framework of an African-American man, Uncle Remus, telling stories to
a little boy. The story of Br'er Rabbit, the hero of the tales, and the
briar patch is one of the most famous.

Afternoon Euchre Club: Euchre became very popular in Red   134
Cloud in the 1880s; most card parties at that time were in the
evening, attended by men and women; afternoon card parties for
women only were a later development.

turned her face to the wall: 2 Kings 20.2 reads: "Then he turned his   135
face to the wall and prayed unto the Lord." The phrase came to be
used to show the nearness and acceptance of death, and by extension, to signify despair.

a company of strolling players sing *The Chimes of Normandy*: Based   141
on an 1877 French operetta *Les Cloches de Corneville*, with a score by
Robert Planquette and libretto by Gabet and Clairville, this popular musical had a plot involving a miser, a lost marchioness, hidden
papers, and a castle. In a 1929 letter lamenting the demise of small-
town opera houses, Cather mentioned the Andrews Opera Company's performances of *The Chimes of Normandy*, *The Mikado*, and

other operas and musicals (Bohlke 185). The Andrews Opera Company, considered one of the best on the road, performed in Red Cloud in January 1889 and in July 1893; Cather may also have seen them perform in Lincoln when she was at the university. The company is mentioned in *The Song of the Lark* as well.

141   the Opera house: The Red Cloud Opera House opened in October 1885, over two ground-floor stores on Webster Street, Red Cloud's main street (see illustration 19). Cather's high school graduation ceremonies were held there, and her letter to the *Omaha World-Herald*, mentioned above, expresses her fond memories.

145   another bilious spell: The nausea and vomiting characterizing a bilious attack were thought to be the result of excessive secretion of bile by the liver.

145   Cleveland: Cather told Ferris Greenslet that two of her father's bulls were named Gladstone and Brigham Young (WC to FG, 24 February 1940); their horses may have been named for political figures also.

146   another baby: Cather's younger sister Elsie was born in January 1890, before Cather left for university; her brother Jack, the youngest, was born in 1892.

146   handkerchief soaked in camphor: Extracted from the camphor tree (*Cinnamomum camphora*), camphor was used for the treatment of pain and in a variety of other ways.

148   irrigated from the South Platte: The South Platte River supplies water for irrigation along its path in northeastern Colorado, the area between Wray and Cheyenne (111) where Skyline is located. The text originally read "North Platte" but the North Platte River flows southeast from central Wyoming into Nebraska; it meets the

South Platte River at North Platte, Nebraska, forming the Platte River.

an old German couple: No prototype for Mr. and Mrs. Heyse has 148 been identified; however, Charles Cather owned a number of farms in various parts of Webster County which he rented to various tenants.

bananas and such delicacies: Regular shipments of bananas from 148 Central America to the United States began in 1872; because of their perishability they remained an exotic and expensive fruit for many years, especially in the Midwest, far from the ports of entry.

honeysuckle vines: There are many species of *Lonicera*, a few native 149 to Nebraska and Colorado; however, a vine trained on a front porch might be a non-native ornamental, possibly a variety of *L. semper-virens*, the trumpet honeysuckle, noted for its clusters of long red and yellow flowers in late May on vines growing to fifteen feet long. In the southern states its leaves are evergreen. Cather may have known of this plant both in Virginia and in Red Cloud, where a specimen was collected for the University of Nebraska herbarium in the early twentieth century.

into the grass country: The town of Skyline is in a hilly area where 149 little but sagebrush (148) grows; the character of the land in this part of Colorado changes as one nears the South Platte River into rolling grassy pasture land and then into the river valley where irrigation made successful farming possible.

"Old Jesse was a gem'man, / Way down in Tennessee": Dorothy 149 Scarborough, in *On the Trail of Negro Folk Songs* (1925), published a humorous song called "One cold and frosty mornin'," the chorus of which ran, "Old Jesse was a gemman, / Among de olden times."

That version was collected from Alabama and was said to have been sung on plantations before the Civil War. Possibly Cather heard the version in the text in Virginia, where a reference to "way down in Tennessee" would be more appropriate geographically than in Alabama. Although the chorus has no relationship to the rest of the text, the first lines of the second verse as printed by Scarborough are of interest in view of Vickie's need for college money:

> Nigger never went to free school,
> Nor any odder college,
> And all the white folks wonder whar
> That nigger got his knowledge.

149 had her father's office to herself: Cather had a desk in her father's loan office on the second floor of a Webster Street store. An 1888 letter expressed her attachment to her place there; she tended the office in her father's absence, and read and studied (wc to Mrs. Stowell, 31 August 1888).

150 wooden cracker-box: Grocery and general stores sold crackers and other goods in bulk, packed in wooden boxes or barrels. When the box was empty, the storekeeper might give it to a favored customer to make room for the next box. See also the more general "goods-box," p. 66.

151 *Joe's Luck*: *Joe's Luck; or, a Boy's Adventures in California*, by Horatio Alger Jr. (1832–99), was serialized in the *New York Weekly* in 1878 and published in paper covers in 1887 as volume 1 of A. L. Burt's Boys Home Library series. As the subtitle indicates, it is one of Alger's stories of western life, although the plot is similar to those of his stories of rags-to-riches in New York. Joe is robbed of his small inheritance by a villain who later attempts to cheat him of the fortune Joe subsequently finds in the gold mining camps.

the second part of *Pilgrim's Progress*: John Bunyan (1628–88) wrote   151
his allegory, *The Pilgrim's Progress from This World to That Which Is
to Come*, in two parts; the first, which follows Christian's journey to
the heavenly city, was published in 1678; the second, which describes the journey of his wife Christiana, her children, and her
friend Mercy, was published in 1684. Cather knew the book well
from her childhood: she owned a copy that was No. 14 in her
"Private Library"; a 1903 article on Cather said she had read it
through eight times in one winter on the ranch in Webster County
(Bohlke 3). A later article adds that she studied the story with her
grandmother — Mrs. Boak, who lived with the Cather family, rather
than her grandmother Cather — and tells how she and her brother
developed the story into a board game that the whole family played
(Bohlke 129). The Cather family library, preserved in Red Cloud,
also contains a copy of Bunyan's *A Relation of the Holy War*; the
inscription shows it was a Christmas present "To Grandma Boak
from Willa."

"Then said Mercy . . .": Mercy was a young neighbor of Christiana,   152
who asks to be allowed to come on the journey; she later married
Christiana's eldest son, Matthew. As the group toils up the Hill of
Difficulty, their guide, Mr. Greatheart, warns them not to sit down
on the wayside but promises that they can rest in the Prince's arbor
when they reach the top, where Mercy's words are spoken.

out of the press: a clothespress, a wardrobe.   154

"Two Friends"

sea-gulls: Of the estimated forty-three species of gulls, with their   161
wide range of habits and habitats, Cather may be thinking of the

kittiwakes (*Rissa tridactyla*), gray-mantled gulls with black wing tips. The common kittiwake is an ocean bird, spending the fall and winter at fishing grounds miles offshore, sometimes following fishing boats and even crossing the Atlantic. In the spring kittiwakes build their nests in great colonies on the ledges of ocean-facing cliffs on the coasts of Canada. A similar passage in *Shadows on the Rock*, Book V, chapter 3, reflects on the rocks to which birds and humans cling.

161 ride the storm: This phrase recalls William Cowper's verse in "Light Shining Out of Darkness," one of the Olney Hymns:

> God moves in a mysterious way,
> His wonders to perform.
> He plants his footsteps in the sea,
> And rides upon the storm.

161 the invention of the motor-car: No one person, place, or event can be credited with the "invention" of the automobile. The relatively light weight of internal combustion engines, developed in the 1860s and 1870s, made self-propelled vehicles practical. Karl Benz and Gottfried Daimler began producing gasoline-powered automobiles in Germany in the 1880s, Panhard began production in France in 1891, and the Duryea brothers established the first American automobile manufacturing plant in 1895.

161–62 the War: World War I (1914–18) made extensive use of gasoline-powered technology for transport trucks, ambulances, airplanes, and early tanks, making it the first "modern" war. The many changes in ways of life and thought in the 1920s were often seen as a result of the war.

Waterloo: Napoleon was finally defeated by the British near this   162
Belgian town in 1815; the German army invaded Belgium, which
had been guaranteed neutrality by Germany and the other European powers, on 4 August 1914, beginning World War I.

in a little wooden town . . .: The town of Singleton (see p. 168) is   162
based on Red Cloud, where Cather and the two men who served as
prototypes for the two friends lived. Like Singleton, Red Cloud was
composed mostly of wooden buildings, although two blocks of the
main street had many brick store buildings by the late 1880s. Red
Cloud was also in a shallow river valley, that of the Republican
River.

Singleton was once the name of a Kansas town in Cherokee
County, in the southeast corner of the state; it was named for Ben-
jamin Singleton, a former slave who encouraged thousands of ex-
slaves to settle in the state. The town later was renamed Baxter
Springs (John Rydjord, *Kansas Place Names* [Norman, Okla.: U of
Oklahoma P, 1972], 202).

Cather had used the name Singleton as the surname of a character in *My Mortal Enemy* when it was serialized in *McCall's*; the name
was changed to Esther Sinclair in the first edition (1926).

St. Joseph: Founded as a French fur-trading post on the Missouri   162
River, St. Joseph grew rapidly as a commercial and cultural center
in the mid–nineteenth century as the United States expanded westward; however, it was superseded by Kansas City to the south before the end of the century.

Chicago: Chicago dominated the midwestern scene, commercially   162
and culturally; the leading merchants, like J. L. Miner and Charles
Wiener, went there for goods for their stores. Those hungry for
culture and art, like Cather's Thea Kronborg and Lucy Gayheart,
went there to study.

162   R. E. Dillon: Cather based Dillon on her memories of James Louis
       Miner (1847–1905), always known as J. L. Miner (see the Histor-
       ical Essay, p. 217, and illustration 22). Like Robert Emmett (see
       below), Dillon is a name associated with Irish patriotism. John
       Blake Dillon (1816–66) escaped to the United States after the Ris-
       ing of 1848; his son John Dillon (1851–1927), an agrarian reformer
       and member of Parliament, was prosecuted by the British and came
       to the United States several times in the 1880s to raise money for
       the Irish cause; a grandson, James Dillon (1902–84), who studied in
       Chicago at one time, was elected to the Irish Parliament in 1932
       and later served as Minister of Agriculture.

163   Robert Emmett: Emmett (1778–1803), an Irish patriot, was ex-
       ecuted by the British for his part in an 1803 rebellion; his speech
       from the dock became famous, especially the part beginning "Let
       no man write my epitaph." Cather knew Robert Emmett Moore,
       known as R. E. Moore, of Lincoln, who owned a Red Cloud bank in
       the 1880s and employed C. F. Cather in his investment company in
       the 1890s.

163   the Caw: The Caw or Kaw River is an unofficial name for the
       Kansas River, which flows east into the Missouri River near Kansas
       City. The Republican River, which flows through Cather's Webster
       County, joins the Kansas River near Junction City, Kansas. One of
       the main lines of the Santa Fé Railroad followed the Kansas River
       between Kansas City and Topeka, where it turned south to Em-
       poria.

163   J. H. Trueman: This character was inspired by Cather's remem-
       brance of William Newman Richardson (1839–1914), usually
       known as W. N. Richardson; see the Historical Essay (220). The
       name may have been a recollection of a Red Cloud minister of the

1890s, the Rev. O. H. Truman, who edited a Populist-leaning local newspaper, *The Nation*. Cather also used the name Trueman in *One of Ours* (1922) for the army doctor on board the troopship that takes Claude to France.

Buffalo: Buffalo, an important commercial and shipping center in western New York, is on Lake Erie, not far from Richardson's birthplace in Dunkirk, which is also on the shore of Lake Erie.   163

Dillon's bank and general store: The People's Bank, with a capital of $15,000, opened in September 1893, after the failure of Silas Garber's Farmers and Merchants Bank (see *A Lost Lady*, p. 78); it was at first housed in the rear of the Miner Bros. store, with a separate door opening on to Third Street (see illustration 22), and later moved into the building next door. J. L. Miner and his brother Hugh built the first brick store building in Red Cloud in 1883; with later additions it extended about 100 feet back to the alley. The local papers described the store as having the largest business in the Republican Valley.   164

on this cross street, two short blocks away, my family lived: The Cather family lived on the southwest corner of Third and Cedar, the second block west of the store at Third and Webster; the Miners lived on the next block, at Third and Seward (see illustration 19).   164

open until ten o'clock: Stores stayed open late to accommodate customers who worked during the day; in "The Best Years" (1945) Cather shows a boy doing his Christmas shopping at 11 P.M. Christmas Eve.   165

buckboard: A light four-wheeled carriage, useful especially on rough roads, was characterized by a flexible lattice or board framework in place of a body and springs; in the late nineteenth century the springy wood framework was supplemented with metal springs.   165

165   steam thrasher: In the days before tractors, a large (and expensive) stationary steam engine powered the thresher, the machine that separated the straw from the grain. Cather spells the word as it is pronounced in the Midwest.

167   billiard-hall proprietor, . . . the horse-trader, . . . the dandified cashier: No specific prototypes have been identified.

167   the crooked money-lender: Cather may be thinking of money-lender Mathew R. Bentley, prototype for Wick Cutter in *My Ántonia*; she described Cutter as a gambler, and one of the Red Cloud newspapers called Bentley a "devotee of gambling" (*Golden Belt*, 3 April 1896).

168   Kansas City: Chartered as a city in 1853, Kansas City, Missouri, quickly became a railroad hub, with more than 50,000 miles of track converging on it. It was a center for the livestock and grain trades, as well as for wholesale goods of all kinds; Miner and Richardson, prototypes of the main characters, shipped livestock to Kansas City.

168   Santa Fé train: The Atchison, Topeka, and the Santa Fé Railroad, chartered in 1859, was a major carrier in Kansas. Two of its lines met at Topeka, one going northeast to St. Joseph, Missouri, the other going east to Kansas City via Lawrence, along the course of the Kansas (Caw) River.

168   the Limited: Ordinary passenger trains stopped at any station that signaled; consequently they were never able to get up much speed. Limited trains, pioneered by the Pennsylvania Limited in 1882, consisted of a few luxurious Pullman Palace cars, a dining car, a sleeper-lounge-observation car, and a baggage-smoker car. This comparatively light load enabled the locomotive to maintain a top

speed of about 60 miles per hour between the relatively few scheduled stops. Being able to command the Limited to make an un-
scheduled stop would be a sign of importance.

Puck: This illustrated humor magazine was published in New York   173
from 1877–1918.

wild plum blossoms: *Prunus americana* and *P. mexicana* are both   174
native wild plums in Nebraska; see note for p. 41 for the former. *P.*
mexicana flowers in late April and is not so apt to grow in thickets as
P. americana.

box-elder trees: *Acer negundo*, the ash-leaved maple, is a hardy,   175
drought-tolerant native tree.

an occultation of Venus: Although to the narrator's eye the "star"   176
(actually the planet Venus) appears to be passing into the moon, an
occultation is actually the temporary disappearance of a star or
planet behind the disc of the moon or a planet; "eclipse" is the name
given to the special cases of an occultation of the sun when the
moon passes between the earth and the sun, or of the moon when
the earth passes between the moon and the sun. Occultations of the
planets are not rare, although opportunities to see them depend on
weather and location. Some summer-occurring occultations of
Venus within the time period of the story were in August 1888, June
and July 1889, June 1891, May 1894, June and July 1895.

The typescript and magazine versions and the first printing of
this story called the phenomenon a "transit of Venus," which may
account for Mr. Dillon's remark that the narrator might never see it
again; transits of Venus — the passage of Venus across the face of the
sun — occur in pairs, separated by eight years, with more than 100
years between each set. Cather may have seen the last transit of
Venus in Virginia when she was nine years old; it was visible over

311

the entire eastern half of the United States in December 1882. It is more likely Cather is referring to an occultation that she witnessed in Red Cloud; Edith Lewis notes that the townspeople had erroneously called it a transit of Venus (*Willa Cather Living* [New York: Knopf, 1952], 161). After her attention was called to the error, Cather changed "transit" to "occultation" in the second printing.

177 about two hundred and fifty thousand miles away from us: At the farthest point in its orbit, the moon is about 250,000 miles from the earth; the mean distance is about 239,000 miles. These distances were known in the nineteenth century: Simon Newcomb, editor of the United States Navy's official Nautical Almanacs, gave a mean distance of 240,000 miles as the distance from the earth to the moon in his *Popular Astronomy* (New York: Harper, 1882). However, in the serial version of the story, Trueman estimated the distance at 300,000 miles, a figure Cather corrected for the first Knopf printing.

178 one fancy house instead of two: When Cather was growing up, Red Cloud had several houses of prostitution; one of the long-established ones was that of Fanny Fernleigh, on the northwest edge of town. Another was known as "the house on the flats," on Fourth Avenue on the eastern edge of town. Mrs. Barton, Jim Johnson, and Nettie Kirk were other names mentioned as proprietors of "bagnios" in the town newspapers of the late 1880s and early 1890s; the periodic campaigns to expel the prostitutes died down in the late 1890s.

179 convent school: Several of J. L. Miner's daughters finished their educations in convent schools associated with Notre Dame in South Bend, Indiana. Miner may well have visited them on his trips

to Chicago. After the death of her mother in 1883, W. N. Richardson's eldest daughter, Winifred, attended school in St. Joseph, Missouri.

Mary Trent: Cather may have been thinking of Red Cloud's Fanny 179
Fernleigh. According to John March's sources, Fernleigh had been
a music teacher in Lincoln before coming to Red Cloud and had a
well-bred, dignified manner. Fernleigh has also been suggested as a
prototype for Nell Emerald, the unusual Denver madam in *A Lost
Lady*.

Hamlet: This tragedy was reverenced in the nineteenth century as 180
the greatest of Shakespeare's plays. Cather's second published essay,
"Shakespeare and *Hamlet*," appeared in the *Nebraska State Journal*
in two parts (1 November 1891 and 8 November 1891) when she
was a freshman at the University of Nebraska.

Pinafore: *H. M. S. Pinafore*, a comic opera by William Schwenck 180
Gilbert (1836–1911) and Arthur Seymour Sullivan (1842–1900),
was first produced in London in May 1878 and ran for nearly two
years. It was quickly pirated and produced in America.

Kansas City Star: William R. Nelson founded the *Evening Star* in 180
Kansas City in 1880 as a concise, newsy paper for the masses. It
soon became a regional newspaper.

Edwin Booth is very sick: Edwin Booth (1833–93), renowned for 180
his Shakespearean roles, especially that of Hamlet, was considered
the greatest actor of his day. He came of an acting family that
included John Wilkes Booth, who assassinated Abraham Lincoln.
Edwin Booth toured extensively in the 1880s; in April 1888 he
appeared in Omaha, where Cather's parents went to see him. (In
My Ántonia the hotelkeeper, Mrs. Gardner, goes to see Booth in

313

Omaha.) When Booth died the obituary that appeared in the *Red Cloud Chief* (16 June 1893) noted that his first serious illness had been in April 1889, forcing his retirement from the stage; he was very ill again in the summer of 1892.

180   *Richard the Second*: Booth was acclaimed by the critics for his interpretation of Shakespeare's weak yet royal king, who is assassinated by his own subjects, but the play has never been a popular one. Although it is possible that W. N. Richardson saw Booth in the role at some point, it would not have been before he came to Webster County in 1870; Booth first played the role in 1875.

Cather may have had a special interest in the play; when she formed the Shakespeare Club to help the Menuhin children gain a better understanding of the English language and literature, she chose *Richard II* as the first reading (Robert Magidoff, *Yehudi Menuhin: The Story of the Man and the Musician* [London: Hale, 1956], 166).

180   Mary Anderson: Mary Anderson (1859–1940) made her debut in 1875 and retired from the stage in 1889. Cather never saw her perform, but "our Mary," as she was affectionately known by many Americans, was one of the great stars during Cather's youth. She was one of the first American actresses to be acclaimed in Europe. In *My Ántonia* the traveling salesmen at the hotel talk of Anderson's great success in London in *A Winter's Tale*, which ran for 164 nights in 1887.

182   the free-silver agitation: The Coinage Act of 1873 had prohibited the production of silver dollars, thus reducing the actual supply of money available in the country. "The free and unlimited coinage of silver at the ratio of sixteen to one" was the demand of the advocates of cheap money, who believed that returning to silver money would

restore prosperity; an increased supply of money would lead to greater demand — and higher prices — for goods, particularly the agricultural products of the West and South.

Bryan: William Jennings Bryan (1860–1925) was born in Illinois and came to Lincoln, Nebraska, in 1887 and was elected to the House of Representatives in 1890. He was nominated for president at the Democratic convention in Chicago in July 1896 and was supported by the Populists as well (see note for p. 184). Although he lost, he was renominated in 1900 and 1908. He later served as Woodrow Wilson's secretary of state, resigning in protest over the United States' entry into World War I. 182

Bryan was a prominent figure in Lincoln when Cather was at the University of Nebraska, and she had opportunities to hear him speak, most notably at the funeral of Congressman William Mc-Keighan in Red Cloud in December 1895, which she called "the greatest speech of his life" (*The World and the Parish* 788). She wrote articles about Bryan and his wife for magazines in Pittsburgh in August 1896 and July 1900; these are reprinted in Curtin's *The World and the Parish*.

Grover Cleveland: Cleveland (1837–1908), who was not running for re-election in 1896, was the only Democrat to be elected president between 1860 and 1912 and the only president to be elected to two nonconsecutive terms: 1884–88 and 1892–96; he was defeated by Benjamin Harrison in 1888. Cleveland had acted to maintain the gold standard in 1893 by calling Congress into special session to repeal the Sherman Silver Purchase Act, which he felt had seriously depleted the gold reserves of the country. This move split the Democratic party. 183

183 Patrick Henry's: Patrick Henry (1736–99) championed the cause of the American colonists. His most famous speech, on 23 March 1775, called for armed resistance to the British. It climaxes in the lines, "Is life so dear, or peace so sweet, as to be purchased at the price of chains and slavery? Forbid it, Almighty God! I know not what course others may take, but as for me, give me liberty or give me death!"

184 Pops: This was a slangy and somewhat pejorative term for members of the Populist Party, which championed the rights of ordinary people against big business, which had come to be aligned with the Republican Party. One of the most successful third parties in American history, the Populists in the early 1890s capitalized on the economic distress of the times and elected many officials even in formerly Republican Nebraska and Webster County.

184 "press . . . gold": A resolution before the Democratic Party convention of 1896 repudiated free silver; Bryan was one of the speakers asked to close the debate. His attack on the gold standard culminated in these ringing words: "Having behind us the commercial interests and the laboring interests and all the toiling masses, we shall answer [the financiers'] demand for a gold standard by saying to them, you shall not press down upon the brow of labor this crown of thorns. You shall not crucify mankind upon a cross of gold." The aroused delegates nominated him for president; the speech was reprinted in newspapers across the country.

Bryan's famous lines were quoted correctly in the *Woman's Home Companion* and in the Autograph Edition. The order of the first phrase is reversed in extant typescripts and in the Knopf edition, reading: " 'You shall not press this crown of thorns upon the brow of labor.' "

part in politics: On 21 August 1896, the *Webster County Argus* noted   185
that J. L. Miner, just back from Chicago, was saying that Bryan was
doing well in Illinois. The next week (28 August 1896) the same
paper reported that W. N. Richardson was back from Chicago,
claiming that Illinois was for McKinley.

Bryan Club: The *Red Cloud Chief* and the *Webster County Argus*   185
reported that a "good-sized" Bryan Club as well as a 123-member
McKinley and Hobart Club, were organized the previous weekend
(7 August 1896).

Bryan Ladies' Quartette: The *Webster County Argus* mentioned the   185
Bryan Ladies' Quartette on 4 September 1896 and noted that
efforts were being made to start a McKinley Ladies' Quartette.

the Merchants' National: The name of this bank may be a com-   186
bination of the names of two then-defunct Red Cloud banks, Silas
Garber's Farmers and Merchants Bank (see note for *A Lost Lady*, p.
78) and the First National Bank, which had belonged to the Moore
family, friends of the Cathers. The new Webster County Bank
became the main rival of the People's Bank until their eventual
merger in 1933.

Hanna and McKinley: Mark A. Hanna (1837–1904), a wealthy and   187
politically active Ohio businessman, engineered the nomination of
Ohio governor William McKinley (1843–1901) as the Republican
candidate for president in 1896. McKinley took little active part in
the campaign, which Hanna managed. The vice presidential candidate was Garret A. Hobart (1844–99) of New Jersey.

Cather was impressed by McKinley, who was already being
mentioned for the presidency in 1894, when he came to Lincoln to
speak. As she wrote in her column, "He has a repose of carriage and
a clear, untroubled face seldom found among the restless, nervous

317

politicians of the Nineteenth century" (*Nebraska State Journal*, 7 October 1894, 13:1).

188 Mr. Dillon died: In the story this would have occurred by 1900, the time of the next presidential campaign. J. L. Miner died in May 1905 in Eureka Springs, Arkansas, where he had gone for his health after an illness of some months.

188 of pneumonia: Before the advent of antibiotics, this disease of the lungs was often fatal.

189 his confidential man: Richardson's chief assistant was Samuel Temple.

189 San Francisco: At the time Cather wrote, San Francisco was California's largest and most important city. She had spent some time there in 1931, when she received an honorary degree from the University of California at Berkeley, and at one time even considered living there herself.

189 sold out everything: W. N. Richardson offered his property for sale in June 1904, nearly a year before J. L. Miner's death. However, no sale was made at the time; a few years later he did sell out, and moved to a smaller property in the north part of Red Cloud, where he lived until his death.

189 a red seal, . . . the piece of carnelian: Carnelian, a red or reddish-brown quartz, has been valued as a jewel since ancient times when it was believed to protect the wearer from evil spirits and weapons; it was often cut into signets and intaglios.

190 the Saint Francis Hotel when it was first built: This famous luxury hotel, first built in 1904, is on Powell Street, facing Union Square. It was rebuilt and enlarged after much of it burned in the San Francisco earthquake of 1906.

what is now Powell Street: According to old maps, Powell Street   190
has always run roughly north–south from the Embarcadero (the
wharf area) through downtown San Francisco to Market Street.

a man whose offices were next his: The first of the surviving type-   190
scripts specified that it was "one of the Huntingtons," presumably
one of the family of California railroad barons.

eucalyptus trees: Eucalyptus, known as the gum tree because of the   190
resinous sap, is native to Australia and a few other countries of the
western Pacific. Some eucalyptus species were introduced into California about 1870; in the 1880s the Tasmanian blue gum tree (*E.*
globulus) was widely planted and quickly became naturalized. These
trees grow to 150 feet tall, with bluish, fragrant foliage and peeling
bark.

ferry-boats: Ferries have transported foot passengers, trains, and   190
later automobiles from the areas across San Francisco Bay from the
mid–nineteenth century up to the present. The Ferry Building, a
San Francisco landmark at the foot of Market Street, was the central terminal for the major ferry lines.

he died about nine years after he left our part of the world: W. N.   190
Richardson died in 1914, about nine years after J. L. Miner's death.

Textual Apparatus

Textual Essay

THIS fifth volume of the Cather Edition presents a critical text of Willa Cather's fifteenth book and her third volume of shorter fiction, *Obscure Destinies*. The book comprises three stories, "Neighbour Rosicky," "Old Mrs. Harris," and "Two Friends," all of which were also published in popular magazines. The first edition in book form was published by Alfred A. Knopf on 1 August 1932.[1] A typescript of "Old Mrs. Harris" and two typescripts of "Two Friends" have recently come to light and have been used in preparing this edition.[2] They permit an unrivaled look at Cather's revising process. No manuscript, typescript, or proof of "Neighbour Rosicky" has been located. The first British edition was published by Cassell in 1932; a Tauchnitz edition appeared in Germany in 1933. The book is included in volume 12 of the Autograph Edition of Cather's works, which appeared in March 1938. No other editions in English were published during Cather's lifetime.

Our editorial procedure is guided by the protocols of the Modern Language Association's Committee for Scholarly

Editions. We begin with a bibliographical survey of the history of the text, identifying any problems it may present. Making a calendar of extant texts, we collect and examine examples of all known texts produced during Cather's lifetime, identifying those forms that might be authorial (i.e., that involved or might have involved Cather's participation or intervention). These forms are then collated against a base text serving as a standard of collation. The collations provide lists of substantive and accidental variations among these forms. A conflation, constructed from the collations, then produces a list of all substantive changes in all relevant (authorial) editions. After an analysis of this conflation, we choose a copy-text and prepare a critical text (an emended copy-text).[3] The collations and their conflation also provide the materials for an emendations list, which identifies changes the editors have made in the copy-text, and an historical collation, which provides a history of the text as contained in its various authorial forms. In a separate procedure, we make a list of end-hyphenated compounds with their proper resolution.[4]

This essay includes a discussion of the composition of the book and the production and printing history of the text during Cather's lifetime, an analysis of the changes made in the text during this period, a rationale for the choice of copy-text for this edition, and a statement of the policy under which emendations have been introduced into the copy-text. The reader will note that page and line references in the essay are to the text of this edition, which usually agrees closely with that of K1.

Composition

Cather's writing of the Nebraska stories that would be included in *Obscure Destinies* was interwoven with the composition of *Shadows on the Rock*; the two volumes, though entirely different in setting, pay considerable attention to childhood and to the metaphor of migratory return. Even the epigraphs printed at the end of each of the three stories place them in the movement of their author's life: the text of "Neighbour Rosicky" is followed by "New York, 1928," that of "Old Mrs. Harris" by "New Brunswick, 1931," and that of "Two Friends" by "Pasadena, 1931."

Surviving letters, memoirs, and prepublication forms provide information about the chronology of composition of the three stories that make up *Obscure Destinies*. Their close connections with Cather's childhood and adolescence in Nebraska, and with her later experiences there, are treated at length in the Historical Essay, pp. 199–241. "Neighbour Rosicky" was written in response to the illness and death of Cather's father (March 1928); it could have been begun at the Grosvenor Hotel in the spring of that year, begun at Cather's new cottage on Grand Manan during the summer and finished in New York, or written entirely during the fall at the Grosvenor. Edith Lewis dates the initial work on "Two Friends" and "Old Mrs. Harris" to March–May 1931, the months Cather spent in Pasadena with her mother, who was convalescing in a sanatorium: "She could not work there on *Shadows on the Rock*, but she wrote most of the short story *Two Friends*, and I think began *Old Mrs. Harris* there" (157).

The epigraph to "Two Friends," "Pasadena, 1931," suggests that the story was finished not later than the end of May of that year, when Cather left her mother and visited her brother in Kearney, Nebraska, on her way back to New York.

An interview in the *Kearney Hub* on 2 June 1931 refers to an upcoming collection of short stories, of which "Neighbour Rosicky" was to be one. Although Cather had published several stories after publishing *Youth and the Bright Medusa* in 1920, only "Neighbour Rosicky" was included in what became *Obscure Destinies*. As the interview indicates, however, by June 1931, about the time she finished "Two Friends," she was thinking of the three stories eventually included in the volume as belonging together. A note in her hand, prefixed to the earlier of the two typescripts of "Two Friends" and dated "August 22nd/18th" [1931], asks her secretary, Sarah Bloom, to copy the story as soon as possible, making two carbons, and to send her the original, the new typescript copy, and one of the carbons. In September she sent "Old Mrs. Harris" and "Two Friends" to Alfred Knopf to read "as a favor" (Knopf, Memoirs).

Production and Printing History

The newly discovered typescript of "Old Mrs. Harris" and the two newly discovered typescripts of "Two Friends" allow a rare opportunity to look over Cather's shoulder as she sits at her desk with a text of her work before her. The process is most obvious in the successive typescripts of "Two Friends," where two typescripts, each revised, present four consecutive texts of the short story. We have, from analysis of the extant typescript of *Shadows on the Rock* and the extant galley proof for *Death Comes for the Archbishop*, evidence of Cather's meticulous attention both to substantive and accidental changes; these typescripts confirm our view that she regarded each successive version of her work prior to its publication in book form as essentially a draft capable of further development and improvement. The changes she makes are almost always stylistic; she does not restructure the text and rarely restructures a sentence. She does not introduce new characters or reconceive characters already introduced. Instead, she alters diction and prose rhythm; she replaces a word or a phrase with a different word or phrase, she clarifies and intensifies her sentences and especially her choice of verb, noun, and adjective. She frequently alters punctuation and sometimes word division. Over and over again, she replaces or omits text that might seem to be redundant, to editorialize too much, or to create a dissonance in the presentation of a character. The revisions continue beyond setting-copy into the proof stages: Cather does not hesitate to make numerous late changes to the text, often at her own expense.

Cather's usual practice was to write her books in longhand, then prepare or have prepared one or more typescripts, always revising in the process. Final typescripts were prepared by a professional typist. Although Cather requested that the original typescripts of her books be returned to her after production, and wrote Pat Knopf that she had destroyed those produced before the move from Bank Street, recent discoveries have confirmed that she retained a number of typed drafts. In the case of *Obscure Destinies* and other books that appeared in the magazines, one typescript would have been used for the magazine version and another, revised, for the Knopf edition in book form (Bohlke 41, 76; wc to Pat Knopf, 19 January 1936; wc to Sinclair Lewis, 22 March 1944; Lewis 127).

"Neighbour Rosicky" was first published in the *Woman's Home Companion* in April and May of 1930; "Old Mrs. Harris" in the *Ladies' Home Journal* in September, October, and November of 1932 (under the title "Three Women"); and "Two Friends" in the *Woman's Home Companion* in July of 1932. The latter two stories were sold in September/October 1931; Cather received $15,000 for "Old Mrs. Harris" and $3,500 for "Two Friends." Alfred Knopf noted that these were fine figures in the middle of the Depression (Knopf, Memoirs), and the amounts attest to the magnitude of Cather's reputation at the time. Knopf's edition, with its felicitous title, was published a month before the first installment of the magazine version of "Old Mrs. Harris" appeared — a most unusual arrangement, as magazine publication normally came first.

The magazine versions of the three stories were never reprinted. Production records show that the Knopf edition appeared initially in both a trade issue comprising 25,000 copies and a limited issue of 260 copies. Knopf had hitherto offered two limited issues of Cather books, one more expensive than the other; with this book, he began offering only one such issue, the number of copies determined by orders received (see note 1). Copies of the limited issue were printed on Nihon Japan vellum and specially bound; Cather signed each copy, and the copies were numbered sequentially. There were six printings of the trade edition prior to Cather's death, and one more hardcover printing before the first in paper.

First printing, 1 August 1932, 25,000 copies
Second printing, August 1932, 5,000 copies
Third printing, September 1932, 3,000 copies
Fourth printing, October 1932, 5,000 copies
Fifth printing, December 1932, 2,500 copies
Sixth printing, September 1941, 1,500 copies.

The eighth printing, April 1953, issued as Random House Vintage Books V-179, was reproduced by offset from an image of the first edition. The presswork for the first six printings, as well as that for the Vintage paperback, was done by the Plimpton Press.

It is clear from the above figures that the book did well initially but that sales dropped sharply after the early printings. Knopf notes that "by August tenth we went to press with another five thousand copies . . . and reported a sale of about twenty-three thousand. By August twenty-fifth it had passed twenty-seven thousand. By September thirtieth, thirty thousand" (Knopf, Memoirs). A favorable review by Dorothy Canfield Fisher in the August 1932 *Book of the Month Club News* might have contributed to the early demand for the book, which was an alternate selection. "Neighbour Rosicky" was widely anthologized and "Two Friends" appeared in two anthologies (Crane 248–49); the extent to which the availability of the stories in such collections interfered with later sales of the book cannot be determined.

All seven Knopf printings were executed from the plates of the first edition (K1); the only changes to the text were two plate corrections, at 143.23 and 212.14, made for the second trade impression. This corrected text was reproduced by photo-offset for the Vintage paperback issue of 1953.[5] The Autograph Edition of *Obscure Destinies*, published by Houghton Mifflin, appeared in 1938; the Library "edition" (impression) of this edition, in 1940. No other U.S. edition appeared during Cather's lifetime. Cassell published the first British edition in 1932, after negotiations with Heinemann fell through;[6] a second British "edition" was issued by Hamish Hamilton in 1965; this was printed by offset from the U.S. first printing and is, bibliographically speaking, either a separate issue of the first printing or a subedition of K1, depending on the terminology one uses. Tauchnitz published the novel in 1933 as volume 5108 in its Collection of British and American Authors.

Changes in the Text I: The Typescript of "Old Mrs. Harris"
Various features of the typescript indicate that it is one Cather herself prepared (substantive variants are in her hand) and that it is composed of sheets from two versions of the work. Many typographical errors and false starts are x'ed

out on the typewriter and the correct word typed in immediately afterward. Lines below the bottom margin of a page
are usually crossed out in ink and retyped as the first line of
the following page. No professional typist would have produced copy with so many false starts and errors. On six pages
there are marginal references to page numbers of another
copy of the text (to 11 on 10, 36 on 32, 47 on 44, 53 on 49, 64
on 59, and 73 on 58). These may be references to a closely
written manuscript or to another typescript; the latter is
more probable because the extant typescript is patched: a
five-line page "1½" is inserted after page 1, and several of the
pages show one or more joint lines where a page from another typescript has been cut and pasted in. Five sheets (15,
20, 21, 23, and 27) are approximately of legal size, the result
of cutting and joining; the rest are of standard size.

Further evidence of the use of pages from two versions
can be seen in the many discontinuities between one page
and the next, and in two cases within a single page: one page
of a version sometimes ends after a few words on its last line,
or text is crossed out or added between one sheet and the
other to provide the necessary continuity. There are other
variations as well. The town name Skyline appears three
times in the unrevised form of the typescript as "Topaz Valley" and once as "town," but five times as "Skyline"; the
surname of the Roadmaster appears five times in the unrevised typescript as "Thomas," corrected in Cather's hand to
"Holliday," but twice is typed as "Holliday." The name
Crummer first appears as in K1 (73.13), but at 109.19 the

331

original reading was "Grubb," revised to "Crummer." At 75.26–76.1 the typescript agrees with κ1 in referring to Mandy as "the bound girl they had brought with them from the South"; Mandy is merely named at 111.25, but the typescript lines out "the bound girl, whom they had brought with them." It is reasonable to conclude that these variations result from the use of two different sets of pages to produce the typescript in its present form.

Some additions and corrections have been typed between the double-spaced lines of text, their place indicated by an inked inferior caret or line. The alignment of these corrections suggests that these typed-in changes were made as the text was being typed. The majority of changes, however, were added in ink, the words in Cather's hand, usually with a caret to indicate their desired position; the original, typed readings are lined out in ink. (See illustration 18.)

Some 650 of the revisions made to the original typescript duly appear in κ1. The following are typical examples of accidental variants; the first reading is that of the unrevised typescript, the second, that shared by the revised typescript and κ1:

72.4	kitchen	kitchen,
85.15	dem	them
94.16–17	have, but	have. But
112.3–4	Democracy	democracy
122.23	preacher.	preacher!

Many of the substantive variants involve no more than a word or two; their general effect is often toward the more specific word or the tighter construction, but sometimes Cather simply writes in a synonym. In the following typical illustrations, the reading of the unrevised typescript is given first: "nice" to "good" (85.14), "that she" to "she" (86.8), "a number" to "some" (87.11), "uniform" to "steady" (91.8), "was uncomfortable" to "felt hurt" (107.11), "white" to "flowered" (124.4), "knew that" to "knew" (141.5), and "grateful" to "thankful" (141.16). As is the case in "Neighbour Rosicky," dialect forms are reduced in number, so as to give the flavor of dialect only: Mrs. Rosen's "dis" and "dan" (81.2, 86.2) are often changed to the usual "this" and "than."

Other changes are more substantial. Often, narrative summary or comment is deleted, so that the characters' words and actions are allowed to tell the story, or so that a judgment by the narrator about a character is softened. These sorts of revisions are especially clear when passages in the unrevised typescript are deleted. At 68.25, for example, two sentences about Victoria Templeton are crossed out: "The best of everything that went on the table was her natural tribute. There wasn't much, to be sure, but what there was was Victoria's." At 133.17 a passage about Hillary Templeton is deleted: "He was still very young in experience, and very much afraid of the world, poor Mr. Templeton, but of course his daughter couldn't realize that." A comment about the "absurdities" of the Templetons is deleted at 86.7, as is one about the "flimsiness and confusion" of their house (89.3).

Many of these longer revisions tighten the text or sub-

333

stitute more vivid language: "room near the kitchen door" becomes simply "room" (67.11), "read aloud" becomes "read *Tom Sawyer*" (76.16–17), "corner behind the striped curtain" is reduced to "curtained corner" (84.7), "from a sense of the heat" is shortened to "from the heat" (88.25), "entirely absorbed" becomes "drunk up into" (114.19), and "just a little" sunlight becomes "a flood" (130.9). At 136.8 Mr. Templeton goes to the barn to "fork" down hay instead of to "throw" it down; at 140.10 "dismiss it from your mind" is tightened to "dismiss it."

Although some fifteen longer passages are crossed out in the typescript and also deleted in к1 (see the Historical Collation, pp. 392–434), there are almost 600 differences between the readings of the revised typescript and those of к1, nearly as many as appeared in к1 as indicated. Changes in accidentals account for more than half of these and follow a pattern seen in several other of Cather's works. Punctuation changes account for almost half the accidental variants, changes in spelling and word division for another 20 percent each. There are relatively few changes in capitalization. The punctuation of к1 is generally heavier than that of the revised typescript; there is a strong tendency to hyphenate compounds that appear in the typescript as two words, and the usual change from U.S. to British spelling for such words as "neighbor" and "gray" is made throughout.

Some 40 percent of the differences between the revised typescript and к1 involve substantives. Many affect only a word or two:

66.12	braided	plaited
76.4	unuttered	understood
79.12	shawl	checked shawl
84.6	One	Two
95.23	a handsome	an attractive
103.21	now stepped up to her	now overtook her
107.13	prods	thrusts
110.6	son's	daughter's
148.14	fourteen	eighteen

Other changes are more extensive, altering word order or adding and deleting several words; a few rework a sentence:

78.25	Victoria away	Victoria was off enjoying herself somewhere
87.17–18	rooms, except the kitchen, were covered	rooms were carpeted alike (that was very unusual),
88.3–4	who was not particular as to how he made his living if	who didn't mind keeping a clothing-store in a little Western town, so long as
106.2–3	listening to his pleasant talk	studying Mr. Rosen's pleasant attentions to Mrs. Templeton
131.3–4	He put his hand on her hair and felt her head enquiringly with his fingertips. "I wonder?" He shrugged and asked her playfully, "Why do you want to go to college, Vickie?"	"Why do you want to go to college, Vickie?" he asked playfully.

Three major changes come at the end of the story. In the revised typescript, Mrs. Harris "felt that she and her bed

335

were softly sinking through the darkness to a deeper darkness, in the silence to a more perfect silence." When Mandy
finds her in the morning, the typescript adds "and she never
regained consciousness." K I deletes the phrase about silence
and the addition. No version of the last sentence of the story
("But now I know.") appears in the typescript.

Although no external evidence positions the typescript in
the sequence of prepublication versions of the text, internal
evidence strongly suggests that it is fairly early, predating the
version in *LHJ*. It is almost certainly not the version sent to
Knopf as setting-copy for K I: it is not marked into galleys
and it is most unlikely that Cather would have sent her publisher a patched-together version of her work with more than
600 revisions indicated, only to make almost as many additional changes in the galleys.

It is also unlikely to have been a final draft for that setting-
copy, worked on after another version was sent to *LHJ*: there
are well over 100 substantive or quasi-substantive variants in
the magazine text that do not appear in the typescript, and
more than 75 of these appear also in K I. Had the typescript
come after the magazine text, one would expect it to include
these 75 variants.

A study of the substantive variants between the typescript
and magazine texts also shows that the two texts agree in over
a hundred instances where K I has a different reading. It
seems likely, then, that at least two copies of a professionally
typed version were made from the typescript and that Cather
then went over one copy and made the changes that subse-

quently appeared in *LHJ*, presumably including the last sentence of the story. It is possible that still another draft was prepared from the other copy before Cather sent the book to Knopf to read in early September 1931; this is not likely, however, because of time constraints: Cather was still on Grand Manan, with its twice-weekly mail boats, and her typist was in New York. Within a few weeks Knopf had sold the story to the magazine. Meanwhile, the revising process continued; by the time the book was published, more than 125 additional substantive (and many accidental) changes had been made, some probably on Cather's copy of the latest typescript, some probably on galley and page proofs.

The revised typescript agrees with the *LHJ* text in substantives more than half the time, with the text of K1 roughly 40 percent of the time, and with neither about 3 percent of the time. For accidentals (ignoring the *LHJ* preference for U.S. spelling, word division, and the use of *s'* rather than *s's* to indicate possession), these percentages are approximately 48, 38, and 14. Examples, all substantive, will indicate the situation (the reading of the revised typescript is given first, followed by those of *LHJ* and K1).

68.24–25	else	but herself	but herself
76.25	on grand-mother's bed lounge	on Grand-mother's lap	on Grandmother's lounge bed
79.21	and sitting on her haunches	and sitting on her haunches	and, crouching beside it
88.3	Jew	Jew	man

337

89.26	sitting with	looking at	looking at
101.11	contributed	donated	donated
111.17	altitude	altitude	altitude of that mountain town
117.8–9	came in	came back	got back
133.13	along three	along three	along about three
157.5	know	feel	feel
157.6–7	so strong	and strong,	and strong,

Changes in the Text II: The Two Typescripts of "Two Friends"
These two typescripts (TF1, TF2) constitute a sequence, the second prepared from the first. The earlier one was fairly heavily revised; the later typescript includes most of the changes indicated in the revised version of the earlier but sometimes reproduces the revised text of the first typescript and then changes it, lining out the typed version and substituting new text in ink. The revisions to TF1 are in Cather's hand; those to TF2 are sometimes in Cather's hand but most often in that of Edith Lewis. The two hands are fairly easily differentiated: Cather's hand is bold and she uses thick strokes while Lewis's hand is smaller and neater and she uses thinner strokes. Both hands appear throughout the typescript, sometimes on the same page. Lewis clearly acted at Cather's direction or served as her amanuensis, and it is likely that Cather went over the typescript after Lewis had finished with it: in at least two cases the revision in Lewis's hand is crossed out and another reading supplied by Cather. We

know that Cather and Lewis often read proof together; the evidence of the typescript indicates that they also sometimes collaborated in the transcription of revisions Cather wished to make. Lewis clearly had Cather's full confidence, and Cather entrusted to her the task of looking at the foundry proofs of *Shadows on the Rock* (Lewis 161). We believe that all the revisions to both typescripts have Cather's authority.

The first typescript is paginated in ink pp. [1]–20, and TF2 is paginated in ink 121–44. The numbering suggests that TF2 was part of a typescript excluding "Neighbour Rosicky," although some pages also show separate, typed-in pagination for this particular story (2–6, 8, 14, 19, 21, 23–24). TF2 is marked into galleys, although the divisions do not correspond to the pagination of WHC or K1; the galley numbers begin with 48 (p. 2) and run through 56 (p. 143). Page 140 of TF2 has been retyped.

The four texts of "Two Friends" thus represented in these two typescripts — the unrevised and revised versions of each — form a continuous sequence. Together with the magazine version and the Knopf first edition, they show the evolution of the text, allowing us to see in some detail Cather's approach to revision once her work reached the initial typescript stage. The following discussion of the relation between the revised forms of the two typescripts, the WHC text, and that of K1 is supplemented by the Historical Collation, which lists the substantive variants of all four of the typescript texts as well as those of the authorial printed texts.

As one might expect, the earlier typescript shows more

339

dramatic revision than the later. The earliest reading of line 4 of the first paragraph of the story is "unalterable facts"; the second word was first changed to "feelings" and then to "realities," a sequence that mirrors changes in Cather's attitude toward the world. Other revisions delete editorial comment by the narrator or change the presentation of a character. At 164.3 the statement that at age thirteen "the grown-up people about one are the chief interest in life" is deleted; at 165.8–9, having just said that Dillon "and his store were one," the statement that he "found his store the most interesting place in town" is deleted. At 170.14–15 no one can tell "just what Trueman knew about anything, or how much he knew"; the "what" phrase is deleted but the "how much" one retained. An entire paragraph in the unrevised version of the typescript is deleted after 174.10, a paragraph including description, information about the narrator, and editorializing by the narrator. At 177.23–24 the typescript leaves a blank space before "million," filled in later with "three hundred thousand"; in K1 a more nearly correct figure for the distance between the earth and the moon is supplied. A passage indicating the narrator's interest in *The Two Orphans* is crossed out at 180.7; one unflattering to Dillon is deleted at 185.14. Editorializing is again deleted at 187.12, and a reference to "one of the Huntingtons" is changed to "a man" at 190.8.

Other changes are less dramatic. At 164.24 "established and easy" becomes "established." At 165.12 "clients" is changed to "customers"; at 166.15 "carnelian" to "onyx"; at 174.14 "smell" to "scent"; at 178.22 "convent school" to "convent." Some revisions tighten the prose, eliminate un-necessary words, or supply fresher language: "he waited" to "waited" (180.16), "such a stupid" to "a stupid" (181.24), "I recall that he asked" to "He asked" (184.10–11), "sit" to "sit tilted back" (190.9–10). One group of changes, involving both typescripts as well as other versions of the text, is con-cerned with the description of the very different activities of Dillon and Trueman on their visits to St. Joseph.

There are between 350 and 400 variants between the re-vised versions of the two typescripts, the version in the *Woman's Home Companion*, and the text of K1. Almost two-thirds of these variants involve accidentals. Analysis shows that three patterns of change account for more than 90 percent of these: (1) WHC alters readings common to TF1, TF2, and K1 (36 percent); (2) TF2 alters the reading of TF1 and is followed by the other two texts (33 percent); (3) the readings of TF1 agree with those of WHC, but the readings of TF2 agree with those of K1 (23 percent). In only four cases for each are the readings of TF2 and K1 unique.

More than 80 percent of the substantive variants fall into two classes: (1) TF2 alters the readings of TF1 and is followed by the two other texts (54 percent); (2) the reading of K1 is unique (28 percent). Only about 9 percent of the variants are readings unique to WHC. There is only one instance of the third pattern mentioned above for accidentals, and there are no substantive readings unique to TF2.

Some two dozen variants, about half substantive and half

341

accidental, follow none of these patterns. Most of the accidental variants arise from the fact that the various texts follow different conventions governing punctuation. The substantive variants are more interesting. K I follows TF2 in six instances and agrees with *WHC* against TF I or TF2 or both in five cases. In one case all four texts show different readings. The table below gives two illustrations of each pattern, in sequence; the reading of TF I appears first, followed by those of TF2, *WHC*, and K I:

ACCIDENTALS

161.1	youth,	youth,	youth	youth
171.8	talk, —	talk, —	talk —	talk, —
162.7	Saint	St.	St.	St.
175.8	off,	off	off	off
167.3	mustache	moustache	mustache	moustache
179.13	banks	banks,	banks	banks,
178.9	added	added;	added,	added:
184.24	with "You	with: "You	with, "You	with: "You

SUBSTANTIVES

162.17	chin with	chin cut by	chin cut by	chin cut by
173.24	pretty	nice	nice	nice
174.25	for idleness	for idleness	for idleness	to be quiet
176.13	sandy	sandy	sandy	farming
170.15	knew	knew	could tell	could tell
180.24	long afterward	years afterwards	years afterward	years afterwards
189.2	wrote him a check, and told	wrote him a cheque, and told	wrote a check and told	and told

The galley "takes" are marked on TF2, indicating that it served as setting-copy for K1; hand collation of TF2 against K1 shows that more than two dozen additional changes were made at the proof stage. The relation of the two typescripts to the WHC text is unclear: although there are nearly 100 readings unique to the magazine text, fewer than a dozen of these are substantive, and most of the accidentals result from the U.S. conventions of spelling, punctuation, and word division followed by WHC. It is likely that, following her usual practice, Cather would have made changes at least to any galley proof and possibly to page proof as well.

Changes in the Text III:
The Magazine Versions of the Three Stories

Two texts that are both authorial and belong more or less to the time of first publication in book form remain to be considered: the magazine versions of the three stories and the first printing of the Knopf edition of them under the title *Obscure Destinies*. The variants between these magazine versions and K1 are numerous, often substantive, and significant.

In addition to nontextual features such as three- or four-column format, the presence of illustrations, the use of different typography and somewhat different paragraph and line breaks, and the breaking up of the stories into short blocks of type visually suitable for column format, the magazine versions impose many elements of house styling on the text. Cather's preference for British spellings, evident well before 1930, is ignored: U.S. spellings are used throughout in both magazines. Her predilection for hyphenated compounds is much less apparent in the magazines; these often appear as two words. More noticeable still is the much lighter pointing of the magazine versions.

The ratio of accidental to substantive variants is remarkably consistent: about 3 to 1 for all three stories. There are more than 1,500 variants all told. Many are minor, involving no more than the addition in K1 of a comma absent in the magazine version. Others entail major changes to the text; for example, K1 includes many passages absent in the magazine version of "Old Mrs. Harris." The percentage of accidental variants by category is shown in the table below.

	"Neighbour Rosicky"	"Old Mrs. Harris"	"Two Friends"
Punctuation	46	33	47
Spelling	6	11	10
Word division	7	14	14
Abbreviation	3		
Dialect forms	8		
Case	3	12	3

Some of the variation in the above percentages has to do with the character of the particular story: "Doctor" is often abbreviated in "Neighbour Rosicky," and there are many dialect forms (here counted as accidentals, but included in the Historical Collation when the spelling changes affect meaning) absent in the other two stories. The high percentage of punctuation variants is characteristic; by a factor of

344

better than 9 to 1 the punctuation of the magazine versions is lighter. Spelling variants are accounted for largely by the difference between the U.S. spelling of the magazine versions and the British spelling of K1: "parlor"/"parlour," "neighbor"/"neighbour," "check"/"cheque," and the like. The high percentage of case changes in "Old Mrs. Harris" is primarily the result of the frequent occurrence of "Grandmother" and "Grandma" and their plural, possessive, and contracted forms in that story: these are often set in lower case in the magazines but capitalized in K1. Word division often follows a pattern as well: two words in the magazine versions are often set as hyphenated compounds in K1.

Although the pattern of accidental variation is clear, its significance is less so. One can argue that the heavy pointing of K1 reflects an attempt to suggest the way a phrase or line ought to sound if read aloud, or that the change from an exclamation point to a period, or from a period and new sentence to a semicolon and a continuing sentence, affects sentence rhythm. Convention, however, dictates that such variants be considered accidentals unless the difference in meaning is significant, and we have followed that practice.

The Historical Collation, pp. 377–454, records all substantive variants between and among the unrevised and revised typescripts, the magazine versions of the three stories, and the text of the first printing of the first edition of *Obscure Destinies*. In the discussion that follows, each story is treated separately. When examples are offered, the magazine reading is given first, then that of the first printing of the book (κ1).

In "Neighbour Rosicky," which ran in the *Woman's Home Companion* more than two years before it appeared in *Obscure Destinies*, one clear pattern appears upon analysis of the accidental variants: the WHC version of the story makes much heavier use of dialect forms than does κ1. Rosicky, for example, uses "an'" and "fur" far more consistently in the magazine installments than he does in κ1. The κ1 text gives the flavor of dialect without overloading the reader with repetitive dialect forms; the more selective use of them is emphasized by extending the dialect to include such words as "lookin'" (32.4) and "preservin'" (42.6), which are spelled with the "ing" in WHC.

The substantive variants in the text of "Neighbor Rosicky" are numerous but rarely entail large additions or deletions; the majority of them involve one or two words only. WHC's "treat" is changed to "they treat" at 9.17; "Peter" to "John" throughout; "around" to "round," "You" to "So you" (14.13–14); "standing up" to "stood out" (18.22); "hand" to "fingers" (21.9). The singular "belt" is changed to plural at 29.3, and "afterward" is changed to "afterwards" throughout.

Some twenty substantive variants, about one-third of the total, affect from four or five words to as many as a dozen or more. The following are typical: "you, and you'll have to look on for a while" to "you" (7.12); "one" to "one (he was still living at home then)" (13.24–25); "life and skimp and save" to "life, not to be always skimping and saving" (24.9).

Several of the variants do not so much add or delete information as revise the wording, word order, or rhythm of a passage: "of Bohemian athletic societies in New York" becomes "in New York of Bohemian athletic societies" (30.16–17); "They were all four musical" becomes "All four of them were musical" (36.12).

In subtle ways the revisions sharpen and clarify the characters. For instance, Rosicky doesn't want "trouble," has "an awful bad spell," and can't get to sleep "at all" in WHC; in K1 he doesn't want "no trouble" (32.6), has "a awful bad spell" (55.18–19), and can't get to sleep "noway" (46.8). In WHC he is a "broad-backed little man" who, when in London, had "not a bit" of money; in K1 he is a "short broad-backed man" (24.23) who had not "a damn bit" (45.12) of money. In the magazine version young Rosicky "never thought of living any other kind of life"; in K1 the negative connotation of "never thought of" (Rosicky is unreflective) is eliminated: his life "satisfied him completely" (27.1). Mary Rosicky's "loud voice" bothers Polly in WHC; in K1 Mary exhibits "hearty frankness" (44.18), a positive quality. Rosicky and his family, in the eyes of others, do not "get ahead" in the WHC text, but in K1 they do not "get on" (16.8); the emphasis in the revision is on the path one takes, not on the material goal.

It is obvious both from the number of the substantive variants and from their nature that they are authorial: they are not the kinds of changes an editor would ordinarily make, and compositors at least try to set accurately the copy they receive. The substantive variants in the other two stories are

347

also authorial, with one important exception, discussed in the next section of this essay. Many of those in "Three Women," as the magazine version of "Old Mrs. Harris" was titled when it was published, are similar to those cited for "Neighbour Rosicky": "braided"/"plaited" (66.12); "natural good manners, nice voices, nice faces"/"nice voices, nice faces, and were always courteous, like their father" (74.22–23); "then looked up"/"looked" (98.2); "had nothing to say for himself"/"never had a thing to say" (125.17). Like those in the earlier story, the substantive variants in this one mostly involve one or two words that are added, deleted, or substituted; the two sets of variants are also similar in that many changes revise word order with or without changes in the words themselves.

The pattern of substantive variants between the magazine version of "Two Friends" and K1 is similar to that for "Neighbour Rosicky." Most of the variants involve only a word or two. Few change more than four or five words, and those that do ordinarily involve word order as well as addition, deletion, or substitution: "his cigar-case in his inside coat pocket"/"his inside coat-pocket" (167.20); "they, with their shadows, made"/"their shadows made" (175.12); "a cloud the size of your hand"/"the smallest cloud" (176.24); "I was just a young man when I first saw Edwin Booth, in Buffalo"/"The first time I saw Edwin Booth was in Buffalo" (180.16–17). A sentence is added to K1 at 179.8–9, and a long parenthesis at 161.16–162.2. The "transit of Venus" error at 176.19 (see Notes on Emendations, p. 376) occurs in both the magazine text and K1.

These changes in "Two Friends" have effects generally similar to those made by changes in the texts of the first two stories in the collection. At 165.19 "thrasher," although not the conventional spelling, emphasizes the midwestern setting of the story. The change from "and" to "or" at 167.10 stresses the force of Trueman's personality: he can stop rowdiness with either a look *or* a remark. When Trueman comes "across" instead of "along" Main Street (169.18), the geography of Red Cloud is preserved and the division between him and Dillon is suggested. The story of Trueman's last days in San Francisco gains more credence when it is told in K1 by a "man whose offices were next his" (190.8–9) rather than by the magazine version's anonymous "man."

Changes in the Text IV:

Passages Omitted from the LHJ *Text of "Old Mrs. Harris"*

The substantive variants between the *Ladies' Home Journal* text of "Old Mrs. Harris" and K1 are unlike the variants between the magazine versions of the other two stories in one important respect: numerous passages in K1 and in the typescript are not present in the LHJ version, and these passages (we treat each as a single variant) are usually considerably longer than the longest variants between K1 and the magazine versions of the other two stories. More than twenty of these passages run more than four lines, thirteen of them run ten

349

lines or more, and the longest of them involves more than ninety lines.

The first such passage describes Mrs. Harris's "hideous, cluttered room," whose few and miscellaneous furnishings reflect her marginal place in the family (69.13–70.3). Other passages establish aspects of her character and her background: her experience as a nurse (119.3–11), her need to keep up appearances (121.14–24), and her desire not to be a burden to others (154.20–22). Some passages detail the routine of her life and depict her relationships with her daughter and grandchildren (83.6–86.10, 113.25–115.2). Others develop characters, like Mrs. Rosen (85.13–86.10, 123.25–124.8) and Mandy (79.22–80.4), or show the relationships between such characters as Mrs. Rosen and Vickie Templeton (88.7–89.3, 92.20–93.11). The passages characterizing Mr. Templeton's reaction to the news of his wife's new pregnancy (148.5–149.8) give a very different slant to his character from that available to readers of the serial version, and the passages describing Vickie as she waits for the letter of acceptance from the University of Michigan (127.23–128.11, 128.16–22) emphasize the contrast between Vickie's intensity and the lassitude of her parents. Finally, the long passage that describes the ways in which the Templeton boys earn money for the family (116.22–117.7) characterizes not only the boys but also Mrs. Jackson; the omission of several passages about this latter character in the magazine version makes her innocuous instead of malicious (for example, 143.11–144.8).

At one point an entire scene is carefully reshaped. In the *LHJ* text Ronald sits on his grandmother's lap while she reads *Tom Sawyer*, and the older boys sit on a box and on the floor; the scene is pictured in the half-page illustration that precedes the story in the *Ladies' Home Journal*, a picture that also shows Vickie (who is not mentioned in the text) lying on the lounge (see illustration 17). When Vickie takes over the reading, Mrs. Harris begins to darn before she falls asleep, neither of which she could easily do with a sleeping boy on her lap. In K1 (76.14–77.9) Ronald lies down on the lounge at the beginning of the scene, one of the twins sits on a sawed-off chair (deleted in the serial text), and Vickie is mentioned as coming in on her way to her room. In this way the awkwardness is eliminated.

The passages omitted in *LHJ* are all present in the typescript, and the typescript is certainly earlier than the setting-copy for the story. It is therefore reasonable to conclude that the passages were present from the beginning and were cut in the *LHJ* version by an editor, presumably because the story was too long for the space available. The omissions are primarily narrative and descriptive, of the sort that an editor pressed for space would tend to cut.

Changes in the Text V: K1, Cassell Edition, Autograph Edition
Collations of the first printing of the Knopf first edition, the Cassell edition, and the Autograph Edition indicate that the Knopf text exists in at least two states. State *a* shows the typographical error "hold" for "told" at K1 143.23 and the

more significant substantive error "transit" for "occultation" at к1 212.14. All copies seen of the first printing belong to state *a*. In state *b* the typo on p. 143 is corrected and lines 12–14 on p. 212 are reset to correct the second error. All copies seen of the second and later printings correct both errors. The publisher's record for the second printing shows a charge for patching the plates of pp. 143 and 212, so it is highly probable that the corrections were made in preparing the plates for this printing, which appeared very shortly after the first. However, because the Hamish Hamilton photo-offset reissue of 1965 corrects the first error but not the second, it is at least possible that some copies of the first or limited printings show this intermediate state. The alternative is that the printer of the Hamilton copies noticed the typo and corrected it; it is unlikely that this change was suggested by Knopf and the more important change ignored. We have found no other variants in the eleven U.S. printings of the Knopf edition.

The Cassell edition of December 1932 exhibits a few substantive and many accidental variants, but these variants show no sign of authorial intervention.[7] "Today," "tonight," and "tomorrow" are hyphenated in Cassell; к1's punctuation is sometimes altered; word division is sometimes different. Occasionally, a word or phrase is replaced with a presumably more acceptable British equivalent: "checkers" with "draughts," "baby-buggy" with "baby-carriage," "goods-box" with "packing-case," "toward" with "towards," "sneakers" with "shoes," "farming season" with "the farming season." Such changes are characteristic of British editions of U.S. books.⁸ At 165.25 Cassell makes a unnecessary "correction," setting "accountant's stools" as "accountants' stools" (following TS1 and WHC). Rarely, an error is introduced: "gentleman" for "gentle man" at 24.5, "bed-spread" for "red spread" at 114.2, and "country" for "county" at 185.8. Only one change is not accounted for in these obvious ways: Cassell changes K1's "donated" to "gave" at 101.11. There is no evidence that Cather had a hand in these changes. Given this fact and the nature of the variants, we conclude that the Cassell edition is not authorial. It does correct the typo at K1 143.23 and change "transit of Venus" to "occultation of Venus" at K1 212.14, but it is not clear whether these changes involved correspondence with Knopf or the use of a second, third, or fourth printing of the book as setting-copy.

There are even fewer variants between K1 and the Tauchnitz edition of 1933. "Oscar" is once set as "Oskar" and "Trueman" twice as "Truemann," both accounted for as slips by the compositor. Lines 49.4–5 of K1 are omitted in this edition, another slip. There are a few changes in accidentals but not many. Again, all variants involve accidentals that do not affect meaning or that introduce errors. There is no evidence, internal or external, that Cather had any hand in this edition, and therefore we do not regard it as authorial. Because it reads "transit of Venus" at K1 212.14, it was presumably set from a copy of the first printing. The typo at K1 143.23 is corrected.

The Autograph Edition is, however, authorial. Scribner's

had wanted to publish a subscription edition of Cather's fiction as early as 1932, but Houghton Mifflin would not release the four novels it had earlier published (Lewis 180; FG to WC, 1 July 1933; Knopf, Memoirs). When Houghton Mifflin itself took up Scribner's idea, Cather worked with Ferris Greenslet, who had been her editor there; after much negotiation Cather agreed to the edition. She wanted W. A. Dwiggins, who had designed some of her Knopf books, as the designer, and she wanted the same type that had been used in the Thistle edition of Robert Louis Stevenson (WC to FG, 18 December 1936). Greenslet did not agree (FG to WC, 21 December 1936), and Bruce Rogers was chosen to design the edition.

During 1936 Cather looked over the books included and made a number of changes, the number varying with the particular title. There are also a few wholesale changes due either to Cather's intervention or, in other cases, to differences in the house styles of Knopf and Houghton Mifflin — the latter, probably, changes in which Cather had no hand. There are relatively few changes in the text of *Obscure Destinies*, which was included in volume 12, *Obscure Destinies and Literary Encounters*. Contractions are expanded: "you'll" at 8.19, for example, becomes "you will." "Though" is changed to "although" at 28.13, "afterwards" to "afterward" throughout. Formal agreement is insisted on at 59.8 ("hearts on their sleeves"); "Shakspere" is changed to "Shakespeare" at 89.16–17; "Grand'ma" and "Grandmother" in their various forms are set in lower case throughout except in direct address.

"Had forgot" at 118.18 becomes "had forgotten"; "check" is changed at 186.8 to agree with "cheque" at 186.12. All such changes are consistent with a movement toward somewhat more formal or more British usage and, in a few cases, with the elimination of inconsistency. House style, on the other hand, probably accounts for the shift from comma and dash to dash alone and from double quotes to single quotes for dialogue, changes made throughout the Autograph Edition.

A few changes could have been made either by Cather or by the compositors: "beasts" at 20.4 to "beast," "gettin'" at 31.21 to "gitten'." Into this class fall the correction of K1's inconsistent "Rudolf" at 44.6 to "Rudolph" and of subject-verb agreement at 57.19: "Rosicky's was" to "Rosicky's hand was." The typo and the "transit of Venus" error in the first printing of K1 are also corrected.

The changes made in the Autograph Edition text, however authorial, are relatively few and relatively minor; most of the substantive variants either make the readings of K1 more formal or more grammatically "correct," or eliminate error or inconsistency. Because the policy of the Cather Edition is to present the text closest to Cather's intention at the time of its first publication in book form rather than a text that represents a later intention for the work, we have not chosen the Autograph Edition text as copy-text. The nature of the variants between K1 and the Autograph Edition texts — the fact that there are not many of them, fewer that are substantive, and of these, still fewer that are significant — lends further credence to this choice.

The Choice of Copy-Text

The copy-text for this edition is a copy of the first printing of the first U.S. edition of the three stories in book form, published on 1 August 1932 by Alfred A. Knopf under the title *Obscure Destinies* (K1). Collation of copies of all the potentially relevant texts demonstrates that eleven of them show evidence of Cather's hand and are therefore authorial: those of the unrevised and revised versions of the three typescripts, the magazine versions of the three stories, and those of K1 and the Autograph Edition. All other texts published during Cather's lifetime were either reprints, separate issues of K1, or derive from K1 without evidence of authorial intervention. The text of the Autograph Edition represents a later intention for the work, in this case one little different from that realized in K1. Although the magazine versions of the stories are authorial and roughly contemporary, they clearly do not represent the intention of the author at the time of first publication in book form nearly as well, either in substantives or accidentals, as does K1. The revised version of the second typescript was probably setting-copy for "Two Friends," but the K1 text, showing some thirty substantive and accidental variants (most are substantive) from the text of TF2 for this story, is still, especially in the absence of galleys, the text that best represents Cather's final intention for her work at the time closest to first book publication. The choice of copy-text in this instance does not depend on a single bit of evidence but on a combination of internal and external evidence, all of which points to K1.

We know, in the first place, that Cather was interested in the magazine versions of her work because they provided additional income, telling Knopf on one occasion that she reacted negatively to the very idea of magazine publication but recognized its publicity value and income potential (wc to AK, 22 November 1922). There is no indication that she took pains with the magazine version of *Obscure Destinies* but ample evidence that she took great pains with the book version. Edith Lewis, for example, notes that Cather insisted on seeing foundry proofs of her novels, and asked Lewis herself to look at those proofs for *Shadows on the Rock* in her absence (161). We have many indications from other works, as well as the testimony of Knopf himself,[9] that Cather took great pains with accidentals as well as with substantives, and that long before 1930 she was insisting on English spelling of such words as "parlour," "colour," and "neighbour" — all of which are routinely given U.S. spellings in the magazine texts of the *Obscure Destinies* stories. Her tendency toward heavy pointing and the use of hyphenated compounds is also far more obvious in K1 than in the magazine texts.

Evidence of a nonlinguistic sort (Jerome McGann, in *The Textual Condition*, calls it "bibliographical") is also relevant. For example, Cather did not like Walter Everett's illustrations for "Two Friends" (see illustration 25); she thought they made her characters look too rough (wc to Carrie Miner Sherwood, 4 July 1932). She would surely not have liked either the uninspired typography or the three- and four-column formats used in the magazines, which some-

357

times have two and sometimes four long, narrow columns of text running the whole length of a page. But she would have objected most of all to the arbitrary divisions of her work in the serial texts. These breaks, usually introduced by large initials or words in large capitals, do not in many cases indicate a change of scene, a substantial lapse of time, or a significant movement from narration to dialogue or vice versa. They usually appear at the chapter indications in K1, but not inevitably, and there are so many of them that one has no sense of a particular story's main divisions, as is given by the K1 text. They seem intended only to give visual relief by breaking up long columns of type. When they come at awkward moments, as they often do, they interpose another, foreign intention on the work.

The substantial passages in the text of "Old Mrs. Harris" that do not appear in the magazine version of the story also suggest the primacy of K1. Although the magazine editor cut them to fit the space available, there can be no question that they significantly enhance the story.[10] Furthermore, K1 and all other printings of the book during Cather's lifetime restore these passages.

In sum: (1) K1 is closest to Cather's practice in the matter of accidentals.[11] (2) Cather is known to have taken strong interest in the book versions of her works, both in accidentals and in substantives, and to have shown little interest in the magazine versions (we have no evidence that she read proof for these stories). Nonlinguistic features of the magazine versions of all three stories, particularly their division into relatively short blocks of type, reflect intentions contrary to those realized in K1. (3) Had Cather regarded the magazine versions of the stories as realizing her contemporary intention for them, she would have sent a copy of the typescript used as setting-copy by the magazines to Knopf to use as setting-copy for the book. She did not do so, but sent a later, newly revised typescript. (4) The long passages in the K1 text of "Old Mrs. Harris" were cut for the *Ladies' Home Journal* from the penultimate typescript. They are certainly authorial, and they add considerably to the development of the story's characters. (5) The typescript of "Old Mrs. Harris" and the two typescripts of "Two Friends" underwent subsequent revision, as did even the second, revised typescript of the latter story. However, revision essentially stops with K1 except for the correction of a few errors and very minor changes in the Autograph Edition text. For all these reasons we use a copy of the first printing of K1 as copy-text.[12]

Emendation and Related Matters

We have emended the copy-text of *Obscure Destinies* under the following circumstances: (1) to correct a typographical error; (2) to change a mark of punctuation when it is clear from many other examples that a particular reading is anomalous — a slip or a rare exception; (3) to resolve inconsistencies in spelling or word division, especially when differences appear in close proximity; (4) to correct a misspelled word; (5) to correct a substantive error that Cather herself asked to have corrected; (6) to correct a substantive error when it is clear from many other examples that a particular reading is a slip or a rare exception. We do not emend to "improve" Cather's wording or grammar, to modernize her diction or usage or use of accidentals, to impose consistency where there is no evidence that consistency was desired, or to correct errors she herself did not address (except when a simple factual error can be corrected without further revising the text).[13]

The emendations accepted into the copy-text by the present editors include four substantive changes (one a correction known to have been made by Cather) and nine changes in accidentals: one involving punctuation, two involving case, four involving spelling (including the correction of one typographical error), one involving word division, and one involving the use of the apostrophe. One of the accepted variants in spelling, and the one involving word division, resolve inconsistencies in the copy-text. The Notes on Emendations explain our choices when the rationale is not obvious. The Historical Collation also lists all substantive variants, except those accepted as emendations, between the copy-text and the texts of the other authorial editions (the unrevised and revised typescript of "Old Mrs. Harris" and the unrevised and revised typescripts of "Two Friends"; the serial texts of the three stories; and the Autograph Edition). Variants from the Cassell and Tauchnitz editions are not included because we do not consider these editions authorial.

In addition, the Historical Collation includes a small number of accidentals that affect meaning and a larger class of quasi-substantives in "Neighbour Rosicky" and "Old Mrs. Harris" involving dialect forms such as "an'"/"and" and "dis"/"this." The latter, because they involve pronunciation as well as spelling, affect the characterization of the speakers. In the copy-text of the former story these dialect forms predominate in ratios from 3 to 1 to as much as 20 to 1. However, we see no reason to impose uniformity; it is obvious from the authorial deletion of several dialect forms in the typescript of "Old Mrs. Harris," for example, that Cather wished only to give the flavor of dialect. The dialect forms retained in the copy-text accomplish this goal.

Records of Cather's direct involvement in the design and production of her works have led us to take special care in the presentation of them. We are particularly concerned with compositor error. By agreement with the University of Nebraska Press, we undertake proofreading in stages to meet the Committee for Scholarly Editions guidelines, which call for at least four readings.[14] Insofar as is feasible within the series format of a scholarly edition, the editors have cooperated with the designer to create a volume that reflects Cather's known wishes for the presentation of her works.

Notes

1. Knopf's title-page advertisement in *Publisher's Weekly* for 7 May 1932, p. [1927] announces the book as "Coming August 5th," and this is the publication date given by Crane (170). However, the same magazine gives 1 August as the date (25 June 1932, p. 2489); Knopf's advertisement for 2 July 1932, p. 20, says that

the book will be "ready the first"; and Harry Hansen's "Among the New Books" column in *Harper's* for August 1932 says that Knopf will publish the book "on August 1st." It is listed in the magazine's "Weekly Record" in the 30 July issue, p. 357. Several printings after the first, including the fourth and ninth, have "Published August 1, 1932" on the verso of the title page. We therefore accept the earlier date, although it is possible that Knopf made a distinction between the "official" date and the date the book was "ready."

The 7 May advertisement also announces a new way of handling the limited issue: "There will also be, as usual, a limited, large paper, signed edition — but, in accordance with the time, this will appear in only one form, to retail at $15.00. It will not be as handsome as we have been able in the past to produce at $25.00 but it will be definitely superior to our former $10.00 editions. The exact number printed of these copies will depend on orders received. . . ." As in the past, of course, the same plates were used for the text of the trade and limited issues, although there were differences in the preliminary matter and format.

2. A typescript of "Neighbour Rosicky" might have existed as late as the 1960s, when an unconfirmed story reports that it was given to a visitor to Cather's cottage at Grand Manan. However, we have not been able to locate the typescript and do not know that it has survived. The typescript of "Old Mrs. Harris" and one of the two typescripts of "Two Friends" were recently discovered in a private collection; copies were kindly provided the Cather Edition editors by the collector, who has asked not to be identified. The other typescript of "Two Friends" is owned by Helen Cather Southwick, who kindly supplied the editors with a copy.

3. For this volume we conducted or supervised solo and team collations of the newly discovered typescripts of "Old Mrs. Harris" and "Two Friends," and three independent solo hand collations and two independent team hand collations of the serial versions of the three stories against a copy of K1 of *Obscure Destinies*. The K1 standard of collation was also hand-collated against a copy of K9, and machine-collated or spot-checked against copies of other printings, including K2 and the Vintage paperback, and against a copy of the limited issue. Three independent hand collations (two solo and one team) were made of the K1 standard of collation against a copy of the Cassell edition and against a copy of the Autograph Edition. Two independent hand collations were made of the K1 standard of collation against a copy of the Tauchnitz edition. The collations were checked twice and again against each other; the conflation was checked three times. The full record of the historical collations, including those of the Cassell and Tauchnitz editions, is on file and available in the Editorial Resources Center of the Department of English, University of Nebraska–Lincoln.

The following copies were used in the preparation of this edition (UNL = Love Library, University of Nebraska–Lincoln; HLPL = Heritage Room collections, Bennett Martin Public Library, Lincoln):

K1: UNL Spec. PS3505 A87O25 1932, Spec. Slote PS3505 A87O25 1932; Cochrane Woods Library, Nebraska Wesleyan U PS3505 A8703; copies owned by Frederick M. Link, Kari Ronning, and Susan J. Rosowski; HLPL 7866615, 7866623, 7866730

K1, limited issue: UNL Spec. Slote PS3505 A87O25 1932bx (copy

34), Spec. Sullivan PS3505 A87025 1932bx (copy 227); HLPL 7866631 (copy 200)

K2: UNL Spec. PS3505 A87025 1932ax

K4: Library of Union College, Lincoln: 813 c280b; a copy owned by Kari Ronning

K7: UNL Spec. Faulkner PS3505 A87025 1932

K9: A copy owned by Frederick M. Link

K11 (Vintage): UNL PS3505 A87025 1974x, UNL Spec. Faulkner PS3505 A87025 1974x; HLPL 7866664; Library of Union College, Lincoln: 813 c280b2

K12 (London: Hamish Hamilton, 1965, by offset from K1): UNL Spec. Slote PS3505 A87025 1965x (showing mixed state); HLPL 7005244 (showing mixed state)

Autograph Edition (titled *Obscure Destinies and Literary Encounters*): UNL PS3505 A87A15 1937bx, v. 12 (Library edition form); HLPL 7 866656 (copy 450)

Cassell edition: UNL Spec. Slote PS3505 A87025 1932cx; HLPL 7866649

Tauchnitz edition: UNL PS3505 A87025 1933.

4. We have resolved end-line hyphenation in the copy-text to establish the form of the word or compound to be used in quotations from this edition. The following criteria are applied in descending order: (1) majority rule, if one or more instances of the word or compound appear elsewhere in the copy-text; (2) analogy, if one or more examples of similar words or compounds appear elsewhere in the copy-text; (3) by example or analogy, if one or more examples of the word or compound, or of similar words or compounds, appear in the corrected typescripts of "Old Mrs. Harris" and "Two Friends"; (4) by example

or analogy, if one or more examples of the word or compound, or of similar words or compounds, appear in first editions of Cather's works chronologically close to *Obscure Destinies*; (5) in the absence of the above criteria, commonsense combinations of the following: (a) possible or likely morphemic forms; (b) examples of the word or compound, or of similar words or compounds, in the Autograph Edition text; (c) the form given in *Webster's New International Dictionary* (1909); (d) the *Style Manual of the Department of State* (1937); (e) hyphenation of two-word compounds when used as adjectives.

5. See also Crane (168–73). Crane does not record the two states of κ1, however. All information corresponds with that in Knopf production records.

6. Heinemann had been the British publisher for all of Cather's books except *The Song of the Lark* until *Shadows on the Rock* was published by Cassell in January 1932. The choice of Cassell in this instance had Cather's approval (Knopf, Memoirs).

7. We follow the usual distinction: substantive variants are changes in wording (including morphemic variations); accidental variants include changes in spelling, case, punctuation, and word division. Typographical changes (in paragraphing, font, spacing, etc.) are neither substantive nor accidental, although they may be discussed; they represent part of what Jerome McGann calls "bibliographical" as opposed to "linguistic" codes. The basis of the distinctions here is the extent to which a class of differences affects the meaning of the text: typography and accidentals often do not but substantives usually do. However, we also recognize a class of quasi-substantives, which includes typographical or accidental variants that *in a particular case* seem clearly to affect meaning. There is a clear distinction, for exam-

ple, between "she wanted to be *there*" and "she wanted to be there" or between "You're hungry." and "You're hungry?" In the case of "Neighbour Rosicky" we accept a fairly large group of dialect forms as quasi-substantive and have therefore included these forms in the Historical Collation. See Bowers, "The Problem of Semi-Substantive Variants"; Greg, "The Rationale of Copy-Text"; McGann, *The Textual Condition*; and Tanselle, "Greg's Theory of Copy-Text." Richard Rust's use of inflection as a basis for distinguishing accidentals that affect meaning has also been of assistance.

8. See Matthew J. Bruccoli, "Some Transatlantic Texts: West to East," in Brack and Barnes (244–55).

9. Knopf, Memoirs. One has only to examine the hundreds of holograph changes in spelling, capitalization, and punctuation in the surviving typescripts of *Shadows on the Rock*, "Old Mrs. Harris," and "Two Friends" to see how meticulous Cather was in specifying accidentals.

10. These additions do not "over-furnish" the story, to use the language of "The Novel Démeublé," an essay first published in 1922. Rather, they represent a type of narration, often "of material things," but excepted from attack on the basis that they "are always so much a part of the emotions of the people that they are perfectly synthesized; they seem to exist . . . in the emotional penumbra of the characters themselves. . . . [They become] merely part of the experience" (40–41).

11. See Greg, "The Rationale of Copy-Text."

12. We are aware of, but do not agree with, the arguments against the possibility of establishing a single satisfactory text. T. H. Howard-Hill has put the matter succinctly: the "insistence that a scholarly editor is not a 'rescuer and restorer' of texts and that

editors 'have been caught out trying to promote the purity of texts' leaves the matter of emendation in doubt. . . . [I]f merely accidental collocations of words will satisfy the needs of literary critics, then editing is essentially unnecessary. Literary theories that emphasize the ambiguity, multivalency, and plurisignification of textual utterances recommend a form of edition in which these textual properties are appropriately acknowledged. Nevertheless, it seems that it would be important for critics who value these textual properties to know the source and (probably) the authority of the specific utterances on which critical attention is to be focused. Only the kind of textual criticism that results in the 'establishment' of a text can furnish this information. It may be polemically advantageous for advocates of new forms of editing to denigrate and dismiss the fundamental functions of textual criticism, but ultimately it is irrational" (52).

13. Whether an editor should emend to correct a factual error not noticed by the author of the work is a complex issue but finally a matter for editorial judgment. We make one such emendation to the text of *Obscure Destinies*, at 148.7, following the rationale stated by Tanselle in "External Fact as an Editorial Problem," especially pp. 42–46.

14. The University of Nebraska Press sets the clear text directly into page proof, running three sets. Two sets come to the Cather Edition editors, who read the clear text against the emended copy-text and the apparatus against the typescript setting-copy, first as a team and then as individuals. At this stage the editors add page and line numbers to the materials comprising the apparatus, keying all references to the Cather Edition text. They also check end-line hyphenation to ensure accurate

resolutions and to gather material for the word-division List B. Also at this stage, the Press proofs the text of the new edition against the copy-text, and the text of the apparatus against the typescript setting-copy. The editors collate their two sets of corrected proof and the Press collates all three sets, sending the final corrected proof to the compositor for correction. When the corrected proofs return from the Press, the editors again make a team collation of the material, correcting any errors in page and line numbers, checking to see that indicated corrections have been made, and compiling the word-division list (List B) for the newly reset text of the novel. The Press, meanwhile, compares pages to corrected proof to ensure that no text has been dropped, and reads the lines that have been corrected. When the Press sends xeroxes of reproduction paper (equivalent to "blues") to the editors, they make a machine collation of these "repros" against the last set of proofread page proofs.

Works Cited

Bohlke, L. Brent, ed. *Willa Cather in Person: Interviews, Speeches, and Letters*. Lincoln: U of Nebraska P, 1986.

Bowers, Fredson. "The Problem of Semi-Substantive Variants: An Example from the Shakespeare-Fletcher *Henry VIII.*" *Studies in Bibliography* 43 (1990): 80–84.

Brack, O M, Jr., and Warner Barnes, eds. *Bibliography and Textual Criticism*. Chicago: U of Chicago P, 1969.

Cather, Willa. Letters to Ferris Greenslet. Houghton Mifflin Collection. Houghton Library, Harvard U, Cambridge.

——. Letter to Alfred A. Knopf. 22 November 1922. Knopf Collection. Harry Ransom Humanities Research Center, U of Texas at Austin.

———. Letter to Alfred A. (Pat) Knopf Jr. 19 January 1936. Knopf Collection. Harry Ransom Humanities Research Center, U of Texas at Austin.

———. Letter to Sinclair Lewis. 22 March 1944. Willa Cather Pioneer Memorial and Educational Foundation, Red Cloud.

———. Letter to Carrie Miner Sherwood. 4 July 1932. Willa Cather Pioneer Memorial and Educational Foundation, Red Cloud.

———. Letter to Irene Miner Weisz. Weisz Collection. Newberry Library, Chicago.

———. "The Novel Démeublé." Rpt'd. in *Not under Forty*. New York: Knopf, 1936. 35–43.

———. "Neighbor Rosicky." *Woman's Home Companion*, April–May 1930.

———. *Obscure Destinies*. New York: Knopf, 1932.

———. *Obscure Destinies*. Autograph Edition, v. 12. Boston: Houghton Mifflin, 1938.

———. "Three Women." *Ladies' Home Journal*, September–November 1932.

———. "Two Friends." *Woman's Home Companion*, July 1932.

———. Typescript of "Old Mrs. Harris." Private collection.

———. Typescript of "Two Friends." Private collection.

———. Typescript of "Two Friends." Collection of Helen Cather Southwick.

Crane, Joan. *Willa Cather: A Bibliography*. Lincoln: U of Nebraska P, 1982.

Greenslet, Ferris. Letter to Willa Cather. 21 December 1936. Houghton Mifflin Collection. Houghton Library, Harvard U, Cambridge.

Greg, W. W. "The Rationale of Copy-Text." *Studies in Bibliography* 3 (1950–51): 19–36. Rpt'd. with minor revision in *The Collected*

Papers of Sir Walter Greg. Ed. J. C. Maxwell. Oxford: Clarendon, 1966. 374–91.

Howard-Hill, T. H. "Variety in Editing and Reading: A Response to McGann and Shillingsburg." *Devils and Angels: Textual Editing and Literary Theory*. Ed. Philip Cohen. Charlottesville: UP of Virginia, 1991. 44–55.

Knopf, Alfred A. Memoirs. Knopf Collection. Harry Ransom Humanities Research Center, U Texas at Austin. Typescript.

———. Production records of Alfred A. Knopf, Inc. Knopf Collection. Harry Ransom Humanities Research Center, U Texas at Austin.

Lewis, Edith. *Willa Cather Living: A Personal Record*. New York: Knopf, 1953.

McGann, Jerome. *The Textual Condition*. Princeton: Princeton UP, 1991.

Sergeant, Elizabeth Shepley. *Willa Cather: A Memoir*. Philadelphia: Lippincott, 1953.

Tanselle, G. Thomas. "Greg's Theory of Copy-Text and the Editing of American Literature." *Studies in Bibliography* 28 (1975): 167–229.

———. "External Fact as an Editorial Problem." *Studies in Bibliography* 32 (1979): 1–47.

Webster's New International Dictionary. 1909 ed. Springfield, Mass.: Merriam, 1927.

Emendations

THE following list records all substantive and accidental changes introduced into the copy-text, the first printing of the three stories under the *Obscure Destinies* title, by Alfred A. Knopf in 1932. The reading of the present edition appears to the left of the bracket; to the right are recorded the source of that reading followed by a semicolon, the copy-text reading, the abbreviation for the copy-text (K1), the reading of the magazine version of the story, the abbreviation S for the appropriate magazine version, the reading of the Autograph Edition, and the abbreviation A for that edition. The abbreviation CE indicates emendations made on the authority of the present editors; although our reading may agree with the reading of another text, it is not made on that authority alone. An asterisk (*) indicates that the reading is discussed in the Notes on Emendations. Page and line numbers refer to the Cather Edition text.

The following texts are referred to:

K1 The first printing of the first edition, Alfred A. Knopf, 1932.

K2 The second and subsequent printings of the first edition, Knopf, 1932 —.

OMH   The unaltered text of the typescript of "Old Mrs. Harris."

TS1   The unaltered text of the earlier of the two typescripts of "Two Friends."

TS2   The unaltered text of the later of the two revised typescripts of "Two Friends."

S   For "Neighbour Rosicky," the version published in the *Woman's Home Companion*, April and May, 1930. For "Old Mrs. Harris," the version published in the *Ladies' Home Journal*, September, October, and November, 1932, under the title "Three Women." For "Two Friends," the version published in the *Woman's Home Companion*, July 1932.

A   *Obscure Destinies and Literary Encounters.* Autograph Edition, v. 12. Boston: Houghton Mifflin, 1938.

*13.6   slyly:] CE, A; slyly; K1–2; slyly, S

*14.20   Doctor] CE; doctor K1–2, S, A

*44.6   Rudolph] CE, S, A; Rudolf K1–2

*47.7   Dere] CE, A; Dey K1–2, S

*47.17   dere] CE; dey K1–2, S, A

*53.23–24   alfalfa-field] CE, A; alfalfa field K1–2, S

*96.16   Templetons'] CE, OMH, S, A; Templeton's K1–2

120.1   told] CE, OMH, K2, S, A; hold K1

*148.7   South] CE; North OMH, K1–2, S, A

*173.10   pretensions] CE, TS2, S, A; pretentions TS1, K1–2

*176.19   an occultation] CE, K2, A; a transit TS1, TS2, S, K1

*184.25   down upon the brow of labour this crown of thorns]
CE, S, A; this crown of thorns upon the brow of
labour TS1, TS2, K1–2

*186.12   cheque] CE, A; check TS1, TS2, S, K1–2

Notes on Emendations

ᴋ regularly uses the colon to introduce a speech.	13.6
In the eleven other cases involving "the doctor" the uppercase form is used, as it is in all eighteen cases involving direct address. ᴄᴇ considers this exception an oversight.	14.20
All other references in the story are to "Rudolph"; ᴄᴇ believes this exception an oversight.	44.6
In all other examples "dey" is used for "they" and "dere" for "there" and "their"; ᴄᴇ believes these exceptions are oversights. See 45.25, for example.	47.7
At 53.15 the compound is hyphenated, as is typical of Cather's practice; ᴄᴇ emends for consistency.	53.23–24
This emendation corrects an error; Cather uses "Templetons'" to indicate possession at 111.3, for example.	96.16
All texts read "North Platte," but Skyline is described as being between Wray and Cheyenne (111.21). Wray, Colorado, is some sixty-five miles south of the South Platte; Cheyenne, Wyoming, is more than seventy-five miles south of the North Platte. The irriga-	148.7

tion project for which Mr. Templeton worked would have involved the south branch of the Platte rather than the north unless one assumes an improbably long commute to work. CE emends because of Cather's known desire to have her facts accurate and because the emendation does not entail any other change in the text.

173.10   The K spelling is idiosyncratic and also inconsistent with that at 172.1–2.

176.19   For Edith Lewis's account of this error, see *Willa Cather Living* (161): "her Red Cloud neighbours had called it a transit of Venus; it did not occur to her to look it up." It is possible that William Lyon Phelps called the error to Cather's attention (WLP to WC, 20 August 1932; letter owned by Beverly Cooper).

184.25   Both the serial and Autograph Edition texts quote the passage accurately. It is possible that Cather deliberately altered it in K1, but the editors believe that her known concern for factual accuracy should take precedence over a possibility for which we can advance no reason other than a change in sentence rhythm. The K1–2 version of the quotation appears in both typescripts but in no other printed text.

186.12   CE emends for consistency with 186.8.

Historical Collation

T HIS list records all substantive and quasi-substantive variants
between the copy-text and the texts of the other authorial
editions (the unrevised and revised forms of the typescript of "Old
Mrs. Harris," the unrevised and revised forms of the two typescripts of "Two Friends," the magazine versions of the three stories,
and the Autograph Edition) which have been rejected in establishing the text of the present edition. The reading of the Cather Edition text appears to the left of the bracket; to the right of the bracket
appear the variant reading(s) and source(s); variants are separated
by semicolons. Ellipsis dots indicate an omission made for the sake
of brevity; they are not part of the CE text. Accidental variants are
not reported when they occur within cited substantive variants.

In reporting variants from the unrevised forms of the three typescripts, we omit not only accidentals but also typographical errors
(whether corrected or not) and text crossed out at the bottom of a
page and repeated verbatim on the succeeding page. If more than
two readings exist in addition to a final revision, the intermediate
ones are treated as belonging to the unrevised typescript: they are
listed after the first reading and preceded by a pointed bracket (>).
Many of the x'ed-out readings of the original typescript seem to
have been false starts immediately rejected; new text in ink replac-

377

ing readings inked out seem in most cases to have been later revisions. There are also typed-in changes and, on a few pages, typed-in or holograph readings that offer alternatives to the final text of the typescript. All such variants are considered in the collation as readings of the unrevised typescript. We report x'ed-out readings only when we deem them significant (usually when they involve more than a false start), but we include all readings presented as alternatives (whether cancelled or not) to the final typescript text. When a typescript shows no revision, it is referred to by title abbreviation only (OMH rather than OMHa or OMHb). If a text is not cited, it agrees with K1.

The following texts are referred to:

S	For "Neighbour Rosicky," the version published in the *Woman's Home Companion*, April and May 1930. For "Old Mrs. Harris," the version published as "Three Women" in the *Ladies' Home Journal*, September, October, and November 1932. For "Two Friends," the version published in the *Woman's Home Companion*, July 1932.
OMH	The unaltered (no changes were made) typescript of "Old Mrs. Harris."
OMHa, b	The unrevised and revised forms of the typescript of "Old Mrs. Harris."
TF1	The unaltered (no changes were made), earlier typescript of "Two Friends."
TF1a, b	The unrevised and revised forms of the earlier typescript of "Two Friends."

378

TF2   The unaltered (no changes were made), later
             typescript of "Two Friends."

TF2a, b   The unrevised and revised forms of the later
             typescript of "Two Friends."

A   Houghton Mifflin, 1938; the Autograph Edition,
             volume 12.

"Neighbour Rosicky"

7.5   summer, dat's all] summer   s

7.12   you] you, and you'll have to look on for a while   s

8.19   you'll] you will   A

9.17   they treat] treat   s

9.20   assented] admitted   s

9.23   Rudolph] He   s

10.3   for] fur   s

10.3   folks] people   s

10.11   Ford] car   s

10.12   for] fur   s

10.12   noway] no way   s

10.16   placed] put   s

11.22   had driven in just] arrived   s

11.22   come back] just come in   s

379

12.5   had to] had had to   s

12.15   spread] put   s

12.21   any way] anyway   s

12.23   out] as loud   s

12.25   smile, put] smile and put   s

13.1–2   fire, and went . . . medicine glass] fire   s

13.24–25   one (he was still living at home then)] one   s

14.1   oughtn't] ought not   A

14.9   and then] and   s

14.10   breakfast!] breakfast.   s

14.13   we] then we   s

14.13   him here] him   s

14.13–14   So you] You   s

14.15   John] Peter   s

14.16   feel] feel that   s

14.17–18   his breakfast] breakfast   s

14.19   I'd] I had   A

15.2   ready fixed] fixed   s

16.5   do!] do.   s

16.8   on] get   s

16.10   rather] sort of   s

16.15   never got] didn't get   s

16.15   couldn't] could not   A

16.24   plucked] shaved   s

17.2   always] usually   s

17.14   for] fur   s

17.23   I'd like dat] I wish she would   s

18.22   stood out] standing up   s

20.1   country] country; so much motion, without hurry
             or sound   s

20.4   beasts] beast   A

20.9   John] Peter   s

20.10   away] up   s

20.11   from the outside] out of the   s

20.13   clusters] grape leaves and clusters   s

20.14–15   coffee-cake of some kind] coffee-cake   s

20.15–16   lunched in town . . . extravagant] ate lunch in town;
             it was expensive   s

20.20–23   out of the oven a . . . plate, and then] the twisted
             cake covered with poppy seeds out of the oven,
             lightly broke it up with her hands and   s

20.25–21.1   coffee. ¶ She] coffee, but she   s

21.8–9   one of the little rolls] a piece of the coffee-cake   s

21.9   fingers] hand   s

21.15   her hair back] back her hair   s

22.4   country-bred; she] country-bred, and she   s

22.8   Ed about it] Ed   s

22.11   round] around   s

22.12   for] fur   s

22.13   for] fur   s

22.23–24   intently, trying to find any change in his face] intently   s

23.19–20   at bottom . . . ideas about life] they had the same ideas about life at bottom   s

23.21   important] worth while   s

24.2–3   short, broad-backed] broad-backed little   s

24.8   They] Without discussing it much, they   s

24.9   life, not to be always skimping and saving] life and skimp and save   s

24.11   they did] themselves   s

24.12   agent] man   s

24.18   I'd] I had   A

24.26   John] Peter   s

25.9   This] That   s

25.14   see] have   s

26.10   nobody's] nobody his   s

26.17–18   often stood through . . . get standing-room] was a
             habitual standee at the opera on Saturday nights.
             He could get in   s

26.22   stage splendour] splendor that went with opera; the
             story   s

26.23   usually] always   s

26.25   a fine] fine   s

26.25   life; for] life and for   s

26.25–27   or so it satisfied him completely] he never thought
             of living any other kind   s

27.11   the odd] odd   s

27.23   the] this   s

28.7   passed, all alike] went on   s

28.8   When] As   s

28.9   and he] and   s

28.13   though] although   A

28.17   a temporary] that temporary   s

29.3   belts] belt   s

29.6   young Rosicky] Rosicky   s

29.10   in an] in the   s

29.13   the articles] articles   s

29.13   read] noticed   s

29.17   have] own   s

30.16–17   in New York of Bohemian athletic societies] of
                Bohemian athletic societies in New York   s

31.4   Ford] car   s

31.11   de car] the car   s

31.13   week] the week   A

31.16–17   "If you and . . . Frank said, "maybe] "You and
                Mother are going to town?" Frank asked.
                "Maybe   s

31.19   and let] an' let   s

31.21   gettin'] gitten'   A

31.25   Saturday night] Saturday   s

32.3–4   did not reply . . . seriously] began to speak to them
                in Czech   s

32.4   lookin'] looking   s

32.5   lookin'] looking   s

32.5–6   It comes hard fur a town girl] It's hard to break a
                town girl in   s

32.6	no trouble] trouble s
32.9	like] want s
32.9	and] an' s
33.24	elbows] bare elbows s
33.25	gently] gently and firmly s
34.1	for] fur s
34.5	goin'] going s
34.21	comin'] coming s
35.4	Halting in the doorway, he] He stood in the doorway and s
35.10	quick!] quick. s
35.12	fumbled] put his hand s
35.13	pants pocket] pocket s
35.20	this] that s
35.23	with] to s
35.25	coal in] coal on s
36.1	draughts] drafts s
36.9	sisters] pretty sisters s
36.12	All four of them were musical] They were all four musical s
37.3	sort of chap] chap s

37.9   all coming] coming   s

37.10   to eat] to   s

37.12   and squeaking] the squeak of   s

37.18   inside] in   s

37.25   one's] the   s

38.2   Rosicky kitchen] kitchen   s

38.4   John] Peter   s

38.5   trees] plants   s

38.6   grown] had   s

38.7   brought] had brought   s

38.12   while] time   s

38.15   at a] in a   s

38.21–25   By chance he met . . . a cobbler. He] The first man
            he met who could speak Czech was a poor tailor
            from Vienna, who kept a repair shop in a
            Cheapside basement underneath a cobbler. This
            tailor, Lifschnitz,   s

39.6   that came Anton's way] Anton picked up   s

39.7–8   lived upstairs] lived   s

40.10   round] around   s

40.11   saying] talking about   s

41.14   we had that] of the   s

41.18   very day] day   s

41.19   and] an'   s

41.23   mind] notice   s

42.6   preservin'] preserving   s

42.8   and he] an' he   s

42.9   round] around   s

42.18   and there] an' there   s

42.19   father and] father an'   s

42.19   you three] all of you   s

43.2   and] an'   s

43.2   an'] and   A

43.9–10   down, and] down an'   s

43.13   gardens an' the corn] corn   s

44.18   hearty frankness] loud voice   s

45.12   a damn bit] a bit   s

45.14   chust] just   s

45.20   and] an'   s

45.22   for] fur   s

45.23   for] fur   s

46.1   round] around   s

46.3   morning] mornin'   s

46.5   and] an'   s

46.8   noway] at all   s

46.10   an'] to   s

46.11   wooden box] store-box   s

46.12   and] an'   s

46.15   and] an'   s

46.17   and] an'   s

46.22   him on the neck beneath his ear] the high top of his
            head   s

46.23   hungry!] hungry.   s

47.5   and] an'   s

47.12   and] an'   s

47.15   twelve o'clock] midnight   s

47.18   chust] just   s

47.24   and talkin'] an' talkin'   s

47.24   and feelin'] an' feelin'   s

47.25   and] an'   s

47.26   talk] speak   s

48.3   beg dem:] talk Czech, an' said;   s

48.6   and give] an' give   s

48.7   and cakes] an' cakes   s

48.9   and] an'   s

48.13   and] an'   s

48.20   and] an'   s

48.22   and] an'   s

48.24   Two three] Two-three   s ; Two-t'ree   A

48.25   and] an'   s

49.8   and] an'   s

49.9   da's] das   s

49.15–16   supper] dinner   s

49.26   Christmas there was no] Christmas, no   s

50.1   February. On] February and on   s

50.4   now the] the   s

50.6   It] That   s

50.12   because] that   s

50.15   blew in] blew   s

50.16   reflection] thinking   s

50.19   himself; now] himself and now   s

50.20   was he] was that he   s

50.21   sure] sure that   s

50.24–25   probably they would . . . a living] they would never
             get much ahead, probably   s

51.24–25   had helped to] had had to help   s

52.1   of the] of all the   s

52.2   cities] cities; doctors, hospitals, undertakers   s

52.9   who] that   s

53.12   it blew] that the wind blew it   s

53.12   that hid] about   s

53.20   and "take] in there and "take   s

53.22–23   insist about the thistles] press them about the
             alfalfa   s

54.6   car, leaving a work-team] car and there was a
             team   s

54.7   to his son's place,] and   s

54.12   Rosicky] He   s

54.19   take] get   s

55.7   out bath towels] bath towels out   s

55.10   on him] on   s

55.11   afterwards] afterward   s, A

55.13   As] When   s

55.17	at last] again s
55.18	Da's] Das s
55.18	a] an s
55.21–22	to your place] over home s
56.1–2	now. It's nice here."] now." s
56.13	comin'] coming s
56.15	was looking] looked s
56.17	face, to regard it with pleasure] face s
57.5–6	Rosicky did] Rosicky s
57.9	colour] color, a talent s
57.19	was] were s ; hand was A
57.24	which] that s
58.1	afterwards] afterward s, A
58.9–10	afterwards] afterward A
58.17–18	bed, though he protested that he was quite well again] bed s
58.20	with his] with the s
58.21	he warned] warned s
58.24	several] some s
59.1	hands] hand s

59.2	John's] Peter's s

59.8   heart on their sleeve] hearts on their sleeves s, A

60.6   wasn't] was not s

60.14   work-horses] horses s

"Old Mrs. Harris"

65.1   cross-stitch] her cross-stitch OMH, S

65.1   in hand] in her hand s

65.10   and, occasionally, the] and the OMH

65.11   letter v] letter "w" OMH

66.12   plaited] braided OMH, S

66.19–20   her neighbour's house] the house OMHa

66.23   homely] homy s

66.25   brown] black OMH

67.2   with her feet wide apart, in] in s

67.5   hour] time OMH, S

67.10   hung] that was hung OMHa

67.11   room] room near the kitchen door OMHa

67.13   embarrassment] embarrassed OMHa

67.14   Thank you] Good day OMHa

67.15   town!] town. OMH, S

67.18	my] de ОМНА
67.18	this] dis s
67.19	so!] so. ОМН, s
67.20	Mrs. Harris] Grandmother ОМНА
67.23	spindle-frame lounge] lounge with spindle frame ОМН, s
68.1	seem] look ОМН, s
68.1	seemed] rather ОМНА; looked ОМНb, s
68.4	complete] complete, unconscious ОМНА
68.5	deft] quick, deft ОМНА
68.9	I would] dat I would ОМНА
68.17	has] drinks ОМНА
68.22	her own] her ОМНА
68.24	come . . . for] go to ОМНА
68.24–25	but herself] else. The best of everything that went on the table was her natural tribute. There wasn't much, to be sure, but what there was was Victoria's ОМНА; else ОМНb
69.3	not all . . . hoped] disappointing ОМНА *as cancelled alternative*
69.11	more] much more s
69.13–70.3	It was a . . . tea-table.] *omit* s

69.17   stood against] against OMHA

69.18   children's caps] caps OMHA

69.19   coats. There was a] coats, a OMHA

69.20–21   A corner of the room] One corner OMHA

69.25–70.1 splint-bottom] split-bottom OMH

70.10   but inscrutable, with] but there was OMHA

70.11   in them] in them. Her eyes puzzled Mrs. Rosen;
             she had never seen any others like them OMHA

70.18   very seldom] never OMHA

70.22   the old lady] she always OMHA

70.25   Mrs. Harris's] the old lady's OMHA

71.17–19   And a . . . shade.] *omit* s

71.23   had!] had.   s

71.24   get . . . others] get past OMHA

72.6–7   eyes . . . breast] eyes OMHA

72.7–8   waited . . . sprang up] and waited. The moment she
             sat down he sprang up OMHA

72.10   rested] settled OMHA

72.13   now became] became OMHA

72.18   anybody."] anybody." She was evidently very proud
             of his accomplishment OMHA

72.20   couldn't] could not   A

72.24   course!] course.   OMHa,   S

72.24   to] mournfully to   S

73.22   this] dis   OMHa

73.23   take anything from] do anything for   OMHa

74.1   "Yes'm. Victoria] "Victoria   S

74.5   yard. The] yard, and the   OMHa

74.10   the baby] Hughie   OMHa

74.11   Hughie] him   OMHa

74.17   ten] twelve   OMH, S

74.20   machine, the rocking-horse] machine   OMHa

74.22–23   nice voices . . . their father] natural good manners,
           nice voices, nice faces   OMH, S

75.4   Mrs.] poor Mrs.   OMHa

75.6   ma'am] Mrs. Rosen   OMH, S

75.9   returned] returned. Victoria would be
           jealous   OMHa

75.11   Victoria Templeton] Mrs. Rosen > Mrs.
           Templeton   OMHa

75.25–26   usual. Mandy] usual, and Mandy   OMHa

76.2–3   when Mrs. Harris . . . been at all] when, according
           to Mrs. Templeton, "Ma rested," had not
           been   OMH, S

76.3	at all restful] restful OMH, S
76.4	understood] unuttered OMH, S
76.5	was not to] must not OMHa
76.7	accepted] usual OMH, S
76.7	order. Nervousness] order, and nervousness OMHa
76.8	repose] real repose OMH
76.9	After the rest of] After OMH, S
76.10	took her place] sat down OMHa
76.13	dozed] dozed for awhile OMHa
76.16	Skyline] Topaz Valley OMHa
76.16–17	read *Tom Sawyer*] read aloud OMHa
76.18–19	Chicago weekly] weekly Chicago OMHb
76.22	anyhow] anyway OMH, S
76.23	coats] coats and caps OMHa
76.24	lay] sat S
76.25	lounge bed] bed lounge OMH; lap S
77.1–2	against the wall] behind the empty stove OMHa
77.3–4	little sawed-off chair . . . served coffee] floor S
77.6–9	Presently . . . stairway.] *omit* S
77.9	own room] room OMH

77.11   you'd] you'll   OMHa

77.19–20   boy on the lounge] boy   s

78.4   Presently] At last   OMHa

78.9   Bert and me'll] We'll   OMHa

78.19   Hughie, the baby] Hughie   OMHa

78.19   room] bed   s

78.21   "beau"] beau   s

78.22   room] room was   OMHa

78.23   was] therefore   OMHa

78.25   was off . . . somewhere] eating sweets
somewhere   OMHa; away   OMHb; off enjoying
herself somewhere   s

79.1   Mrs. Harris] she   OMH, s

79.2   lounge bed] cot > lounge bed   OMHa

79.5   Miz'] Misses   OMHa

79.12   checked shawl] shawl   OMH, s

79.14   down] down beside it   OMH, s

79.15   untied . . . and took] and took   OMHa

79.21   tub and, crouching beside it] tub, and sitting on her
haunches   OMH, s

79.22–80.4   Mrs. Harris . . . lantern.] *omit*   s

79.24   solace] comfort and solace   OMH

80.2   Mandy] she   OMHA

80.5–6   Mandy . . . asleep] Mandy dropped off more than
          once   OMHA

80.10   as soon as she] at once when she   OMHA

80.10   was in bed] lay down   OMHA; went to
          bed   OMHb, s

80.12   comfort] rest   OMHb

80.13–14 would begin] began   OMHA

81.2   this] dis   OMHA

81.2   left?] left behind him.   OMHA

81.4   felt of] felt   OMHA

81.8–9   her mattress. There] the mattress of her bed and
          there   OMHA

81.9   knew] knew that   OMHA

81.14   often felt] felt   OMHA

81.15   Sometimes her] Often the   OMHA

81.19   possessions] personal possessions   OMH, s

81.22   had married] was married   OMHA

81.24   After she was] Once   OMHA

82.1–2   rambling old] old rambling   OMHA

82.3   splint-bottom] split-bottom   OMH, s

82.6   indeed, there] there OMHa

82.10   possible] possible. She was simply following where the road led OMHa

82.12–13 all her life] for so many years OMHa

82.13   apple trees] trees OMHa

82.14   which] that OMH, s

82.16   which bore] that used to bear OMHa

82.24   she] that she OMHa

83.1   folks] people OMHa

83.6 — 86.10 And if . . . so much.] *omit* s

83.10–11 only at a distance] only OMHa

83.14   room] room full of coats and caps and toys OMHa

83.15   would get] got OMHa

83.15   wash] washed OMHa

83.18   in two] in the two OMHa

83.22   folding] putting OMHa

83.23   smoothed] folded OMHa

84.4   little rented house] house OMHa

84.6   Two] One OMH

84.7   dresses hung] dress always hung OMHa;
       dress hung OMHb

399

84.7   curtained corner] corner behind the striped
curtain OMHA

84.8   fourth] third OMH

84.18   afterwards] afterward OMH, A

84.21   enjoyed] had OMHA

84.23   In winter the boys] They OMHA;
In winter they OMHb

85.8   But even] But OMHA

85.8–9   Albert] Ronald OMH

85.15   them] dem OMHA

85.16   good] nice OMHA

85.19   infancy] babyhood OMHA

85.22   teasing] twinkling OMH

85.24   your children] children OMHA

85.24   comfortably] humanly > unnaturally OMHA

86.1   her] dose OMHA

86.2   than] dan OMHA

86.2   takes] does OMHA

86.3–4   can he expect to] can he get > get OMHA

86.4   you?] you OMHA

86.7   about the] about the absurdities of the OMHA

86.9   she] that she   OMHa

87.5   and a] and there were a   OMHa

87.11   some] a number   OMHa

87.14   Skyline] Topaz Valley   OMHa

87.17–18   rooms were carpeted . . . unusual),] rooms, except the kitchen, were covered   OMH, s

87.19   scattered on] on   OMH, s

87.20   were] were all   OMHa

87.20   dark] the same dark   OMHa

87.21   engravings] water colors — sketches made by Mr. Rosen on his travels — and   OMHa

87.21   some] There were some   OMHa

87.22   a castle] some castle   OMHa

87.23   another] one very dark one   OMHa

88.3   man] Jew   OMH, s

88.3–4   who didn't . . . so long as] who was not particular how he made his living if   OMHa; who was not particular as to how he made his living if   OMHb; who didn't mind keeping a clothing-store in a little Western town as long as   s

88.5   philosophy] philosophy, and "keep up with what the new German and French men were doing."   OMHa

88.6	Jewish family] family OMH, S
88.7–89.3	Last August . . . nice, too.] *omit* S
88.7	August] summer OMHA
88.7	Skyline] Topaz Valley OMHA
88.8	were burned] burned OMH
88.9–10	sand-hills . . . south] sand-hills OMHA
88.10	blew] blew in OMH
88.10	singed] burned up OMHA
88.11	lawns] yards OMHA
88.11	taken to] got into the way of OMH
88.12	upon] one [*sic*] OMHA
88.14	other cool] cool OMHA
88.15	home . . . roof] home OMHA
88.18	corsets] corset OMH
88.21	little] tiny OMHA
88.25	from the heat] from a sense of the heat OMHA
89.1	within] within and the elegance and order of her surroundings OMHA
89.3	her own] the flimsiness and confusion of her own OMHA
89.5–6	to admire] admire OMHA

89.7	cross-legged on] on s
89.14	*what*] what s
89.15	guess] think omha
89.23	do] do her omha
89.25	looking at] sitting with omh
90.2	the church] a church omha
90.15–16	it . . . while] it omha; it for a while omhb, s
90.19	There] Then omha
91.3	it doesn't] you don't omhb
91.5	through] lamely through omh, s
91.8	steady] uniform omha
91.10	even gave] gave omh, s
91.12	Vickie] her omha
91.13	apathetic] apathetic. She was perpetually interested, and usually pleased omha
91.14	nearly always played] was nearly always playing omh, s
91.14	about] somewhere about omha
91.15–16	something] things entirely outside herself omha
91.24	darkened] darkened a little omh
92.1	cheeks grew] cheeks (there was a tinge of orange in it in sunlight [*last two words a cancelled alternative*]

somewhere) grew OMHa; cheeks (there was a
tinge of orange in it somewhere) grew OMHb, s

92.3   if she] when she OMHa

92.4   betrayed it] betrayed it, betrayed it OMH, s

92.4   one felt] one was greatly OMH

92.6   to the] in the OMHa

92.12   future] education OMHa

92.14   sort; . . . up] sort, OMHa

92.20–93.11   Sometimes . . . know?] *omit* s

93.2   grey skin] gray OMH

93.3   white] white, like a pavement OMHa

93.3   fell . . . with] lost her heart to OMHa

93.5–6   romantic. Mrs.] romantic, not a cloak but
              Mrs. OMHa

93.10–11   said: . . . know?] said, "But it's not a cloak, it's an air
              from Rigoletto!" So it was, — but why should
              Vickie be so delighted > charmed by it? OMHa

93.12   Vickie's whole] But Vickie's entire OMHa

93.13   finer] more delicate OMH, s

93.16   the milk] her milk OMHa

93.22   this] dis OMHa

94.7   most houses] any other house > most
        houses   OMHA

94.8   parlour] cool parlour   OMHA

94.9   looked] was   OMH, S

94.10   a pleasantness] something pleasant   OMHA

94.11   didn't] did not   A

94.14   had time to see you] *omit*   OMHA

94.15   that] that all   OMH, S

94.21–22   them; and some were] them,   OMHA

94.24   might] would   OMHA

94.25   cookies] cookies and ice cream   OMHA

94.25   sent in] sent in, perhaps   OMHA

94.25–95.1   in, but she . . . always ready to] in, perhaps; but she
        offered anything they had to a caller, she
        would   OMHA; in; but she offered anything they
        had to a caller, she would   OMHb; in; but she
        offered anything she had to a caller. She would   S

95.3   never] never, never   S

95.4   Templeton (people usually] Templeton, he looked
        so boyish that people often   OMHA

95.6   debts . . . boyish] debts. Neither he nor his wife had
        learned that people won't use you well simply
        because you think well of them and are too
        considerate to press your claims. Mr. Templeton's
        boyish   OMHA

95.8   old] little OMHa

95.13   came] first came OMH, S

95.17   into the] in the OMHa

95.18   dirt] both dirt S

95.19   packing-cases] a number of packing cases S

95.21   the town] town OMH

95.23   an attractive] a handsome OMH, S

95.24   warm and genuine] very individual? OMHa *as*
            cancelled alternative

96.1   ladies] belles OMHa

96.2   but with] with just OMHa

96.3   too, as] as OMHa

96.4   and to do] and do OMHa; and eagerly seeking to
            do S

96.4   thing] thing. She was simple, direct, and
            hearty OMHa

96.5   While . . . party] During the party OMH

96.6–7   next . . . other] so near together OMH

96.8   blizzard. Mrs.] blizzard, and Mrs. OMHa

96.9–10   she laughed] laughed OMH, S

96.11   up to] to OMHa

96.14   right!] right. OMH, S

406

97.3	easy] comfortable OMH
97.6	Mrs. Rosen] she OMHA
97.9	corsets] corset OMH, S
97.9	challis] cashmere OMHA
97.15	snugly] comfortably OMHA
97.16	still talking] and talking OMHA
97.19	flushed] pink OMHA
97.20	Mrs. Rosen] Mrs. Rosen who had always wanted children OMHA
97.21	were] seemed OMH, S
98.1	turned on] turned OMHA
98.2	looked] then looked up S
98.4–8	And he . . . "We think] "WE THINK S
98.24	Rosen had] Rosen OMHA
99.4	arc. When he] arc and OMHA; arc, then OMHB
99.4–5	he looked . . . with] looking up with OMH
99.8	following] carefully following S
99.8	knew] knew that S
99.13	in a] lying in a OMHA
99.16	Skyline,] town OMHA
99.16	on] and it was on OMH

99.17   sage-brush] sage ОМНа

99.19–20   turn . . . on] keep the sprinklers going ОМНа

99.20   hours] hours, to keep the lawn green ОМНа

99.20   grass] grass. They couldn't have managed the lawn-mower ОМНа [*after* lawn-mower *four typed lines are interpolated.*]

99.25   ponies] little burrows ОМНа [little burrows *resumes original page*]

100.6   dig up] exterminate > obliterate ОМНа

100.7–8   the naked] the sand [*last words on cut and joined sheet*] the naked ОМНа

100.9   a miniature arroyo] *omit* ОМНа

100.9   which ran across] that ran through ОМНа

100.12   twins] boys ОМНа

100.19   vacation] school vacation ОМНа

100.21   party. When Mrs. Holliday] party. There was no Presbyterian church in Skyline, so Mrs. Holliday attended the Methodist church, and when she ОМНа

100.22   she always] she ОМН, s

100.23   Aid Society] Aid ОМН, s

100.24   place] place. It was the largest yard in town, and was shaded by fine old cottonwood trees ОМН

101.1   was a] was OMHA

101.3–4   everything. They got] everything, got OMHA

101.5   Before noon] In the morning OMHA

101.6   brought] brought out OMH, S

101.9   ladies . . . receive] Ladies opened up the kitchen to
                receive > Ladies came out and opened up the
                kitchen to receive OMHA

101.11   donated] contributed OMH; gave A

101.12   expected to send a cake] asked to contribute OMH

101.17   church] church > denomination OMHA

101.18   church suppers] suppers OMHA

101.19   June evening] midsummer night OMH

101.19   set out] went OMHA

101.20   first. They] first, and OMHA; first; OMHb, S

101.22   moon] moon, which was OMHA

102.4   seemed] looked OMHA

102.8   carried] seemed to carry OMHA

102.14   the rustling tree-tops] their rustling tops OMH

102.23–24   father. But good] father, but OMHA;
                father. But OMHb

102.24   laundresses] wash-women OMHA

103.1–2   didn't like their children to] wouldn't let their
                children OMH, S

103.3   came out] came   OMHA

103.4   leaned] and leaned   OMHA

103.4–5   fence . . . Maudes] fence   OMHA

103.15   which] that   OMHA

103.16   just selected] selected   S

103.19   take care] be sure   OMHA

103.21–22   overtook her . . . manner] stepped up to her and
             said in his very courteous and gentle manner asked
             her if she wouldn't 'have ice-cream with
             them.'   OMHA; stepped up to her and in his very
             courteous and friendly manner said   OMHB;
             stepped up to her and in his most courteous and
             friendly manner said   S

104.5   their table] a table   OMHA

104.7   moved] sat   OMHA

104.19   sat] enjoyed   OMHA

104.19   glad] pleased   OMHA

104.21   for her] under her   OMH

104.25   her over] over   OMHA

105.1   was] looked   OMHB

105.3   as much] quite as much   OMHA

105.4   looks] appearance   OHM

105.6   with her] by her   OMHA

105.7   He thought her] Her ᴏᴍʜᴀ

105.7   just] he thought just ᴏᴍʜᴀ

105.8–9   anything patronizing] a false accent ᴏᴍʜᴀ

105.10   too casual] casual ᴏᴍʜᴀ

105.18   had been keeping] kept ᴏᴍʜᴀ

105.22   tones] tones. One could never be sure just how much she meant to hurt people ᴏᴍʜᴀ

105.25   the more] more ᴏᴍʜᴀ

106.1   When she] She ᴏᴍʜᴀ

106.2–3   studying Mr. Rosen's . . . Mrs. Templeton] listening to his pleasant talk ᴏᴍʜ, s

106.3   she] when she ᴏᴍʜᴀ

106.13   deliberately separated] separated ᴏᴍʜᴀ

106.16   kept] had ᴏᴍʜᴀ

106.19–20 it!" he declared] in it!" ᴏᴍʜᴀ

106.23–24 would be . . . cook-stove] would be to forget I had a cook stove > would be never to build a fire in my ᴏᴍʜᴀ

107.2   the craftiness] 'smartness' in the country sense, the coarseness ᴏᴍʜᴀ; the 'smartness' in the country sense, the craftiness ᴏᴍʜb; smartness, the craftiness s

107.3   to the] at the ᴏᴍʜᴀ

107.4–5   she regarded] regarded   OMH, S

107.5   as an] as   OMH

107.10   is a] was a   OMHA

107.11   felt hurt] was uncomfortable   OMHA

107.13   thrusts] prods   OMH, S

107.14–16   The neighbours . . . mother] If people came to see
her mother, they took sides against herself, it
seemed. Therefore she must keep people out-out
of a house that had always been open and
hospitable, where everyone was welcome and no
one was ever allowed to go away without
'refreshment' of some kind, if it were only a glass of
lemonade.   OMHA; The neighbors who came in to
see her mother took sides against herself,
apparently   OMHB, S [*except* herself∧]

107.17   Templeton] Templeton all evening   OMHA

107.19   knew] knew that   OMHA

107.20–21   them to go] them that they must go   OMHA

107.23   some peppermint tea] a hot toddy   OMH

108.3–18   [*The earliest extant version, here reproduced within
brackets, is crossed out at the bottom of p. 32 and the top
of p. 34 of the typescript. It was replaced by text at top of
p. 33, treated below as* OMHA: Mrs. Harris sighed and
began to turn down her bed. She knew, as well as it
(*sic*) she had been at the social, what kind of thing

had happened. Some of those prying W.R.C. or
W.C.T.U. > Womans Relief Corps, or Womans
Christian Temperance Union women had been
intimating to Victoria that her mother was "put
upon." Nothing but (*part cut off*) small attentions
paid to Mrs. Harris 'over her head". Whenever she
'bridled' or withdrew herself, something of that
kind had occurred. (¶) Mrs. Harris got into bed,
said an *Our Father* and The Lord is my Shepherd,
and went to sleep lying gratefully on her back and
snoring comfortably.]

108.3	Left alone, Mrs.] Mrs. OMHa
108.5	happened] occurred OMHa
108.8	upon."] upon.' Victoria was naturally hearty and warm-hearted and good-humored OMHa
108.9	Victoria] her OMHa
108.10–11	because] mainly because OMHa
108.13	a belle] called the reigning belle OMHa; "belle" OMHb
108.14	but] and OMHa
108.15	wore] had OMHa
108.16	her mother] Grandmother OMHa
108.16–17	somehow to blame; at least] to blame s
108.22–23	usual . . . town] usual, and thought the situation over before the house was stirring OMHa;

413

usual, before the house was stirring, and thought
about their position in this new town OMHb

109.1   place in the family] position OMHa

109.2   perfectly regular] traditionally correct OMHa

109.2   Mrs. Harris] As Mrs. Harris OMHa

109.2   replied to] told OMH, s

109.6   the South] Tennessee OMHa

109.7   the fault . . . Vickie] Grandmother's only criticism
           of Vickie OMHa

109.9   have] bear OMHa

109.14   older] old OMH

109.15   mother or] mother or a s

109.16   help] working women, working with them OMHa

109.18   had been] were OMHa

109.19   Crummer] Grubb OMHa

109.22   did] came to do OMHa

109.25   but] who were but OMH, s

110.2   Miz'] Misses OMHa

110.2   good] the good OMHa

110.2   and a] and OMHa

110.6   managed] ruled OMHa

110.6	daughter's] son's OMH, S
110.9–10	young friends] friends OMHA
110.11–12	there they ordered life] they ordered life there OMH, S
110.13	friends] own friends OMH, S
110.16	"blood"] blood OMH, S
110.21	carriage] carriages S
111.1	and became] as became OMHA
111.2	gratefully] gratefully, as the tired apple orchards accept winter OMH
111.6	little] babies OMH
111.6	his] that his OMHA
111.8	good] very good OMHA
111.12–13	managers . . . mining] mining OMHA
111.15	got a promotion] done better OMHA
111.16	of that mountain town was] was OMH, S
111.18	ill most of] sick all OMH, S
111.19	Hillary Templeton] Hillary OMHA
111.25	helper] helpers OMHA
111.25	Mandy] Mandy, the bound girl, whom they had brought with them OMHA
112.5	out to] keen to OMH

415

112.6–7	understood . . . matter] knew what had happened oмнa; understood just what had happened oмнb
112.8	knew] only knew oмнa
112.14	marks] any mark oмн, s
112.21	every] in the oмнa
112.21	gingham] calico oмн
112.23	as these . . . did] the usual morning costume of these brisk housekeepers oмн
113.3	means went on decreasing] means decreasing oмн
113.10	either in] in either s
113.14	own ways] ways oмнa
113.18	German] Swede oмнa
113.19	help] help with the housework s
113.19	but now] now oмнa
113.20	her. Grandmother's] one. Her oмн
113.20	improve only] only improve oмн, s
113.22	that of the family] the general family comfort oмн
113.25–115.2	That was . . . important.] *omit* s
114.4	Ronald and Hughie] they oмнa
114.9–10	if her feet . . . little low] Mrs. Harris felt a little low, if her feet ached more than usual oмн

114.10   did] knew   OMH

114.14   feeling that] feeling   OMHA

114.16   children running down] children's feet on   OMH

114.19   drunk up into] entirely absorbed   OMHA

114.21   explaining their] their   OMH

114.22   and underwear] or underwear   OMHA

114.24   suddenly the] the sunshiny morning   OMHA

114.24   the] all the   OMH

115.2   sunshiny] as sunshiny   OMH

115.5   The day] The second morning   OMHA

115.5   didn't] did not   A

115.12   Miz'] Misses   OMHA

115.15–16 threw . . . and went] went   S

115.16   children] twins   OMHA

115.22   Ronald] him   OMHA

116.6   cat] blue cat   OMH

116.11–12 Holliday's] Thomas'   OMHA

116.15   Holliday's] Thomas'   OMHA

116.17   forgot] almost forgot   OMH

116.21   in which] where   OMH, S

116.22–117.7	Mr. Holliday . . . Grandma.] *omit* s
116.22	Holliday] Thomas omha
116.25	the sum] of the money omh
117.1	milk every Saturday] milk omh
117.4–5	Jackson next door] Jackson omha
117.7	Grandma] Grandmother omha
117.8–9	got back] came in omh; came back s
117.11–12	Roadmaster . . . invited] Roadmaster invited omha
117.14	always whizzed] whizzed omha
117.16–17	sage-brush] sage omh, s
117.18–21	Sometimes the . . . good work.] *omit* s
117.22	boys] twins omha
117.22	Holliday] Thomas omha
117.23	late] about four omha
117.24	Ronald and Hughie] the two little boys omha
118.3	coal-shed] coal house omha
118.4–6	Bert . . . Blue Boy.] *omit* s
118.5	didn't] did not a
118.11	cried] asked omha
118.16	up] by omha

118.17–19	She patted . . . "Where's] "Where's s
118.18	forgot] forgotten A
118.20	part her] her s
118.22	people kind of] people omh, s
119.3–11	Back in . . . more.] *omit* s
119.5	distress] stress omh
119.6	Miz'] Mrs. omha
119.8	diphtheria] diphtheria at once omh
119.13	die] go omha
119.14	and] so omh, s
119.19	at] about omha
119.23	herself went] went omha
119.24	shed] coal shed omha
120.19–21	They stood . . . "You git] "YOU git s
120.22	a spade] the spade omh
121.16–18	That was . . . thoroughly.] *omit* s
121.25	overbearing] overbearing > (stern) omha *as cancelled alternative*
122.2	me beforehand] me omha
122.4–5	went with] followed omh, s

419

122.6   That's] but that's OMHA

122.7   dying] dying. I wish you could have kept this one,
             though OMHA

122.8   Maybe . . . have] You can have OMHA;
             How'd you like to have OMHb, s

122.9   afternoon? And] afternoon if you want to,
             and OMHA

122.13   ring] ring in the yard s

122.14–24   They knew . . . about it.] *omit* s

122.22   terribly] very much OMH

123.1   their] the OMHA

123.2   came to the show] came OMHA

123.4   if] that if OMHA

123.9   into the house] home OMHA

123.12–16   Grandmother . . . lemonade.] *omit* s

123.13   stayed] sat OMHA

123.13   unusual] unusual, and Hughie went to sleep on the
             sofa OMHA

123.17   widout] without OMH

123.19   right smart] a good deal OMH

123.23   I am] I'm OMHA

123.25–124.8   Mrs. Templeton . . . was due.] *omit* s

123.5   tumblers] glasses OMHA

124.2   her neighbour's] her OMH

124.4   flowered] white OMHA

124.12   overdoing it] overdoing OMHA

124.19   her] her all we can OMHA

124.20   bridled] tossed her head and bridled OMHA

125.1   Templeton's either] Templeton's OMH, s

125.5   Professor] young Professor OMH, s

125.9   Vickie."] Vickie; I know her." OMH

125.10–11   Mrs. Templeton] dear lady OMHA

125.15–16   Chalmers, myself] Chalmers OMH, s

125.17   never had a thing to say] had nothing to say for himself OMH, s

125.21   you know] Mrs. Templeton OMHA

125.23   insisting upon] reminding her of OMHA

126.4–5   soles. She . . . rocker.] *omit* s

126.5   rocker. Mrs.] rocker, leaving Mrs. OMHA

126.6   sat chatting] gossip a little OMHA

126.8   professor] man OMHA

126.8–9   come to Skyline] come OMHA

421

126.10	stayed three months] spent the summer OMHa; stayed the summer OMHb, s
126.12–18	at their . . . hand up] out at their camp. They said s
126.13	day in a light] morning in a OMH
126.14–15	them at . . . town] them OMHa
126.21–22	once have . . . came upon] have perished. Farther down, they came on OMHa; have perished. Deeper down, they came on OMHb, s
127.1	about a] about the OMH
127.1	a memorial] the OMHa; the memorial OMHb, s; memorial A
127.1–2	at Ann Arbor, which] that OMHa; at Ann Arbor, that OMHb, s
127.2	Colorado] the state of Colorado s
127.6	Holliday] Thomas OMHa
127.9	examination] examinations OMH
127.10	with] with the OMH
127.10	the Denver] the OMHa
127.23–128.11	While . . . success.] *omit* s
128.8–9	University of Michigan] University OMHa
128.11–13	as she . . . what] herself what s
128.16	the weeks] these weeks OMHa

128.16–22   During the ... complete.] *omit* s

128.18   into] in OMHA

129.2   from] out of OMHA

129.4   hid the letter] hid it OMH, s

129.5   striped blazer] blazer OMHA

129.13   in at ... and said] in and said s

129.16–17   Mrs. Rosen ... stove.] *omit* s

129.22–24   Mrs. Rosen ... intently.] *omit* s

129.24   floury] a little floury OMHA

130.1   *be*] be OMH, s

130.1–2   on de front] on the OMH, s

130.2   round] plump OMH, s

130.7   come home] come OMHA

130.7–8   sitting, a book in his hand, in] sitting in OMH, s

130.9   where] with OMH

130.9   a flood of] just a little OMHA

130.9   streamed] streaming OMH

130.10   dark green blind] dark blind, a little German book in his hand OMHA; dark green blind, a book in his hand OMHB, s

130.10–14   He smiled ... behind him] He smiled at Vickie and waved her to a seat s

130.12–13   The dark engraving] His dark etching OMH

130.13   cypresses] poplars OMH

130.17   their visitor. She spoke] the visitor,
speaking OMHa;
their visitor, speaking OMHb, s

130.21–22   scholarship?] scholarship at Ann Arbor? s

131.3–4   Why do . . . playfully] He put his hand on her hair
and felt her head enquiringly with his finger-tips. "I
wonder?" He shrugged and asked her playfully,
"Why do you want to go to college,
Vickie?" OMH

131.11–17   She had . . . voice.] *omit* s

131.17   voice] voice and in his eyes OMHa

131.20   to keep] keep OMHa

131.21   *n'est*] *c'est* OMH

132.8   the twitch of] something that happened to OMHa

132.14   give] teach OMHa

132.20   the] that s

132.25   said] meekly said s

133.2   thought] thought that s

133.6   Vickie] SOON Vickie s

133.11   two] three OMH

133.13   about three] three OMH, s

133.15   this] this second   OMH

133.17   embarrassed] embarrassed. He was still very young
          in experience, and very much afraid of the world,
          poor Mr. Templeton, but of course his daughter
          [Vickie *as cancelled alternative*] couldn't realize
          that.   OMHa

133.19   spare] lay hand on   OMH

133.22   wouldn't count . . . I just have] won't count next
          year. I've just got   OMH, s

134.10   everyone] the family   OMHa

134.15–16   to have . . . streak] stubborn and hard   OMHa

134.22   took] had   OMHa

135.3–4   began to wash her face] washed her hot face and
          neck   OMH, s

135.6   sitting . . . lounge] sitting.   OMHa

135.12   cushions] pillows   OMHa *as cancelled alternative*

135.16   was] is   OMHa

136.5–6   Templeton, but opportunities] Templeton herself.
          Opportunities   OMH, s

136.8   next saw] saw   OMH, s

136.8   fork] throw   OMHa

136.16   whisk-broom] broom   OMH

136.16   kept there] kept   OMHa

136.19   right now] just now   OMHa

136.25   right now] just now   OMHa

137.10–11 meant they could] means they can   OMHa

137.14   at that moment] just   OMHa

137.16   play] sit   OMH

137.16   here] here in his buggy   OMH

137.23   her to] her to reach   OMHa; her reach   OMHb, s

138.2   so much] something   OMHa

138.6   went] had gone   OMH

138.7   Mandy] to Mandy   OMH

138.12   you to come] you   OMH, s

138.17   hand] purple-veined hand   OMH

139.1   her] the   OMH

139.5–6   sickness in . . . before] sickness before   s

139.9   over] about   OMHa

139.13   borrow] try to borrow   OMHa

139.14   it] you see, it   s

140.4   would] that would   OMHa

140.6   her arm] the back of her hand with the cord-like
           purple veins   OMHa

140.8–9   You know . . . young.] *omit*   s

140.8   the old] de old   oмнa

140.8   than the] dan de   oмнa

140.9   take] can take   oмн

140.9   away] off   oмнa

140.10   dismiss it] dismiss it from your mind   oмнa

140.13–16   Mrs. Rosen . . . excited.] *omit*   s

140.17   slowly filled] filled   oмн, s

140.24   purple-veined] purple-spotted   oмн

140.25   home] back   oмнa

141.2   felt!] felt! In a few minutes she was fast asleep in her chair.   oмн

141.5   knew] knew that   oмн

141.9   and] so   oмн, s

141.11   gloved] encased   oмнa

141.13–15   Then she . . . gate.] *omit*   s

141.16   thankful] grateful   oмнa

141.16   friend] neighbor   oмн

141.21–23   *The Chimes* . . . Victoria] The Chimes of Normandy at the opera house   s

142.2   something wrong] something   oмн, s

142.3	Miz'] Mis'es OMHA
142.13	for once she lay] she, for once, lay OMHA
142.21–23	responsible . . . said:] responsible, though Mr. Rosen had said: s
142.23	speak of] mention OMHA
142.24	And] But OMHA
143.7	All her] her OMHA
143.9	two] three OMHA
143.9	do everything!] get ready! OMHA
143.11–144.8	She thought . . . set.] *omit* s
143.12	people] real people OMHA; refined people OMHB
143.15	disagreeable] humiliating OMH
143.18	find her] find out she was OMHA; find she was OMHB
143.18	round] about OMHA; around OMHB
143.20	call] come OMH
143.25	Miz'] Mrs. OMHA
144.2	the colic] colic OMH
144.3	Miz'] Mis'es OMHA
144.6	yesterday] that OMH
144.9	day] morning OMHA

144.13   over her] over   OMHa

144.16   where] right where   OMHa

144.16   I'll] an' I'll   OMH

144.20   Immediately after] After   s

144.22   still on] on   OMHa

145.4   and I] and   OMH, s

145.6   you're going to] you   OMHa

145.13–14   Things did seem] The house seemed   OMHa;
            The house did seem   OMHb, s

145.15   While] When   OMH, s

145.16–17   narrowly observing] observing   OMHa

145.20   Instead . . . office] Immediately after
            breakfast   OMHa

145.21–23   Soon . . . After] Soon he brought Cleveland, the
            black horse, out with his harness on. Mandy
            watched from the kitchen window. When   OMH;
            When   s

145.26   most] most brisk   OMH, s

146.1   back] home   OMH

146.4   these] such   OMHa

146.6   on] by   OMHa

146.8   her] the   OMHa

146.9	bent over] leaned over her OMHA
146.16–17	dropped . . . doze] went to sleep OMHA; dropped off into a doze OMHB
146.18	Mrs. Templeton] Victoria OMHA
146.18–19	bed alone] bed OMHA
146.25	then about at] at OMHA; then glanced about at OMHB, s
147.12	She had had] She had OMH, s
147.13–14	some time before] sometime before OMHA sometime, before OMHB, s
147.22–148.2	Life hadn't . . . tried!] *omit* s
147.24	right] well OMHA
147.25	dress] look OMH
148.1	to keep] and keep OMHA
148.2	Mrs. Templeton] She OMH, s
148.3	smothered] tried to smother OMHA
148.5–149.8	Hillary . . . Tennessee."] *omit* s
148.6	up into] into OMHA; and up into OMHB
148.6–7	that was irrigated] irrigated OMH
148.8–9	on the way] as he lounged in his buggy seat OMHA
148.9	Victoria] that Victoria OMHA

148.14   the eighteen] of the fourteen   OMHa;
           the fourteen   OMHb

149.15   milk toast] toast   OMHa

149.17   children at noon] children, when she gave them
           their dinner at noon,   OMH

149.21–22 invited] asked   OMHa

149.22–23 hotel (he boarded there] hotel where he
           boarded   OMHa; hotel, he boarded there   OMHb

150.1   offered to] said they would   OMH

150.5   whisky] a little whiskey   OMH

150.6   like to make] make   OMHa

150.14   sat in the morning] sat   S

150.15–16 He brought this down] He got this   S

150.22   After] When   OMHa

150.23   fetched] got   OMHa

150.25–151.1   red cotton] red   OMHa

151.3   his] the   OMH, S

151.5   Having] When he had   OMHa

151.7–11   The windows . . . sunlight.] *omit*   S

151.11   sunlight] sunlight that poured in   OMHa

151.12   gazed] looked   OMHa

151.24   so many] many OMHa

152.3   home] in OMH, s

152.4–6   He said . . . listen.] *omit* s

152.8–13 She and . . . eyes.] *omit* s

152.11   her, it seemed] her seemed OMH

152.25   old] and old OMHa

153.2–4   Mandy . . . out.] *omit* s

153.3   biscuits] biscuit OMH

153.7   Miz'] Miss' OMHa

153.11   very well] all right OMH, s

153.12   upstairs] up to her room OMHa

153.14   and no clothes] or no clothes OMHa

153.14–16 Nobody . . . "when] Nobody seemed to take the least interest but Mr. Rosen, "when OMH, s

153.18   Vickie] everyone went to bed early but Vickie. She OMH, s

153.18–19 read; she] read, and she OMHa

153.19–20 and when . . . bed] and she would come in and go upstairs OMHa

153.21   ran] went OMHa

153.23   slipped] came in and kissed their grandmother goodnight and went OMHa;

432

came in and kissed their grandmother
goodnight and slipped   OMHb, s

153.23   stairs to their room] stairs   OMH, s

153.25   Miz'] Miss'   OMHa

154.7   out on her] out   s

154.8   with the back of] with   s

154.13   answer] reply   OMHa

154.15–16   back in] in   OMHa

154.18   said] knelt down to say   OMHa

154.20–22   She dreaded . . . care.] *omit*   s

154.25   glad] glad that   OMHa

155.2   that . . . sick] how sick her old neighbor was   OMHa

155.13   away, too] away   OMHa

155.16–17   doctor . . . peaceful] doctor. No words could tell the
          dread she had of lying helpless on this lounge and
          being beholden to a family where she had always
          paid her way. And that was not to be. The Lord
          would take her and she need ask nothing of
          anybody.   OMHa

155.24   Grandma] She   OMHa

155.24–25   home: what] home and what   OMHa

156.1   had always been] always was   OMHa

156.6   darkness] darkness, in the silence to a more perfect
          silence.   OMH, s

156.7   Old Mrs.] Mrs.   OMH, S

156.9   morning] morning, and she never regained consciousness   OMH

156.14–17   The inquisitive . . . her nay.] *omit*   S

156.17   never] never in the least   OMHA

156.18   object] centre   OMHA

156.19–20   a little . . . home] to the family about twenty-four hours after she died to herself   OMHA

156.21   Thus] And thus   S

156.21   Templetons'] Templeton   S

157.5   feel] know   OMH

157.6–7   and strong] so strong   OMH

157.7   and] and because I   OMH

157.7   much. But now I know."] much."   OMH

"Two Friends"

161.2   untried] strange   TFIa

161.4   realities] facts > feelings   TFIa

161.5   things] things, a sure foundation   TFI

161.5   These] Sometimes these   TFIa

161.5   may be] are   TFIa

161.6–8   memories, which in some unaccountable and very personal way give us courage] memories which are

in themselves ideas or ideals. They may be very
homely; the only thing we can say of them is that in
some curious and very personal way, they satisfy
us TF1a;
memories which are in themselves ideas or ideals.
They may be very homely; the only thing we can
say of them is that in some unaccountable and very
personal way, they fortify us TF1b, TF2a

161.8   that] that > which TF2a

161.9   that] that > which TF2a

161.10   tides] waves TF1a

161.11   even they] they TF1a

161.12–13   remote islands] islands TF1, TF2a

161.13–14   and lonely ledges that are their breeding-grounds]
             that are their breeding grounds, to lonely ledges
             where they creep into well-known holes and caves,
             into mere fissures and cracks in the rock TF1a;
             that are their breeding grounds, to lonely ledges
             where they creep into mere fissures and cracks in
             the rock TF1b, TF2a

161.16–162.2 motor-car (which . . . after Waterloo)] motor car s

162.3   a shallow Kansas] a shallow TF1a;
             the shallow Kansas TF2a

162.3   valley] valley of Central Kansas TF1

162.7   "connections"] business connections TF1a

435

162.16	prominent] very prominent TF1a
162.17	cut by] with TF1
162.17–18	with a] and a TF1a
162.19	black] thick TF1a
162.21–22	Yet on meeting him] Yet TF1a
162.22	an imperious] merely a handsome imperious TF1a
163.5–6	and proprietor] the proprietor TF1a
163.7	fine] big cattle TF1a
163.11	Trueman] He TF1, TF2a
163.12–13	West . . . man] West TF1a
163.14–15	in his] in the TF1, TF2a
163.21	this] that TF1a
163.25	anything . . . small] any meanness or smallness TF1a
164.2–3	ten . . . thirteen] ten to thirteen TF1, TF2a
164.3	thirteen] thirteen — years when the grown-up people about one are the chief interest in life TF1a
164.5	one . . . them] had more experience and more money TF1a
164.5–6	Dillon . . . intelligent] Dillon was the more intelligent of the two TF1a
164.6	had, perhaps,] had TF1, TF2a

436

164.11   going on] on   TF1a

164.13   Its] the   TF1a

164.24   established] established and easy   TF1a

164.24   So many] Most   TF1, TF2a

164.25   hopper] grasshopper   TF1, TF2, s

165.3   often see] see   TF1a

165.5   were both] were   TF1a

165.5   found] found together   TF1a

165.9   never] never, of course   TF1a

165.10   wire-screened] wire-screeded   TF1

165.11   called on] called on because he found his store the
        most interesting place in town   TF1a

165.12   customers] clients   TF1, TF2a

165.15   and on] and in   TF1a

165.19   or to buy] or buy   TF1a

165.19   thrasher or] thresher or to   s; thresher or   A

165.21   passed] went   TF1a

165.22   going round] around   TF1; going
        around   TF2a, s

165.23   catch sight] catch a sight   TF2a

165.25   accountant's] office   TF1a; accountants'   TF1b, s

166.3   about . . . them] about   TF1a

166.4–5   from a] at a   TF1, TF2, S

166.7   blue] dark blue   TF1a

166.8   hair] hair, with high knuckles   TF1, TF2, S

166.12   Each of the] Both   TF1, TF2a

166.12   a ring] rings   TF1, TF2a

166.12   his] their   TF1, TF2a

166.13   Dillon's was] Dillon   TF1a

166.14   Trueman's] Trueman   TF1a

166.15   onyx] carnelian   TF1a

166.24   crowd] company   TF1a

166.24   Trueman's] Dillon's   TF1a

167.1   evenings] nights   TF1, TF2a

167.1–2   but there . . . proprietor] but the billiard-hall
             proprietor   TF1a; but three tireless poker
             men were always on hand; the billiard-hall
             proprietor   TF1b; but three tireless poker
             players were always on hand: the billiard-hall
             proprietor   TF2a

167.4   the] and the   TF1a, TF2a

167.5   the] and the   TF1, TF2a

167.5   Dillon's] Dillons, they were always on hand   TF1a

438

167.6   gamblers] poker players TF1a

167.10   look or] look and TF1, TF2, s

167.11   freeze] always freeze TF1a

167.11   And his] His TF1, TF2, s

167.18   he was] was TF1a

167.20   his inside] his cigar-case in his
inside TF1, TF2, s

167.25   a contemptuous word] contemptuous
remarks TF1, TF2a

167.25   "poker bugs"] poker bugs TF1

168.2   other] rival TF1a

168.9–11   ready . . . signalled] ready they stepped aboard the
Santa Fe and went; one of the fast California trains
was always signalled TF1a; ready, they packed
their bags and stepped aboard a Santa Fe and went;
the California limited was signalled TF1b; ready,
they packed their bags and stepped aboard a fast
Santa Fé train and went; the California limited was
signalled TF2a; ready, they packed their bags and
stepped aboard a fast Santa Fé train and went; the
California Limited was often signalled TF2b

168.12   made some . . . of us] made us TF1a; made some
of us TF1b, TF2a; made the rest of us s

168.15   shirts] shirts, the cuffs and collars one with the
garment TF1a

168.17   which were] and they   TF1a

168.18   was] were   TF1, TF2a

168.19–21   waistcoats . . . were] waistcoats, and their
                suspenders, I thought, were > waistcoats, often
                removed their coats; their suspenders, I thought,
                were   TF1a

168.25   hand up] hand   TF2a

169.4–5   I returned] returned   TF1a

169.6   spring and summer] long, free summers   TF1a;
                spring and summers   TF1b

169.7–8   Spring began early] Summer began in May   TF1a

169.8   often . . . hot] often in the first week of April   TF1a

169.10   bring] bring out   TF1

169.11   out to] out on   TF1a

169.12   office] desk   TF1a

169.13   which] that   TF1, TF2, S

169.14   spreading] sprawling   TF1a

169.15   higher] higher than the back   TF1, TF2, S

169.15–16   would spend] spent   TF1, TF2a

169.16   would sit] sat   TF1, TF2a

169.16   light] lit   TF1, TF2a

169.18	across] along	TF1, TF2, S
169.20	out to him] out	TF1, TF2, S
170.12	talked] would talk	TF1a
170.13	talked] would talk	TF1a
170.13	made] make	TF1
170.14	could tell] knew	TF1, TF2
170.14–15	how much] what	TF1a
170.15	anything] anything, or how much he knew about anything	TF1a
170.16	diffidence] diffidence, one knew	TF1a
170.19	often sat] would often sit	TF1, TF2a
170.22	told] would tell	TF1, TF2a
171.1–2	low . . . never] low, rather indistinct, and his speech never	TF1, TF2a
171.4	into] onto	TF1a
171.7	But I] I	TF1, TF2a
171.9	Dillon] He	TF1, TF2a
171.9	enunciation, and] enunciation, very vibrant vocal chords, and	TF1, TF2a [cords]
171.14	humorous] gay and droll	TF1a
171.16	alive] alive, and keen	TF1a

441

171.20   closeted . . . in his] closeted   TF1a

172.11   talk] talks   s

172.13–14   lingering] hanging about   TF1a

172.14   them, and] them. They   TF1a

172.18   perched on top of] sat on   TF1a

172.19   there] and there   TF1a

172.20   several of these] two or three   TF1, TF2a

172.22   those two] them   TF1a

172.23   one] that one   TF1, TF2a

172.24   talked of] talked about   TF1a

173.3   speech] sppech [*sic*] at all   TF1a

173.8   discussed] talked   TF1a

173.9   and joked] joked   TF1, TF2, s

173.9   the policies] well known policies   TF1a

173.10   pretensions] empty pretentions   TF1a

173.13   town] streets   TF1a

173.14   "G.O.P."] G.O.P.   TF1, TF2a, s

173.18   went] drove   TF1a

173.24   nice] pretty   TF1, TF2a

174.4   an amusing sight] something amusing   TF1a

174.4   turned in at] drove down to   TF1a

174.10   laugh] laugh. [¶] On those spring nights both men
wore their coats, Trueman kept his hat on as well.
For me, there were still lessons to get — school
went on through May — so I seldom lingered in the
shadows about those two men all evening. But that
was not because I didn't find their talk interesting.
Any presentation [discussion *as alternative*] of
human occupations is interesting if the speaker is
deeply interested, knows and cares. Human speech
all about me was so vague that I found it fascinating
to hear exactly how a new kind of cultivator
worked, or all the reasons why Hereford cattle did
so well in our country.   TF1a

174.11   Those] The   TF1a

174.14   scent] smell   TF1a

174.15   evenings] nights   TF1a

174.17   idleness] indolence   TF1, TF2, S

174.17   Then there] There   TF1a

174.17   school, and] school —   TF1, TF2

174.25   to be quiet] for idleness   TF1, TF2, S

174.25   My two friends] My two aristocrats   TF1;
My two aristocrats > Dillon and Trueman   TF2a

175.5   them all as] all them as   TF1a

175.8   supply] large supply TF1a

175.10–11   features] faces TF1a

175.12   their shadows] they, with their shadows, TF1,
               TF2, S

175.15   Across . . . was] The street was TF1a

175.21   rickety] the TF1a

175.23   faded blue] blue TF1, TF2, S

175.25   melted] at night melted TF1a

176.2–4   with here . . . shutter] with tilted patches of sage
               green TF1a; with here and there a tilted patch of
               sage-green that had once been a shutter, a faint
               smear of blue door that took the moonbeams like
               the reflection in a waxed floor TF1b, TF2a

176.9   lay soft] soft TF1a

176.11   or] nor S

176.13   farming] sandy TF1, TF2, S

176.14   from the] from TF1a

176.22–23   little while] little TF1, TF2a

176.24   the smallest cloud] a cloud the size of your
               hand TF1, TF2, S

177.3   as I] for I S

177.4   chance to see it] see it TF1, TF2a

177.10   had been watching] had watched TF1, TF2a

444

177.12   bright wart] wart   TF1, TF2, S

177.14   fast] rapidly   TF1a

177.21   matters] things   TF1, TF2, S

177.23–24   two hundred and fifty thousand] *blank space* million
               TF1a; three hundred thousand   TF1b, TF2, S

178.4   then it] that   TF1a

178.8   he said] Then he added   TF1a

178.9   Then he added: "Mustn't] "Mustn't   TF1a

178.17   When . . . St. Joseph] Twice or three times a year
the two friends left us for a fortnight on their
excursions to big cities. Even when they went to
Chicago they always stopped off in St.
Joseph   TF1a

178.18   they stopped] They always stopped   TF1a

178.22   of a] in a   TF1a

178.22   convent] convent school   TF1a

178.22–23   there . . . him] there. He always went to see her and
she gave a dinner for him. He knew all the sisters,
and his visits were great events at the convent. The
nuns made much of him, and he enjoyed their
admiration and good food and all the ceremony
which attended their dinners   TF1a; there; he went
to see her often and she always gave a special dinner
for him   TF1b; there; he went to see her often, and
she always gave a special dinner for him. The nuns

445

made much of him, and he enjoyed their admiration
and all the ceremony with which they entertained
him TF2

178.25–179.2   When . . . friends] While his two daughters were in
school there, he gave theatre parties for them, took
all their friends and a group of the sisters TF1a;
While his two daughters were going to the convent
school, he used to give theatre parties for them;
invited all their friends and the nuns who were
their teachers TF1b; When his two daughters
were going to the convent school he used to give
theatre parties for them; invited all their friends
and the nuns who were their teachers TF2a;
When his two daughters were going to the convent
school, he used to give theatre parties for them,
inviting all their friends and some of the nuns who
were their teachers TF2b

179.8   money] money there TF1a

179.8–9   He was . . . too. The] He had rather questionable
women friends there, too, as he had been a
widower for many years. The TF1, TF2a;
The TF2b, s

179.12   house] house in St. Joe s

179.12–13   She must . . . she had] She was intelligent and a
good business woman, had TF1, TF2, s

179.14   any sort of trouble] trouble TF1a;
any sort trouble TF1b

446

179.15–16   school . . . young] knew how to manage
             young   TF1, TF2a; school   s

179.16   women] women, and was quoted as saying that all
             any girl needed was opportunity   TF1a; women,
             and was quoted as saying that 'all any girl needed
             was opportunity'   TF1b, TF2a

179.17–21   interesting . . . companionship] interesting. Dillon's
             tongue played sharply enough with men who
             allowed themselves indulgence in loose company.
             Trueman wouldn't have stood for the slightest
             interference from anybody. So Mr. Dillon must
             have shut his eyes, been resolutely blind; and that
             was a measure of the great value he put on
             Trueman's companionship   TF1a; interesting. Mr.
             Dillon must have shut his ears to these rumors —
             that was a measure of the great value he put on
             Trueman's companionship   TF1b, TF2a

179.22   did not see much] saw little   TF1;
             did not see a great deal   TF2a

179.24   They . . . day] They dined together
             occasionally   TF1a; They dined together at the
             end of the day   TF1b, TF2a

179.25   afterwards went] they went   TF1a;
             afterward went   TF1b, TF2a, s, A

179.25   theatre] theatre together   TF1a

180.2   It was] That was   TF1a

180.5   had come] came   TF1, TF2, s

180.6   city,] city, with supplies of new shirts and neckties, and always with new hats, and sat on the sidewalk in the evening again   TF1a; city, and had sat on the sidewalk in the evening again   TF1b; city and sat on the sidewalk in the evening again   TF2, s

180.6   sometimes to] to   TF1, TF2, s

180.7   recalling] recall   TF1, TF2a

180.7   effects] effects. An evesdropper [*sic*] could pick up a good deal from their talk, but it was years before I could find out what really happened in "The Two Orphans" about which they talked a good deal   TF1a

180.7–8   Occasionally] Sometimes   TF1, TF2, s

180.14   a young man] very young   TF1, TF2, s

180.16   waited] he waited   TF1a

180.16–17   The first . . . in Buffalo] I was just a young man when I first saw Edwin Booth, in Buffalo   TF1, TF2, s

180.19   "I don't] "And I don't   TF1a

180.23   had seen] saw   TF1; say > saw   TF2a

180.23   St. Louis] as Juliet in Chicago   TF1a; Kansas City   TF1b, TF2, s

180.24   years afterwards] long afterward   TF1, TF2a; years afterwards   TF2b; years afterward   s, A

180.25   Catholic girl] Catholic   TF1, TF2, s

181.19 as far] to as far TF1

181.24 a stupid] such a stupid TF1a

182.1 "tainted"] tainted TF1, TF2a

182.4 it was the] the TF1a

182.6 Chicago] that Convention TF1a

182.8 all about] about TF1a

182.10 in . . . way] with his masterful stride TF1a

182.11 Dillon] him TF1a

182.11 had found] left TF1a; found TF1b, TF2a, s

182.12 whether] and whether TF1a

182.12 had had] had TF1a, TF2a

182.13–14 Trueman] he TF1a

182.17 was a] was that TF1a

182.21 noticed that] noticed TF1a

182.24 orator] orator, J.H. TF1, TF2a

183.1 memorable] great TF1a

183.5 from him] him TF1, TF2, s

183.10 around] about TF1a

183.12 voice] speech TF1, TF2, s

183.15 It was one] One TF1a

183.18–19 "Glad I . . . Trueman] I won't have any
grandchildren," said Mr. Trueman with grim

humor. "And thank God for it, if they'd be brought
up upon that sort of tall-talk   TF1

183.20   like a] like a show-off   TF1a

183.21   an unsound] unsound   TF2a

183.24   provokingly] provolkingly [*sic*] when he laughed
like that   TF1a

183.25–184.1   anyhow. By] anyhoe [*sic*], and by   TF1;
anyhow, and by   TF1a

184.1   dyed-] died-   TF1a

184.6   turned] went over to the   TF1b, TF2a

184.8   rose] got up   TF1a

184.9   watching] sat watching   TF1a

184.10–11   He asked] I recall that he asked   TF1a

184.13   by the] by the new   TF1

184.15   time in my life] time   TF1a

184.16   Whoever] Whomever   s

184.19   had] has   TF1a

185.1   mankind] humanity   TF1a

185.5   politics. But] politics before, but   TF1

185.6   subject] subjects   TF1a

185.7   his customers] customers   TF1a

185.8   convincing] talking to   TF1a

450

185.10–11	Quartette] Choir TF1
185.12	for Mr. Dillon] for him TF1a; for Dillon TF1b, TF2, S
185.13	and it] —it sat TF1a
185.13–14	Even his . . . in it] His voice became unnatural, there was a sting of come-back in it, something that resented opposition and meant to get even TF1a; Even TF1b
185.18	on him.] on him? TF1, TF2a, S
185.22–23	but . . . grim] kept his ears open and looked grim TF1a
186.2	Trueman] he TF1
186.2–3	some of his friends] his poker-playing circle TF1, TF2, S
186.4	which] that TF1, TF2, S
186.8	Dillon's] Dillon's bank TF1a
186.8–9	balance] deposit TF1a
186.17	men] people TF1a
186.22	and there] but there TF1a
186.22	group of men] group TF1a
186.25	to the post-office] for the mail TF1a
187.7	sure] so sure TF1, TF2, S
187.8	were] had been TF1, TF2a

451

187.11   was . . . to] annoyed   TF1a

187.12   time now] time now. [¶] When families quarrel
          about politics or religion, when two brothers
          turn bitterly against each other, it is usually
          the expression of some indefinable personal
          antagonism, an old grudge or jealousy, ashamed to
          show its face, that seizes the mask of a righteous
          cause. But with Dillon and Trueman I know this was
          not so.   TF1a; *same except* which seizes   TF1b, TF2a

187.14   Dillon and Trueman] them   TF1, TF2a

187.20   his gains] money   TF1a

187.23   "principle"] principle   s

187.23   anyone] any man   TF1, TF2, s

187.24   take] accept   TF1a

188.6   rich] rich, satisfied   TF1a

188.7–8   full and satisfying] calm and   TF1b;
          full and absorbing   TF1a, TF2, s

188.11   true] balance   TF1a

188.12   Formerly, when] When   TF1, TF2a

188.13   figures] objects   TF1a

188.13   with] with two   TF1a

188.15   some law] a relation   TF1a

188.16   relation] understanding   TF1a

188.17   which] that TF1a

188.18   pleasure.] pleasure, like geometrical perfection or
           musical division [intervals *as cancelled*
           alternative] TF1, TF2

188.23   us] us that TF1a

188.24–25 tell Mr. Trueman] Mr. Trueman's office to tell
           him TF1, TF2, s

189.2   and told] and wrote him a check and told TF1a;
           wrote him a check and told TF1b, TF2;
           wrote a check and told s

189.3   informed] told TF1a

189.4   that he] he TF1a

189.6   stop] get off TF1, TF2a

189.12   everything he owned] everything TF1a

189.14   town lots] real-estate TF1, TF2a

189.15   now . . . common] only common TF1a;
           only the common TF1b, TF2a

189.16   would be left] left TF1a

189.22   seemed absent-minded] looked thoughtful TF1a

189.23   recall] think of TF1, TF2a

189.23   from] off TF1

189.24   red seal] seal TF1a

189.25   into] in TF1, TF2, s

190.1   said evasively] said evasively, as if trying to escape
           from something. I have it still   TF1a; said
           evasively. I have it still   TF1b, TF2a; said   s

190.3   left . . . He] left us, and spent   TF1a

190.4–5   moved into . . . built] lived at the Saint
           Francis   TF1a; lived at the Saint Francis
           Hotel   TF1b, TF2, s

190.6   an office] what he called an office   TF1, TF2, s

190.6–7   top of what is now] top of   TF1, TF2, s

190.7   Street. There] Street, where   TF1, TF2, s

190.8–9   a man whose offices were next his] one of the
           Huntingtons   TF1a; a man who officed next
           him   TF1b, TF2a; man   s

190.9–10   sit tilted back] sit   TF1a

190.12   watching] but watching   TF1a

190.18–19 More than . . . where] Often in Southern countries,
           when   TF1 TF2a

191.1   sleep.] sleep. It left a scar.   TF1, TF2a

191.1–2   old scar] scar   TF1, TF2a

191.2   chance] accident   TF1

191.3–4   something . . . mended] *inked through in*   TF1

191.5   truth that was] truth   s

191.6   want] would like   TF1b

Word Division

L IST A records compounds or possible compounds hyphenated at the ends of lines in the copy-text and resolved by the editors as one word or as hyphenated compounds. See the Textual Essay (pp. 364–65) for a discussion of the criteria for resolving these forms. List B contains the end-line hyphenations that are to be retained as hyphenations in quotations from the present edition. Page and line references are to the present edition. Note that hyphenated words that obviously resolve as one word ("com-/ pound," for example) are not included in either list.

List A

7.14	triangular-shaped
8.14	desk-chair
12.16	oilcloth
14.1	milk-cans
15.17	buttonhole
17.9	goose-fedder
17.25	India-ink

25.9	drinking-water
26.12	overtime
27.15	sleeping-room
27.17	low-pitched
31.14	jack-knife
33.15	old-fashioned
39.8	bedroom
56.24	yellow-brown
57.19	quicksilver
60.14	work-horses
61.8	undeathlike
66.24	goods-box
69.20	oilcloth-covered
69.25	rocking-chair
74.20	sewing-machine
77.15	wash-stand
78.13	hallway
82.2–3	hand-woven
87.3	dining-room
88.18	hourglass
89.24	cross-stitch

97.4	oil-chromos
101.6	wagon-load
103.8	ice-cream
104.18	ice-cream
109.24	barefoot
116.14	drayman
117.16–17	sage-brush
126.11	sand-hills
126.15	Roadmaster's
128.6	downhearted
134.16	love-affair
139.21	red-brown
141.10–11	travelling-hat
150.5	toast-water
150.14	cracker-box
152.25	play-room
156.11	self-absorption
161.16	motor-car
164.15	cross-street
167.2	billiard-hall
167.4	horse-trader

457

167.22–23	cattle-sheds
168.1	billiard-hall
169.13	half-circle
170.8	old-country
171.16	unaccented
172.17	moonlight
175.25–176.1	moonlight
176.1	velvet-white
179.6	poker-playing
185.14	come-back
188.7	outflowing

List B

12.4–5	self-consciousness
14.20–21	close-clipped
19.8–9	mowing-machine
26.14–15	self-indulgent
53.9–10	wheat-fields
53.23–24	alfafa-field
57.24–25	"gypsy-like"
67.20–21	rocking-chair
68.19–21	coffee-cake

69.21–22	red-striped
69.25–70.1	splint-bottom
72.9–10	full-gathered
77.24–25	yellow-brown
82.2–3	hand-woven
87.24–25	water-colour
91.10–11	reddish-brown
95.8–9	money-grubbers
96.1–2	high-spirited
99.21–22	lawn-mower
101.11–12	cake-bakers
102.5–6	sage-brush
106.23–24	cook-stove
108.1–2	good-night
117.16–17	sage-brush
130.2–3	good-natured
141.10–11	travelling-hat
152.6–7	rocking-chair
154.20–21	heart-ache
161.13–14	breeding-grounds
162.16–17	cheek-bones

165.20–21	post-office
167.1–2	poker-players
167.9–10	over-heated
167.22–23	cattle-sheds
169.10–11	arm-chairs
178.12–13	Good-night
189.23–24	watch-chain